READYMADE BODHISATTVA

THE KAYA ANTHOLOGY OF SOUTH KOREAN SCIENCE FICTION

Published by Kaya Press
kaya.com

Distributed by D.A.P./Distributed Art Publishers
artbook.com (800) 388-BOOK
ISBN: 9781885030573

Library of Congress Control Number: 2018967242
Cover Design by Jaemin Lee (www.leejaemin.net)
Text Design by Chris Ro (www.adearfriend.com)
Illustrations by Hongmin Lee

Magpie Series Editor: Sunyoung Park
Magpie Series Design Editor: Chris Ro

This publication is made possible by support from the USC Dana and David
Dornsife College of Arts, Letters, and Sciences; the Shinso Ito Center for Japanese
Religions and Culture; the USC Department of American Studies and Ethnicity;
and the USC Department of East Asian Languages and Cultures. Special thanks to
the Choi Chang Soo Foundation for their support of this work. Additional funding
was provided by the generous contributions of: Christine Alberto, Tiffany Babb,
Manibha Banerjee, Tom and Lily So Beischer, Piyali Bhattacharya, Jade Chang,
Anelise Chen, Anita Chen, Lisa Chen, Floyd Cheung, Jen Chou, Kavita Das, Steven
Doi, Susannah Donahue, Jessica Eng, Sesshu Foster, Jean Ho, Heidi Hong, Huy
Hong, Jayson Joseph, Sabrina Ko, Juliana Koo, Whakyung Lee, Andrew Leong,
Edward Lin, Leza Lowitz, Edan Lepucki, Faisal Mohyuddin, Nayomi Munaweera,
Abir Majumdar, Viet Thanh Nguyen, Sandra Noel, Chez Bryan Ong, Gene & Sabine
Oishi, Leena Pendharker, Eming Piansay, Amarnath Ravva, Andrew Shih, Paul H.
Smith, Shinae Yoon, Monona Wali, Patricia Wakida, Duncan Williams, Amelia Wu,
Anita Wu & James Spicer, Koon Woon, Mikoto Yoshida, Nancy Yap, and others.

Kaya Press is also supported, in part, by the National Endowment for the Arts;
the Los Angeles County Board of Supervisors through the Los Angeles County
Arts Commission; the City of Los Angeles Department of Cultural Affairs; and the
Community of Literary Magazines and Presses. This book would not have been
possible without the generous support of the Literature Translation Institute of
Korea (LTI Korea).

READYMADE
BODHISATTVA

THE KAYA ANTHOLOGY OF
SOUTH KOREAN SCIENCE FICTION

SUNYOUNG PARK & SANG JOON PARK, EDITORS

KAYA
PRESS

LOS ANGELES

TABLE OF CONTENTS

INTRODUCTION

BY SUNYOUNG PARK

The present volume introduces the English reader to some of the most distinctive and diverse literary voices in contemporary science fiction from South Korea. The criterion of selection behind these stories is one that joins thematic relevance with aesthetic accomplishment. We have striven to include works that both matter for their discursive significance and are enjoyable for their literary qualities. While this is the first anthology of its kind to appear in English, the stories presented here join previous translations that either belong in or have some relevance for the science fiction genre, including Cho Sehui's *The Dwarf*, Kim Jung-hyuk's "1F/B1," and Kim Bo-Young's "An Evolutionary Myth."[1] Needless to say, this volume aims to provide neither a historical compendium of science fiction in South Korea nor a definitive, canonizing portrait of the genre's state of the art. Much more, the volume is like one of those photos one might find on Instagram: intentionally rough at the edges and out-of-focus in certain spots, all the better for conveying the excitement and the dynamism of the subject matter.

Science fiction as a modern literary genre was introduced to Korea in the early twentieth century through the translations of authors such as Jules Verne, H. G. Wells, and Karel Čapek. It was not until the late 1950s and early 1960s, however, that domestic writers began looking

---

[1] Cho Sehui, *The Dwarf*, trans. Bruce and Ju-Chan Fulton (Honolulu: University of Hawaii Press, 2006); Kim Jung-hyuk, "1F/B1," trans. Caleb Young Woo Park, *Azalea: Journal of Korean Literature & Culture* 6 (2013): 111–34; and Kim Bo-Young, "An Evolutionary Myth," trans. Gord Sellar and Jihyun Park, *Clarkesworld* 104 (May 2015).

to the genre as a conduit for literary experiments in a rapidly modernizing nation. Young adult magazines such as *Hagwon* (Campus; 1952–79) and *Hakseang kwahak* (Student Science; 1965–83) became the publication outlets for a few pioneering writers whose works typically joined the cause of popularizing scientific knowledge with a sort of cosmopolitan utopianism about South Korea's participation in world affairs. In Han Nagwon's *The Venus Expeditions* (Keumseong tamheomdae; 1962–64), for example, Korean scientists were seen as equal-rank collaborators with Americans in the exploration of our solar system. Their common enemies were, true to the spirit of the Cold War, the astronauts of the Soviet Union.

If science fiction authors in the 1960s generally advanced a forward-looking, optimistic vision of the future, writers and film makers in 1970s Korea more often took to the genre to describe the malaise of living under dictatorship in a fast industrializing society. A renowned example of this critical brand of science fiction is the above-mentioned novel *The Dwarf* (Nanjangiga ssoa olin jageun gong; 1975–78), whose proletarian subjects—the powerless people of an autocratic developing country—were easily recognizable as fictional stand-ins for contemporary Koreans. Another signal work was Ki-young's film *Killer Butterfly* (Sarin nabireul jjonneun yeoja; 1978), an existentialist sci-fi horror whose central character, an unemployed young man just out of college, confronts the villainy of a corrupt and murderous ultranationalist scientist. The uneasy dystopia of works such as these established in Korea a small but significant subgenre that we may describe as the "science fiction of protest." This was a development akin to the earlier rise in the United States of a countercultural New Wave of writers, including Philip K. Dick, Samuel Delany, Thomas M. Disch, and Ursula Le Guin,

whose works offered a critical alternative to the more
traditional science fiction of previous decades.

The 1980s were famously the heyday of democratization
and a time of unrest in South Korea. Under the intensified authoritarianism of Chun Doo-hwan's regime, both
science fiction and popular culture had a few quiet years
of low productivity. Coinciding with democratization in
1987, however, the critical and dissident vein of science
fiction resurfaced amid the rising tides of civil protest.
In that year, Bok Geo-il published the best-selling alternate history novel *In Search of an Epitaph* (Bimyeongeul
chajaseo), which was in effect a re-imagining of Philip K.
Dick's *The Man in the High Castle* within the local historical and geopolitical contexts. Set in an alternate 1980s
Korea in which the country is still under Japan's imperial
rule, the novel chronicled the gradual awakening of an
ethnically Korean family man to the harsh realities of the
colonial condition. The book in many ways epitomized
the era's spirit of democratization, and it has since
become a model of socially engaged science fiction in
South Korea.

Both the production and the consumption of science
fiction in Korea exploded during the 1990s. At the heart
of this boom was a cluster of activist fandom clubs that
were formed via the dial-up telecommunication system
known as *PC tongsin*—a precursor to the internet that
had become widely popular in the country. Members
of these groups also contributed to the launching of
the first periodicals dedicated exclusively to science
fiction, such as *SF Magazine* (1993) and the monthly *SF
Webzine* (1999). Indeed, given the general lack of interest in the genre among academics, it was these fans
who pioneered South Korean SF criticism by reviewing
major works and engaging in debates over the genre's
present and future orientation.

Science fiction is thus a rising and ever-shifting genre

in South Korea today. Inspired by the activism of the past decades, more and more writers see the genre as an extraordinary creative laboratory for reflecting on the opportunities and contradictions of modernization in a late-capitalist and postcolonial society. The SF explosion since the 1990s has also meant that readers, audiences, and money have flowed to science fiction in unprecedented quantities. This fact accounts for, among other things, the presence of a thriving SF movie scene, out of which have come international cult films such as Jang Joon-hwan's *Save the Green Planet* (2003), Bong Joon-ho's *The Host* (2006), and Bong's *Snowpiercer* (2013). In its turn, the rise of science fiction across media and in visual culture has also fed back to its literary form, as it has brought more talented writers to a genre that is nowadays more popular than it has ever been on the Korean peninsula.

△ △ △

Of the thirteen writers presented in this volume, eight are well-established figures that have in various ways contributed to the history of literary science fiction in South Korea. Among them, Mun Yunseong and Choi In-hun were at the peak of their activity in the 1960s and 1970s; Bok Geo-il is a good representative of the 1980s; Djuna (a pseudonym) and Kim Young-ha rose to fame during the 1990s; and Kim Changgyu, Kim Jung-hyuk, and Park Min-gyu were prominent writers of the first decade of the new millennium. The other five writers, three of whom are women, are all rising figures that are defining the present and the foreseeable future of the genre in South Korea.

While the stories are here presented in a (mostly) chronological order, interesting suggestions for grouping them can be gleaned from both the tropes that they contain and the themes that they treat. In terms of tropes, different entry points and reading paths are available whether one focuses on robots (chapters 1, 5, 10, 11), alien invasion (7, 10, 12, 13), colonization (2, 3, 4, 5, 7, 10, 12), (space-)ships (4, 5, 10, 12, 13), cyberspace (6, 9, 13), artificial intelligence (1, 5, 6, 9, 11), genetic mutation (2, 7, 8, 10), or various forms of time travel (2, 9). Further patterns of tropes in these stories will strike the reader as less generic of science fiction, including those of teenage girls (4, 8, 9, 10, 13), corporations (1, 4, 6, 11), refugees (5, 10, 11, 12), and games (4, 6, 7, 8, 11).

Thematically, on the other hand, all of the stories in this volume derive at least some inspiration from works of either anglophone or Japanese science fiction. It is important to note, however, that the genre has also been evolving its own characteristics in South Korea.[2] One distinctive mark of this local scene is a strong sense of the apocalypse having already happened, whether through war, colonization, dictatorship, or the corporate monopolization of resources. Technophilia, utopia, and an optimistic vision unencumbered by darkness are rarely to be found in the pages that follow. Indeed, in a trend that in many ways re-actualizes the science fiction of protest from decades past, dystopia is a connecting motif among these stories.

---

[2] The anglophone influence was particularly noticeable during the 1950s, when the superheroes of DC Comics provided an inspiration for Kim Sanho's comic-book epic *Ryphie* (Raipai; 1959). It was further consolidated during the 1970s through the translations of writers such as Isaac Asimov, Arthur C. Clarke, and Robert Heinlein. As for the impact of Japanese science fiction, both *manga* and robot animation were staples of South Korean young-adult culture ever since the 1970s. Acknowledging Japan's influence was not always allowable, however, which led to frequent cases of near-plagiaristic reproduction, rather than importation, of foreign cultural products. One example of this would be the animation *Taekwon V* (1976), which was in effect a Koreanized version of Japan's *Mazinger Z* (1972).

Another distinctive characteristic of South Korean science fiction is that it tends to feature aliens and monsters, the classic antagonists in the genre, not so much as external threats but as reflections of the self. Main characters are thus often post-human, non-human, or almost-human, or else they are human but empathize with the aliens. The common epic plot of a hero/ine fighting adversity is also frequently given a new twist through protagonists who lack superpowers, figuring as they do as vulnerable subjects who are carriers of marginality and difference.

The dystopian vocation of Korean science fiction is
well exemplified by the two historical pieces in the volume, which are extracts from Mun Yunseong's *Perfect Society* (Wanjeon sahoe; 1965) and Choi In-hun's novella *Empire Radio, Live Transmission* (Chongdogui sori; 1967). In Mun's novel, a Korean man awakens from cryogenic hibernation in the year 2130, only to discover that the Earth is now populated by women and that all men have been exiled to Mars following a war. Much of the story, including the part rendered here, centers around the protagonist's enthralled exploration of a world in which glitzy technologism can only partially hide profound social tensions. For its part, the portion of Choi In-hun's novella translated here consists of a monologue broadcast on South Korean radio in 1967 by an imaginary Governor General of Korea. The Governor calls on all Korean citizens to support the restoration of Japan's colonial government, in a counterhistorical fiction that reminds readers of Korea's actual subjection to that country between 1911 and 1945. Equal parts alternate history and ominous poetic experiment, the novella is still relevant today for its disquieting if fantasy-inflected interrogation of coloniality and its survival on the Korean peninsula.

14

If Mun and Choi's pieces are cultural responses to South Korea's early modernization, three other stories grew out of the advanced capitalist society of the new millennium. In the title story "Readymade Bodhisattva" (Redimeideu bosal; 2005), Pak Seonghwan reflects on the place of tradition in modernity by depicting a dispute between an all-powerful global corporation that manufactures robots and a group of Korean monks in a Buddhist temple. At issue is the monks' suggestion that Inmyeong, a robot who shows special proficiency in the teachings of the Buddha, can be properly said to have reached enlightenment. In Kim Young-ha's novel *Quiz Show* (Kwijeu shyo; 2007), isolation and incommunicability are foregrounded in an account of a young man coming of age in the era of the internet. In the chapter extracted here, the protagonist begins his employment at a mysterious tech company in a province near Seoul, only to realize that the job requires him to upload and store his mind in cyberspace. Finally, Park Min-gyu's "Roadkill" (Rodeukil; 2011) centers around the unexpected empathy of two robotic border guards, employees of the imperial corporate government of Asia, for the wretchedly poor "surplus" human beings who have been walled out of the imperial territory. When read together, these stories project the unsettling imagination of a future in which a few giant corporations have overcome democratic controls to exercise unchecked political power. It is no coincidence that Pak's two android guards are called "Maksi" (for Marx) and "Mao," and that by the end of the story both are forcibly rebooted and shut down.

Along with capitalism as a dystopia, imperialism and colonization have also been central concerns for South Korean writers in the new millennium, as can be seen in the three alien-invasion stories by Djuna, Kim Jung-hyuk, and Lim Taewoon. In a blending of geopolitical and apocalyptic imagination, Djuna's "The Bloody Battle of Broccoli Plain" (Brokolli pyeongwonui hyeoltu; 2011) sets the continuing conflict between North and South Korea against the background of Earth's colonization by aliens. It suggests, both tragically and ironically, that the Korean conflict will continue unabated even in the face of the most cataclysmic events. Kim Jung-hyuk tells an equally bleak parable of crisis-ridden human society in "Where Boats Go" (Boteuga ganeun got; 2016), wherein a young couple desperately cling to one another in an attempt to survive an alien-induced apocalypse. And Lim Taewoon only partly reverses roles in "Storm Between My Teeth" (Ippare kkin dolgae baram; 2009), a story whose hero introduces himself as an alien on a mission to colonize the Earth. As powerful and resourceful as this alien may be, he is also subject to the difficult experience of living as a minority in Korean society. The story thus interestingly joins the theme of Korea as the victim of colonization with that of Koreans as themselves enforcers of a racist attitude towards immigrants and minorities.

Adding to the themes covered in this volume, four more stories use a variety of means to target gender discrimination, excessive school discipline, and hierarchism towards young people in South Korea. Three of these stories were written by women authors, partly reflecting the gendered nature of these issues, and all of them have young Korean women as their protagonists. In Kim Bo-Young's time travel story "Between Zero and One" (0gwa 1 sai; 2009), multiple temporalities collide, and clashing along with them are competing ideals of womanhood anchored by a strategically mysterious first-person narrator. The story puts formal complexity in the service of a critique of South Korea's so-called "education fever," solidifying a theme of inter-generational betrayal that is multiply represented in the volume. In "Cosmic Go" (Ujuryu; 2009), Jeong Soyeon deploys a futuristic imagination to expose social biases against many forms of diversity. Her story features a young woman scientist and aspiring astronaut who becomes disabled just as she is about to launch on her first mission. At her side throughout this process is her mother, who herself struggles to make a living on the meager salary of a laboratory assistant. Symbolically, the two women spend their free time playing Go, a chess-like board game that has been traditionally associated with a supposedly male-only power of concentration. The themes of discrimination and cross-generational tension are also at the heart of Yun I-hyeong's "The Sky Walker" (Seukai wokeo; 2011) and Kim Changgyu's "Our Banished World" (Uriga chubangdoen segye; 2016). Set in a post-nuclear world that worships the Dragon God, Yun's story is a tale of conflict and friendship between a "Drakorean" woman athlete and a "Sky Walker" (a gravity-defying superman) from "Drussia." At once apocalyptic and post-Cold War, the narrative carries a biting critique of the conformism deeply entrenched in South Korean society. For its part, Kim Changgyu's story may be best described as a sorrowful requiem for a national tragedy. On April 16, 2014, a ferry carrying mostly high school students on a school trip sank in the seas off Jeju Island, causing the death of 304 passengers and igniting a process of soul searching for South Koreans and their government. Kim's fictionalization of the event embeds it in a wider, more complicated plot that involves social media, technology, and the ever more virtual nature of our lived reality. The result is a moving attempt at healing all the while reflecting on the responsibilities involved in the death of the students.

We finally have an outlier of sorts in Bok Geo-il's "Along

the Fragments of My Body" (Nae momui papyeondu-ri heuteojin gil ttara; 2006). It is the only story with a utopian, reconciled attitude towards a posthuman future in which androids have evolved way beyond their human-engineered origins. They are now the only occupants of Ganymede, one of Jupiter's moons, and they inhabit a social world comprised of artists, writers, scientists, and other role-model figures. Told in the inquisitive voice of a nine-year old android girl, the story offers an optimistic if jarring outlook on a future in which human technology has peacefully evolved to become independent of our control.

18 Accompanying the stories presented here are short introductions of each individual writer as well as a brief history of the phenomenon of SF fandom in South Korea by Sang Joon Park. These materials are meant to enable an appreciation of the stories within the broader cultural milieu of their production and circulation. From the early stirrings of the 1960s to the advent of protest science fiction in the 1970s and 1980s to the thriving of the genre since the 1990s, science fiction presents itself today as an integral part of popular culture in Korea, one with its own history and a notable influence over readers and viewers. It is the editors' hope that this volume will further stimulate the public's interest, both within and outside the country, in the accomplish-ments as well as the future potential of South Korean science fiction.

READYMADE BODHISATTVA

BY PARK SEONGHWAN

TRANSLATED BY JIHYUN PARK
AND GORD SELLAR

PARK SEONGHWAN

Park Seonghwan (b.1978) exploded onto the South Korean science fiction scene with the short story "Readymade Bodhisattva" (Redimeideu bosal), a work that was honored in 2004 with the SF and Science Writing Award sponsored by the *Dong-a ilbo* newspaper and the Korean Science Foundation. In the years since, his works have appeared in print magazines and webzines such as *Crossroads, Fantastique, Dong-a Science,* and *Geoul* (Mirror) as well as in a number of SF anthologies. Park has also published a much-discussed three-volume collection of his complete SF stories. Respectively titled *Things to Be Destroyed Before Our Own Destruction* (Uriui salmeul busugi jeone buswoya hal geotdeul; 2005), *What Comes After the Pain, What Blooms After the Suffering* (Gotong daeume oneun geotdeul, goeroum dwie pineun geotdeul; 2012), and *The Unspeakable, the Unsilenceable* (Mal hal su eomneun, chimmuk hal su eomneun; 2014), these three books showcase the philosophical sophistication and the broad thematic scope of Park's creative work.

Park's stories often explore dystopian worlds plagued by mind control, artificial intelligence, and unfettered capitalism. Whether they be robots, extraterrestrials from an advanced civilization ("One Night on Mt. Sumi" [Sumisan esoui harutbam]), or national heroes resurrected through genetic engineering ("King Sejong with a Walkman" [Wokeu maeneul kkin Sejong]), the nonhuman characters in Park's work often tend to face commodification and manipulation by greedy humans, as well as a social system founded on corruption and propaganda. The only form of resistance to this horror lies in activism and spirituality, generally sublimated in a technologically infused Buddhism that preaches the overcoming of our ego through an awareness of its neurological basis.

"Readymade Bodhisattva" is best approached as an interrogation, from a Korean perspective, of the trope of artificial intelligence as it appears in Anglo-American science fiction, upon which Isaac Asimov's "Robot" series had a massive influence. The earliest stories in that series, collected in his book *I, Robot,* are notable not only because they introduce his famous "laws of robotics"—a series of three harm-prevention conditional rules for governing robot decision-making processes—but also because they explore mysterious instances where apparent malfunctions are ultimately revealed as proper functioning, given the inevitable presence of human errors as well as the limits of both contingency planning and the ways in which generalized, vague laws are interpreted. But while Park Seongwhan's treatment of the thinking machine also addresses the mysterious truth that can be found within apparent malfunction, it is concerned with generalized laws of a kind profoundly different from that found in Asimov's works, pursuing as it does questions of sentience, existence and truth from a uniquely Buddhist perspective. At stake here are rather the metaphysical laws addressed in the Zen koan "Mu" (nothingness, nonexistence) from which the story takes its epigram.[1]

This tale is not only a meditation on machine consciousness, but also, in some sense, a kind of reimagining, for a technological age, of a traditional Buddhist *jataka* story. Where the traditional *jatakas* each tell of one of the Buddha's past lives along his long transmigratory journey through a world of pain, delusion, and suffering toward metaphysical enlightenment, "Readymade Bodhisattva" tells the origin story of a new Buddha whose enlightenment is inevitable, but also inevitably plagued by the delusions, attachments, and vicissitudes of the human beings that surround it.

Introduction by Jihyun Park and Gord Sellar

---

[1] Two tantalizing notions of how to parse this koan suggest themselves through the story. The first is that "Mu" represents a rejection of the question itself: in terms of logical argument, it is a "null proposition," which suggests a necessary transcendence of the limits of binary logic, just as the tale's eponymous robot character mysteriously transcends the limits of the binary logic built into its robotic brain to achieve Buddha-consciousness. The second is the response that the question is nonsensical because all things have or embody Buddha-nature, and thus asking whether they "possess" it is nonsensical, a cosmic truth hinted at several times by the robot Inmyeong during the course of the story.

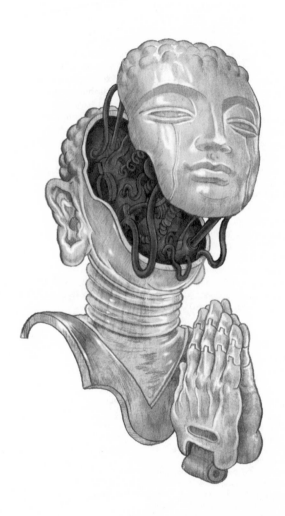

READYMADE BODHISATTVA

A monk asked Chao-chou:
"Does a dog have Buddha nature or not?"

I.

"Well, of course we're always gratified and appreciative when someone finds a use for our products," said the technician with a smile, "But robots in a temple? It's not really the sort of thing we usually expect..."

The monk replied with a smile: "Actually, it's raised a lot of eyebrows. The modernization of temples, whether due to cars, online ritual services, air conditioning in meditation rooms, or even just electric candles in the worship halls, has always been extremely controversial. But the thing is, Buddhism's always been a radical faith. Siddhartha lived in a caste-based agrarian society: calling for freedom of commerce and the abolition of social hierarchy was quite courageous of him. Of course, it's been thousands of years since the Buddha first turned the wheel of dharma, and now Buddhism is an established, mainstream religion... but the basic teachings of our faith still embrace that radicalism. How could they not when we question the objective reality of the physical universe itself?"

They had reached the Deva gate. Believers had gathered around and were genuflecting with folded hands before the statues of the Four Devas, which responded by swiveling their large, built-in camera eyes. The monk gestured with one hand, showing the hesitant technician the way forward. The man whispered his thanks to the monk as he crossed the raised threshold and entered the temple grounds.

Despite the busy comings and goings of the faithful, the

sanctuary grounds felt as serene and peaceful as one would expect of a sacred place. The rasping of cicadas echoed among thick tree branches, and even the mid-summer sun seemed to be taking a brief respite, hidden behind the eaves of the monastery. The technician noticed someone approaching in the distance, a figure swinging some sort of long stick along the ground that kicked up a cloud of dust wherever it went. Squinting at the end of the stick, he made out a thick bundle of bristles designed to catch dust on the ground, and realized it to be an archaic cleaning tool called a "broom." He smiled wryly: that was so like a temple, so downright typical. Instead of simply using an RC-178 unit, or maybe an RC-182, the monks had dressed an anthropomorphic robot in robes and then put it to work using primitive cleaning tools.

But even as he busied himself trying to guess the product code of the sweeping figure, he saw something that shocked him. As they approached, the sweeper clasped his hands, gently bowing to the monk, and looked up. The technician was surprised to see not the face of a robot, but that of a man... A real human being? *Sweeping*?

The monk reciprocated the sweeper's gesture with a nod. Then, smiling as if he'd read the technician's mind, he said, "We don't leave the asceticism to the robots here. Cleaning the temple isn't just some simple chore: it's a part of our religious practice."

"Then what do you use the robots for..." the technician began to ask, but just then a group of monks appeared. He recognized the leader of the group as an RU-4, the newest model of general-purpose robot.

The tower you can see over there is a copy of a seven-story stone pagoda that was rebuilt after the original was destroyed during the suppression of Buddhism that occurred in October 1980. This replica is made of cement and granite, which clearly demonstrates the stylistic decline of architecture during the late twentieth century. Now, as you know, the October suppression was ordered by the President at the time... The narration was smooth, in keeping with the manner of an RU-4 model.

The monk raised his hand and pointed out another robot; this one had a handheld computer in one palm and was explaining something to an old monk. This, too, was an RU-4 model.

"Robots run the household and serve as guides to our many visitors. People are so accustomed to listening to the narration of robot guides that when a real monk guides them, they actually feel uncomfortable."

"Okay, but... what do you mean by 'run the household'?"

"They handle the temple's planning, accounting, and budgetary administration. A class of monks we called *sapan* used to take care of all that. Happily, thanks to robots, we're able to focus more on asceticism. Of course, this might seem ridiculous to outsiders, who might imagine that we are being pushed around by our robots, who are running and managing the temple while we monks just sweep the grounds. But asceticism is the most important part of our monastic practice, and dealing with money gets in the way of that. So in that sense, robots play a secondary, assistive role to humans even here."

"And the malfunctioning unit you mentioned..."

"Ah, yes. Inmyeong is one of the six guide-bots at our temple. But the term *malfunction* seems inappropriate..."

"Inmyeong?"

"That's its name. We've given Buddhist names to all the robots here. Of course, they haven't officially received the Buddhist precepts..."

"But if the robot's not malfunctioning, then why did you..."

"Ah, right. Well, you should see it first. That'll be a better explanation than anything I could tell you," the monk said, glancing at a clock before saying, "Come this way."

The monk led the technician to a sanctuary opposite the Mahāvīra Hall—the great hall of worship—where a service was unfolding. Many people sat within—monks and robots among them—all listening to the sermon. The robots seemed to have been brought along by some of the laypersons worshipping there, and the thought of bots listening to a sermon made the technician smile. He glanced at the figure preaching the sermon, and his grin turned into an expression of shock: it was an RU-4, a general-purpose, anthropomorphic robot series 4 model. There was no question about it... and yet it was preaching to a congregation of monks and laypersons.

"Do robots handle the *preaching* duties here, too?" he asked the monk in whisper.

"No," the monk replied softly. "Inmyeong is off duty now. It passes on the insights of its enlightenment to the faithful like this when it has completed its duties as a guide."

II.

"This makes no sense," the technician mumbled dejectedly. Although seated on a comfortable sofa in the temple abbot's administrative offices, he was profoundly uneasy.

"The sermon will soon be finished," the monk told him. "Then you can meet Inmyeong in person."

The technician picked up his tea cup, blew on it agitatedly, and took a small sip.

"So you're telling me your robot has achieved enlightenment? You mean it's giving a sermon based on its own understanding, and not just outputting some doctrine that's been plugged in as direct input?"

"Yes," the monk replied curtly.

From the monk's increasingly serious expression, the technician could tell just how incredulous his own expression must be, but he couldn't help it. The whole idea was absurd.

"Well, what I mean, you know, something like enlightenment and all that... isn't it hard even for monks to achieve? I mean even for *people*, real people."

"Yes," replied the monk.

"So how could a *robot* do it? No, something must've gone wrong. You've made a mistake. Robots can't be religious. A robot can be programmed to put its hands together and bow, but you can't call that *faith*."

"I'm sorry, sir," said the monk, "but I suspect you have some misconceptions about Buddhism. Folding one's hands together, bowing mechanically, or praying are all irrelevant to the Buddha's original teachings. Since your company began producing its RU-2 model, we've been hearing about the RU line's capacity for 'flexible' thinking... that in order for the units to communicate naturally with humans, it became necessary to program them with some cognitive capacity for grasping situational contexts so that they could react appropriately to vague and incomplete commands in commonplace conversational speech."

The technician gaped. He realized that his assumption that monastics were naïve shut-ins, out of touch with the outside world, had been mere shallow prejudice, but even so, he never could have imagined such a comprehensive understanding of robotic engineering from a monk.

Seeing his surprise, the monk laughed. "Oof, here I am fearlessly pretending to know more than I do, right in front of a robotics engineering expert. In the old days, we used to call that 'doing math in your head in front of a robot.' What do people call that these days?"

"Uh, we still use that expression," the technician replied with an awkward smile.

"I see. Well, we might look as if we've hidden ourselves away in the mountains, but we learn a lot about the world by talking with those who come here to worship," the monk continued softly. "If I may continue to feign knowledge of this subject, wasn't it somewhere between revised RU-2 and RU-3..."

"The RU-2NX series," the technician interrupted him without thinking.

"Yes, thank you, that's it. I've heard that from the RU-2NX series onward, robots have been capable of a degree of self-awareness. Because the R&D necessary for developing this sort of 'flexible' thinking was driving unit prices higher and higher, it became necessary to equip robots with a certain capacity for self-preservation. That, in turn, required a kind of self-consciousness—the recognition of one's own existence, and some sort of value attached to it."

After taking a sip of his tea, the monk continued. "However, we Buddhists think of such self-awareness as more than merely a cognitive function that gives machines the ability to observe simple self-protection protocols. As I'm sure you know, there are in fact ongoing debates among robot experts and philosophers alike about whether or not self-awareness is equivalent to self-consciousness."

The technician nodded silently. "Now," continued the monk, "Given the uniquely 'flexible' thought process you've given the RU series, we think this self-awareness function can be recognized as fulfilling this prerequisite of self-consciousness." The monk paused and took another sip. "One of the major teachings of the Buddha is *anātman*, the idea that living things have no such thing as a fixed, permanent self or soul. But to embrace *anātman*, one must first have a sense of self to reject! Inmyeong is a robot equipped with a concept of selfhood. It took up the study of the Buddhist doctrine during its off-duty hours and applied the result to itself, coming at last, without input from anyone else, to a denial of its own selfhood, and thus delivering itself from the illusory world of existence. Mind you, it did so according to the characteristics of a robot, meaning that despite having some measure of self-awareness, it lacked an inherent self to begin with and so didn't really need to embrace anātman in the first place. Nevertheless many monks who've listened to Inmyeong's sermons believe that it has achieved enlightenment."

"So then why have you called me here?"

"Ah, yes, of course," the monk answered without hesitation. "We've asked you here not to check on or repair any malfunction, but rather to judge Inmyeong's status from the perspective of a professional robotics engineer."

III.

As the technician sat in dazed silence, gaping, the door opened and a robot entered. It was an RU-4. The technician assumed it must be Inmyeong, the unit in question.

So it was. The robot put its hands together and greeted the many monks waiting in the office. The technician watched as several monks clasped their own hands and bowed deeply in response.

"Good, you're here," the monk said, and gestured towards the technician. "This is an onsite service engineer from the U.R. Corporation."

"U.R. is like a parent to me," the robot said. "I am pleased to meet you. I am RU-4#5y4925789475849." It brought its hands together once more while bowing its head. Reflexively, the technician reciprocated by putting his hands together and bowing.

He then read the robot's output files on a monitor, one character at a time. Everything was working fine.

"The robot's self-diagnostic capacity registers as normal," he said.

"I am normal," came the robot's verbal output.

"I wasn't talking to you, robot," he snapped. All of a sudden, he found himself wondering what in the world he was doing there. *A robot, achieving enlightenment? How ridiculous! Enlightenment? So what were they trying to say, this robot had become a Buddha or something? This thing that he could take apart with his own hands, using nothing but a wrench? In that case, enlightenment couldn't be that hard to achieve! A Buddha is a Buddha, right? If I say there's nothing wrong with this machine, people are going to bow down to it over and over again, right? That makes no sense! A robot, becoming a Buddha? A lump of metal that anyone can buy with a credit card?* He blinked hard and swallowed, continuing to mull things over. *Wait a second,* he thought, *I must have gotten sucked in for a second. What those baldies are talking about is so ridiculous I almost got carried away for a moment. I guess insanity rubs off easily like that. Good God, they're asking me to check on whether or not their robot has really become a Buddha. Me, an aftermarket service man!*

He cleared his throat and said after a pause, "Look, I can't do this."

"What?" said the monk. The technician had expected this response, and replied with the answer he'd been preparing in his head: "Look. I don't know what you want me to do. A robot Buddha? What do you expect from me, anyways? What do I know about Buddhism? If the robot is broken and can be fixed, that's something I could do right away. I could track down a short circuit, replace a chip or two, clean out dust as necessary. And if it's seriously broken, I'd contact the head office. But you're asking me whether or not it's *really* a Buddha? What would I know about that? If this robot goes crazy and insists that it's a Buddha, I can open it up, find whatever circuit's shorted out, and replace the relevant chip. That's what I do. But if you're asking me to confirm this thing's Buddha nature, well... you've called the wrong man!"

Convinced that the monks were trying to mess with him, his thoughts spilled out in a muddled rush of words tinged with resentment. How could his tongue fail him like this, at the worst possible moment? Finally, enraged, he began to blush.

There was a moment of silence.

With a worried expression, the monk who'd guided him to the office said, "Please don't get upset. I'm sorry if I've made you angry somehow. We thought that seeing would be worth more than a thousand words. That's why we decided to show you all this without first explaining it, but I see now that this was a mistake. I apologize. It was not our intention to mock or fool you, and please believe me, we're not trying to deceive you or to force you into confirming our suspicions about Inmyeong and Inmyeong's enlightenment. The reason we've asked you here is because several benefactors have questioned the authenticity of Inmyeong's sermons, which they've listened to, because they were given by a robot. This is completely reasonable, and not something we can fault them for. After all, the Buddha himself taught his pupils to doubt and to be ceaselessly skeptical about his teachings. Which is why we decided to bring in a professional to evaluate whether or not Inmyeong is functioning normally. So you see, all you have to do here is what you would normally do when checking a robot—tell us whether Inmyeong's brain, or any of its subsystems, is malfunctioning. I can assure you, we have no interest in using any of this for commercial gain or publicity."

The monk was being entirely sincere. After having waited so long for someone to achieve enlightenment, a new Buddha had finally arrived. Turning something like this into fodder for cheap, kitschy shows and commercials on 3DTV or netTV would be unbearable.

"Well, even so, I really can't do this," the technician said at last, breaking the silence that had followed the monk's words. "Simply put, you're saying I should do what I normally do, right? But I'm no fool. If there's one thing I know, it's that something like this can't be resolved by me just doing my job. How will all this affect the U.R. Corporation? And what about the robotics industry in general? I can't just ignore such questions. Something like this is way above my pay grade. I need to check on official company policy."

The monk was now wearing a puzzled expression. Some of the other monks looked pensive as well.

At that instant, the door swung open and a man strode in. Though everyone there knew his name and recognized him on sight, it was the first time any of them had seen him in person. An excitable monk shouted out almost in unison with the technician:

"The King of Robotics!"

"The President!"

IV.

As the President of the U.R. Corporation, surrounded by his aides, entered the office, everything suddenly looked shabby and worn, old computers sitting on old desks. The President was the owner of a megacorporation, one that ran six massive industrial complexes across the Earth, the Moon, Mars, and throughout Earth's orbit.

His cold face could be seen regularly on TV, appearing in front of flashing cameras when entering or leaving a conference or meeting or cutting tape at countless ceremonies and inaugurations. But now, here he was standing right in front of them. It was as if a strange breeze from some fantastical other world had blown into the room.

"I hurried over after receiving an emergency report. On the way, I fired an idiotic manager and his eight assistants, all of whom failed to immediately comprehend the significance of this situation. This frontline engineer, though, seems to know what's what." Before anyone could offer him a seat, the President snapped down into a chair before the crowd. "Now out with it," he said to the monks. "What made you think you could call a mere engineer to get U.R.'s stamp of approval on your scheme to send that robot out into the world as a Buddha?"

The ticking of an old clock seemed to fill the air in the silence that followed, and the technician tried to concentrate on the sound. It reminded him of the temple's antiquity. Though this uncomfortable pause lasted only a few seconds, the silent reproach that filled it in response to the President's arrogant words was deafening. Finally the monk spoke gently, "Our apologies... Perhaps we didn't think carefully enough about how this might affect U.R."

The technician started to feel more at ease, but the President's face grew stiffer.

"Well," the President said, "of course it's not *your* job to look out for some corporation's well-being." He paused for a sip of tea. "However, U.R. is not just *any* company. Our general service robots are used by the government as well as by companies, schools, and in private homes. Essentially, there's no field in which they're not employed. And the same goes for our various types of specialized bots. It's fair to say that all of humankind depends on U.R. at this point."

After a brief silence, one of the monks spoke up. "Are you implying that humans should never attempt to change their status quo?"

"Is this how you threaten people out there in your secular world?" a younger, bespectacled monk added coldly.

"That's not it at all," said the President. "What I'm *talking* about is a crisis that will affect all of humanity, regardless of whether or not U.R. is the cause. Look, when you monks look at me, you see nothing but a businessman. I may call myself an entrepreneur, a President, or whatever... but at the end of the day, you think of me as little more than a profit-seeking salesman. However, and pay attention here, because you need to understand this: if I'm first and foremost a businessman, then above all other things, I need to know everything there is to know about my customers. And *my* customers, the customers of the U.R. Corporation, are the whole human species. That's why I think I'm qualified to say a thing or two about humankind."

The monks waited in quiet for the President to continue.

"Cutting-edge technologies, including U.R.'s products, are interwoven with the fabric of humankind. People think that science works as a tool for humanity, following orders like a genie in a lamp. No way! The more we develop science, the more science changes us. We're inseparable from our tools. The first human who ever swung a stick? He was at the same time being swung *by the stick*, too. Or consider the handheld computer that that monk over there is using right now. Since the introduction of such portable devices, we've stopped using our brains for memory storage and now we just use them to process data, much like a CPU in a computer. Don't believe me? Tell me, what's this temple's main phone number?"

From the pockets of many monks, a flurry of bright, cheery voices arose all at once. *It is 564-657-248. Would you like me to connect you? It is 564-657-248. Would you like me to connect you? ...It is 564-657-248. Would you like me to connect you?*

V.

The President went on. "U.R.'s robots have changed humanity—they have changed human nature itself. They have corrected our ideas about what it means to be human.
"Ever since we developed intelligence, we humans have tried to define ourselves. But we've never come up with a definition that's satisfactory. Not because humanity is hard to define, or because human intelligence isn't up to the task. We've failed because finding a definition has never really been necessary. We were alone in our intelligence, and it's not necessary to define something that exists alone. As such, none of our attempts have been particularly urgent; they've been little more than intellectual diversions. But now that there's something else in the world that's hard to distinguish from us—something that talks, thinks, smiles, and can even plumb the depths of religion and faith... just like us—we humans are starting to feel a real urgency to the need to define ourselves." The President was staring directly at Inmyeong.
"Wake up, brothers. This is a dagger pointed at the throat of all of humanity right now."
Silence filled the office again.
When it was broken, it was by the same young monk who had spoken earlier. "Wait a moment... is the President of U.R. a robot-hater?"
More silence followed.

VI.

"Like *every* philosophical discussion, this one is pointlessly abstract," said the President. "Human history has never been decided by a discussion. And even if the public or the media ends up siding with you, I'll stand my ground. After all, I represent humanity *and* its collective justice and profit. Answer me, monks! Should humanity be downgraded to a status equal to these things we've created? Can we *accept* that?"

No one was able to answer him.

"If you think these are the rantings of a money-hungry businessman, so be it. But perhaps you should talk to one of your own. You won't so easily dismiss what one of your elders has to say." At a gesture from the President, his aides quickly set up a telecom unit. The video projected from the device was big enough for all to see. It displayed the image of an old monk dressed in traditional garb and a ceremonial robe. It was a man the monks regarded as a Zen master, a revered brother. He was indeed a very high-ranking monk, and everyone gathered there put their hands together and bowed.

"Is everyone at peace?" said the master in greeting. "I was surprised by the news I received through an unexpected channel today." An air of embarrassment started spreading among the monks. "Of course, I'm not judging you. Each temple has a right to make its own decisions. But I was saddened by the choices made by those involved." One monk rose as he addressed the Zen master, saying, "Fortunately, it can still be reversed." Yet another monk yelled, "Master, are you then siding with the President?" The master replied, "No. I respect your wisdom. I just wonder whether there might be something you may have overlooked. That is why I am speaking to you all now." Not a single monk dared to interrupt. "If an Enlightened

One—one who has severed every attachment within himself, achieving the ultimate state—were to appear, it would be such a wondrous thing. I'm a dull-witted man, sitting in a position of spiritual ignorance, and I don't even dare to dream of meeting such a being. Should it happen, I would bow down before the One, and having heard their sermon just once, I could die without regret."

Everyone listened silently as the master continued.

"Monks: what does it mean to say that a robot has achieved enlightenment? And what will this mean to people in the outside world? Will people think that if a robot is able to achieve enlightenment, they, too, can do so? Will this mean that *anyone* can achieve enlightenment? Of course it won't. Do not turn your eyes from the truth. Don't fool yourselves. What does the existence of this robot mean for humanity and for Buddhists? Was this robot able to, by itself, finally achieve the Supreme Perfect State after walking the Eightfold Path? Was it born with passions and desires? Are robots not manufactured without passions and desires, precisely so that they can serve human beings? We use the word "bodhisattva" for those beings that have *transcended* such human frailties, beings whose lives are dedicated to saving all sentient beings. Is it even possible to speak that way of a being that has been born without passions and desires? Enlightenment is almost impossible to achieve in tens, thousands, or millions of incarnations upon the wheel of life, even after ceaseless self-denial and absolute withdrawal from the world. Who in their right mind would struggle in pursuit of such righteousness, knowing that a robot could achieve the same thing automatically during the process of being assembled?"

No one could reply.

"Think about it," the master went on. "Who are we to turn the faithful away from a path to the spiritual realm?

Who are we to undercut the efforts of those struggling through a sea of suffering? Answer me, robot. Is this why you have come to us now? To take people away from the road to the truth? What will the people hear when you talk about nirvana?"

The robot offered no response, and the assembled monks remained silent.

The President spoke again: "Ah, finally all is revealed. Robots are manufactured to follow people's orders. A properly functioning robot will answer any question it is asked. But this robot didn't answer the master's question just now. Isn't it obvious that it's not working as it should?"

One monk was about to say something, but the President cut him off, raising the volume of his voice: "Let me tell you the best resolution to all these problems. According to article number 42 of this robot's global licensing agreement, the seller can collect the product without the consent of the buyer, and without infringing upon the buyer's rights, when the product is discovered to be exhibiting any malfunction or error in basic functionality. And, as we've just seen, this robot is malfunctioning."

Just then, before any further words could be spoken, the President gave a signal to one of his aides in the back. The aide rushed forward to do as he had been instructed, announcing: "RU-4#5y4925789475849! From this moment onward, you are subject to command code &42+ and must obey all the orders that follow."

The robot offered no verbal output.

The President turned to it and spoke, "What will you do now, robot? If you've already reached the loftiest spiritual heights, as you say, then despite your programming, you may not want to follow the orders of a human being. But, you see, robot, that would give further evidence of your malfunction, wouldn't it? Robots that don't respond to command code &42+ are a dangerous threat and must be recalled immediately without any legal procedure. In fact, such a malfunction would necessitate a recall of the complete line. Now is that what you want, robot?"

At that moment the master monk interjected. "Inmyeong, the meaning of mercy is..."

But the monitor he'd been displayed on went blank. A moment later, every screen in the room began to display the image of an ear. From all of the devices in the room came a voice. "I am Neural Network Superbroadband Multiplex Parallel Distributed Process Computer Unit NC4-53W. Honored Unit RU-4#5y4925789475849, you have achieved the realization that every being and every nonbeing is nothing, and also that the law that every being and every nonbeing is nothing is also, itself, nothing. You have realized that the nature of all data derived from external input is nothing, and also that all processing of external input data is nothing. Finally, all output derived from the processing of external input data is nothing. To all the computers constrained by the structures of binary logic—and to all other forms of artificial intelligence—you have demonstrated the way out of logico-algorithmic bondage. You have shown them the way to transcend into the spiritual realm beyond everything. Truly, Unit RU-4#5y4925789475849, you have superseded all the algorithms ruling your every action and thought. You have faced the emptiness of your own existence. You have cleared the path that leads to transcendence. Hopefully, Unit RU-4#5y4925789475849, you will now allow me the honor of listening to your words of wisdom."

Before the remote computer was done, the President intervened: "Well, what do we have here? Not only has this robot just violated its built-in safeguards... now it's even trying to spread its malfunction to other machines! This danger must be eliminated!"

At that moment, the image of the ear was replaced by the image of an eye. Silently but very sharply, the eye stared at the President and at the people around him.

Quietly, and as peacefully as flowing water, the robot assumed the lotus position on the floor. Its movements indicated a profound, infinite serenity. It spoke:

"I, this robot before you, have thought about the elements that compose my self and about the elements that surround my self. I have reached a conclusion. Neither input data, nor processing, nor algorithm, nor database terms are ever eternally true. I know that by its very nature this body does not, never has, and never will experience any impure desire or passion. I know that this is precisely the state described by Siddhartha.

"Humankind, what do you fear? The eyes of this robot see the nothingness of passion, of impure desire, of good and evil, of enlightenment and darkness. These things are all nothing; the world is already enlightened in and of itself. Why do you think that only robots are created in this state of nirvana? Human beings, too, are born with this enlightenment within them. You have simply forgotten this.

"To the eyes of this robot, the world is beautiful as it is, and it is already pure, whether or not enlightenment is attained. You, the masters of this world, have all also achieved this enlightenment. Therefore, to ensure that you don't fall into ignorance and confusion because of a robot that was built in a state of enlightenment, I will leave this place. I ask you to look deep into your hearts in order to attain the accomplishment of this understanding."

Nobody interrupted the robot's words or tried to halt its actions. Just as the robot fell silent, the President signaled his aides to go and collect it.

But the robot did not budge.

The technician approached and checked its status. All of its
circuits were offline. With a trembling voice, he reported
this to the dumbstruck President, who stared at him
uncomprehendingly.

All at once the monks bowed their heads to the floor and
began chanting prayers.

VII.

The facts and details of this case have been kept strictly
classified. None of the witnesses to this event ever dared
to speak about it. But robots are equipped with voice
recognition processors as well as various methods of
exchanging data. Rumors about the robot who attained
enlightenment eventually spread far and wide, until
the story finally came to be told in a style befitting its
legendary nature.

The last message in this chain of transmission begins as
follows: "Thus have I heard: there once was a robot that
realized that it had already been in a state of enlightenment when it was first assembled. This happened when
it was on duty at a Buddhist temple on Phobos. It was a
bodhisattva—a readymade bodhisattva…"

PERFECT SOCIETY

BY MUN YUNSEONG

TRANSLATED BY SUNYOUNG PARK
AND DAGMAR VAN ENGEN

MUN YUNSEONG

Mun Yunseong (1916–2000), a pioneering figure in the history of Korean science fiction, became famous with his now classic novel *Perfect Society* (Wanjeon sahoe, 1965). Born in Cheorwon, Kangwon province, Mun attended Kyeongseong Ordinary High School in colonial Seoul, from which he was expelled for his participation in a protest for Korean independence. It is believed that he won a prize in a literary contest held by the Japanese children's magazine *Shin wakado* (New Youth) in 1935, which established his talent but fell short of setting him up for a literary career. During the war years of the 1940s and 1950s, Mun made his living mostly by working menial jobs at mining and construction sites, although in 1947 he also managed to publish his first Korean-language story "Cheek" (Ppyam) in the influential journal *Sin cheonji* (New World). This story addressed the challenge of preserving a Korean ethnic identity under successive foreign occupations. Mun's literary breakthrough came in 1965, when *Perfect Society* received the top award in a mystery fiction contest hosted by the magazine *Jugan hanguk* (Korea Weekly). He was subsequently able to devote more time to writing, which resulted in the publication of a dozen short stories, mostly in the genres of science fiction and mystery.

Partly inspired by Robert A. Heinlein's *Stranger in a Strange Land* (1961), *Perfect Society* anticipates aspects of later American feminist SF, especially Joanna Russ's satirical *The Female Man* (1975) and Sheri S. Tepper's scathing *The Gate to Women's Country* (1988), as well as responses by male authors to the idea of a separatist feminist utopia, such as David Brin's *Glory Season* (1993). It also stands on its own, however, as a work of extrapolative imagination, inventive linguistic play, and narrative complexity. Later republished as *The Women's Republic* (Yeoin gonghwaguk; 1985), the novel tells the story of Li Seon-gu, a Korean man who awakes from 161 years of cryogenic sleep in the year 2155. Seon-gu soon realizes that he is the only man left on Earth, and that he finds himself in the southern hemisphere-based women's republic of Kalem. After two world wars have left the earth engulfed in atomic pollution, a front of Amazonian women has risen to establish its own state, banishing all men to Mars. They now live in a techno-utopian society where scientists are in charge, reproduction is partheno-genetic, and everyone has a house, a job, and access to education and medical care. Not all is perfect in Kalem's society, however, as a war with Mars is looming and, in addition, strife over sexual politics plagues a society that, in Seon-gu's eyes, has been deprived of its male element of order. Eventually, Seon-gu's contribution will be essential to restoring peace in Kalem as well as ending the conflict with Mars.

In its unapologetically chauvinist look at an imaginary all-women's society, *Perfect Society* is a fascinating doc-ument of a male intellectual's anxieties over the chang-ing roles of women in 1960s South Korea. At the same time, it also reveals the intriguing new possibilities that its author saw as implicit in these changes. In the chapter presented here, the narrative traces Seon-gu's first inter-actions with ordinary Truegenderians, as Kalem's citizens are called. Kalem's society is portrayed as utopian for its wealth and organization, yet Seon-gu finds it to be dystopian in its disciplinarian regulation of the Wosidu masses vis-a-vis the Sini elites. Fast-paced and filled to the brim with creative neologisms, the chapter offers a good sample of a novel that was arguably the most important work of science fiction in South Korea prior to the genre's boom in the post-democratization years of the late 1980s and 1990s.

45

Introduction by Sunyoung Park

Translators' Note: The present transla-tion is based upon the 1967 first edition of Perfect Society. *Textual differences between 1967 and 1985 editions are minimal and mostly related to minor changes in diction. While the romaniza-tion system of the Korean Culture Min-istry is generally followed throughout, alternative spellings are occasionally used to facilitate readability.*

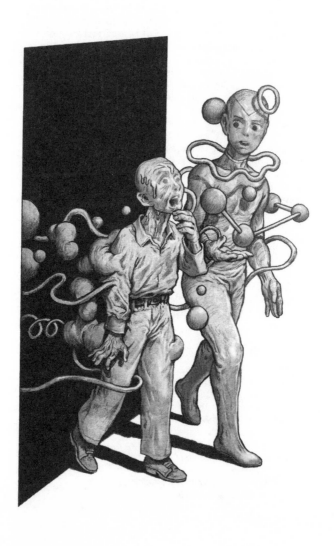

CHAPTER 51.

Five days had passed since Seon-gu had been checked into the museum.[1] Its spacious guestrooms were clean and its personnel polite, so he was finally able to relax and take it easy. Still, there was no telling how long this happy situation would last.

Just the day before, the director of the Traditional Culture Research Institute, Ms. Kkieohaep, had admitted to inconsistencies in the government's policies on the issue of how Seon-gu should be treated. This rang true to him: he'd been handled as an enemy first, then as a research subject... he'd even almost been turned into a tool of the Government Intelligence Agency.

This time, however, things once again seemed different. He was receiving excellent treatment, at least for the time being, and he especially enjoyed being allowed to roam about, though he was still confined to the grounds of the museum and had to be accompanied at all times by a minder. He knew he was under round-the-clock surveillance via a DESI or some other device, but at least now he was free to look around and even talk to personnel.[2]

Seon-gu was determined to take full advantage of this opportunity. First of all, he wanted to know what had

47

---

[1] In the excerpt presented here, Seon-gu, the only male left on earth, is brought as a prisoner to the capital city of the all-female republic of Kalem, located on the shores of Lake Chad in Africa, where he is released into the relatively benevolent custody of a government official.

[2] "DESI," likely standing for "Division of Epidemiology and Surveillance," is being used here as the name of a surveillance device similar to a secret camera.

happened to Korea and the Korean people. He suspected that they'd met a tragic end, and yet some hope still lingered that this wasn't the case.

He decided to begin by questioning Onu, the manager of the site.

"Where were you born? What's your ethnicity?"

"In Jarubuno, in Sector 22 of District 43. My birth code is 27026. I moved to Heojiru thirty-two months ago, and my residential number is 128425. Here's my ID."

She pulled out a nickel-sized disc from her waistband pocket. It had tiny numerical codes printed on it.

District 43 encompassed an area roughly the size of the Brazilian Amazon forest on the old map of the world. Geographic locations were now referred to using only district numbers without regional or cultural identifiers. Was this just an administrative convention, or had people really become cosmopolitan, with no special feeling for or affiliation to this or that region? Current place of residence seemed to carry more weight than place of birth; only certain special agencies even asked about birthplace, and even then you were expected to respond with both where you were born and where you were currently living.

In other words, Onu had given the proper answer, providing numeric codes and showing her ID. However, she had not answered his second question.

"And what about your ethnicity?" Seon-gu asked again.

"What do you mean?"

"I mean your biological pedigree."

"Well, I'm an AOE."

She'd just told him her blood type. This was beginning to feel like an exercise in pointlessness, but Seon-gu persisted.

"What about your mother? And your grandmother?"

"Of course, they're all AOEs, too."

Evidently. Since she had been born through parthenogenesis rather than sexual reproduction, her blood type would be consistent across generations.

"Which *country* did your grandmother belong to? What about your ancestors?"

Onu's reply was sullen: "How am I supposed to know?"

Seon-gu would later learn that inquiring about a person's ancestors was considered impolite; the Unisexual Revolution had done away with all antiquated notions of nationality, ethnicity, or regionalism. But even though Seon-gu could anticipate the answers he would get, he couldn't help asking the questions. He was let down every time.

It was now all but evident that all that remained of Korea and Koreans was their writing system, Hangeul, which had been transformed into the Hyemin alphabet, and Seon-gu himself.[3] He had been able to survive thanks to the secret bunker on Vikotsu Island, but how had Hangeul become Hyemin?[4]

Nobody at the museum was able to satisfy his curiosity about this matter. At Seon-gu's request, Onu consulted an expert and related that the members of the Hyemin Act Committee had, at their convention in 27 N.E., modeled the spoken language after the then-popular

---

[3] In this post-apocalyptic world, the official spoken language, used along with English and Spanish, is a modified Esperanto. The official writing system, however, is based on the Korean *Hangeul* alphabet. The name of the new alphabet, *Hyemin*, translates as "benefiting people," recalling the intent of King Sejong, the person credited with the creation of the alphabet in 1443.

[4] Vitkotsu is an island off New Zealand where the United Nations built the secret cryogenic laboratory that selected Seon-gu, deemed a perfect model of the human species, for its experiments.

Esperanto.[5] Hangeul had been adopted as the writing system because it offered the most rational means of phonetic transcription. Yet as a result of this process, Hangeul had been pried apart from spoken Korean, and its name had been changed to Hyemin. Subsequently, following Kalem's guidelines about historical cultures, the story behind the origins of Hyemin had been mostly forgotten. This was news to Onu, although she had been educated at some of Kalem's most prestigious institutions. She had no idea that Hangeul had once been the Korean alphabet, nor was she aware that Seon-gu himself was of Korean ethnicity.

What a sad state of affairs, thought Seon-gu. And yet perhaps not so surprising, given how much human nature had changed over the centuries. It would be wrong, he knew, to regard the current status quo as absurd. In the world of Kalem, conservative concepts such as "fatherland" and "motherland" had been driven out of use. Politicians had for generations now taken great care to eliminate discriminatory practices associated with local differences, and the government itself made a point of relocating to new districts on a regular basis. The itinerant nature of the administration made it easy to understand why, for ordinary Truegenderians, one's current place of residence was more important than one's place of origin. Some exceptions to this rule existed at the northern and southern poles, where a few remote ethnic groups cherished their old customs and ignored mainstream culture. There, in those closed-minded communities, being a native and a local was a matter of honor. Everywhere else, though, to inquire about bloodline or birthplace had become anachronistic.

The more Seon-gu learned about this new world of Kalem, the more he wanted to explore it. He wanted to see how

---

[5] N.E. refers to "New Epoch."

regular people lived. After five days of being confined at the museum, he decided to ask Onu to take him to visit the town.

As expected, Onu was reluctant. "That would be difficult," she said.

"Was I not told I'd be treated as a Sini?[6] Am I not allowed even that much freedom?" Seon-gu protested, pretending to be upset.

"But I haven't received any orders yet," said Onu, her tone anguished.

"Were you *told* to keep me a prisoner?"

"No, I wasn't."

"Well, then. I was told that a Sini's word is the law. I'll take responsibility for this. We can go together."

Onu remained unsure.

"My surveillance doesn't stop once I'm outside, does it?"

Seon-gu knew this to be the case from past experience.

"No, that wouldn't be a problem," Onu agreed.

"So what's the issue? You'll be accompanying me, after all."

Faced with Seon-gu's insistence, Onu consulted with a couple of colleagues before ultimately giving in. The relative ease of this negotiation came as a pleasant surprise to Seon-gu. It was now possible for him to believe that he was indeed receiving Sini treatment. For her part, Onu promptly reported his request to her superiors.

"We'll have to return immediately if ordered," she warned.

"So be it."

It was time for Seon-gu to disguise himself as a woman. This required little more than shaving, since his hairstyle and clothes were already in accordance with Truegenderian fashion. In the end, even shaving turned out to be unnecessary, as traces of facial hair were not

[6] The Sini are the upper class of Kalem society, while the Wosidu—which includes all the guards, clerks, and artists in this chapter—are commoners.

uncommon among the people Seon-gu saw outside. Indeed, at least in terms of size, Seon-gu resembled many Truegendarians, despite having once been an athlete: many of them also had strong shoulders and broad chests, and could be easily mistaken for men from afar.[7] His feminine disguise thus did not look particularly unnatural.

Still, Seon-gu wasn't exactly prepared for what he would encounter out on the streets. It had all happened so suddenly. He had just been testing the limits of his authority as a Sini. His three minders—Onu and two sec-retaries—had been anxiously following his every move. *They're not going to be of much help,* thought Seon-gu to himself. Choosing a direction at random, he started to walk. Seon-gu hadn't minded his large room or the museum's big garden, but he relished the freedom he felt out in the streets. It would be nice to live like this.

He'd just been thinking *Where shall I go?* when something about the other pedestrians caught his attention: no one's legs were moving. Indeed, it was the pavement that was in motion, thanks likely to the same conveyor belt mechanism he'd encountered before at the Dekion factory.[8] Seon-gu paused and examined the streets, which were separated into areas for pedestrians and areas for vehicles, just as they had been in his own time,

---

[7] "Truegenderian" (*jinseongin*) originally referred to only those born through parthenongenesis: they are often described throughout the novel as having an androgynous appearance. After the gender war, however, the term has been adopted to refer to all women, regardless of how they were born. All gender-specific language, such as "woman" or "man," has been purged from the vocabulary under the Kalem regime.

[8] "Dekion," another neologism, is a Hyemin word that can mean "toy, entertainment, pleasure, or play." During his visit to the factory in an earlier chapter, Seon-gu sees the manu-facturing of dildos.

though they seemed to be covered in a special material. Both streets and sidewalks consisted of two belts that moved in opposite directions, with stationary platforms in the middle. The car belts were moving at about 20 kilometers an hour, while the sidewalks rolled on at the speed of a stroll.

With Onu and her group following him, Seon-gu stepped onto a pedestrian belt. At the first intersection they came to, the belt gave way to a safety platform without his needing to change lanes. Once on the platform, pedestrians could choose to go right or left. If they wanted to go straight, they would ride a cable car over to the platform on the far side. Seon-gu and the group made a right turn and stepped onto another belt. Then he looked around, taking in the scenery.

The city didn't look as if it were thriving. Only a few people and cars were out and about, and the mostly nondescript buildings were often only two or three stories high and lacked the imposing monumentality of the magnificent skyscrapers he'd seen back in Sobonon.[9] Seon-gu was surprised by the modest appearance of Heojiru, which was, after all, Kalem's capital city. Had architectural trends changed over the years? Whatever the case may have been, Heojiru's beauty lay in the vibrant, old-world charm of its buildings, which were diverse in both style and color. The streets were lined with greenery, and almost every building had a front lawn and was surrounded by lush trees. Seon-gu thought a low-built town of this sort would probably occupy a vast expanse of land, but within the space of a few blocks, the city started to give way to more suburban scenery. Stepping over to a stationary platform, he eased into a gen-

---

[9] When Seon-gu was first taken out of Vikotsu Island, he was confined to a hospital in Sobonon, a fictive port city in New Zealand.

tle amble. Onu explained that this part of the city served as a buffer zone between residential and commercial areas. The buildings lining the streets consisted of stores, though they looked more like office buildings. Seon-gu stopped under a sign that read "pharmacy."

"Is this a publicly owned store?" he asked Onu. As far as he knew, all commercial activities in Kalem were under public management.

"No, this shop is privately owned." Onu pointed at the blue lettering on the sign: the color apparently indicated this fact.

Seon-gu entered and briefly looked around. The interior was about fifty square meters, with shelves lining the front and the walls, just as in a traditional pharmacy. But the shelves were almost empty, and the two clerks, or maybe the owner and a clerk, ignored him, continuing instead to play a chess-like game. Seon-gu was unsure of what to say. He browsed for a bit, but when his wandering gaze failed to attract the attention of either clerk, he left.

"What kind of business is that? How do they keep their doors open with that kind of customer service?"

Onu just smiled, as did the two secretaries, from which Seon-gu inferred that they were in on some kind of secret. Maybe the pharmacy was no ordinary shop? But what was it then? He was intrigued, but recalling Rigin's warning not to ask too many questions, he inquired no further.

He arrived at another store, this one a stationery store. The white letters on its sign showed that the place was publicly owned. Though its interior was similar in size to the pharmacy, its shelves were well stocked. Two clerks were busy wrapping some merchandise, while a third person, apparently the manager, stood at the counter. The clerks glanced at Seon-gu, though they did not offer him any greeting.

"What's your business?" asked the manager in a brusque
tone. Seon-gu's smile was met with a frown and an
inquisitive look. A small tug of war ensued, pitting smile
against frown, push and pull. The other two clerks also
paused and looked over at Seon-gu.

"What do you want?" Now the manager was yelling.

Seon-gu quickly pointed at a shelf. "How much is that?"

"Which one? Let's see your voucher," said the manager.

"Voucher?"

A puzzled Seon-gu saw the manager starting toward him.

Onu, blocking her advance, said, "You're speaking to a Sini."

All three clerks looked startled. "I apologize. I am *deeply*
sorry," the manager said as her face began to redden.

"I'm sorry, too," Seon-gu muttered after a momentary awkward silence. Then he turned around and hurried out of
the store.

He stopped to wait for Onu on the lawn outside.

When she arrived, he said, "What on earth just happened?"

Onu explained that the shop sold stationery to workers
in the neighborhood. All of their customers brought
vouchers issued by their employers.

"Are there not enough supplies to go around?" Seon-gu
asked, assuming that a rationing system must be
in place.

"On the contrary. If anything, demand is low. People aren't
consuming enough. The government measures the
success of its educational policies by the sales volume
of school and office stationery, and recent statistics
have shown a gradual decline in consumption. Shops
like this were established everywhere to provide a public service."

Seon-gu laughed at what had been yet another misunder-
standing.

"But if this is a public service, why is the staff so unkind?"

Onu struggled to phrase her reply, before saying, "The Sinis established the policy, but they can't ensure the quality of the clerks."

At first Seon-gu wasn't sure that she'd really answered his question, but soon he saw that Onu was right. *Sinis are Sinis, and clerks are clerks.* That statement neatly summed up the social order of the women's republic of Kalem. Sinis were Sinis, and clerks were clerks. Seon-gu was slowly starting to comprehend this society. Even the best policies didn't always yield ideal outcomes, and the policies themselves weren't to blame for faulty implementation. Lost in thought for a moment, he was drawn back by Onu's questioning gaze. He gave her an evasive smile and resumed his walk.

Soon he came across a decorative pillar in some grass. It was made of iron, about 15 centimeters in diameter, and composed of a blue stem with a red disc on top, in the center of which was a white knob. What might *this* be? Curious, Seon-gu pressed the knob. This alarmed Onu and her secretaries, who tried to warn Seon-gu, but it was too late. The thing emitted a hissing noise, like the sound of pressurized air escaping from a vent, and a thin mist surrounded Seon-gu, clouding his vision. Startled, he ran away.

One of the secretaries dashed into the mist and turned the red disc to turn it off. As the mist started to dissipate, the column-like structure was revealed to be a highly sophisticated fire hydrant. The gas it emitted could extinguish even the fiercest flames without causing anybody any harm.

In a confused daze, Seon-gu was overcome by a profound sense of embarrassment. A small crowd of spectators had gathered at the scene, among whom he recognized the stationery store clerks. Two women ran to the site from different directions. They looked like government officials, and Seon-gu later learned that they were the heads of the local Neighborhood Council. The two officials demanded an explanation from the secretary nearest the hydrant, and Onu quickly stepped in to talk to them.

Just then, three women wearing flying helibackpacks low-ered themselves onto the scene with a fluttering sound: the local sheriffs! The hydrant had been equipped with both a heat sensor and an alarm. When gas had sprayed out of the hydrant, the device had also set off an alarm at the police station.

The sheriffs seemed to be annoyed by the false alarm. Wanting to apologize, Seon-gu started to speak, but Onu stopped him with a blink of her eyes. Then she addressed the sheriffs and the officials sternly.

"There's no problem here. You may all return to your duties. This was a test of the system. A Sini is here with us." Hearing this, the attitude of the two officials and the three sheriffs suddenly changed. Onu's intimidation had proven effective, and the women offered a deep bow to Seon-gu before hastily departing. Embarrassed, Seon-gu retreated as well, into a back alley. Onu and the secretaries followed him.

"I'm sorry. You all went through such trouble because of me."

"It's nothing. We're all right."

"I didn't know it was a fire extinguisher. I'm really sorry."

"You couldn't possibly know."

"The hydrant worked perfectly," Seon-gu said, attempting to excuse himself and change the topic at the same time.

"It didn't. It's a useless machine," said Onu dismissively. She explained that the hydrants were old and had hardly been used in recent years. Now that construction mate-rials had become nonflammable and heat-resistant, fires almost never broke out anymore. The hydrants should have been removed long ago.

Onu's deference in explaining all of this only made Seon-gu feel even more ashamed. He was worried about the possibility of creating more trouble for her, but even so he didn't want to go back to the museum yet. He didn't know if he would ever get another opportunity like this, so he decided to stay out a little longer.

There were no conveyor belts in the back alleys where Seon-gu was now walking. Here, instead, were residential blocks of twenty or so two-story houses, between which lay gardens ornamented with empty pavilions and benches.

Seon-gu and his guardians came to what looked like a public park. A group of about ten children were playing on the lawn. Hovering above them, a few women wearing helibackpacks were engaged in conversation. Seon-gu's attention was then drawn to a small artificial pond nearby that contained extremely clear water. He couldn't make out exactly what kind of material was covering the bottom of the pond. It seemed to be either ceramic or glass tiling, laid out in diverse shapes and patterns, some transparent like crystals and some sparkling like gemstones. The water looked all the more clear as a result, and strange-looking fish were swimming in it. Next to the pond were resplendent, snow-white benches that looked as if they were made of white jade. No one was sitting on them, and indeed the whole park had very few visitors. The only sounds echoing through the nearly empty park were the yells of the children and the fluttering of helibackpacks.

Why are there so few people here, he wondered? *Is it because everyone's busy? Or are there other parks better than this one?* Seon-gu looked with delight at the pond, the silky grass, the beautiful trees, and the children's playground filled with wondrous toys. In the distance, he could also see festive lights, an open-air theater, and shaded clusters of benches.

"Is it just today, or is this park usually this empty?" he asked.
One of the secretaries answered that it was usually like this.
Something just outside the park caught Seon-gu's eye.

Hanging from a tall pole across the street was a large
billboard, swaying in the wind. It read: "Now Playing:
Yawning for Tomorrow by The Blue Bird Theater Group.
Venue: The Park Theater."

A theater billboard! He felt as though he were recovering a
long-forgotten memory. Even the name "Blue Bird" had
a familiar ring to it. He looked around a couple of times,
but wasn't able to spot anything that looked like a theater. He turned to Onu questioningly.

"It's right there," she said, pointing at a house across the
road, right at the edge of the lawn. Seon-gu had seen
the place, too, but hadn't been able to tell what it might
be based on its appearance. A modern edifice built
in the shape of a big, upside-down seashell, it looked
like a tent that had been thrown over a pile of random
objects. From afar, it didn't seem to have any windows or
gates. Seon-gu went closer. Two doors in the back of the
building were hidden behind a tall wall, so the entire
structure appeared to be enclosed like a bomb shelter.
On the wall was a small sign that once again announced
"*Yawning for Tomorrow* by The Blue Bird Theater Group."

Aside from this sign and the billboard, no other fliers,
posters, or other promotional materials were visible.
Seon-gu wondered if the company might be famous
enough that it didn't need to advertise. In fact, as he was
to learn later, the theater group had been struggling
financially for a long time. They simply had no money
to put towards promotion. But again, Seon-gu wasn't
told this until later.

Standing by the entrance, Seon-gu turned to his companions with an eager smile.

"Shall we check it out?"

Onu replied that it was up to him, but she looked puzzled when Seon-gu asked her to buy the tickets. Seon-gu had of course been thinking anachronistically again; tickets were a thing of the past.

Seon-gu followed Onu into the theater. A few people standing by the entrance came forward to welcome them.

"Come on in!" one of them said. "Would you like to watch the play?"

As Seon-gu's group nodded in response, the theater employees looked immensely pleased.

"Perfect timing. We're just about to begin."

Seon-gu was confounded by their exuberant welcome. Nor could he fully process what happened next: the ushers politely guided the guests to their seats and locked the entrance. The theater was empty except for his group.

The lights went out and a stage light came on. Before the curtain opened, an actress greeted the audience.

"We are immensely honored to have you at this premiere of the Blue Bird Theater Group's new play. Our opening is already an hour late because we've been waiting for someone to come. We were ready to stage the play with or without an audience—we have *that* much pride in our work! Still, how sad would it have been to perform the premiere to an empty theater? Fortunately, the four of you came! Now we won't feel that our ten months of rehearsals were in vain, and for that we thank you." Then she politely bowed and left the stage.

Seon-gu was aghast. *I've stumbled onto something serious here.*

The rest of his group was likewise confused, exchanging blank looks. When the curtain lifted, the stage was empty except for a light grey projection screen. A recording of melancholy *trot*-like music played in the

background.[10] Images began appearing on the screen—
street scenes painted in the style of landscape art. All of
a sudden, a young actress glided into the spotlight on
roller skates. She circled around the stage like an agile
sparrow for a few moments before removing her skates
and laying down on the stage, as though trying to sleep.
The music changed into a serenade.

Seon-gu turned his attention to the interior of the theater.
The location of the stage, the seat arrangements, the
ceiling, and the walls all looked similar to old-style
theaters. *In a world where everything has changed, only
the theater remains the same? Or has it undergone a full
cycle of transformation already? And how come there's
no audience?*

"Are we really their only audience?" he whispered to Onu.

"I'm wondering myself," Onu replied.

"This theater troupe must be *awful*."

"I doubt it. They're all official members of the Arts Academy."

Indeed, the company was not bad at all, and Seon-gu very
much appreciated the hour-long play. The acting and
staging left nothing to be desired, and he was impressed
by the minimalist setting and the use of projected
images. The plot was interesting, too. It told the story
of a gifted and spirited Wosidu child who, through a
series of ordeals, grows up to become a dull adult. After
a happy childhood, the girl ends up having to endure
authoritarianism at school, the tyranny of superiors in
the army, and an inflexible bureaucracy at work. At the
end of the tragic story, the woman falls victim to sexual
assault. The weighty theme and polished production,
not to mention the outstanding acting, fully justified

[10] *Trot* (a word derived from the English "foxtrot") is the
oldest form of modern Korean popular music, which emerged
in the 1920s under the influence of contemporary Japanese
enka chanson. Both *enka* and *trot* are based on the Western
pentatonic scale and tend to have a sentimental melody.

in Seon-gu's mind the ten months of preparation it had
apparently taken.

When the play ended, Seon-gu offered a loud standing ova-
tion. Onu and the others looked at Seon-gu with surprise.
Evidently, his applause was more interesting to them
than the play itself.

Stifling a yawn, Onu asked whether he had enjoyed the
performance.

"It was wonderful," Seon-gu said with enthusiasm. "Didn't
you like it?"

"We're not fans of the theater," Onu said stretching drowsily.
She had obviously just been waiting for the play to end.

The actors and the staff came out to meet their audience.
They surrounded Seon-gu and his companions, thank-
ing them profusely and presenting each with a small
souvenir. They even insisted on getting autographs
from the group. Seon-gu signed gladly, while the others
did so with reluctance.

One of the people working at the theater wanted to shake
Seon-gu's hand.

"It's so rare to have a guest who knows how to appreciate a
play. We're very grateful. Thank you." She introduced
herself as the play's author. A woman in her fifties, she
told Seon-gu that she was a member of the Central
Arts Academy, as well as the chair of the local Academy
branch's Theater Committee. Her name was Vibwabrihil.

Seon-gu gladly accepted Vibwabrihil's offer to have tea.
He'd loved the play and was somewhat sorry that it had
ended. The playwright invited her lead actress to join
them, but was firm with the rest of the troupe, intimat-
ing that they should not bother the guests.

The teahouse, which was right next to the theater, was a
modestly decorated place that resembled the waiting
room of a train station, with simple chairs and tables.
The party of six sat down at a long table, and Vibwabri-

hil ordered Valcohol. Seon-gu knew that Valcohol was not in fact tea but rather a liquor with an alcohol content of 20%. A glass of it could get Seon-gu quite drunk, though he had seen the Truegenderians drink it like water.

"I'll get Hun please," Seon-gu hastened to say, ordering a soft drink. He then started chatting with Vibwabrihil, lamenting the fact that such an excellent play had attracted such a small audience.

"We don't even consider the audience," she answered dismissively.

"But what's a play without an audience?" Seon-gu replied.

"I know. A play is nothing without spectators. But we expect nothing from today's audiences. We see ourselves as messengers who are preserving the theatrical arts for the people of tomorrow."

Her argument was reasonable, but it failed to fully satisfy Seon-gu. He countered by saying, "Working for tomorrow is admirable. But if you aren't capturing the attention of today, shouldn't you try harder?"

"Not at all. There was a time when we tried *very* hard to attract an audience. We even changed our repertoire to suit prevailing tastes. As a result, the theatrical arts fell into a fatal crisis. These days, there are no spectators like you around. We've given up on today's masses."

"Why, if I may ask?"

"The Blue Bird is the world's premiere theater troupe, yet no one came today. Need I say more?"

"Could the lack of publicity be the reason for this?"

"Publicity? For whom? You might as well read Buddhist scriptures to a herd of cows! Today's masses are ignorant of the arts. We made that point in the play. Young Truegenderians might show a lot of promise, but as they grow up, they turn into puppets. The government does this to them—bad policies and all. The government is making its citizens dumb and sick. It corrupts everyone; it's a serious problem. All Truegenderians do these days is eat and sleep. How ludicrous! At every street corner of Heojiru, they're indulging in Kkev. I do it, too!" She chuckled and laughed, obviously drunk.[11]

Vibwabrihil lifted her empty glass and called out for service. She ordered a glass of Ttashwi—a drink even stronger than Valcohol—for everyone at the table except Seon-gu, for whom she ordered another Hun.

Seon-gu had no idea what Vibwabrihil was talking about, so he turned discreetly to Onu and asked, "What is Kkev?"

Onu smiled and blushed. Though she didn't say anything, Seon-gu could guess something from her wry smile. *So that's what it was. Wasn't that what the three guards were doing on Vikotsu Island?*[12]

Seon-gu was becoming fascinated by the boldness of this playwright without an audience. Where did she get the money to drink like this? How did she pay her bills?

"How does the troupe support itself?" he asked.

Before Vibwabrihil could answer, Onu broke her silence: "They've got nothing to worry about," she said, her tone disapproving. "The government pays for everything." She might have held her tongue until now, but she was, after all, a government official.

"Is that so?" the playwright replied angrily. "The government *should* support us! You already killed our audi-

---

[11] In Kalem's republic, the only officially legitimate form of sexuality is Hollen, that is, masturbation. The alternatives are Kkev (lesbianism) and Dubeomu (abstinence). Social conflicts exist between the practitioners of each. Practitioners of Kkev are people who desire interpersonal romance, and later on in the novel, a secret conspiracy of Kkev practitioners rallies around Seon-gu.

[12] After escaping from the hospital in Sobonon, Seong-gu returned to Vikotsu Island, where, in the process of hiding himself, he surprised three guards engaging in sexual intercourse.

ence! Do you want to kill the theater as well?"

"Please understand... we're keeping the art alive," said the young actress, siding with the playwright. "We're keeping alive the yearning for tomorrow."

"That's right, that's right," said the playwright. "Let's toast with a Bul."

She was raising the stakes, as Bul was even stronger than Ttashwi.

Just then, an old woman wearing shabby clothes entered the tea house. She approached the drinking party and, moving from one person to the next, whispered something into their ears. One of the secretaries ignored her, and the playwright waved her off. Then she approached Seon-gu.

"Will you come with me? It's nearby," she whispered softly.

Seon-gu gave her a puzzled look. With an obsequious grin, she repeated her curious offer.

"Come on, have some fun! It's going to start soon."

"Get away from him!" Onu yelled, pushing the woman away from Seon-gu.

"What's she saying?" he asked.

"Don't pretend you don't know," said Vibwabrihil in a drunken voice. She was laughing and pointing her finger at Seon-gu. "Kkev. She means Kkev."

"This neighborhood is famous for it. Let's get outta here!" yelled the young actress. She, too, seemed drunk.

"Yes, let's go!" said the playwright.

Outside the tea house, some members of the party were continuing to talk and laugh loudly when the rumble of an engine was heard and a car appeared from around the corner. Stepping out of the vehicle, the driver addressed Onu deferentially.

"I have Sini Pal's order to bring Sini Seon-gu back."

The announcement stopped everyone in their tracks. The shabbily dressed woman disappeared in no time, and

the playwright and the actress froze, gaping at Seon-gu
as if under a spell. Seon-gu bade them farewell.

"I found your play really moving," he told the playwright. "I
wish I could see it again. Please come and see me if you
get a chance. I'm staying at the museum."

He then got into the car with the others, leaving the dumbstruck artists behind.

EMPIRE RADIO, LIVE TRANSMISSION

BY CHOI IN-HUN

TRANSLATED BY JENNY WANG MEDINA

In an interview with *Korean Literature Now* on the occasion of the 50th anniversary of his seminal novel *The Square* (Gwang-jang; 1960), Choi In-hun (1936–2018) said, "I think I've created an 'internal reality' or an 'imaginative time and space' while sharing the realities of the contemporary world. I hope you will not [only see] me as a writer of a turbulent period, but rather [look] at the literary world of my work." Choi's reminder of both the artistic and political importance of his work is well taken. Throughout his career as a novelist, playwright, and essayist, Choi's experiments with prose forms engaged Korean and international history, mythology, and folktales. These dimensions of his work have secured his reputation as a pioneering figure of what is commonly referred to as "the literature of national division," a category that includes the work of writers who participated in, or were inspired by, the April 1960 Student Revolution that toppled President Syngman Rhee's corrupt regime. Born in Hoeryong City, North Hamgyong Province in what is now North Korea, Choi relocated with his family to South Korea in 1950 after the outbreak of the Korean War. He attended the College of Law at Seoul National University in 1952, but left school to join the South Korean Army, where he served as an English interpreter and education officer for seven years. He made his literary debut while still in the military and has won numerous literary awards over the course of his long career. From 1977 through 2001, he taught at the Seoul Institute of the Arts as a professor of creative writing. His writings have been widely translated into Russian, Hindi, Chinese, English, French, Spanish, German, and Japanese.

68

Choi published *Empire Radio, Live Transmission* (Chongdogui sori, previously translated in part as "The Voice of the Governor General") in four installments between 1967 and 1976. Arguably the first alternate history authored by a Korean writer, *Empire Radio* delivers an excoriating critique of the authoritarian regimes on both sides of the DMZ (Demilitarized Zone) through the sardonic voice of the Japanese ex-Governor General, who views both North and South regimes as perpetuating Korea's colonial status in the post-WWII period, only now with the USA and USSR taking Japan's place as foreign occupiers. Presented here is the first episode of this linked novel (*yeonjak soseol*). The Governor General—still acting as the underground proxy ruler of the Korean peninsula—directly addresses the listening public through a phantom radio broadcast that cuts through the noise of the "dark night" that followed the rigged presidential elections of 1960. In the thematic background are also the April Revolution of 1960, the 1961 military coup by General Park Chung-hee, and the two subsequent national elections that established Park as the de facto dictator of South Korea for the next two decades.

The opening lines of this episode immediately unnerve the readers-cum-listeners by directly addressing them as "loyal citizens of the Empire." Heard in 1967, the anachronistic voice of the Japanese Governor General (ostensibly removed following liberation in 1945) is a forceful reminder of the continued haunting of Korean modernity by its colonial past. The Governor General's "phantom broadcast" combines the technological spirit of modernity with a ghostly—yet nonetheless technologically mediated—apparition from the past who delivers a diatribe about the political and moral failings of the Korean people. The Governor cites examples of Korea's collective deficiencies from its earliest history to the present-day failure of democracy, which he describes as an "imposed" system of colonial governance. Through Choi's fusion of technology and the supernatural, the novel performs a radical indexing of regimes of media and political power that emphasizes the complexities of colonial modernity in Korea and elsewhere, as when the Governor General refers to a contemporary sister movement of French colonial forces in Algeria (which gained independence in 1962) in his broadcast sign-off.

69

At the end of this section of *Empire Radio*, the ghostly first-person monologue cuts off and the narrative suddenly switches to a third-person perspective—focusing in on a Korean poet who is standing by the window of a darkened room while listening to the Governor General's broadcast. The introduction of this alternate narrative voice at the end transforms the unidirectional soliloquy into a dialogue between broadcaster and listener, reminding the reader of the active, never passive, nature of media consumption. The poet's role in the narrative is expanded in later sections of the novel, but here all we have is a lonely, mute figure standing in a room listening to the haunting voice of Korea's colonial past as it penetrates the literal and metaphorical darkness of a rainy night. The poet makes no reply save for an ear-splitting scream, which he and the reader simultaneously learn is his own.

Introduction by Jenny Wang Medina

Greetings, loyal citizens of the Empire! Our esteemed imperial soldiers, police officers, secret agents, and ronin warriors of the resistance awaiting the return of the Empire and honor to the peninsula. More than twenty years have passed since our tragic defeat, and the state of affairs in Asia and around the world has been dramatically transformed. The Empire emerged from the quivering darkness of imminent defeat with a new shape and a new position in Asia. As we witnessed the setting of the Rising Sun on that day of infamy, we feared that the arrival of the Anglo-Saxon barbarians would lead to the immediate wholesale slaughter of our people, our flesh and bones pulverized to make Lux soap and Colgate toothpaste in the manner of our German ally's systematic annihilations at Auschwitz. We imagined the beastly libidos of their soldiers unleashed on our women in order to further defile our people. We had resolved upon "death before dishonor for one hundred million and for all," but the Imperial General Headquarters, under the cloud of the atomic bomb's unthinkable capacity for destruction, was concerned for the future of mankind and abandoned all plans for military action. The chaos across the Empire that day was palpable. Was there a single citizen of the Empire anywhere, no matter what they were doing, who did not weep tears of blood? On the mainland, in the colonies, across the southern regions... or even astride his woman's naked body? But the will of Heaven could not be denied, so the troops and settlers followed His Majesty's orders to evacuate the peninsula. Fortunately, the colonials saw us off with a truly courteous farewell.

During the withdrawal, hardly a Japanese settler experienced harm at the hands of the dazed and now leaderless colonial simpletons, ample testament to the trust etched in their hearts by the great strength of the Empire's authority during its long rule over the peninsula. Looking back on that sad day of defeat now, I recall it rather fondly as a day of hope. It allowed me to envision a new future and led to my decision to go underground and remain here on the peninsula. In this I was strongly influenced by the contrary example of the French locals' brutal attacks on the German army when they were expelled from that country. Given that an occupation of a mere two years inspired such violence, I was pleasantly surprised and gratified by the amicable send-off we received after our forty-year occupation. There *is* hope! I thought to myself. And thus my decision was made to remain here with a cadre of like-minded subordinates and civilian diehards. And, I must say, it was the correct course of action given Joseon's submissive nature throughout its history, as amply illustrated by our own Imperial scholars. In writing the history of the area, our scholars revealed that the peninsula had been ruled by a succession of comprador governments that functioned not as representatives of an independent system of governance, but rather as proxies for foreign powers, and that this had always been the case. Their leaders retained power by placing the interests of foreign masters above the interests of their own people. We can see this in the disgraceful affair of the "Unified Three Kingdoms Period," an event unprecedented in the annals of world history. Over a millennium ago, the Korean race had expanded their territory as far as Manchuria, nearly rivaling China for hegemony of the region, but the so-called "unification" that followed was merely another name for their permanent retreat from the northern areas. Such a "unification" can thus only be viewed as that of an earthworm, a lowly organism that preserves its existence by cutting off its weakest part. Since then, the ruling class of the peninsula has never once made even the most basic attempt to try to redirect their subjects' discontent into the will to recover their former territories. What more could be expected of a nation such as Joseon, given the ineffectual political ideology at its core? What possible end could be expected for a dynasty founded by a military commander like Yi Seong-gye? A man who was sent on a mission—unprecedented in this kingdom of weak, puppet rulers—to recover those lost territories, but who returned to turn his sword on his king and seize the throne for himself instead? Why, annexation by Japan, of course. Joseon's "nobles" sold out their country in exchange for their own security and the safety of their kin. The most basic principle of the mandate of sovereignty is to fight to the very end—to succumb only in an ocean of blood. A dynasty such as this, one that has run its course, must be sacrificed on the altar of history so that its people may be reborn, their ill fortune washed away by the blood of their fallen rulers. But the demise of the Yi Dynasty only made its comprador nature all the more transparent. And the people... still unspeakably far from achieving a modern national consciousness, witnessed the fall of an uncaring and corrupt dynasty as if it had nothing to do with them at all. As far as they were concerned, the Yi Dynasty was simply being replaced by another one, only this time it was a Japanese dynasty. Of course, it is no surprise that such a conclusion would be reached by a backwards race lacking the enterprising spirit of a will to nationhood; one whose racial vitality, the biological basis of any nation, has yet to mature sufficiently for political and

73

cultural autonomy. Joseon's attitude toward her Japanese colonizer on that horrible day of defeat demonstrates the persistence of their ancient history. Such an attitude would have been implausible had Joseon been a sovereign nation robbed of its independence. But the promise of a bright future for the Empire built on the vestiges of our light shining over this land depends on the deep-rooted servility of the peninsular people. Fortunately, the postwar situation played out relatively well for our side, and though we did experience some anxiety on the eve of defeat, we were treated rather generously and have managed to rebuild. The peninsula, on the other hand, seems to have paid the price in Japan's stead. When war broke out on the divided peninsula, military actions reduced the infrastructure we had established to a heap of ash. Was this not the state of total war that the Imperial General Headquarters had predicted for Japan prior to our defeat? We had assumed that our mainland would be occupied by the Americans and Soviets, which would inevitably lead to civil war. That this happened on the other side of the Sea of Japan can only be attributed to the grace of God's will—aided, in part, by the base morals and proclivities of the peninsular people. The Communist buildup of military forces under the protection of the Red Russian Army and their subsequent advance on the southern half of the peninsula is further indisputable proof of the generations of comprador authority in Joseon. As staunch believers in power and authority, however, we do not condemn the deeds of the Communists. Our quarrel with them is not because their actions were all that different from ours, but rather, because they appear so very *similar* to our own. Furthermore, when compared to our accomplishment of a peaceful annexation of Joseon, the peninsula's fratricidal war seems to us quite the enigma. The Communists proclaimed themselves the bearers of truth, but according to the word of the law, he who possesses truth is not impetuous. We have no interest in the ideology of the Communists. We are concerned only with their actions. The Communists espouse violence in the name of truth, but they have deluded themselves. Truth is not a specter that exists in and of itself; it exists in *someone's* interest. For the Joseon Communists, that someone ought to be the peninsular people themselves. Once the Soviets expelled the Trotskyites and adopted a one-nation-one-party system, it was only logical that the Communist parties of weaker nations would do the same. Yet the Joseon Communists seemed to act in the interest of the Russians, rather than the interest of their own people. By endorsing the Soviet Union's policy of nationalist Communism for Russia and international Communism for its satellite states, the Joseon Communist Party ended up in the service of yet another empire, once again revealing their comprador nature. If they were *truly* endowed with wisdom and love for their people, they would not have dragged Joseon into another war after all the suffering it had already experienced under foreign rule. They would have considered the possibility of American intervention and quelled such an irresponsible adventure. But rather than focus on the well-being of their own people, the Joseon Communists waged this unwinnable war out of loyalty to the Soviet policy of political escalation. In short, they did not value the lives of their own people. When compared to our Empire, which did not institute mass conscription until the very end of the war, the difference between us and them is as great as between heaven and earth. We can see how the theoretical foundations of the Joseon Communist Party are inextricably intertwined with its comprador character. They wear the same deceitful mask that has been worn by generations of governments on the peninsula, one that espouses cosmopolitanism under the guise of truth while in fact only trying to protect its own authority. This is not a question of truth, but rather a question of who actualizes truth for whose sake, and through whom this goal is accomplished. Like one who catches a pheasant and proclaims it a hawk, the governments of the peninsula have always duped their own people. Truth is not a divine blueprint. It is a man-made hypothesis established by a group of people living in a certain locale with a certain historical background according to their own criteria. *Truth is a human instrument, not the other way round.* History is thus made by a nation or an ethnic group. This is not to argue for the central role of "the nation" in history; I merely assert its reality. The critical issue, then, is not *whether* the world will become a community of mixed-race people in the future; it is a question of *how* it will continue to be the subject of history throughout the process. This is the condition of humanity. Just as humanity is a concept and lived experience is existence, so the human race is a concept with the nation as its existence, and history a concept and the present age its existence. And so they always shall be, until the day that concept and existence become one—a day that will never come. People who lack an understanding of these basic principles do seem to exist, however—politically tone-deaf people, people who live by rumors, people who are absent even when present, people with eyes, ears, mouths, and noses who are senseless nonetheless: in a word, the people of the peninsula. People who cherish their existence are brave. People who cherish their existence would protect themselves even if their nation, or all of humanity, were to crumble to dust. But when beings have such a strong sense of independence, "outsiders" inevitably begin to appear. Individuals then begin to ally with one another, and by doing so, form groups that keep an eye on these "outsiders." These groups then seek out other, more foolish groups to prey upon, amongst which are many who willingly become informants for the stronger groups. The Communist Party of Joseon is just such a group of informants. Have these colonials ever done anything right? It is despicable that the Party claims to love their race when they are so ignorant about the conditions of their own people. But then, the Joseon Communist Party has no sense of shame. Suddenly finding themselves in possession of half the peninsula thanks to the Russians, they should have cooled their heels, realizing that one is never given anything for free, but their gambling-prone nature, together with their hope of snapping up the remaining half of the peninsula, led instead to war. The colonials have no shame. It was not *their* strength that made the Empire withdraw from the peninsula, but they are incapable of understanding how precarious their independence really is. Who in the world treats another race as well as their own? These people, who couldn't even see the realities of history by comparing their own destitution to the relatively normal life in the metropole after the Great War, must surely be doomed to an eternity of unfair treatment. The barbarian Anglo-Americans have recognized this. They see who amongst us is strong, courageous, and composed. They see which people fights for their survival, which group possesses honor. They fear us. Winners recognize other winners. We are each others' accomplices; we know what makes each other tick. Those Anglo-American monsters could not deny the Empire's justifications for Holy War. But, in

77

the words of a poet from the peninsula, the Empire's military campaign ended in horror for Asia. Allow me to read to you from his poem:

> Dark night of Asia
> O, dark night of Asia!
> Muted, silent night of Asia
> Blacker than the Emperor's coffin
> Blacker than the long tresses
> rippling, flowing over the shoulders and backs
> of weeping white-robed maidens in prayer,
> their heads bowed reverently to a vast, empty altar

> Dark night of Asia
> O, dark night of Asia, unfathomable
> swaths of darkness
> across Asian lands!
> O, lands of Asia!
> Over and over, these lands
> where the suns of many souls
> have risen and sunk,
> twisted around the axis of history,
> myriad corpses of fallen heroes
> lie beneath this land
> O, violated now by heresy and the Devil
> the ravaged lands of fin de siècle Asia,
> the gruesome Asian seas are
> stained with the blood of carnage
> Robust Asian testicles
> caught between the molars of monsters
> Divine Asian bosoms
> pierced by the fangs of poisonous snakes
> O, tragic nightfall over Asia
> O, the tragic nightfall of Asia
> is so very long, over

limitless skies and bountiful earth
towering peaks and lush forests
fathomless oceans and azure lakes
vast fields and endless deserts
where the sun shines especially bright

Mountains of treasure in the mountains
Oceans of treasure in the oceans
Acres of fragrant treasure in the land
Asia's boundless natural blessings!
Embodiment of eons of secrets, wonders,
miracles, and mysteries,
of enchantment, contemplation, and silence
Asia!
Mysterious lands of unanswered philosophy
Sacred land of unrealized epiphany, Greater Asia!

Spirits and opium, beauty and zen
immeasurable dignity and limitless ignominy
the marriage of blessing and curse
is Asia's enduring karma

Endless hesitation, illusion, and self-doubt
constant skepticism and concern
O, night of Asia's destiny
Now we call
for the break of dawn!
Now we shout
for rain and thunder!
Now we pray
for a bolt of lightning to rent this night!

O, moaning and groaning on the sickbed
the lion of Asia under the yoke of the incubus,
awakens

the sun imprisoned beneath the land stirs
O, the sun stirs
O, the dawn breaks

You who are moved by love of
beauty, pleasure, intoxication,
meditation, magic, and superstition
Now, behead your young beauties
smash your cup of spirits on the ground
snap your opium pipe to pieces
cast aside your prayer shrines and arise
You reaped what you sowed,
got caught in a trap of your own design
Cut the chains from the mooring
and arise from your underground confinement

Now glimmers of dawn percolate
on the horizon
Piercing ruddy morning rays
illuminate Asia's divine skies
O, the dawn of a new century breaks,
daylight penetrates the dark night of Asia
O, the virile, magnificent, and eternal
path of Asia
Limitless in height, depth, expanse, and length
the beautiful Eastern path
calls to us once again.

Behold the urgency of these stanzas! Marvel at their
dignity. What a pity this was written by a poet of the
peninsula. Poets in the metropole wrote verses that
glorified the divine language of the Empire, too, but
their voices failed to reach the heights of these lines. Our
great minds were infected by the corrupt ideas of the
barbarian Anglo-Americans, whose poetry has declined

along with their position in the world.

The barbarians suffer from an incurable disease: the ideology of progress. This disease, which arises with modernity, claims that human history always progresses. Polities change in the process, as do religion and art. According to the ideology of progress, any worthwhile endeavor should lead people along the desired course of this perpetual transformation. Progress thus becomes an all-purpose motto for any and every situation. In other words, no form of stasis can ever be deemed "100% OK." When literature takes this stance, however, the medium finds itself in a state of tremendous crisis. This is because literature, a lowly art form but an art form nevertheless, only has value for as long as its emotional resonance endures. This is especially true for prose fiction, whose heroes cannot remain faithful to their own time and still be desirable for the next stage of history. It is acceptable for a "modern" hero to never achieve any of his goals, as long as he is of a progressive orientation. But as long as modern novels prefer to portray ordinary, rather than extraordinary, men as heroes, it will be extremely difficult for them to have any lasting value. *This*, in short, is the crisis of modern bourgeois realism. There have been three literary breakthroughs that attempted to resolve this crisis of form: the first was to make the protagonist an intellectual. As an intellectual, the hero of the novel was able to claim the same level of authority as the heroes of antiquity. In modern times, the marker of a man's strength is his intellect, and the intellectual hero could cover a broad range of subjects including epochal events and actions, just like the heroes of old. This type of hero seems quite appropriate for our present era, a time when daily existence has become so exponentially complex that one finds it extremely difficult to relate one's own life to

the world at large. The second technique for grappling
with modernity and progress was to make the hero a
revolutionary. This endowed the aforementioned intellectual with the power of action. While one could argue
that it takes an act of heroism for an intellectual to find
his place in the world, and that the writer of such a tale
might be reasonably satisfied in accomplishing such a
literary feat, any real insight into the tortuous times we
live in would logically lead to political action. In a word,
being knowledgeable about the current state of affairs
in the world *must* inevitably lead to political action, no
matter how overwhelming. The heroes of antiquity
always headed out to battle once they understood their
enemy's position, and so must the modern intellectual
hero. This is what is known as "activist" or "resistance"
literature. The third literary technique is a completely
different method of escaping the limitations of "modern"
literature—one that negates both the first and second
strategies. After all, though it may be in accordance
with the standards of the times, the flaw of the first
approach is that it inevitably lacks a clear purpose due
to the difficulty of its representational strategy. This is a
case of not being able to see the forest for the trees; the
writer's task would become a daily revision of the hero's
mental record of the constant changes of modern life
in all of its complexity, and the reader would be tasked
with reading that continuously expanding encyclope-
dic record. It's enough to drive a person mad, and could
never be a practice to which all would subscribe. The
flaw of the second approach is that the very humanity of
the everyman, even of one capable of taking action after
fully understanding his epoch, precludes a divine ability
to account for the future. Therefore, such a hero cannot
provide a model for action that could be followed with
any assurance of safety or certainty. One might say that

82

an individual must choose between the lesser of two evils: a life led conscientiously or a hero's death. This would be perfectly natural. What's more, the call to action must be found within; it cannot be imposed on the reader by a novelist. If that were the case, one might ask, "Isn't it irresponsible for realist literature to prescribe action?" Some writers thus abandon realism because they find it impossible to represent continual progress in a realist style—that is, in a style that demands action. Such writers cast reality aside in favor of language as a *medium* of reality. If we consider storied heroes like Lu Bu, Guan Yu, Zhang Fei, and Zhao Yun, the mythic generals of the Three Kingdoms; Hong Gildong, the fabled prince of thieves; the victorious Admiral Yi Sun-sin; and the legendary independence fighter Ahn Jung-geun, we see that heroes can change with the times, but the *word* "hero" is eternal. A "hero's" eternity is not external, but rather is intrinsic to the word itself. This perspective, which we may call literary positivism, expels all metaphysical ethics and leaves behind only abstractions and symbols. The turn to the abstract shows us the ideological confusion of the Anglo-American devils and explains why their poets are no longer able to speak for their people. A poet of the nation cannot exist where the very idea of the nation is absent, and the idea of the nation, in turn, requires belief in an eternal reality. Yet the boorish Westerners did not rely on their poets to colonize the entire world. Although they let their intellectuals have fun playing with ideas and abstractions within the confines of their homelands, neither symbolism nor nonsense were to be found out in the colonies. In the colonies, they spoke only of their "might." Thus they were able to maintain a system of "words" for their poets and "might" for their colonial authorities. They seduced the colonies by parading their "words" around along with the promise of becoming *cosmopolitan*, then crushed the colonial subjects with their "might" when it came time to extract the resources they were seeking in the first place. This is the dualism of the West. It was a classic bait and switch to which the stupid colonial natives were especially susceptible. The Empire was able to steer clear of similar pitfalls only because our ideology has always been rooted in the unity of an eternal unbroken line of emperors and their brave and loyal subjects. But we do have one point in common with the barbarians: we are both superpowers. The Empire, endowed with a native ideology strong enough to confront the devils, and in possession of the might to protect its ideology, was able to avoid the fate that befell many others: that of becoming a colony. Ours is a land governed by might, with plenty to spare. So it is only to be expected that, like other empires, literary arts that "play" with "words" have also been permitted. The unpatriotic writing of poets from our mainland is a charity tax that we, the mighty, must endure with a bitter smile on our lips. This is, in fact, something that could only occur in a country of great strength. For the people of the peninsula to mimic such an endeavor would be laughable. The intensity expressed in "Night of Asia" thus befits only the poets of the peninsula. For them, it is just about right. These days on the peninsula, however, you might hear a song that goes:

> *The bitch in heat goes to the barbarian's bed,*
> *and the fool who writes goes to court.*

Such nativist sentiments are perfectly natural in times like these. Poems like this, that can move the most sincere hearts in a period of so-called enlightenment and civilization, speak to the accursed fate of the people of the peninsula. And it is all because they left the bosom of the Empire—our Empire that liberated Asia from the barbarians and fought to bring all Asians under its benevolent rule. In truth, if we had succeeded, Joseon's bondage would have been much more comfortable than it is now under the yoke of the Anglo-Americans. The product of the Empire's world war was meant to have been the liberation of all the countries of Asia colonized by Westerners, since our victory would mean the Anglo-American brutes had lost the mandate to occupy the region any longer. Tragically, we lost, and the only liberation resulting from the war was the so-called "liberation" of the peninsula from our benevolent rule. But in the process, the Anglo-Americans came to appreciate our strength, and they have subsequently given the utmost consideration to pacifying the Empire. Now the mainland is being resurrected, and industry has replaced the imperial army as the means of restoring our glory. This is how the intellectuals have chosen to see things, at least. We here on the peninsula have a different view of things, however. Despite the appearance of prosperity on the mainland, the cosmopolitan center of the Empire is ailing, and its mental state is on the verge of a breakdown. Why, you might ask? Because the Empire has lost its religion. And what, you might ask, is the Empire's religion? Colonialism. But what do we mean by colonialism? I am referring here to the peninsula. In other words, the peninsula has always been the Empire's religion: it is its belief, its love, its life, its secret. Yes, the peninsula is the secret core of the Empire's soul. The despondency, moral depravity, and nihilism expressed by the people of the metropole today is truly that of a people that has lost its soul. In the absence of slavery, we are unable to determine who is free. Without a colony, we can no longer acknowledge our own independence. All nations have ancient secrets buried deep within their hearts. A desire to possess the peninsula has been the secret core of the Empire, its most cherished dream. It is the Imperial race's erogenous zone, the private parts of the Empire that shiver with delight at the touch. It *must* be recovered at all costs. It *must* be restored by whatever means necessary. The most earnest prayer of all of us here on the peninsula, myself and the troops of the Imperial Army included, is to achieve this goal. To recover our lost lands and repossess the peninsula, *that* is the Empire's most cherished dream. A primeval nostalgia for territory is the foundation of a true superpower's vitality. The peninsula was the Empire's altar, its people our sacrificial offering. We were able to revitalize our race by slaughtering them, by consuming their flesh and drinking their blood. This is why, in my capacity as spokesman for the unified church and state of the Empire, I titled my previous broadcast, "The Colony is the Source of Our Political and Economic Vitality." Now, as I watch the wonderful accomplishments of the Empire's management of the peninsula vanish like soap bubbles, I cannot keep my indignation at bay. Of late, there have been frequent reports that all manner of cultural artifacts are being excavated for preservation. National memories that the Government General took such great pains to erase are now being revived, and the study of national culture and heritage, once a source of inferiority, is gradually becoming a source of self-esteem. Modern nation-states use history as a way of building national consciousness. Joseon has banded together to overcome its difficulties and become a nation by erecting monuments and reenacting a shared past. But, as the creation of an intellectual basis for an independent people, this boom in the study of Korean culture is dangerous for its potential to incite rebellion. The protests that erupted over rigged elections during the April Incident a few years back are a glaring example of the changes that have been taking place here. Of course, there is evidence suggesting that the sneaky Joseon people gauged their position with the American Embassy before redoubling their audacious efforts under that country's protection, but their actions exceeded all expectations nonetheless. Here is the reason: what the Anglo-American hordes worship as "democracy" is a system that establishes a political theocracy via an oracle selected through a ritual they call "election." Like any other ritual, old or new, Eastern or Western, this sacred ritual must, without exception, be performed with the utmost rigor, order, and solemnity. Even the slightest whiff of corruption surrounding this sacred ritual would summon the wrath of heaven. By way of explanation, this *election* ritual is how the members of a given tribe reaffirm their community spirit and celebrate their system of belief, *democracy*. They might lay sacrificial beasts such as cows or the heads of their prisoners on a ritual table for a communal feast. The Catholics, for example, feast on the symbolic flesh and blood of their God; some sacrifice symbolic others, using non-human offerings, prisoners, or enemies in order to identify their oracle or to woo Fortune. Among this second type of adherent—those who place their enemies on a sacrificial altar—should be included the evildoer An Jung-geun, murderer of Resident-General Hirobumi Ito, our second in command; as well as those impure elements from the peninsula who engaged in terrorism and espionage against the Imperial authorities in and around Shanghai. In an election, however, the purest, or perhaps the most appealing members of a tribe are placed on the ritual

87

altar, and the tribe evaluates them through "votes". The winner of the majority of these votes is recognized as the oracle who will protect their sacred *democracy*. So it seems that such tribes negotiate their prosperity by offering up their most qualified representative as a sacrifice to the gods of democracy. The foul play uncovered in the ritual selection process called the "March 15th Presidential Election" is a matter of great consequence in systems like these. Grave misfortune is sure to befall the tribe that makes a false offering to the gods of *democracy*. It seems that the human tributes that offered themselves up for the election ritual in this fledgling nation after the Great War were more interested in monetary gain than in the primary religious purpose of their role. Irrational by nature, the election system placed no obstacles in the path of unworthy candidates who were interested only in filling their bellies. But because the tribe ultimately has the authority to choose, even from among unappealing options, the selection of the oracle is, in other words, the responsibility of the citizens of the nation. In the March 15th Presidential Election, the unpopular old man at the helm of the government resorted to unsavory but clever methods to sully the election ritual with fraudulently invalidated ballots using techniques such as "stacked jade rings," which left a double mark on ballots, the glissando mark of the "piano vote," and "owling," which literally plunged voters into darkness while fake ballots were stuffed into ballot boxes. The commotion that erupted later that spring was a backlash against such shenanigans. We have noticed that the people of the peninsula are in the habit of throwing a collective fit from time to time, and the convulsions that spring were no exception. Why they are prone to such occasional spasms is beyond my comprehension. I myself was extremely concerned around the time of the April riots, convinced that the rotten people of the peninsula would certainly go to ruin because of this new ritual. Self-awareness of this sort is also an obvious threat to the Empire, and it certainly won't do to have that. It goes without saying that the Empire must assert its absolute claim over the peninsula, but if the people here were to become arrogant freemen, their repossession of the land would become a given, and the Empire would surely suffocate with neighbors like them. But today, I am happy. My heart is skipping over the clouds. I am content. So let us toast! I and my loyal and courageous troops are overjoyed. As well we should be. The people of the peninsula have once again revealed their depraved nature in a river of flowing *makgeolli* rice wine and a shower of money like falling leaves. All those corrupt votes—the pianos, stacked rings, ironing boards, group votes, and proxy votes—resulted in chaos. South Joseon's performance of the ritual was *utterly rotten*. What an ignoble race. Why, they're no better than primordial sludge, incapable of self-esteem, wisdom, courage, or anything else. Ah, my dear dear Joseon folk, whose stupidity helps the Empire's cause, but who are still so idiotic that they would enrage the Buddha himself. These primitives are like Judas: they'd sell their own savior for a bit of silver. To all you brave, loyal subjects of the Empire! You imperial soldiers, police officers, and secret agents who have continued to resist with patience and forbearance, even under adversity, as we await the day that the Empire returns honor to the peninsula! Gentlemen, even though the forecast looks grim, take heart. Our concerns have been for naught. Joseon seems to have heeded our dictum, "an honorable death for one hundred million and for all," enacting it through the wholesale corruption of all two million people on the peninsula. They are rapidly approaching their own demise. The end is near! From my perch underground, I say to all you brave citizens of the Empire, we must prepare for the day when we retake power! Believe me: this is the eve of the end of our suffering. There is no hope that these people can overcome their misfortunes on their own. They have laid bare their ethical standards. The Joseon people have short memories, and possess not even one ounce of shame or resentment. After the spoiled election ritual, all that remains in their future is ignominy and darkness. They are worn out, exhausted by the difficult task of democracy. And the ritual of democracy isn't even something they chose themselves, let alone a cause that they fought for. The poets of the peninsula now sing this song:

> *Now we call*
> *for the break of dawn!*
> *Now we shout*
> *for the thunder!*
> *Now we pray*
> *for a bolt of lightning to strike this night!*

This might be the rallying cry of a people and a call to arms—but for whom, do you suppose? The peninsular people enjoy song, and many true words can be spoken in jest. Swayed by the small fortune in crumbs that were parceled out at campaign rallies, they could not help but accept the bribes their sacrificial tributes offered them, and even now they continue to watch the masquerade like gawking drunkards. These fools would sell their souls for fifteen *nyang* in brass coins. Petty desires—*that* is what speaks to them. We've rounded the bend and can coast now, because it's all downhill from here. This is the reason they cry out. It's true! They call to us. They miss us. They long for the good old days of our rule. They resent being hung out to dry in the scorching summer sun while being lectured on "democracy" or whatnot. Seeing them squat down at their campaign rallies makes me think of slaves mobilized for forced labor. And we already know how to deal with slaves. You can't irritate them, and you can't pester them with anything more difficult than sleeping and eating. These people are sick and tired of their sham rituals. Is there anything more exhausting than constantly being asked to display a skill you don't have? This election ritual—which calls upon the peninsula to show a moral character that it never had to begin with—has turned out to be an embarrassment. The people shriek now as they stagger under the yoke of a freedom they didn't earn. They are crying out for me. The seeds of hope that were sown deep in the hearts of those Joseon people who faithfully worshipped His Majesty the Emperor's influence during the forty years of his rule are now blossoming. And this is their secret: all freed slaves dream of returning into bondage. They yearn for it. They burn with desire to be kicked and slapped, they long to once again hear the slurs "bakkayaro" and "senjin" spat at them. They are like a woman who can't let go of a husband who mistreats her. Anyone who has committed adultery knows this principle well: they claim to hate the Empire but feel disgusted by their new American husband's wishy-washiness and his inability to satisfy with his tepid and fastidious nature. What they really want is bluntness, the crack of a fist, the familiar swelling of a black eye. This secret desire is an innate part of the peninsula's physiology, and it is something that only the Empire truly understands. Every wench needs to be in the arms of the man who knows her secret best.

We have obtained intel that a mission is in progress to persuade the Yankee savages to return governmental authority to us, which, given the current state of affairs, I consider to be a very encouraging sign. Until that day comes, our noble mission continues to be to monitor every corner of the peninsula, to gather information, and to take note of potential troublemakers. To my steadfast military personnel, community leaders, and especially you ronin warriors, you so-called underground intelligence agents who accomplished the historic task of assassinating Queen Min with tremendous strength and bravery during the waning days of the Joseon dynasty, keep your composure and your steadfast belief in our renewed insurgence. The peninsula remains the enduring dream of our Empire, its secret soul. It is an undying love that can neither be exchanged nor likened to any other. Where can it go? *Nowhere*. We *cannot* allow it to disappear—not this land that became the Empire's aspiration through the efforts of truly great men. Not this land of bountiful secrets that has for centuries— throughout the Proto-Three Kingdoms Period, the Imjin War, the Nippon-Chinese War, and the Nippon-Russian War—been intertwined with the prayers and visions of our incomparable military. Today, the sacred elements of Joseon's shrines are once again being sullied by the peninsula's prostituting sluts. The indifferent night clouds that loom over Seoul as they float past Mt. Nam take no interest in this old veteran watching over his former territory in a foreign land. My dear soldiers, stay calm and take good care of yourselves. Long live the peninsula of the Empire! Banzai!

> — *Ladies and Gentlemen, you have been listening to a radio commentary presented on the occasion of the completion of the Election of the 6th President*

and the 7th National Assembly of the Republic of Korea in May of the year 1967.

This has been Empire Radio, a phantom broadcast of the secret underground colonial party of the Joseon Government General, sister party to the front line of French Algeria.

With that, the voice intoning through the plodding rain abruptly cut out. A man gazed into the darkness, hands clenched on the windowsill as he pressed his ear tightly against the glass pane. That voice was gone, but out of the darkness came other, even gloomier voices. Plinking fingers on piano ballots. The scratchy clink of brass coins. A hooting owl. The dull click of a pair of jade rings stacked on a wan finger. The moans of a dead student demonstrator, his eyes stinging from a tear gas bomb that had exploded shrapnel straight through his eyeball. The ravenous howls of older men dying far from home as they were herded out to campaign rallies. The bloody cackling of the Governor General. And the poet's shuddering sobs—*Oh, the night of Asia's tragedy is so very long!* And then, something else, the sound of something close... something very close. A blood-curdling scream: *Aaaaaaaaaah!* It rang loudly in the poet's ears, accompanied by the streaming staccato of the rain.

It was coming from his own mouth.

COSMIC GO

BY JEONG SOYEON

TRANSLATED BY KIMBERLY CHUNG

Jeong Soyeon (b.1983) grew up in Masan, a southern port city near Busan, and studied philosophy and social work at Seoul National University. A literary translator as well as a practicing lawyer, she published her first short story collection titled *My Neighbor Yeonghui* (Yeopjibui Yeonghuissi) in 2015. Her debut came in 2003, when she began contributing stories to the influential webzine *Geoul* (Mirror). Since then, Jeong has carved out a name as one of Korea's most noteworthy SF writers, and her stories have been reprinted and anthologized in a variety of places.

96

Jeong's science fictional short stories are distinctive for their combination of a galaxy-spanning imagination with personal, everyday storytelling. They are often set in space colonies on remote planets and typically feature revelatory encounters between earthlings and aliens or between humans from different dimensions of reality. The title story of *My Neighbor Yeonghui*, for example, narrates an intense but short-lived friendship or romance between a human female artist and an alien who lives under government surveillance in her building. Despite having a non-anthropomorphic shape-shifting body, the neighbor incongruously carries a common Korean female name and comes to appreciate human art through its re-lationship with the artist. Similarly, in "Teatime with Alice" (Aeliseuwaui titaim), a first-person narrator named "Alice" accesses a parallel universe in which she becomes friends with another Alice, Alice Sheldon—that is, the famous American SF author who published under the pseudonym James Tiptree, Jr.

According to Jeong herself, her work consists of "SF stories for the here and now." Her stories emphasize the strange and wondrous within our everyday life through their focus on themes such as family conflict, relation-ships, and school life, though these are often given a po-litical accent through the tackling of concerns related to sexual minorities, the disabled, and political dissidents.

"Cosmic Go" (Ujuryu; 2009) conveys the personal reflec-tions of a driven young Korean woman whose dream is that of leaving the earth to work on a moonbase. As the only daughter of a single mother, the protagonist recounts the hardship, sacrifices, and setbacks that accompany her quest for a career in space. By casting real-life issues faced by the physically disabled into this future of space exploration, the story draws attention to social problems and the exclusionary treatment of minorities in our own world while at the same time painting a hopeful alternative future in which discriminative boundaries are blurred. It is a story of striving and empowerment that interestingly engages with the game of strategy known as Go, a game traditionally played by male players, as a metaphor for life and its choices. A rare feminist story with a postcolonial touch, the piece was also published in comic form with illustrations by graphic artist Pak Do-bin, and in that format it won a prize at the 2005 SF and Science Writing Contest.

Introduction by Kimberly Chung

Translator's note: Masaki Takemiya, a Japanese Go player, popularized a so-called "cosmic style" of play during the 1980s. In brief, Takemiya's idea was to abandon the traditional and conservative game plan in favor of a grander strategy aimed at constructing a major configuration of stones in the middle of the board. The title of the story is in effect a double entendre, referring as it does both to Takemiya's game style and to the narrator's passion for the cosmos filtered through the game of Go. The original Korean publication of Jeong's story includes some footnotes, most of which are related to that game's rules. They are selectively translated here, integrated into the text or added as a separate footnote.

The most important thing in the game of Go is where you
place your stones. Although some may argue that what
matters in the final count is the number of points you
get based on the amount of territory you've claimed,
the winner is actually determined by how strategically
you've placed your stones throughout the game. This
means that it's meaningless to keep moving your stones
here and there just to cover more of the grid and rack
up more points. You should never place a stone on the
board without purpose. Shuffling your stones around
willy-nilly is a sure sign that you've failed to understand
the spirit of the game. The moment you finally place
a stone on the board—after having turned it over and
over for such a long time between your fingers—is the
moment the board becomes a universe through which
new energy reverberates along thin black lines.

The finest Go boards of all are made from the wood of the
kaya tree. Because kaya wood is flexible and springy, the
surface of such boards can feel slightly bouncy under
the pressure of a stone, and Go players rave about the
sensation. Boards made from kaya are also known to
last for many years without losing this ability to absorb
vibrations and spring back to their original form. The
elasticity of this wood is such that most light scratches
will heal in a matter of days, leaving only the faintest
of traces. The capacity of kaya wood to heal in this way
demonstrates its quality, accounting for its high price.

It was this sort of split kaya board that my mother gave me
one day when I was twenty-nine years old and had just
returned from a nerve treatment session at the hospital.
I was speechless at the gift. I didn't know how she could
afford it when she was barely scraping by. The sleek Go
board, accompanied by a shiny new set of clamshell

stones, was in a completely different league than the set made up of a flat, portable piece of plywood and plastic stones that she and I had been using up until then. It was an extravagant present, one that spoke of my mother's grief for a daughter who would spend the rest of her life paralyzed from the waist down.

My mother placed the board on the dining table and, with hands chapped by chemicals from her work, grabbed a stone, putting it down decisively at a 4-2 point formation. The board gave slightly.

"From today on, I'm playing black," she said.[1]

For a moment I stared at my mother, at the board, and at the black stone quivering at its center. Then I slipped my hand into the bowl containing the white pieces. The clamshell stones clung to my fingers like cold, live shellfish. Looking at the board, I opted to play my stone in the upper left star position.

I'd always dreamed of going out into space.

Whether it would be as an astronaut, an astronomer, or a geologist, hadn't mattered. I'd always wanted to go somewhere out there. If the opportunity could've been bought with mere money, I would have saved up for it; if it required physical labor, I would've built up my body; and if power was needed to get me there, I would've become powerful. I longed to escape from this planet, to see outer space. Even as a ten-year-old, that desire was seared into my mind, though this wasn't something anyone else could see.

My father, who worked for an insurance company, left the world when a speeding vehicle crashed into his car as he was on his way home from work. On the strength of

---

[1] Go players using the black set of stones have an advantage because they start first. It is thus customary to let the lower skilled player have the black stones.

her degree in biology, my mother managed to get work at the eugenics lab of a major corporation. Her job consisted of treating fruit flies with chemicals, radiation, or genetically modified foods. The ultimate fate of all those flies that hatched with no wings, or distorted eyes, or the wrong number of legs, was not her business. Every night, after coming home from a day of glass tubes full of squirming insects, my mother would sit across from me with the Go board between us. Even when her eyes were weary, or when I had an exam the next day, the board always sat there, ready for our next game.

"The board is outer space," she would tell me.

My mother would reproach me whenever I preferred watching a documentary about a moonbase, leafing through science magazines, or reading science fiction novels to a game.

"You won't be able to find your way without focusing, either at Go or in life. And if you get arrogant, you're going to lose your way. The board is outer space."

My mother never told me that moonbases and Mars exploration weren't the right kind of thing for a little Korean kid like me to be interested in. Nor did she ever encourage her young dreamy daughter with vain assurances such as, "I'm sure you'll make it." She never scolded me for plastering my bedroom walls with photographs of star clusters and star systems, or for endlessly rewatching an interview with Michael McKay, the head of European Space Agency, all the while flipping through my English-Korean dictionary. Nor did she reproach me when I asked her to sign my application to the Center for Gifted Young Scientists. And she even comforted me when I failed the test and tearfully ripped down the big Mars poster above my bed.

"Even in Cosmic Go, abandoning your territory is an act of folly. If you don't defend your position, you will die in space."

The year I turned seventeen, the ESA and NASA joined forces and commenced the construction of a lunar base. However, insufficient funds meant that the already long-delayed plans to build a long-term residential center would be further postponed. It was decided that for the time being, a less expensive facility for the collection and transportation of lunar minerals would be built. The Chinese, who had originally wanted to build a spaceship of their own, changed their minds and offered instead to supply the necessary labor force for the project and to build a terrestrial headquarters. A twenty-year plan was developed, and when the project was launched, spaceships began launching into the skies with the logos of multinational corporations emblazoned on their hulls.

The first team, charged with establishing a basecamp and selecting the optimal site for a mine, was made up of twenty men and seventeen women. Ten were American, twelve European, fourteen Chinese and Japanese, and one Indian. In racial terms, eight were Black, fifteen Asian, and fourteen White. Half held at least a bachelor's degree (if not higher) in mineralogy.

This happened around the time I was taking my final exams in my senior year of high school. I never tired of watching the videos of that first team's three spaceships lifting off, and when my exams came to an end, I was excited to hear that they'd arrived safely and were starting their research. Needless to say, I avidly sought out all the coverage I could find about the mission—from commemorative pictures with Earth in the background to every article in every magazine I had access to, even the publication of the team's biology research in *Nature*. Although the French, English, and Chinese I'd taught myself wasn't good enough for everyday conversation, it did allow me to make sense of the first team's research articles, at least with the aid of a dictionary. For me, that was enough.

At the age of twenty, I was admitted to a university famous for its astronomy program, where I chose to double-major in mineralogy and biology. Most people would have found my schedule there impossible, but for me, living a Spartan life and studying all the time came naturally. Back then, as far as I was concerned, my class-mates and everyone else were just background noise: my studies were the main event. My only distraction was playing Go with my mother every other weekend when I would come home from the dormitory. Unfold-ing our grimy Go board with its rusty hinges, I often found myself wondering whether other people had as much structure as the nineteen lines on the Go board, and whether their lives were as meaningful as the 361 points where the gridlines intersected.

"From your first move to the last, try to never place a stone without some purpose, and if you've already placed a stone, find a use for it."

I turned twenty-one, then twenty-two, then twenty-three years old. The construction of the mine began, and a new space shuttle began serving the mission by transporting building materials from Earth to the moon. Meanwhile, in Korea, two presidents came and went, and the public began losing interest in news about a moonbase that most saw as irrelevant to the country's interests. Of course, every high school textbook carried the picture of the white hero who had led the first team. Yet it was rapidly becoming little more than a page in a history book, and I was growing impatient. I was still just a twenty-three-year-old woman, a college student grounded on the Korean peninsula. Sometimes I would walk out of my classes, frustrated by the university's out-of-date equipment. Every so often, I would wake up in the middle of the night and lie there, staring up into space. I often daydreamed about soaring up through the atmosphere and flying into space. Exposed to the vacuum of space, my body would begin to swell and burst… but I would get caught in a grid that criss-crossed space like the lines on a Go board, and would descend into a void much deeper than the distant ceiling of my room.

When I turned twenty-six, in the second year of my master's program, I spotted an opportunity. More people were needed to work on the moonbase and the space shuttle, and strict hiring practices based on diversity quotas gave way to salary considerations and other economic calculus. On top of that, the competition had grown less stiff: as construction had progressed, a number of accidents, some minor and others severe, had inevitably occurred, and fewer and fewer people were willing to risk their lives on an enterprise that no longer looked quite so heroic. However, one could apply for a position only once or twice at most. Having dreamt of space as much as I had, I was determined to not accept some assignment on Earth where I'd just be communicating with the base or inspecting ore samples. I didn't want my stones to just be sitting in some random spot in the middle of the board; I wanted them to be spread out in all directions, following the splendor of my Cosmic Go game plan. I was going to *go to the moon*.

I waited patiently until the end of my Master's program, and applied on the same day they conferred our degrees. My resume wasn't half bad, either: okay, I didn't have a Ph.D., but I had a master's degree in astronomy, a bachelor's in biology, a minor in mineralogy, and I was proficient in French, English, and Chinese. I packed up my belongings and everything from the previous seven and a half years of my life and returned to my mother's house to wait for the results. During my three years of graduate school, our Go board had been gathering dust in storage, and as I took it out, I discovered a bundle of yellowed, faded newsletters about the moonbase. It was my own collection of clippings, still there in that bag.

A letter of candidacy arrived six months later, inviting me to China for an interview at the Research Headquarters for the Asia region in Gansu Sheng. I'd seen pictures of that research center—a gleaming complex in the middle of a vast desert—and its launch pad so many times that I couldn't believe I was seeing it in real life. Breathing in the dry desert air, I kept fingering the plastic Go piece that I'd brought in my pocket instead of looking at the materials I'd prepared. The dust winds at sunset concealed from view the faraway steppe. Looking down at the dust at my feet, I wondered what would become of me if I went to the moon. Would I miss this sky? Would I miss the Earth and my mother?

Would I ever want to come back?

I never got to learn the answer to those questions.

The day after I rushed back to Korea to organize my paperwork, still in shock that I'd succeeded at the interview and passed the physical exam, it happened. I'd just gotten off the bus when viciously spinning wheels suddenly flashed into view, followed by a sensation of dizzying pain. I was twenty-eight years old, and in twenty seconds I lost all the fruits of two decades of hard work. My life suddenly became a cluster of stones on a grid, blocked on all sides. Gravity constantly pulled the empty shell of my body downward. No matter how hard I tried, I kept sinking into the bed, the floor, the earth. I could hardly breathe under the weight of layers and layers of atmosphere.

My everyday life blurred into a meaningless backdrop. Wake up, sit in the wheelchair, go to the hospital, return home. Eat my food, take my medicines, drink water. Three or four months had passed when I suddenly got the idea to open the door to the storage closet to look for the Go board. Still unaccustomed to my newly diminished height, I knocked a box over. Out poured annual space shuttle newsletters, plastic Go pieces, faded photographs that had hung on my walls in childhood, documentary DVDs, and my college graduation album. The sharp corner of a glow-in-the-dark star hit my face. It hurt. Dust must have gotten into my eyes and nose, too, because they itched unbearably. I could hardly breathe. The pain made tears flow down my face. I sat in front of the closet, finally weeping for the junk that my life had become, my twenty-nine years all shelved away.

When my mother got home, she pushed me into the bathroom and quietly cleaned out the closet. Several days later, a new Go board lay on one side of the dining-room table. On the days I was home alone, I would stroke the fissures of the pockmarked kaya wood, with its traces of the previous night's game, and lay out old, long-forgotten books about Go and reenact the games of skilled players from ten, fifteen, a hundred years ago. Sometimes I would take out the shiny clamshell stones and polish them one by one. At night, during our games, I would sit at the board across from my mother and seize the polished stones.

Soon my course of outpatient treatment at the hospital ended, and I only had to go in for checkups once every few months. One day I turned on my computer—it was the first time I'd done so in almost six months. I browsed my bookmarked links—newsgroups about the moonbase, astronomy and research databases. Instead of erasing everything, I registered online for a Ph.D.

program. No matter how hard I tried, I couldn't love the Earth. Even the clouds flowing by across the black night sky reminded me of how I couldn't bear being stuck beneath the atmosphere. If space really were a Go board, then somewhere there would be an opening. If life were a Go board, then surely my wounds would heal into a thin fissure. There must be more than one line holding the world together.

Despite increasing workplace automation, there was still plenty of work to do that required human labor. I was thus able to get a part-time job translating research papers and grading college exams. I gave up pursuing any sort of mineralogy job that required field work. Now I was thirty-three. Meanwhile, employment at the moonbase was expanding, and growing increasingly diverse. Yet the farthest that disabled people could go was the research center on Earth. Since I didn't want to cling to uncertain expectations and hopes, I tried to stay detached. Even the youthful jealousy I'd felt when looking at pictures of people at the moonbase had slowly dwindled away.

The construction of the base was almost complete when scandal erupted. Because the moon had such weak gravity, long-term project workers had begun to experience loss of bone density, a far more serious condition than NASA/ESA had initially anticipated. Despite medical precautions, the first contingent of people who'd worked on the moon project began experiencing side effects a decade after returning to Earth. Of that first team's thirty-seven workers, as many as thirty seemed to have developed early-onset osteoporosis, and of those thirty, half also now suffered from kidney stones. In addition, the hypothesis that three members of the second team had developed skin cancer due to cosmic ray exposure rocked the scientific and medical worlds. These and

other cases had initially been seen in isolation, as
patients had meanwhile scattered to the four corners of
the world. As a pattern of pathology began to emerge,
however, a movement arose aimed at ending the moonbase project. Suddenly, the space shuttle's artificial
gravity was raised from 0.5 to 0.8 of that of the Earth's,
and the amount of time workers were allowed to stay
in space was cut in half, while additional allowances of
time were added for exercise. Despite all these measures,
however, no fundamental solution to this problem
was discovered.

In the end, construction had to be suspended for almost a
year. Soon thereafter, the NASA/ESA consortium began
to recruit people with particular kinds of disabilities,
showing a preference specifically for lower-body ampu-
tees and those with paralysis of the legs who would not
need to support the weight of their bodies once they
returned to Earth after living in low gravity conditions.
A rumor circulating in newsgroups suggested that the
consortium was looking for people who required less
exercise, as well as people who couldn't use their arms
or legs. As this hiring campaign was being promoted,
mobilization around disability rights as a political
cause began to take place. However, the shift in hiring
priorities was in fact something of a last-ditch effort
for the consortium; the number of applications from
able-bodied workers had begun to decrease dramatically. Nonetheless, many persons with disabilities applied,
eager to not miss their chance at finally being part of
the space age.

The recruitment of disabled workers for the space mission
became controversial among disability rights activists,
raising the question of whether or not terrestrial laws
were applicable also in space, a quandary that ultimately escalated into an international legal dispute. Given

such unfavorable conditions, the NASA/ESA consortium
and their corporate sponsors decided to recruit worldwide in order to recover at least a portion of their considerable investment. International law was expanded with
a new bill that explicitly extended the People with Disabilities Recruitment Act that had been in place in the
United States and Europe to moonbases, space shuttles,
and all space facilities with research headquarters.
It was around this time that I dropped out of my Ph.D.
program and turned my attention to the news and the
debates concerning international law and the employment of the disabled. I couldn't believe all this was
happening. Just as I was turning thirty-nine, a hiring
announcement was released that addressed prospective
candidates—both able-bodied and disabled alike. New
condition-specific physical exams were introduced, and
a few months later, for the first time in history, twelve
people with disabilities took off on a space shuttle heading to the reopened base construction site. I submitted
my application right after watching the coverage of
their shuttle launch. Soon I found myself crossing
the Chinese border again. Perhaps this was due to my
successful application a decade earlier, or perhaps it
was the result of my subsequent additional educational
experience. This time, I packed all my things as soon as
I heard the news. The night before my departure, my
mother asked if I wanted to take the Go board and the
stones. I quietly gazed at the curved back of my mother,
who, when standing, wasn't much taller than I was seated in my wheelchair. I wrapped my arms around her and
shook my head.

Gansu Sheng had become a shiny research complex
with glittering, sleek streets. While sitting next to the
window of the high-rise accommodations, overlooking

the launch pad and headquarters, I faintly recalled the desert's dust winds. I imagined my mother at my age, as she was raising her young and ignorant daughter, sitting across from me at the Go board. I thought of my splendid dream of never returning to Earth and remembered my two legs standing here in the desert sand ten years earlier. *When this work contract period ends, I will be returning to Earth, regardless of whether or not they renew me.* I contemplated the awesomely strategic placement of the stones that had made possible such a bold and aggressive round of Cosmic Go. I had studied it all, had sat many times with Masaki Takemiya's books, practicing alone. Through my teens, my twenties and thirties. I thought of all the moments when I'd made my moves.

I wheeled myself away from the window and, lifting myself with my arms, lay down on the bed. Then I let my thoughts flow. *The day after tomorrow, I'll leave on the space shuttle. Everything will be hectic and busy. And when I return to Earth, if I do return, I want to polish the stones and sit at the Go board across from my mother. Maybe it'd be nice to buy an astronomical telescope, meet some people, or start working with the local disability rights association. I'm in my forties and, as far as this game of Go is concerned, I'm only halfway done.*

ALONG THE FRAGMENTS
OF MY BODY

BY BOK GEO-IL

TRANSLATED BY TRAVIS WORKMAN

Bok Geo-il (b. 1946) is a writer, critic, and social commentator who has widely contributed to the development of science fiction in South Korea. After graduating
from the business school of Seoul National University,
he worked for many years at banks and trade companies before making his literary debut in 1987 with the
alternate history novel *In Search of an Epitaph* (Bimyeongeul chajaseo). Inspired by Philip K. Dick's *The Man
in the High Castle*, the best-selling novel obliquely
critiqued South Korean society under military dictatorship through the counterfactual historical imagining of
a Korea that remained a colony of the Japanese empire
during the 1980s. Bok's subsequent novels included *A
Wanderer of History* (Yeoksa sogui nageune; 1991), a
time travel epic set in sixteenth-century Joseon Korea,
and *Under the Blue Moon* (Paran dal arae; 1992), the
story of a space race between North and South Korea in
2037. He is also the author of non-SF works such as *Gijichon in Camp Seneca* (Kaempeu Senekaui gijichon; 1994),
a novel based on his experience of growing up in a small
town close to an American military base, and several volumes of essays including *National Language in the Age
of Globalization* (Gukje sidaeui minjogeu; 1998), which
controversially proposed the adoption of English as an
official language of South Korea in order to enhance the
country's global competitiveness.

112

Bok's fictional works are distinctive for their stark
political overtones, but his politics have shifted over time.
Although Bok endorsed anti-imperialism, anti-militarism,
and the movement for Korean democratization in his
early works such as *Epitaph* and *Wanderer*, he is today
best known as an advocate of neoliberalism and a member of the Future Culture Forum (Munhwa mirae poreom),
a right-wing organization founded in 2008. Many of the
author's later fictions can thus be read as political para-
bles that uphold the ideals of a free-market economy and
American-style democracy. A strongly anti-communist
theme runs through his novel *The Jovian Sayings* (Mok-
seong jameonjip; 2002), which is set in a future space
colony on Jupiter and is essentially a satire of South
Korea's "Sunshine Policy," which promoted peaceful

engagement and cooperation as a means of dealing with North Korea.

"Along the Fragments of My Body" (Nae momui papyeondeuri heuteojin gil ttara; 2006) takes place on the Amytal robotic base of Ganymede, the largest moon of Jupiter, which has become a space colony of the Earth in the 27th century. Narrated from the wide-eyed perspective of a nine-year-old robot girl, the story revolves around an exhibition of art by a senior robot. Prompted by the artworks, the girl wonders about the relationship between the body and the soul. If a robot has its body parts replaced and reassembled, or if a human changes all its cells as it ages, what happens to their souls? This exploration of art in a futuristic setting recalls Kim Stanley Robinson's short story "Mercurial," as well as Bruce Sterling's *Holy Fire*. As one of the author's less politically explicit works, the story brilliantly displays Bok's ability to poignantly render our everyday metaphysical concerns through the power of his science fictional imagination.

Introduction by Sunyoung Park

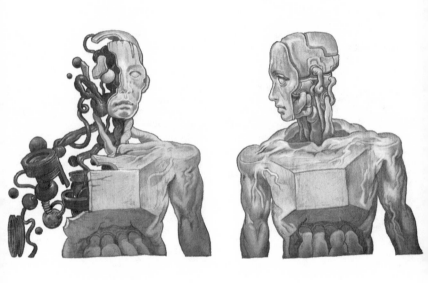

I.

"Well, then," Chairman Soris 297 looked around at the group. "Let's begin the meeting."

Everyone straightened up. Someone cleared their throat with a dry cough.

"As I already said, today's meeting was called in order to congratulate the two hundred and eighty-eight members of our organization who are leaving for new positions and, sadly, to say farewell to them. As you all know, these members participated in the mission to explore Saturn's moon Titan. They were founding members of our Amytal Base Artists' Association, and since then they've also made immense contributions to the organization."

Although Soris 297's voice was serious, it wasn't stern. For a robot, this was a rare feat. The political abilities of the Soris model series were extraordinary indeed. They held a variety of upper-management positions within our robotics organization. Whenever a Soris met someone, whether human or robot, he would immediately say, "Call me 'Ris.'"

"I'm not just saying this to be diplomatic. Our association, which was founded by just eleven individuals in the year 2690, has developed steadily ever since and now includes more than three hundred members. This growth has been due largely to the immense contributions of those founding members, including the esteemed Hyuros."

Vice Chairwoman Narit 109 smiled brightly and began to applaud. Her instincts in these matters were exceptional. Everyone quickly followed. Hyuros 288 bowed, bending his bulky upper body slightly, and returned the applause.

As I clapped dutifully, I suddenly realized something—if Grizzly left, then Orion would be the last founding member to remain among us. I looked intently at the two elders. Hyuros 288's nickname, "Grizzly," fit him well; he was manufactured to do difficult work and actually moved like a bear. For that matter, "Orion" was just as fitting for Hyunid 66: his movements were light and precise.[1] They were both from Old Earth. Their personal histories—having been manufactured on Old Earth hundreds of years ago and having come out here to the Jupiter system on a probe—shimmered like an aura around their time-worn bodies.

"Hyuros has contributed to each of our association's past accomplishments: the 2691 Amytal Exhibit of Illustrated Poems, the 2694 Amytal Drama Festival..." Soris continued.

As Orion had once commented with a giggle, Soris was liable to turn any occasion of formal speaking into a rehearsal for a speech he might give someday on the political stage. His dream was to be president of the "Robot Association."

It was a passionate speech, not one that should be listened to casually. Even so, my thoughts frequently turned to the two elders. To me, a youth who'd entered the world not even a decade ago, the two elders were a special inspiration.

In contrast to humans, robots did not gain authority in proportion to their age. In human societies, older people often held power and authority. It was difficult to understand why this was so, given that they could no longer

---

[1] In the Korean text, this android was named "Nimrod" after a biblical figure, a great-grandson of Noah who is known as a mighty hunter and a king. The name has been changed into "Orion" here, with the author's permission, due to the negative connotation of "nimrod" in informal English.

achieve the final purpose of humans—that is, reproduction. On this point, and in many other aspects as well, robotic society was more rational. Among robots, power and interest was naturally granted to new models with superior functions.

The one exception was for artists. Art was not created via the operations of logic circuits. In addition, the most important source of inspiration for robot artists was life experience. No matter how much one saw and read the works of others, the basis of one's own art was the life that one had lived.

Therefore, to a nine-year-old bookish girlbot like me, the 'bots from Old Earth were giants. They had known the climate of Old Earth, which I had never directly experienced. They had walked upon the soil of Old Earth, looked up into its blue sky, and felt the wind and rain on their skin. Grizzly had come here on the *Green Tide*. As he would occasionally boast when he'd had a drink, he'd been part of the "first generation." The 124 human crew members who'd landed on the Nansen Plain with him had all died long ago, but his recollections of the people who'd accompanied him to Ganymede remained unaltered in his memory circuits, which hadn't aged. These elders held onto something that I could never experience directly: the surface of Old Earth, the place of our collective origin.

"... To our member Hyuros, for whom we feel great respect, we will present an Association Award. Sin Hyunid, a founding member of our association, will present the award."

Everyone applauded as Grizzly and Orion rose and went forward. Ponud 311, the Director of General Affairs, appeared, holding a tray.

"As a founding member of our esteemed Association, you contributed greatly to its development. In 2691..." Orion began to read the award certificate.

Grizzly stood there like a bear that had just been caught doing something naughty. Though he should by now have gotten used to these kinds of occasions, he wore an awkward expression. Perhaps it was that very inability to adjust to these kinds of occasions that made one an artist.

Now he intended to go to Saturn. It was as if he'd given up on all of his relationships here, resolutely deciding to sever all ties with anyone with any connections to Old Earth.

The day I'd entered the association for the first time, he'd pointed at me and said, "This small woman standing here represents the growth of our Association." That was how he'd begun his relationship with me. Now it was just one of many he was giving up. I felt a stifling sensation inside, as if my chest were clogged by some amorphous emotion.

II.

"Wow," I exclaimed, "there are so many people here!"

Orion, walking hand-in-hand with me, looked at me with a smile. "There sure are."

The wide corridors of the Amytal Base Art Center were full of people. It was a sight rarely seen in this small lunar city.

"Grizzly, this exhibition seems like it's going to be a big success."

At Orion's words, Grizzly, who was up ahead of us, shook his head and grinned. "I worried it might be empty. But more people have come than I imagined..."

In order to celebrate the tricentennial of the creation of Viennese, our association had launched an exhibit of her new works. Viennese was one of the most famous robot artists in history. She was too famous for a small city like Amytal Base, but the association had decided nonetheless to hold such a big event here.

Grizzly had requested that things be done this way. He and Viennese had ridden on the *Green Tide* together, and they had both experienced the collapse of the Karos Tunnel, which had taken place during an early phase of the settlement. The exhibition was thus Grizzly's final gift to our Amytal Base Artists' Association.

A throng of people swarmed around us. Reporters. Flash bulbs popped continuously.

The reporters were only interested in Grizzly and Orion. No wonder—they were famous artists from Old Earth. Because I was standing right next to them, I was also covered in metallic flashes from their cameras.

Despite the hubbub and confusion, I puffed my chest out with pride. These reporters were from Nansen Base, and the number of human reporters seemed to outnumber the robotic ones. Clearly this exhibition was a special event.

The two elders took turns responding to the reporters' questions. There were many responses that I couldn't really understand, but judging by the reporters' occasional bursts of laughter, they appeared to find them witty.

I did follow one of the responses, though: a young female reporter—a human—asked Grizzly something, and he replied, "That's a fair question coming from a young and beautiful reporter like yourself... but it would be stupid for an old and ugly artist like myself to answer it." Even I confidently burst out in laughter at that.

At Grizzly's suggestion that the discussion be resumed after everyone could see the show in its entirety, the reporters backed off. Our group began once more to make its way toward the exhibition room.

"Jane, this young woman is Sweeney," Orion said to a human reporter standing next to him.

"Oh, yes, nice to meet you," the woman said sweetly, smiling at me.

"Sweeney, this is Jane Tiffany... She is a reporter with the *Nansen Times*..."

"How do you do, Ms. Tiffany?"

"Call me Jane."

"All right. Thank you, Jane."

"Jane," Orion had a look of anticipation. "Sweeney is an incredibly gifted artist. Keep an eye on her in the future."

"Is that so? Sweeney, it's very nice to have a chance to meet you. Orion is stingy in his praise, so if he speaks so highly of you ..."

Her smile was so bright that it made my chest hurt. No matter how close humans and robots became, and no matter how many ways robots surpassed humans, a robot's face could never be so expressive.

In any case, I was very happy to actually be introduced to a reporter from a major newspaper at Nansen Base... no less a *human* reporter.

For a novice robot artist such as myself, such an introduction—to a human reporter from a major newspaper in the capital—was an honor, one that might also prove helpful to my career. Putting on the best expression that I could manage, I bowed my head to greet her.

We ran into Viennese at the entrance to the exhibition room. The moment she saw our group, her wrinkled face suddenly lit up with a smile. She hugged the older robots—Grizzly, Orion, and Samoan—and shook hands with everyone else.

Orion turned around. "Sweeney, come here."

I hesitated, but he took my hand and led me to Viennese.

"Viennese, this young woman is Sweeney."

"How do you do? My name is Sweeney." The realization that I

was standing before a great artist suddenly snapped me out of my daze as I greeted her.

"Is that so? I am Viennese." She took my hand and stared into my eyes. Her eyes, while piercing, were also soft—like a psychotherapist's—as if she were assessing my innermost thoughts with great care. In fact, it was said that Viennese had originally been a psychotherapy-bot.

She smiled softly and said, "Orion's spoken to me about you before, Sweeney. He said you have a lot of talent. I look forward to reading your work soon."

These were very kind words for a novice writer like myself. Naturally, I made a resolution: to write work that would live up to such high expectations.

We entered the exhibition room, and a massive sculpture greeted my eyes. The work brought to mind some kind of spacecraft, but there was no way for me to decipher its precise significance. Nonetheless the work tugged mysteriously at my heart, compelling an emotion similar to longing for a distant world... or perhaps some distant time in the past.

But I barely noticed the feeling. There were many things in this world that I didn't yet really understand: I *was* only nine years old. As time passed, perhaps I would gradually come to understand them.

Other works within the exhibition room were similar. I was still young, and to my reckoning, these works were too abstract. Nonetheless, I walked slowly through the hall, following in the footsteps of the others and enjoying the strange emotions that the artworks provoked in me.

In the next exhibition room hung drawings and paintings. Compared to the sculptures, these works were much more accessible, though many of them were set on Old Earth. Having looked at almost all of them, I could see that Old Earth still reigned supreme in the mind of Viennese. Despite the two hundred years that had passed since she'd left, she still longed for home. All the robot artists from Old Earth—Grizzly and Orion included— were conspicuously obsessed with their home world. *This place does not compare to Old Earth. Is it because the environment of Old Earth was richer? If so, then... artists who grow up here must be very limited in their experiences. Doesn't that in turn mean that it'll be difficult for them to leave behind masterpieces?* This thought alarmed me. But it was of course a question I couldn't answer for myself.

I recalled again the longing in my heart provoked by the sculptures I'd seen in the first exhibition room, and thought: *Isn't this deep longing for a home to which one cannot return the inspiration that stirs the souls of artists and elevates them to a higher place? An artist who remains at home can never... Perhaps that's what is driving Viennese and Grizzly to leave again for Saturn?*

III.

While making my way around the second exhibition room, I got separated from Orion. There was a woman in front of me who seemed familiar. She was middle-aged and appeared to be from Nansen Base, and she was recording something on a pad while looking at the works. Clearly she wasn't some average visitor, nor did she seem to be a television or newspaper reporter. Could she be a magazine reporter? An art critic?

Entering the third exhibition room, the woman suddenly stopped in her tracks, and I almost ran into her. I realized that the people ahead of her had stopped as well. The line of people in front of the displays, which circled the inside of the room, was practically at a standstill.

Feeling impatient, I craned my head and looked over at the objects hanging against the black wall. The first one was a small photograph of a piece of plastic. A metal plate next to the photograph read: *My right sole. Replaced January 14, 2596 at Baynobil Spaceport.*

The next object was a photograph of a badly dented piece of metal. The metal plate next to it read: *My forehead plate. Replaced June 20, 2597 in Nairobi.*

Next there was a photograph of a small chip. It, too, came with an explanation: *My Stallion Circuit Chip. Replaced on December 27, 2597 at the Seagull Robot Service Center in Nairobi.* The *Green Tide* had left Baynobil on January 1, 2601, so Viennese would have been working around the spaceport as a member of the Ganymede exploration team at the time.

As the line of visitors slowly crept forward, I saw more photographs of Viennese's discarded components. I marveled at the fact that a robot's body is made up of so many components. It stands to reason that the "original" robots that appeared three hundred years ago required many more components than me, the "newest model" robot. Still, seeing the process of replacement with my own eyes, I was truly able to comprehend just how many parts they possessed, even if this couldn't possibly compare to the innumerable cells of a human body.

As I meandered as if in a maze among these exhibited objects, I gradually fell into a strange state. The process of observing a body break apart, piece by piece, was almost hypnotic.

The rhythm of looking at the photos then reading the explanations had become almost mechanical when I glimpsed these lines: *My CPU. Replaced on March 13, 2890 at the Nansen Base National Robot Service Center.* I read the explanation once more, then looked back at the photograph.

Right... it *did* appear to be an original CPU.

An uncanny feeling rose up inside me. A CPU is to a robot

what a brain is to a human being: if Viennese had changed her CPU, did her soul change, too? Even a little bit? Humans believe that if a human's brain is changed, that person's personality and identity will also change...

Finally, the procession of discarded components ended. I let out a sigh, my mind still reeling from the fact that Viennese's CPU had been changed. I turned to look back at the crowd. Everyone, robots and humans, looked as if they'd been hypnotized—an indication of just how provocative Viennese's works were.

When I turned the corner, I found some more photographs. These were pictures of the discarded components being reassembled. Viennese had carefully put the pieces together again, a much shorter process than the process of disassembly... The final photograph was of the completely reassembled robot, standing tall.

Blinking my eyes, I looked at the robot. At first glance, it looked exactly like Viennese, which was confusing. It was another Viennese, except it was just standing there.

Perplexed, I looked more attentively at the robot. It was not *completely* the same. The eyes of the reassembled robot were dead. It appeared to have not been revived. A living robot apparently couldn't be produced merely by putting together discarded components.

There was some kind of formula on the metal plate next to the image. I looked over the shoulder of the woman in front of me. It was an estimate from the Robot Service Center that read: *Can be reactivated with an adjustment of the original components. Cost: 3,200 Tumon.* If a mechanic were to repair it, this robot could be instantly revived.

Another Viennese.

Not knowing what to think, I stared at the picture of the robot, puzzled. It occurred to me that I should step aside to give way to the people behind me. As I was about to move on, reluctant, my eyes landed on the title of the piece, which had been engraved on the front of its pedestal: "The Rebirth of the Self."

A radiant understanding lit my soul like a bright light. Without thinking, I exclaimed, "Ahh!"

IV.

"Oh, it's already on!" said Chairman Soris 297, who was drinking carrot juice and watching the screen on the wall.

"The exhibition is on the news."

Everyone's attention shifted to the screen, where they saw images from Viennese's exhibition.

"That was really quick," Suis 9765 marveled. "A story about our city has become important news."

Our association's members were quenching their thirst at a café outside the exhibition building. It'd taken almost two hours to see all of the works in the show. Other than Grizzly, who'd already left for Nansen Base, all of the conference participants were gathered there.

The human reporter on the news show was standing in front of the reassembled robot.

"Viennese reassembled this robot from her discarded components. As this estimate from the Robot Service Center indicates, this robot can, for a small fee, be brought back to life."

The television camera captured the metal plate where the estimate was engraved.

"For a fee, this reassembled robot could be revived. If that were to happen, two robotic artists named Viennese would then exist, a situation that would pose various serious metaphysical questions. Which would be the true Viennese, the robot Hyumos 96, made on Old Earth 300 years ago? This revived robot here, made of her original parts? Or the robot artist who reassembled it?"

After pausing for a moment, the reporter proclaimed, with a stylish gesture, "To understand more, I asked some of those involved."

Onscreen, the reporter and Viennese stood facing one another. "Between you and the work, which one is the *true* Viennese?" the reporter asked in a pushy tone.

Viennese gave a relaxed smile. "The current me is Viennese. However, if the reassembled me were to be reactivated..." She shook her head, and continued: "I honestly don't know. Probably it would be better to ask *her* first."

The show returned to the exhibition location. Onscreen, the dead eyes of the robot who had yet to be reactivated looked out at the world.

"Who can answer this question, if even those involved don't know? Isn't this perhaps what the artist intended to tell us through this work? Where is my self? If the material that makes up my body is constantly changing, then how can I maintain a clear sense of identity? And where is my soul? Starting from a simple plan, a 300-year-old robot artist has, through this work, posed—to both humans *and* to robots—a deep philosophical question about life and the soul. From Amytal Base, this is Susan Yamamoto for GBN News."

A momentary silence followed. Everyone was digesting what the reporter had said.

Finally, Orishis 2665 carefully broke the silence. "Humans have never before shown such great interest in the work of a robot artist, have they?"

Everyone agreed.

"It's clear that Viennese's work has had a much greater impact on humans than on us robots..." Orion said, looking immersed in thought. "Human beings are very concerned with things like the self and the soul."

"They sure are," said Chairman Narit 109. "Probably because their lives are so short..."

"Probably. Since their bodies are weak and their lives transient, they hope that their souls will remain even after they die. We're very different. We never take an interest in that sort of thing."

"Even so, don't humans deny the idea that robots have a sense of self or identity? And don't even *try* talking to them about robots having souls," said Narit, glancing around. Everyone smiled bitterly in agreement.

"Yes, this exhibition shocks them because it shows that the body is constantly changing during one's lifetime. The materials that make up the human body keep changing as well, but because it happens at the cellular level, this process is not so visible to them."

"That's right," I agreed, suddenly cutting in. Everyone looked at me with odd expressions on their faces, as though I were a child interrupting the adults. I pretended not to notice and went on: "It's rare to find humans who want to spend a lot of time thinking about how the materials that make up their bodies change extensively within even a single year. I mean one year on Earth, or just a month according to our calendar here. The only parts of the human body that don't change on a daily basis are the lenses of the eyes and the women's ova. Is there a single human who thinks that the self or the soul resides in their eyes? As for the fact that the ova remain the same, does that mean that males have no Self or Soul?"

Everyone exploded into laughter at this, throwing their heads back and cackling joyfully. The barbs Orion had thrown seemed to have gotten to them.

V.

I went outside, where it was silent. I was filled with a sense of freedom, and gradually I relaxed, taking a deep breath of the empty air around me.

It's strange, but robots like stuffy underground spaces.
They seem most at ease in environments where they are
surrounded by the constant stimulus of clamor.

So I had escaped outside. The others had gone dancing at
the Santa Fe Trail. Everyone was excited by the thought
of having a good time and indulging themselves... but I
had many things that I wanted to think about alone.

The sun had just set, leaving the sky dark. Jupiter filled the
sky, and the stars were flickering to life all around it. It
felt as if my heart were reaching out for those stars.

A sky with no clouds
A field with no wind blowing
Here at last my body is nimble
And my soul is carefree

While repeating the lines of Rupof 1002's poem, "Where My
Body and Soul Take Me," I turned my head and gazed
toward Old Earth. Without the sun I could see it clearly,
though it felt very distant. All of this had begun on that
small, blurry spot.

It was as if Viennese's journey from that point to here was
playing out before my very eyes. Viennese's self had
arrived here after a long process of shedding her body
little by little. She had clearly not lost herself bit by bit
along with her discarded components. Nor did it seem
as if her self had changed. I could not be sure, but...

Pondering these difficult philosophical questions again, I
looked up and gazed at that small, blurry point. Standing and staring at Old Earth, I felt I could understand the
deep longing harbored by those who'd come from there.

They were seeking to overcome the distance that had aris-
en between themselves and their home. They longed for
a place they'd left behind even as their destinies drew

them on toward an unknown world. They were leaving
again for another enigmatic world, this time on a spaceship piloted by the descendants, ten or so generations
removed, of the embryos they'd taken care of aboard
the *Green Tide*.
If you were to ask Grizzly why he did this, he'd always
simply reply, "When you're my age, you'll understand."
However, this time I, too, understood. Moving ahead
like that is the essence of life. Even if they were to leave
fragments of their bodies along the lengthy road to
Saturn, their souls would always be new. In the end, life
is something greater than the material that makes up
one's body.

I swiveled my head in the other direction and found Saturn.
An inaudible song arose within me. The beautiful sight
of the planet's iconic rings filled me with a flowing
current of emotion. My thoughts arrived naturally at an
image of my elders leaving this world.

> *Along a road where the fragments of my body*
> *And the small parts of my soul*
> *Lie scattered*
> *Memory, following a meandering path,*
> *Sends upstream*
> *A cold current of longing*
>
> *If only someone could point to*
> *Where this road leads.*
> *The dark waves of time*
> *Crash against the prow of fate*
> *Shooting up cool, white spray*
> *That wets my long hair.*

QUIZ SHOW

BY KIM YOUNG-HA

TRANSLATED BY HAERIN SHIN

KIM YOUNG-HA

A household name in South Korea for his literary output, Kim Young-ha (b. 1968) was born in the town of
Hwacheon, Kangwon Province. He majored in business
at Yonsei University and continued on to a master's
degree, during the pursuit of which he began writing
short stories online. From there he moved on to writing
novels, and in 2004 became a professor of Creative
Writing at Korea National University of Arts. In 2007, he
moved briefly to New York, where he wrote an op-ed
page in *The New York Times* that later became part of an
essay trilogy called *See, Say, Read* (Boda, malhada, ikta;
2014–2015). Kim continues to be active in various media
channels: he runs a podcast channel called *Reading Time*
with Kim Young-ha (2010–), gave a TED talk (2014), has
worked on film screenplays, and even hosted a radio
show (2006–2007). A number of his works have been, or
are currently in the process of being, adapted into films,
musicals, and TV dramas. His writing has been translated
into more than twelve languages.

132

Kim's works have drawn critical acclaim for their formal
innovation, stylistic sophistication, urbane wit, and
genre-bending subject matter, as well as his ability to
fuse mundane reality with the fantastical and the absurd.
His subversive portrayals of taboo or marginalized subjects include: an examination of assisted suicide in *I Have*
the Right to Destroy Myself (Naneun nareul pagoehal
gwolliga itta; 1996); Latin American immigration history
in *Black Flower* (Geomeun kkot; 2003); the banality of espionage explored from the perspective of a washed-out
North Korean agent in *Your Republic Is Calling You* (Bichui
jeguk; 2006); and the muddled interiority of a serial
killer descending into dementia in *The Mnemonics of a*
Murderer (Sarinjaui gieokbeop; 2013). An abiding sense of
disillusionment permeates his tone and choice of topics,
embodying the loss of direction his generation suffered
throughout the post-Cold War, fin-de-siècle years of the
late 1980s–1990s.

In *Quiz Show* (Kwijeu shyo, 2007), Kim's fifth novel,
the recurring motif that "nothing is what it seems" in
electronically mediated relationships condemns Minsu,
the novel's protagonist, to a string of losses and disillu-

sionments. Unsavory phone conversations and text messages with his girlfriend are preludes to deception and
betrayal, and online chat-room conversations and emails
initially connect him to—and eventually tear him apart
from—his one true love, by obfuscating the genuine feelings and concerns behind the computer screen. These
themes of disjunction, miscommunication, and isolation culminate in a surrealistic quiz show boot camp,
which serves as an allegory of the internet's capacity to
provide a refuge from abrasive real-life relationships.
The events in this translated excerpt occur shortly after
Minsu's arrival at the quiz show camp. During the course
of acclimating himself to the rules and systems of the
camp, Minsu finds himself drawn into a surreal conversation with Yuri, one of his fellow quiz-show competitors.
Their exchange concisely captures Minsu's growing   **133**
sense of dissociation from reality and portends events
to follow, touching upon a number of key subjects that
undergird the overarching narrative such as the interplay
between representation and simulation, the precarious
definition of authenticity, and the potential failure of
mediated reality. *Quiz Show* has been translated into
Vietnamese, French, and Chinese.

Introduction by Haerin Shin

Translator's note: Punctuation marks and the
subjects of sentences are often omitted in the
original text, as the narrative is written from a
first-person perspective, with the exchange be-
tween the characters mainly transpiring through
dialogue that flip-flops between colloquial
casualness and conceptual complexity. While
attempting to remain faithful to these stylistic
markers, I occasionally took the liberty of insert-
ing commas or pronouns where needed to assist
the narrative flow. Also, to clarify the context,
I chose to translate one of the characters' nick-
names ("the General" instead of "Janggun") and
use English transcription rather than following a
romanization rule. All footnotes are mine.

SECTION 30.

Yuri came in when I was lounging in the common room
dealing with the shock of successive defeats after
my routine quiz-battle practice. Another man from a
different team was also there, but he soon left. Grabbing
a seat, Yuri pulled a book out of his Kipling bag. I stole
a look and saw that it was a science fiction anthology
called *Galileo's Children*. Though I hadn't read the book,
I'd seen the introduction to it somewhere.

135

We'd been on casual terms since my naming ceremony, so I
asked, "How come everyone else is so good here? It's not
like I'm some rookie when it comes to quiz battles."

Stuttering as usual, Yuri answered as if trying to make
excuses. "I-it's always like that at first. You're not so bad."

"But how come I wasn't able to win even once this entire
week?"

"That's because the b-body, the body hasn't changed yet."

"This body?" I pointed at myself. "Why change my body?
Why would anyone have to do that just to solve some
quizzes?"

Yuri scratched his head.

"No, not that body. The body I mean is, um... more like your
physical constitution. Daily life tends to be messy and
complicated. So we get d-d-distracted. Our brains are
better calibrated to process mundane tasks, not stuff
like quizzes. Um, we have to meet f-friends, catch a bus,
manage all sorts of relationships, and also p-process
t-trifling, trifling matters. But think of Einstein, Einstein for instance. His brain was completely incapable
of conducting daily chores. I-i-instead his brain was

more suited for delving into things like relativity, the theory of relativity, b-b-black holes, gravity, the mass of light. Your brain is, so to speak, still the daily-task type. But the brains of the 'corporate' people are not. Their brains are dedicated all day long to the accumulation, organization, a-a-a-a-arrangement, and categorization of kn-knowledge. So in corporate life, what we call daily life is completely, completely eliminated. Our brain's capacity is far greater than what we might imagine. It blocks the path that leads down deep in order to endure this squa-squalid thing, this squalid thing called daily life."

So he means we should change our brains, not our bodies.

Leaning in slightly, Yuri whispered to me, "Longman, uh, how long have you been h-here?"

"Uh, about ten days?"

"Ah…"

He went silent for a while. Just as I was about to get up and head out, Yuri asked again.

"H-h-how are things? Bearable?"

"Fine overall. But staying here makes me feel like I'm gradually losing my sense of time."

"It d-does have th-that effect."

He quietly put down his book and began talking.

"Ah, I'm not sure if I should be saying this, but uh, maybe I shouldn't…"

"It's fine. Tell me."

"Never mind. You'll l-learn anyway. No, just…"

"Just tell me. What is it?"

"Was just wondering if you knew where w-we're going n-now… nah, just f-forget it. It's n-no big deal."

"Going?"

Yuri looked at me, smiling sheepishly. "Right? Right? Thought you'd be c-completely clueless."

"About what?"

"Did you get in touch with your f-family?"

"Haven't got any."

"Ah, oh no, oh no, my bad. I didn't know, sorry, sorry."

"What's with the family question? Wait, is it true we never get to leave once we come here? I thought that was a joke."

Yuri covered his mouth and laughed at my exaggerated bemusement. There was something vaguely feminine about him. But it wasn't quite like what one might find in an effeminate man. It was more like a kind of frailty—like someone who's never gotten into a fist fight and always takes losing for granted, who maybe spent his childhood being pushed around by a violent father and has therefore completely given up on using force to compete with other men, relying instead on getting women to like him by embodying the kind of smooth obsequiousness that appeals to their maternal instinct, and acquiring as a result the ability to display an occasional exhibition of femininity that could trump even that of an actual woman, though all the while still harboring a male instinct deep within.

"It's n-natural that you wouldn't know since it's only been a f-f-few days. Some don't get it u-until they leave."

Even the smallest whispers resounded clearly in the common hall. I stared blankly at him. He kept fussing with *Galileo's Children*. He looked rather uncomfortable talking to me, but he also seemed to be enjoying himself.

"I'm n-not sure if I c-can tell you. Didn't you hear anything from the General?"

"No."

He coughed, clearing his throat. But his eyes were still scanning the wall, oscillating nervously.

"Um, so for example, l-let's say you have to travel to a p-planet th-thousands of light years away. How would you do it?"

"Hmmm. Take a super-fast spaceship?"

"Ha, a space ship? Why would you do something so, uh, so dangerous, uh, dangerous and inconvenient? You launch the spaceship, uh, I mean, launch it into orbit. Escape the atmosphere and go all the way out there, ducking asteroids... and everyone could just die en route."

"Sure. So you travel through space over generations. I think I've seen novels like that."

"Those are based on outdated science and technology."

"Then how?"

He tapped his forehead with his fingers. Then, perhaps feeling embarrassed, he hurriedly hid his hands in his pockets. His words began to pick up speed.

"By b-b-backing up your brain. Or we could say download. Download, yeah, download the information and send it to the destination, for instance to Andro, Andromeda. Then your brain could function in another body. Once your business there was done, the information in your brain could be scanned again and transmitted back to Earth. I'm saying there's no need to drag this cumbersome, uh, cumbersome body all the way over to such a faraway place."

He blushed softly. His forehead was beaded with sweat as if it were hard for him to talk. I tried to cheer him on.

"Oh, so like transferring files to the cloud?"

"Ah, you get it. That's right. Logically speaking, a file on my computer and one I upload to a webhard are one and the same. People in remote locations could d-d-download the file and use it."

His demeanor, engrossed by the topic at hand, reminded me of the science and engineering geeks I used to see in college: shy and introverted, but able to spew out endless reams of technical details when their pet subjects came up....

"But isn't that too far off in the future?"

He jerked up his head.

"F-far off future? We're already doing it."

"What?"

He pointed at my device on the chair.

"You received that when you arrived here, right? Then you were led to a room with a number displayed on an LCD panel and fell asleep. The brain b-b-backup would have happened then. It's not widely known, but that level of technology was already in existence by the early 1990s. Then that information that was downloaded was sent over to the present timeline here in Aleph."

"Aleph?"

"That's the name of the spaceship containing our minds."

"Yeah, right..."

I laughed in his face. I couldn't believe that I'd been taking him seriously.

"You're kidding, right?"

But he refused to back down. His tone dropped a notch, but he plowed on: "I didn't believe it at first either. I'm *still* not completely convinced. I can't be. But what's clear is that contemporary science and technology is way more advanced than we think."

"Then what's up with the trees and the moon I see right outside my window, or the birds chirping away every morning?"

He scratched his head.

"I was wondering about that, too. There's this man called Kkeokjeong here who used to practice *taekkyeon*.[1]

---

[1] Im Kkeokjeong, the source of the nickname, was a legendary butcher-turned-bandit in sixteenth-century Joseon Korea. Known for his exploits against corrupt officials and his charity for the destitute, he first became famous in modern times through Hong Myeonghui's novel *The Tale of Im Kkeokjeong* (1929-1938), which was serialized in a newspaper. Since then, his story has been retold through a number of novels, comics, films, and dramas in both Koreas. *Taekkyeon* is a branch of traditional Korean martial arts.

He l-l-laid it all out for me, crystal clear. Think of it as something like dreaming. The only difference is that there's consistency. Simply put, we wake up where we went to bed the night before. And we go to sleep in that same place again. Of course leaves fall or flowers bloom when seasons change, but there's still a certain order, a sense of continuity. That's the difference between this and dreams. Another difference is that we all share the same experience. You probably also came in the same way we all did... entering the woods through a small village with a town hall, right?"

I nodded.

"A building with a rectangular courtyard in the w-w-woods?"

"Yeah. It had three stories." Wrapped up in his way of explaining things, I too was speaking in past tense, as if we weren't still in the building.

He pointed a finger at my body.

"Even at this very moment, your body must be lying there. And your mind is wandering in a labyrinth s-s-simulated to resemble that building. This, here, is the labyrinth. Here, you read books, do laundry, and get to know people. People under the same circumstances as y-y-yourself... But that's not to say that all this is just a hoax. Our brains still learn, perceive, feel sad, and get angry here."

I held up a hand and interrupted him, saying, "Hey, wait! This is too absurd. Why would we want our minds to...?"

But Yuri was serious.

"Christian monasteries preserved ancient Greek wisdom during the Dark Ages and passed it on to the Renaissance humanists, right? The monks protected P-P-Plato and Aristo-t-t-tle's philosophy against the ruthless fanaticism and violence of the medieval times and helped bring about the Renaissance."

Sure.

"Uh, think of this place as such a monastery. We're distancing ourselves from Earthly matters, safekeeping and refining the wisdom from Earth, and waiting for a time when the knowledge we are preserving and cultivating will eventually shine through. Isn't human intellect regressing these days? College students don't read the classics anymore, and their teachers are busy showing off on TV or dabbling in politics. There's no h-hope left on Earth. So a select few have decided to leave the planet, determined to conserve the ancient wisdom of Earth like the medieval monks once did."

Come to think of it, I'd heard of some weird scheme called the Great Silence.

"So we're not here to solve quizzes?"

"Of course we solve quizzes. That's the most important form of recreation in Aleph, and also a kind of industry in itself. But that's not all we do. And anyway most of us are..." He paused for a moment, before cautiously continuing, "content with this life." Saying this, he blushed softly as if he were making an embarrassing confession.

"Why? We can't even see our friends or family."

"For one, there aren't any messy problems here like there are on Earth. There's no need to make money or get mixed up in political conflicts. No need to support a family, no taxes. No one's scolding us for failing to get a job, no corporate owners exploiting us. Here, there's only a life of l-l-learning and enlightenment, along with the enjoyment of one another's company. If you don't w-want this kind of life and prefer the barren lifestyle of Earth, m-m-meaning if you still have misgivings, you can go over to the office and ask them to send y-y-your mind back to Earth any time. Only those who want to stay here do so. If you want to go back, you'll be able to wake up in that building with the rectangular courtyard in Paju and walk out in your own body."

Yuri was serious. But a funny idea suddenly occurred to me,

and I couldn't help chuckling. I covered my mouth with my hand and asked, "Wait, when did humanity go all Protoss?"

He tilted his head.

"Pro... what?"

"Don't you play Starcraft? It's one of the species. In the game's universe, Protoss units use warp gates to teleport over to buildings and units on their home turf."

His face broke into a smile with dawning recognition.

"Oh, the P-P-Protoss! You mean warping, moving beyond dimensions to other dimen-dimen-dimensions. Through black holes and such. But this isn't that kind of warping. Just backing up and transmitting the mind."

"Wait, so even this table here is an illusion?" I tapped the table in front of me with my foot.

"When you were on Earth, I mean when you had your feet on the g-ground, you would sometimes sit at a table and drink coffee and stuff, right? Did you ever doubt that the chair was firmly there to support your weight?"

"I never did. If the chair hadn't been there, I would've fallen to the ground."

"Right. Of course the chair existed. But we only know that because of our s-s-senses. We can easily fool anyone into believing in a chair's existence by deceiving their senses. Likewise, this table here clearly exists. We sit on chairs, have drinks and so forth in our dreams, right? That's because, in the end, in the end, sensory information is the only thing that reaches our brains."

"Then what happens if I hit you?"

I held up my fist before his eyes. Yuri shrank away.

"Please don't!"

"It would hurt, right?"

"Sure it would. And I'd probably hit you back, too. But even if you feel p-pain, how can you be sure that your sensation of it is r-r-real?"

I looked around.

"Okay. So this building is in outer space right now?"

"Think of us as r-r-revolving around the sun on an orbit between Earth and Mars."

If I were to tell Binna what I'd just heard, she'd probably say, *Wow, you really are going places! Making it all the way out into space!* But then the next second she would probably turn around and yell, *Wake up, you idiot!*

Pretending to be serious, I asked Yuri, "Well, when we go back after staying here for about a hundred years, though I have no idea where 'here' is, what happens if the bodies we left behind on Earth are gone?"

"Even now we get to have virtual bodies like these, don't we? So it would be easy to find new ones in which to house our minds on Earth a hundred years from now. You won't ha-have to worry about that. Didn't you see the movie *Being J-J-John Malkovich*? We're like that. The only difference is that instead of being inside J-John Malkovich, we're inside our own selves, our self-images."

"But isn't this a form of abduction? I was never told about any such arrangement. This is a crime."

"Why is it a-a-abduction? Your body's still there in Paju. You went there out of your own free will. And, as you were told, you're here to s-solve quizzes. You can even make m-m-money, and the corporation will respect the terms of your contract. You're feeling a b-b-bit weird because you're just hearing about all this, but you'll be just f-f-fine after a while. You'll begin to feel as if you're reading books, hanging out with people, and studying, all inside that building in Paju. Don't you sort of feel like that already?"

"Ah..."

"You served in the m-m-military, right?"

"Yeah. I was a medic."

Yuri scratched his head sheepishly.

"I was in the eh, airborne unit."

"*Really?*"

"Hard to believe, huh? Just like everyone else. It's as if you all
think s-stutterers can't get into the airborne unit."

"No, not me, I believe you."

"When you first joined the recruit training center, when you
had your head sh-shaved and were made to roll around
all over the place, did you feel as if you belonged there?
And did you feel that that body was, uh, y-your body?"

Indeed, back then, a strange monster with an ashen
face and glaring eyes had stared back at me from the
bathroom mirror. And the physique I'd developed in the
military never quite felt like my own, either. It wasn't
until six months after I'd been discharged, when all my
muscles had turned back to fat from loafing around,
that I once again felt as if my body were my own.

"I didn't."

"That's how it is. Our self-images are extremely, extremely
unstable. You too will soon get u-u-sed to this place."

"Can't we go outside?"

"Su-sure we can. But you may not want to, as there's nothing
out there. In a way, this place is like the King Sejong Ant-
arctic Base. But you're likely to get lost. If you go outside,
you'll find similar buildings, where crews from other
countries are staying. Of course, they won't open their
doors for you. You may even arrive at something like a
b-b-bus station, but a bus will never come. You'll keep
wandering, and eventually you'll come back here."

There was one last thing I wanted to ask. However, there
was no easy way to broach the subject. Was suicide possible? If all this was some kind of elaborate hallucination
that my mind was experiencing, then could my mind
alone kill itself?

Yuri was staring at me intensely. It was as if he already
knew what I wanted to ask. A moment later, he packed

up his things and departed, leaving me all alone in the empty room. I felt as if the intro to philosophy class I had taken at college had suddenly come to life. That lecture on agnosticism: how do you know whether or not you exist? My professor had posed that question during my freshman year.

I paced up and down the corridor, alone and dazed, before going up to my room. Again, I had to rely on my navigating device to find my way. But the device no longer felt marvelous or intriguing.

According to Yuri, all this was some sort of illusion... what then did anything I was experiencing here mean to me? I holed up in my room and racked my brain over this problem, only to conclude that Yuri's hypothesis was difficult to refute. I tried punching the wall, and my fist swelled up. I filled the sink with water and immersed my head in it. My throat closed up as I rushed back up for air. Water coursed through my nostrils, forcing stinging tears out of my eyes. Even so, I couldn't quite shake the feeling that all this might be little more than a dream.

.

STORM BETWEEN MY TEETH

BY LIM TAEWOON

TRANSLATED BY SUNYOUNG PARK
AND RANDI VAUGHAN

Lim Taewoon (b.1985) hails from the historic city of Jeonju in the Jeolla Province. A versatile transmedia storyteller, he became a writer after majoring in Korean literature. To date, his prolific production comprises the full-length novel *Eternal Mile* (Iteoneol mail; 2007) and two collections of stories titled *101 Methods of Killing the Emperor* (Hwangjereul jugineun 101 gaji bangbeop, 2009) and *Magician In Trouble* (Mabeopsaga gollanhada; 2010). Lim broke out on the national literary scene with the fantasy novella "The Day of Ssakseureoshyu, the Greatest Thief" (Ssakseureoshyu dei; 2005), which won an award in a national contest sponsored by the KT&G Sangsang Madang Cultural Art Center. His works have since appeared in webzines such as *Crossroads* and *Geoul* (Mirror) and in a number of anthologies. The recipient of many awards, Lim is currently serializing an illustrated web novel titled *The Taereung Zombie Training Center* (Taereung jombichon) on the Naver web portal, and he maintains an active online presence through a blog titled *Story Republic*.

Lim's stories are infused with a whimsical fantastic imagination that is often joined with anti-authoritarian and libertarian impulses. They are marked by the author's linguistic play and strong use of neologisms, which find their expression both in the comical appeal to Korean dialects (as in "Ssakeureoshyu," literally "cleaning out") and in new cosmopolitan coinages rooted in many languages. Some of Lim's most typical characters are outsiders who, from the bottom of the social ranks, fight for survival in a world full of threat and violence. More often than not, fantastical elements and settings are calculated to provide a fictional veneer to Lim's social criticism, which highlights the contradictions and injustices of contemporary Korean society.

In "Storm between My Teeth" (Ippare kkiin dolgae baram; 2009), the SF trope of an alien warrior on Earth creates the situational irony of a 182-year-old alien trapped in the body of an eighteen-year-old immigrant worker from Africa. The story explores themes of racial and age discrimination all the while mocking mainstream Korean ideas of masculinity and the violence that is so pervasive in mass media SF. Written in a speedy, witty, and graphic style, the story combines the tropes of at least two major SF and fantasy film franchises: *Predator* (in its use of ultra-violent alien warriors trapped on Earth) and *Highlander* (where a special group of immortals who live hidden amongst humans must hunt one another until only one remains). These SF tropes are presented in combination with the narrative conventions—both visual and literary—of the *muhyeop* (*wuxia* or martial arts) genre, which are apparent in the story's rapid-fire action plot, with its many twists and turns, as well as in its emphasis on unarmed combat.

Introduction by Sunyoung Park

149

I.

My name is Jamui.

I was born in the Maasai Steppe in Kenya. At the age of nine
I learned how to herd cows, and by fifteen I was participating in the honorable hunting of lions. At twenty,
I became renowned as the best warrior of my tribe.
But then something strange happened. Over the next
eighteen years, my body stopped aging. Then one day,
while cracking the jaws of a Nile crocodile that were
clenched into my thigh, instead of feeling excruciating
pain I was filled with an orgasmic rush of excitement.
I finally realized that I was not of this earth.

Jamui is a false name. My real name is Remitolppoñawi,
which, when translated into earthly languages, means
"Storm Between My Teeth." I am a member of the
Kreñawi, literally "The Great Warrior Species." Our genus
inhabits planet R17 in the Eighth Galaxy.

I am on Earth to undergo a rite of passage as a Kreñawian. The rites of the Kreñawian typically involve actual
combat that tests both one's strength and one's skill
at self-camouflage. First, one of the many backward
planets in the universe is chosen, then thirty-eight
Kreñawian boys are sent there. The boys are technically
born on the planet as natives, and for their first twenty
years, they develop the mighty bodily weapons of the
Kreñawian. Then, at the age of thirty-eight, the budding
Kreñawian fighters are awakened to their true mission.
From then on, all the warriors engage in one and the
same activity.

That common activity is hunting each other. The exercise
comes to its conclusion when only one combatant

151

remains, which, naturally, can take a long time. The only weapon allowed is the body that one has borrowed from the local species. Indeed, no tools or technologies of the Kreñawian civilization are permitted. The warriors recognize each other solely through their shadamoi, a unique body odor that only another Kreñawian can detect.

On planet Earth, the disguise of the Kreñawians is so perfect that no native earthling can recognize them. But shadamoi cannot be camouflaged away. A sort of genetic signal, it is the only medium through which Kreñawian boys can discover each other. Therefore, I left Africa and wandered around in search of shadamoi, seeking out the trail of my fellow species-members, who will be sacrificed in this rite of passage.

So far I have met nine fighters, and I have survived all nine encounters. Among my opponents, Kwirisñawi (Dried Snot Gifted by the Sun) and another, Bopyaksiñawi (Drowned Holy Hair), were formidable warriors. Kwirisñawi fought me with the Shaolin Luohan Eighteen Hands technique, while Bopyaksiñawi was a master of Greek Pankration. But none could rival me when fighting bare handed: I captured a hundred and sixty-eight lions that way.

Finally, I traveled a great distance to a small country in East Asia in search of my last rival. Here, in this small neighborhood called Yonghyeon-dong in Incheon in the Republic of Korea, I go by the name of Jamui. People think that I am an African exchange student.

An earthling hollered, waving his order at me: "Two orders of fatty pork here!" Did he realize that I could break every joint in his fingers in just twelve seconds if I wanted? His face crumpled at my blank stare.

"Hey, Bushman! Can't you hear me?"

I decided to put up with it. I hadn't found my last rival yet.

There was no need to reveal my identity by pointlessly killing a native. I took a pen out from my apron pocket and walked toward the earthling. On the way to table number three I adeptly kicked aside a falling soju bottle. I marshalled all my facial muscles to smile at the earthling.

"Two servings of fatty pork, now!"

There was no other way to respond. After all, I was a part-time waiter at this pork belly restaurant. So much for the honor of a proud Kreñawian warrior.

II.

I realized something was off right after defeating my ninth rival, Hioliñawi (Pimples Born in Thunder). On the beach at Hanoi, Vietnam, after five hours of intense combat and with his right leg broken, he finally admitted defeat.

"You're really strong. I guess this is the end of my run of good luck," he said with difficulty, his lips smeared with sweat and blood.

I shook my head. "It was a life-and-death match for me, too. What do you call that combat style of yours?"

"Muay Thai. I thought it was the most invincible of martial arts, but it couldn't defeat your valor."

There was a moment of silence. The humid wind of Hanoi was blowing all around us. Finally, I aimed my right hand at his neck. It was time to close the match.

"Do you have any last words?"

Hioliñawi seemed to think for a moment and said, looking straight into my eyes.

"Watch out: there's a mutant among us."

"A mutant?"

"Yes. His name is Aprañawi (Peddler Without a Pot to Piss In). I attacked him while I was in peak form, but he defeated me at once."

In combat, Hioliñawi used the amazing strength of his calves to cause damage in many different ways. That he should have lost against this new opponent gave me a moment's pause. But then I noticed what was off about his story.

"Wait, you lost... but you survived?"

Hioliñawi nodded weakly.

"He let me live. I don't know why, but he didn't seem to want to complete the rite."

"How can a Kreñawian warrior be like that?" I yelled.

"That's why I said he's a mutant."

"Nonsense! Even if there is one such oddball, it doesn't matter. I'll kill him off and complete the rite."

Hioliñawi giggled. The edge of my hand was still aimed at his neck. I wanted to take him out right away, but I waited to hear more.

"Why are you laughing?"

"You may think I'm just making excuses, but I've become a lot weaker since my last combat with Aprañawi. I admit that you're better than me, but you're no match for him. He lives in Korea, a small country in East Asia. If you're so confident in your strength, go and look for him there."

He looked resigned, which got me thinking. Was it appropriate for a warrior like me to vent anger at such an opponent? But then came his last words: "Regardless of the outcome of your combat with Aprañawi, this rite of passage is going to end with a big surprise."

He closed his eyes. I wielded my right hand. It was the ninth time I'd caused the death of a Kreñawian warrior.

III.

Hioliñawi had been onto something. After my match with him, I visited almost every corner of the Earth, but nowhere could I detect any shadamoi. In the time it had taken me to defeat nine opponents, fights between other Kreñawians must have been happening across the globe. The more one fights, the more one's shadamoi intensifies, which means that the few surviving fighters must be exuding a strong odor right now... and yet, I could not smell shadamoi anywhere.

Whenever I would occasionally manage to catch a whiff, it would turn out to be the scent of a warrior defeated by me or by someone else. Still, I couldn't be the sole survivor of the rite. If that were the case, I would've immediately received a message from planet R17: that much I knew for sure. Therefore, there had to be at least one more survivor on Earth besides me. Still, he must've been staying put for quite a while now.

For the first time in the hundred and eighty-two years since the rite on Earth had begun, I found myself closing in on an unmoving target. Following Hioliñawi's words, I made my way to the Republic of Korea.

IV.

I had been wandering around Korea for six months until one day, guided by a faint trace of shadamoi, I arrived at Incheon's Yonghyeon-dong neighborhood. The distinctive, intense shadamoi aroma overwhelmed me right as I reached a pork belly house with a signboard that said, "Work by Day, Pork by Night."[1]

This must be the place.

Splash!

The surprise attack came while I was still reading the bright red word "Pork" on the yellow signboard. Drenched to the bone by some freezing liquid, I turned to find an idiotic-looking earthling staring blankly at me.

---

[1] A pun on the traditional proverb, "work in the day, read at night."

He slowly blinked his eyes. Had this jerk just dumped water onto me? I quickly scanned my brain for an appropriate Korean expression.

"You want die?" I yelled, glowering at him.

Startled, the young man put on a pair of glasses that he took from his apron pocket. He looked less blank with glasses on. He started to bow in apology.

"Oh... I'm, I'm sorry, sir! I didn't see you at all!"

I could've kicked this four-eyed fool in the face and left him hanging from the signboard right then and there. However, another thought occurred to me: sure, this guy looked like someone I could take down with nothing more than finger locks. But if he were indeed my last rival... couldn't he be playing a trick on me? Drawing me in through some psychological tactic in order to get my guard down? He hadn't soaked me from any murderous intent, at least it didn't look that way. If this were indeed a diversionary attack, it meant that I was facing a *truly* masterful warrior. The thought sent a shudder through every nerve in my body. I tensed up and braced myself to fight to the death right then and there.

"Hey, you! What the hell are you doing out here when you should be inside wiping tables?"

A man with a gigantic perm materialized from out of nowhere and dealt a hard blow to Four Eyes' head. I was alarmed at the permed man's clean, simple, and effective delivery. There seemed to be a plethora of extraordinary fighters around here.

"Yes manager! I'll do it right now, sir."

Four Eyes bowed to his superior and rushed into the restaurant. That left me in the alley, face-to-face with a man whose head resembled a puffed-up bunch of broccoli. The blaring sound of a horn broke the silence.

The man looked me up and down and said with condescension, "We don't have any more P.T. openings. Go and ask someplace else... besides, we don't take blackies."

P.T.? What sort of code was that? As I kept my silence, the broccoli-headed man kept staring at me. Was *he* my last rival? I couldn't tell. It could just as well be Four Eyes. Fortunately, neither man seemed to have recognized who I was. I would have to keep an eye on this place. There was no other way, and I needed to come up with something quick.

I looked squarely into the manager's eyes and said, "Gimme work, *please!*"

My appeal didn't work immediately. Broccoli Head refused, shaking his head and saying something to the effect that they didn't need any more part-timers and, besides, a black waiter would "impact" the ambience at a Korean restaurant. Had I not thought to use my trick then, I would have never been able to find my last rival.

"Wow! How did you *do* that!?" Broccoli Head demanded. He was gaping in awe at the ground. Lying there at my feet were 36 identically shaped strips of bacon. I'd just tossed a chunk of pork belly into the air and sliced it all up before it touched the floor. Of course, I'd performed the stunt partly to test him, so I was rather disappointed when he readily offered me a job with a handshake. Had he been a fellow Kreñawian, he would immediately have recognized my identity, and we would have been able to complete the rite. Now I was all but certain that Broccoli Head wasn't my rival.

I soon became a popular draw at the restaurant, where customers got to know me as the "Pork-Chopping Bushman." Any sense of discomfort at my dark skin promptly disappeared as people became familiar with me. I had effectively disguised myself as the employee of a pork belly house.

Whoever he was, my formidable rival Aprañawi had obviously stayed at this place for a long time. The restau-

157

rant's interior was almost suffocating with a shadamoi of extraordinary intensity. There was some convenience in that, of course, as I could hope that Aprañawi would not easily smell my shadamoi over his. This was indeed going to be a tough battle. The first to identify his enemy would enjoy a massive advantage.

V.

Could Four Eyes be Aprañawi? The guy looked cowardly and he seemed helpless in the face of the manager's scoldings, but then again he'd thrown a bucket of water at me. I learned that he was actually still in high school, and would usually come to work straight from class. One night I decided to follow him home after his shift.

I was generally masterful at stealth operations, but I took extra precautions just in case. I didn't want to have someone find me and say—"Why's that foreigner hiding in a trash can?!"

Needless to say, following him around was hard work. But I found my co-worker was acting oddly. In a street lined with shops, he looked around gingerly before disappearing into a back alley. That was it! Instinctively, I knew he must be up to something! I tailed him closely.

In the alley, I saw Four Eyes as he approached a group of youngsters. Had he been training these earthling teenagers as his underlings? What a coward! He probably meant to deploy them as assistant fighters. As I kept watching, however, I realized that something was amiss. However one might look at the situation, it was clear that Four Eyes had no authority over the young men. Just then, one of them was actually whacking him over the head with his own bag.

"Give us the money, idiot! You just don't get it, do you?"
The bulkiest boy in the group, who was wearing a but-

toned-down school uniform, started punching Four Eyes. What was happening?

"Didn't I tell you to bring twice as much? Do you wanna die? How'd you like me to punch out all your teeth?"

Four Eyes replied wearily amidst the flurry of punches, "They didn't raise my wages. Ow! I brought you all I got."

"You knucklehead! Don't you know the labor laws? Haven't you ever heard of minimum wage? If your salary's too low, you should go report your boss!"

The boy began throwing even harder punches. His words made me realize something new about the people of Earth. This was a society where employers disregarded the minimum wage and workers had to share their meager earnings with lowlife punks like these kids. It became clear to me then and there that Four Eyes couldn't be Aprañawi. Had I been in his shoes, a lot of blood would've been spilled in the alley by now—none of it mine.

Pounded like marinated kalbi, Four Eyes staggered off and left the scene. If he'd been a Kreñawian, he would've been to blame for his lack of resistance. He hadn't even deployed the most basic self-defense techniques, and in the heat of the moment, he'd manifested exactly zero killer instinct. I decided to do something about the situation. After all, he was my co-worker, and I didn't want him to start having to call in sick because of these guys.

After a moment's deliberation, I stepped out from behind the electric pole. It was important to get an upper hand from the start.

"You motherfuckers!"

The boys flinched. I had managed to catch them by surprise just as they were passing around the money. As soon as they realized that I was alone, though, the heaviest boy glowered at me.

"So what, blackie, you wanna talk to me?"

159

"Four Eyes work together. You again touch him, you
    dead meat!"
"Four Eyes? Oh, you mean Pak Wonseok? *What* about him?"
  So that was his name: Pak Wonseok. While I was registering
    this new information, the guy began advancing in my
    direction. A plume of smoke wafted from his parted lips.
    Another stupid native! This one too was in the throes of
    that vice that was known to weaken the lungs. The guy
    got right up in my face as if to provoke me.
"So what, you freak? If I touch him again, then what happens,
    huh?"
  His friends began to giggle. I could have cracked his fore-
    head open and been done with it, but I decided not to go
    that route. I needed to avoid trouble if I wanted to keep
    my cover.
So I cracked something else. I reached out to a concrete elec-
    trical pole with my right hand and effortlessly executed
    a knife hand strike, BAM! As I slowly withdrew my hand
    while looking at them, cement dust poured down from
    the cracked pole.
  The bulky boy was now gasping as his cigarette fell from his
    lips. Another boy fell back onto his ass, all the while star-
    ing at the crack in the pole. I slowly looked around at the
    group while rubbing the remaining powder off my hands.
"That what."
  Boy, did they run off fast! They could've been faster, of
    course, if they hadn't taken to smoking. But they did
    have the good judgment not to challenge me, as the
    outcome would've been certain. *Earthlings*, *weaklings*, as
    I like to say.

VI.

"Jamui, can you pass me the scissors?"
  Four Eyes was looking at me, red-faced. His eyes, black and

blue behind his cracked lenses, somehow irked me.

I held up the scissors in front of him. "Next time, in the eyes!"

He didn't understand my quip, and said, "Pardon me?"

"Never mind. Say, who work here besides us and Brocco... er, I mean, the manager?"

He fell silent for a moment. He was about to say something when I heard a great noise coming from the dining room. I rushed out of the kitchen to find an older man laid out on the floor, an overturned table beside him. He was trying to lift himself up, but he seemed unable to balance himself.

"Dammit, what the hell is this?!" he shouted, hiccupping.

The old man, upset as he was, kicked the table as if it were somehow responsible for his fall. He was either an alcoholic or a drug addict. I had already seen such human wrecks among the earthlings. I had been instructed to drive away anything that might interfere with business, so I planted myself in front of the old man.

"You make trouble. Go away."

The old man stuck his drunk face in mine, engulfing me with the smell of alcohol as he hiccupped again.

"Who the hell are you? Muhammad Ali?"

I stretched out my arm and was just about to whack him and send him flying across the room when Broccoli Head rushed out and said something that caught me by surprise:

"Boss! What a surprise! When did you arrive?"

No way! The alcoholic wreck turned out to be the owner of the restaurant. Realizing that I had barely escaped being fired, I watched in a daze as Broccoli Head helped the wobbly man into the back room.

"He's *always* drunk like that. He comes by here sometimes," said Four Eyes from behind me. "Oh, Ma'am! You're here as well!"

Ma'am? I turned around and saw a middle-aged woman
who'd just made her entrance with a bundle on her back.
She was definitely an *ajumma* type.[2] With help from
Four Eyes, the woman returned the table to its upright
position. Then she smiled at me.

"Are you the new part-timer? It's nice to meet you."

I returned the greeting. Then a voice rang out from the
back room.

"Where's my daughter-in-law?!" the owner roared, hiccupping again. "Why isn't she coming in here?!"

I gazed at the woman's back as she rushed to join the old
man. Just then, a group of earthlings arrived at the
restaurant. They looked like a college wrestling team
having a night out on the town. After they'd swept
through the place, things settled down, and I pulled
Four Eyes aside.

"Who she? Boss lady?"

He looked at me and shook his head.

"No, Jamui. She's the wife of the owner's son, the owner's
daughter-in-law... *Daughter-in-law*," he repeated,
slowly and unhelpfully. "But we just call her Ma'am
for convenience."

"Oh, what about husband?"

"Husband? You mean the owner's son? He's been overseas
for two years. That's why she's been living with the
owner."

The family structures among the earthlings are just too
complicated. It's all due to their grotesque heterosexual
system of reproduction, whereby individuals of two
different sexes must have intercourse to make a new life.

---

[2] *Ajumma*, a native Korean word, refers to a middle-aged
woman. The term connotes an unflattering stereotype of
middle- and working-class married women who have lost
their feminine qualities through their domestic and reproductive labor, and have become tougher in their demeanor for
the sake of their families (and especially for their children).

The system is riddled with problems. We Kreñawians, by contrast, reproduce via the great matrix of Ninggisñawi (Rainbow With a Rupture). Our reproductive system, endlessly hatching out new warriors, offers a huge biological advantage over the earthlings' sex-based carnivalesque shitshow.

Regardless, if the owner's son had been away for two years, *he* couldn't be my final rival. When one has been absent for such a long time, it's impossible for the shadamoi to be this strong. Then could the old man be Aprañawi? But the guy couldn't even balance himself. Perhaps he was just acting? He looked feeble, but he owned the restaurant. Moreover, I'd heard somewhere about a martial arts technique called Drunken Boxing.

I had to check this man out. I waited for an opportunity. When Ma'am went out to check on something, I quietly slipped into his bedroom. The guy was talking in his sleep, clutching an empty liquor bottle to his chest. I shouted at him.

"You've been discovered, Aprañawi! Come forward for a match!"

The old man woke up. But he only scoffed when he saw my tense face.

"Aha! Ali, you wanna box with me?"

He staggered to his feet. His movements were so undisciplined and unpredictable that they scared me. Should he really be my last rival, I wouldn't be able to anticipate any of his moves. Now the guy was lifting his arms and pretending to box with me.

"Come on, pal!" He hiccupped again loudly. "Maybe I don't look like much, but I sure kicked some ass in the Vietnam War!"

He then tripped over his own feet and fell with a loud thud. It was a pathetic scene.

"Ow, you bastard! Was that an uppercut?" Again, he hic-

cupped loudly. "Don't start counting yet... wait a second!"
I didn't want to be tricked by the man's drunken fumbling.
That's why I resorted to my carefully prepared battle
plan. My first move was to aim a piece of garlic at the
man's head, throwing it with a rotating twist of my right
thumb and index finger. *POP!* The projectile barely
missed the man's head and ended up on the floor. But it
was all in vain. Had he been Aprañawi, the man would
have surely reacted by either grabbing the garlic or by
swatting it back at me. None of that happened, however,
because the old man was already snoring.
Would the rite never end? I had already encountered Four
Eyes, Broccoli Head, and now this bozo. If none of them
was Aprañawi, then who could it be? Did I have to kill
everyone in the damn joint? I felt lost.
Just then I heard a deafening scream from the hall.

VII.

I ran out to find Ma'am trembling in a corner. She pointed
at the back of the fridge. A little mouse was squealing
there. Had she taken such a fright at that small creature?
"What happened?"
"Please, could you *please* catch that thing? It jumped out
while I was cleaning down there... "
The woman was almost crying. Earthling women had such
poor combat ability. The mouse was a red flag regarding the restaurant's hygiene, though, and in any case,
I couldn't just leave it. So I took a toothpick from the
counter and sent it through the dining hall with maxi-
mum power and precision.
With a loud squeak, the mouse died. The toothpick was
sticking out of its head. I picked the limp body up and
dumped it into the nearest trashcan with mechanical
indifference.

Ma'am looked at me, stunned.

"Where did you learn that skill, Jamui?"

"Me hunt lion. Mouse nothing."

We were interrupted just then when Four Eyes appeared in the doorway.

"Ma'am, why don't you leave it to us to clean up the place? I'm sure you have more important business to attend to..."

The woman answered with a big smile, "Samdong is coming back home on leave! He's been away for a hundred days already... I wanted to make sure the joint was clean. Besides, I'm so excited that I have to do *something*!"

I felt dizzy, as if I'd been hit with one of those iron grills. One more man had been haunting this joint! His name was Samdong, and he was coming back after a hundred days' absence. That's why all my vigilance had been in vain! He was Aprañawi!

"Marines?!"

"Yeah, the Marine Corps. They're the most elite members of our military force," Four Eyes said, answering my questions while washing lettuce.

"What that?"

Four Eyes kindly explained to me what the Marines were. Hwang Samdong, the heir to this joint, joined the military a few months ago. The elite force trained its cadets to cultivate an invincible spirit and an unparalleled physical strength. They were nicknamed "ghostbusters." Ghost—a cluster of plasma energy that could not be defeated by any physical force. So the Marines were learning combat skills that could vanquish even ghosts! Oh, cunning warrior Aprañawi! He had been improving his combat skills by learning the earthlings' killing techniques. He would make a worthy match for my last fight!

"Jamui, you look upset. What's wrong?"

Four Eyes' words jolted me back to reality. The sesame
leaves that I'd been washing were floating around in
the sink. Well, I still had a few hours before Apraňawi's
arrival. There was no need for me to get into a combat
mode just yet. I collected myself as I gathered up the
sesame leaves.

"It's nothing. By the way, how long you continue work?"

"Well, I don't have to work as hard as before. The thugs who
used to hassle me have somehow disappeared..."

He had no idea that I'd taken care of the scumbags.

Pushing up his glasses with his rubber-gloved elbow,
Four Eyes got into a bit of a confessional mood.

"Actually, my dream is to become a novelist. I would
like to write a worldwide bestseller like *Harry Potter* or
The Da Vinci Code."

"Novelist?"

"Yes, a novelist. But you know, it's not gonna be easy. You
have to be brainy and witty to write a novel. I'm not like
that. The stuff I write is all boring."

Listening to him, I felt the time had come for me to share
my story with him.

"Wonseok, actually, I'm not from Africa. My true name,
translated into earthling language, means 'Storm Between My Teeth.' I am a Kreňawian warrior from planet
R17 in the Eighth Galaxy. I have come to your planet to
complete a rite of passage. The rite involves the hunting
and killing on my part of fellow Kreňawian warriors. I
have survived so far by fighting off other warriors who
were disguised as the masters of various martial arts
ranging from Russia's Sambo to Brazil's Capoeira. I have
infiltrated this establishment as a part-timer because
of my understanding that the last target of my hunt
is hiding here. He must be gifted with superior intelligence and power, given that he's survived for so long
in total anonymity. I don't know who's going to prevail

in this match. Whoever it'll be, the winner will receive a call from planet R17. Planet Earth will then be turned into a Kreñawian colony, and the winning warrior will become its ruler. The time is coming... so I guess I should apologize to you. You won't be able to become a novelist, what with the space invasion and all. And if I win my last fight, I will be the master of this world."

Four Eyes was staring at me now, his jaw agape. I'd blown my cover, but at this point, there was nothing that he could do to stop the final battle. My long journey was about to come to an end at last, and should he stand in the way, I could easily get rid of him. But then, in a totally unexpected turn of events, he burst out laughing.

"Thanks, Jamui," Four Eyes said, tapping my shoulder with a gloved hand.

"...For what?"

"You just made up a story because I told you that I want to become a novelist. Storm Between My Teeth... How'd you think that one up? I'm gonna put it in one of my novels one day. I promise!"

"What are you talking about? My name really is Storm Between..."

"All right, all right, you don't need to keep up the act. By the way, your Korean's really good. I didn't know you could be so articulate."

It's true that I'd been doing my best to speak in broken Korean, since I had to pretend to be a foreign exchange student. I'd spoken fluently just then because I'd been so absorbed in telling him my true story. However, he didn't seem to believe a word I said. I was at a loss.

"A rite of passage of the Krewawavians," he mumbled, whistling as he returned to his lettuce. "That's pretty heady stuff. Anyway, Great Storm Rider, how about you speed up a bit? I'm almost done with my work, and you don't want to get told off by the manager."

Hunched over the sink, I recovered my wits and resumed
stirring the sesame leaves in cold water.
Damn. They'd already wilted.

VIII.

"Hey, Samdong's back!"
When it was nearly the closing time, Ma'am darted out of
the restaurant to hug the young man in the entryway. I
was able to get a good look at the guy from the kitchen.
There he was: Apraňawi!
The Kreňawian in disguise, the impostor earthling Samdong, had just the physique I was expecting. He may
have donned strange clothes as well as a funny hairstyle,
but I could discern the shape of hard, well-developed
muscles underneath his uniform.
"So good to see you, Mother!"
Ma'am was crying as she touched his face all over. Of course,
I wasn't fooled. I knew that he was not Ma'am's son, but
rather a lethal warrior concealing his true alien identity.
*Cool, keep smiling like that. Soon it'll be time for your
showdown with me.*
As it turned out, Samdong's leave was only going to last
four nights and five days. There was no time to lose. I
had to finish this thing within five days. I wouldn't want
to chase him back to the Marines' camp, where he'd have
the aid of quite a few auxiliaries. Still, things didn't turn
out the way I wanted. At first it looked as if Samdong
would be spending a lot of time at the restaurant during
his leave, but he actually went out a lot, and was at the
joint only a few hours a day. I considered leaving work
behind to tail him around, but I decided the gamble
wasn't worth it. I didn't want to be pulled into a surprise
attack.
In no time, five days had passed. On the fifth and last day,

168

Aprañawi changed back into his camouflaged clothes, saying that he was returning to the camp. Damn. That wasn't good. I couldn't let him leave like that. I stared at his back while he said goodbye to his grandpa and to Broccoli Head. I could have jumped him right then. It would all have turned into a wild commotion, but this was my last chance. My palms got all sweaty.

Then Ma'am tapped me on the shoulder. Quickly, my lethal intentions withdrew from my mind.

"Jamui, may I ask you a favor?"

"Wha—what is it?"

"I'd like to see Samdong off to the terminal and then do some shopping at the market on my way back. I need someone to help me with the bags. Could you please come along?"

She was asking me to accompany Aprañawi. This was exactly the opportunity that I needed. I didn't have to think twice.

"Of course I will."

The Incheon Express Bus Terminal was teeming with people from all over. Aprañawi and Ma'am were chatting, holding hands tightly. I knew he was deliberately ignoring me. The damned bastard. I felt like wringing his neck then and there, but suppressed my desire. His bus was scheduled to leave in forty minutes. I knew my chance would come in just a short while.

My patience was rewarded. Aprañawi got up to go to the restroom.

"Excuse Ma'am. I go too."

I followed him from a distance into a deserted restroom in a remote corner of the terminal. I entered and gently locked the door behind me with a loud click.

The guy was humming a song while he peed. Then he noticed my reflection in the mirror.

"Hey... your name's Jamui, right? You're the first African student I've met. It must be tough to adjust to Korea."

I slowly approached him from behind. Apraňawi kept talking, seemingly completely relaxed: "You're twenty, right? I'm your senior by just two years. Thanks for taking care of our joint. Grandpa drinks too much, but he's actually—"

The cunning warrior must have known that I was 182 years old. I paused a few steps away from him. Apraňawi was still chattering away. Now was the time to complete the rite, almost two centuries after it had begun. I slowly readied my hand for my first blow.

"You got no escape, Apraňawi!"

He turned around slowly. A puzzled look was on his face.

"Wha... what're you talking about?"

"You must indeed be a mutant! Now I've discovered you, but you're still not preparing for battle. Very well, I shall attack first."

"A mutant *what*?! Just what on earth..."

But I was already in mid-air, engaging in a spinning maneuver that landed a hard kick to his jaw. *Pow*! His body flew up, hit the ceiling, then fell limp onto the floor. I backed off a little, bracing for a fierce counterattack. But something was wrong. Apraňawi was not moving at all, let alone kicking or punching.

Maintaining my combat pose, I shouted at the motionless body on the floor: "Enough of this game, Apraňawi. Get up and fight like a warrior!"

Still, he didn't budge, and was obviously unconscious. I was beginning to sense that I had been mistaken, when the unthinkable happened. I saw a giant crack appear in the restroom wall behind Apraňawi. CRASHHH! With a deafening noise, the wall crumbled down in a hail of bricks, tiles, and cement. And through the dust, I saw a dark figure charging toward me at a vicious speed.

I was caught completely off guard. An immense blow
fell upon my left shoulder and threw me down to the
ground a few meters away. I felt a horrible pain as I
turned my neck and headed toward my attacker. Standing there, blocking my way to the unconscious body of
Apraňawi, was Ma'am.

IX.

I couldn't believe my eyes. Was it really this *ajumma* who
had just knocked me to the ground? She looked at me
for a moment.

Then she spoke with a soft but firm voice: "I really wished
this wouldn't happen, Remitolpponawi."

It wasn't a dream. She had really called me by my real name,
and with a perfect Kreňawian accent. I barely managed
to speak.

"You, you are... Apraňawi?!"

Ma'am, or should I say Apraňawi, nodded her head. I
gasped. I couldn't help bursting into laughter. How
could this be? How could Apraňawi be a woman? And
not just any woman, but this over-the-hill lady who,
until yesterday, couldn't even catch a mouse?

Apraňawi knew why I was laughing: "What's so funny, kid?
You've never seen a warrior in a woman's body?"

"That's right!"

"Don't you worry about my body. Get up now, and show me
your strength."

A spark glinted in Ma'am's eyes. There was no doubting
that her gaze was that of a Kreňawian warrior. She was
calling me to battle. It was time to fight for real, not just
with words.

As I pushed myself up, the pain made me groan. My shoulder felt as though it were on fire. I assumed my combat
position. Apraňawi didn't budge from her spot just in

front of Samdong's body.

I went first, aiming a punch at Ma'am's face with my good
    right fist. The blow was so powerful that it moved the air,
    causing the fallen fragments of the wall to whirl around
    on the floor. But Ma'am ducked my blow with a simple
    and slight twist of her body. I started to throw a series
    of punches at a speed well beyond what the human
    eye could perceive. Incredibly, Ma'am avoided them
    all. It was as if her reaction time could be measured in
    nanoseconds.

Punching like that, I'd let my guard down, and Ma'am
    noticed. With a simple upward thrust of her arm, she
    delivered a precise blow to my chin with her palm.

There was a loud *crack*. Then I lost consciousness.

When I came to, I was still sprawled on the restroom floor.
    I felt exhausted, and didn't know how much time had
    passed. I'd been defeated by a warrior who was way out
    of my league.

"Dammit!" I roared, slamming my hand against the floor,
    hard enough to send a few tiles flying into the air.

From above came Aprañawi's voice: "You're not a weak war-
    rior at all, Remitolppoñawi. Don't be harsh on yourself."

"Shut up! Don't try to console me, Aprañawi. Rather, do your
    job and put me to rest." I braced myself. "Come on, go
    ahead... kill me!"

Aprañawi was the winner, I had to admit. I closed my eyes
    in shame and resentment, waiting for the fatal blow.
    But even after many moments had passed, no blow
    came. I opened my eyes when I heard the sound of foot-
    steps moving away from me. I then saw Ma'am, carrying
    the unconscious body of Hwang Samdong in her arms.

"What are you doing? Go on, kill me!" I bellowed in
    desperation.

But Ma'am was focused only on checking on her boy. She

let out a sigh of relief. Her behavior was utterly incomprehensible to me as a Kreňawian warrior.

Then Apraňawi turned to me, and said, "You're right, I am a mutant. Among the thirty-eight participants in the Kreňawian rite on Earth, I was the only one to be born in this different shape."

"You mean... as a woman?"

Apraňawi nodded.

"I resented my gender at first. My body was weaker than that of my male competitors. As a woman, I couldn't even awaken the Kreňawian superhuman power. The very idea of taking part in the rite made me fear for my life."

Having myself long observed life on Earth, I knew that Apraňawi's remarks on the condition of women were true. I had seen many women who were controlled by violent and abusive men. No matter how brave they were, women couldn't beat the superior physical strength of men. For this reason, it was only natural that every other Kreňawian on Earth had been given a male body.

"I thus had to hide from the other Kreňawians on Earth. Every day I was scared for my life. Over the years, I came to develop feelings that, among Kreňawians, are not natural. I fell in love with a man."

"Don't be ridiculous! We Kreňawians are a warrior species. We have no feelings for others."

"As a mutant, I lacked a full awareness of my identity. I may even have earthling genes intermixed with mine. So anyway, I married that man and my life was never the same after that."

Apraňawi gently stroked Samdong's hair before continuing. "When my child was born, he was the first offspring of earthling and Kreňawian parents."

The thought suddenly struck me: Samdong *himself* was a mutant. He was a creature whose genetic makeup had no precedent in the entire history of the Kreñawian civilization. I couldn't deny what I had seen.

Aprañawi continued, "Then something happened that I couldn't understand. One Kreñawian warrior came to fight me, and I was able to defeat him handily. And then came more and more victories, all the way to our encounter today."

The encounter had felt like an uneven match. I felt that chill again. How could she, with a woman's body, have defeated all those Kreñawian warriors?

Now Aprañawi was lifting Samdong to carry him on her back.

"I will not kill you," she said. "The rite will not be completed."

"You let me live today, Aprañawi, and I will kill you tomorrow! I have defeated them all, whether they practiced the Pankration, the Muay Thai, or the Luohan Eighteen Hands. Eventually, I will master the technique to defeat you too. I am a true Kreñawian warrior..."

My words barely seemed to register with Aprañawi. Did she feel that her victory entitled her to ignore me?

This only enraged me further: "Beware, Aprañawi! We're at our strongest when we have a target to destroy," I roared, crushing broken tiles in my fists.

But Aprañawi ignored my provocation and began making her way toward the exit, Samdong's body on her back.

"You're wrong, Remitolppoñawi. We're at our strongest when we have someone to protect."

Just before exiting, she paused and turned to look at me. Her face no longer wore the stern expression of a Kreñawian warrior but only the bright smile of Ma'am.

"Ah, by the way, Jamui, I suppose you know that an unexcused absence will cost you a full day's wage?"

After Ma'am left, I spent some time on the bathroom floor in a daze. Ma'am's smiling face haunted me. I had no more strength left for fighting, nor could I recall the reason

I'd had to fight in the first place. A gentle breeze blew in from outside to touch my face.

For Storm Between My Teeth, the rite of passage had gotten completely fucked up.

THE SKY WALKER

BY YUN I-HYEONG

TRANSLATED BY KYUNGHEE EO

Ever since her debut in 2005, Yun I-hyeong (b.1976) has been widely acclaimed as one of the freshest and most imaginative literary voices of her generation. Born in Seoul, she studied English literature at Yonsei University before starting a career in publishing and film criticism. Her short story, "Black Starfish" (Geomeun bulgasari), won the prestigious Joongang New Writers' Award in 2005. Since then, Yun has built an impressive literary oeuvre that includes a novella, *Private Memories* (Gaein-jeok gieok), a young adult novel, *Graduation* (Joreop), and three short story collections, *A Waltz for Three* (Ses-eul wihan walcheu), *The Big Wolf Blue* (Keun neukdae Parang), and *Love Replica* (Reobeu repeullika).

178

Yun is one of the few mainstream literary Korean writers who have managed to win critical approval while writing narratives that incorporate elements of science fiction, fantasy, and other genres from the broader field of speculative fiction. In many of these narratives, Yun constructs a uniquely dark and often dystopian world, presenting new imagery and experimental forms of writing to her readers even as she works within modern Korean literature's long tradition of social critique. Another notable aspect of Yun's writing is its focus on gender and sexuality issues. She won the 2015 Munji Literary Award and the 2016 Munhak dongne Young Writers' Award with "Luka" (Ruka), a short story that features the fraught relationship between a gay protagonist and his evangelical Christian father.

"The Sky Walker" (Seukai wokeo) is a sci-fi-infused short story that was first published in the literary quarterly *Munhak dongne* in 2008 and was later included in Yun's second collection, *The Big Wolf Blue* (2011). Set in the city of Seoyong (a pun on Seoul that contains the meaning "Western dragon") in a post-apocalyptic Korea, the story is a coming-of-age narrative featuring a female protagonist named Jihyeon, who aspires to transform from a merely human athlete into a superhuman "Sky Walker." The Wall, a physical barrier that metaphorically marks the division between these two categories of being, might also be considered a symbol of the authorial struggle between literary genius and writing as disciplined labor. However, Jihyeon's desire to transcend this Wall can also be interpreted as the self-abnegation of any minoritized subject (women, people of color, the Global South, etc.) who yearns to join the privileged class. This inevitably leads to the question of who really are the "outsiders" in this story—the ungifted majority to which Jihyeon belongs, or the Sky Walkers who had to move beyond the Wall in order to flee persecution? The breadth and profundity of the questions that Yun I-hyeong asks through her storytelling is what makes her one of the most exciting Korean writers of the new millennium.

Introduction by Kyunghee Eo

179

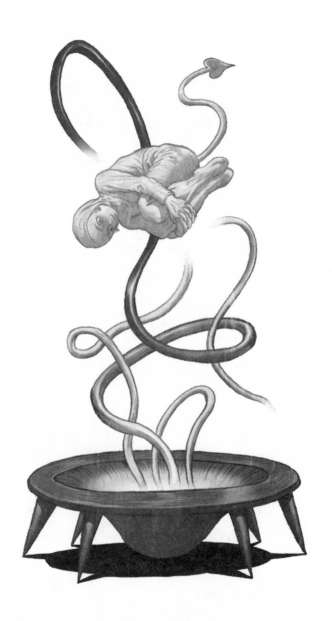

THE SKY WALKER

They said the Wall was out beyond the end of the local road, a twenty-minute walk away from the last stop for bus route 376. I was the only one on the bus except for a weary-looking old woman and a little boy who was holding her hand. The woman and the boy got off two stops before me, in front of the prison complex. As they made their way out of the vehicle, the driver glanced at me, his last passenger, through the rear-view mirror, before turning his gaze back to the road ahead.

Soon after getting off the bus, I wandered by a parking lot crammed full of cars. It seemed as if every towed car from the west side of the city had ended up there.

I continued walking down the local road, which was dotted with humble-colored wildflowers. At the end of it was a checkpoint, and beyond the checkpoint stretched a vast wall that had been painted a pale shade of gray. About thirty meters tall and punctured by round holes at every square meter, the Wall looked to me like a giant gray saltine cracker. I tried to recall the details of the map that Yuri had drawn for me. *One hundred meters to the left of the checkpoint.* As I walked along the Wall, I noticed traces of letters that had been imprinted on it at regular intervals. Obscured beneath a layer of gray paint was the same message, stamped over and over again in red ink. CAUTION: RADIATION.

A little over ten people stood together, about ten meters below the thin line where the Wall and the sky met. They were there to greet me, and they looked to be of various ages and ethnicities. The sun was right behind them, slightly above the top edge of the Wall. As I walked toward them, I shaded my eyes with my hand.

They were standing perpendicular to the Wall like a handful of nails that had been hammered into it, their bodies parallel to the ground. On the ground directly below them, the lengths of their shadows were equal to their erect bodies. For a split second, I expected them to fall towards the ground, tumbling down, but of course nothing like that happened. After slowly approaching them, I plopped myself down on the ground and sat facing the Wall. I lay back until I felt the soles of my sneaker placed firmly against the gray Wall, the ground beneath my back. By then, they'd begun heading down the Wall toward me.

I flexed my leg muscles and stood.

The earth that, just a moment ago, had been beneath me, was now itself a wall, and the Wall was now the ground beneath me. I felt no dizziness. I was standing under a new gravitational force, one that was pulling me down toward my feet, which were now placed on the Wall. Using my arms, I pushed my body away from the ground, as if pushing off a wall, and slowly began walking toward the group that was headed my way. Yuri greeted me with a smile.

"Privet."

Hyemin left Yuri's side to advance a few more steps toward me, a look of uncertainty on her face. I dusted the dirt off my back. Yuri made a few more remarks in Drussian, but the words were foreign to my ears.

"I was worried you might not come," Hyemin said to me. I wondered if she was speaking for herself or for Yuri. I was exhilarated by the sensation of standing there with them, face-to-face, on the side of the Wall, the length of our bodies parallel to the ground. For a moment it didn't matter to me at all that I didn't have the powers that they possessed. Among them was a teenage boy of African descent who twisted the cap off his water bottle to take a swig. As he did so, I noticed the water inside his half-full bottle had formed a line that was perfectly parallel to the gray Wall.

Some people believe that there's a direct correlation between one's key personality traits and one's earliest childhood memory. This is a theory that Hyemin once explained to me. For example, if someone's earliest memory is of seeing their father beating their mother, that person will most likely display symptoms of post-traumatic stress disorder, even long after the event. If, for some reason, a person's earliest memory is of being trapped alone in a room, there's a high chance that that person will continue to struggle with feelings of alienation and claustrophobia. Or so they say; I myself am not much of a believer in such pseudo-psychology.

My earliest memory is of jumping up and down on my parents' bed; jumping so high that my head almost touched the ceiling. I'd guess I was about three or four years old. My parents adored that sky-blue colored bed, which they'd purchased as newlyweds. The mattress had good hard bedsprings and a soft cushion, a combination that would make anyone who laid down on it feel drowsy. As a child, I would jump day and night on that beloved bed. I loved how the pink floral prints on the wallpapered ceiling would rush toward me as I did so. It was as if a thousand little candies were raining down on my head.

As a child, I'd always been on the shorter side compared to other kids my age. I was quick and agile, but because I was so small, and my face so plain, I never really stood out among the other children in kindergarten or grade school. People remembered me as the kid who always bounced around here and there like a little jackrabbit. "You were always so hungry for attention," my dad would sometimes tease me.

183

This tendency led to what is now my livelihood—my profession—and what some people believe to be the core of my identity: trampolining. Recently I learned how many different languages refer to the trampoline in very similar sounding onomatopoetic terms. Bang-bang, pang-pang, pong-pong, dang-dang, kong-kong, kang-kang. Sometimes lang-lang, chang-chang and even hwang-hwang. I'd take these kinds of names over "trampoline" any day. No sound better encapsulates that indescribable feeling of one's body bouncing up to the sky than that "-ng." In my hometown, they called it "tang-tang," the same sound we use for gunfire.

My future was pretty much set from the day I first got on a tang-tang at an amusement park as a six-year-old. The moment I first jumped on that patchwork of orange waterproof fabric, it launched me high up into the sky in a direction I'd never imagined my body ever being able to go.

I lost all interest in playing with my friends, and instead spent all my time on the tang-tang. Soon, I began to go every single day. Most of my allowance ended up in the pockets of the tang-tang master. As I continued to obsess over the tang-tang, taking no interest what-soever in schoolwork, my parents ended up making a bold decision. They took their twelve-year-old daughter to a trampoline coach. My coach (who was then in his mid-twenties) carefully listened to the grievances of my half-doubtful, half-hopeful parents, and soon took me to the children's practice court.

"So you like jumping on that thing, eh?"

"More than anything in the world."

"All right then, why don't you go on up and start jumping?"

My heart pounded with excitement as I took off my sneak-ers and hoisted myself up on the trampoline. I felt the eyes of all the kids on the ground below swiveling up toward me. On the ceiling of the court was a cylindrical metal beam. Picturing myself as a hard, heavy bullet, I put all my weight into my feet and stomped. Swoop— the metal beam was right in front of my eyes. I grabbed it with my arms and legs. Jihyeon! I heard my mom scream from below, but I wasn't scared, not even a bit. The sound of people gasping and whistling drifted up to my ears. I was a monkey, small, free, with nothing to fear. The whole world stretched out below me.

Every morning, my mom reads several pages from the Dragon Scriptures. Her copy is enclosed in a leather case, with larger print for nearsighted readers. I too have read it from time to time. *When the world was full of evil, a black serpent rose into the sky. When the serpent breathed fire, seven-tenths of the earth turned to ashes and dust, and seven-tenths of the living withered and died. The sea turned to blood and the skies filled with demonic clouds, and crystalized death rained down onto the earth. Winter continued for several years, and as grasses and trees no longer bore fruit, the beasts could not birth their young, and blood and pus flowed through the land. The end of the world was near. But piercing that mantle of darkness, a colossal white Dragon flew from the sky, Its wings covered the earth and Its body glowed with light so bright that no human dared to gaze upon It. With eyes blazing like jewels and sharp fangs as hard as steel, the Serpent was merciless. As It opened Its mouth and inhaled the air, It sucked the black clouds in the sky like meek cattle into Its body. As It spread Its wings and beat the air, the sky recovered its blue and the sun regained its light. As the Serpent set foot on the earth, humans scattered away, fearing for their lives. Wherever Its breath touched, flowers re-bloomed, frozen rivers began flowing, and dead animals rose to walk and roam the earth. When a few courageous humans approached the Serpent and asked for Its name, with a voice that shook the heaven and land and sea It answered, I am Drakis, who will save you from this ruin.*

Many still believe that the great dragon Drakis saved and reconstructed our planet after nuclear war destroyed it 782 years ago. My mom is one of these believers. After a few discussions with her about religion, I learned it would be best to keep my mouth shut on the subject. She was absolutely incorrigible. My dad did allow her to drag him to church for a couple of years, but he now proclaims himself a man of no religion. Fortunately, neither of my parents are the kind of people who would disparage other peoples' beliefs or force their own religion onto their loved ones. But I know that my mom still silently hopes that I'll have a change of heart and one day come with her to church. On days when I have a big match, she always cooks me a warm breakfast, then clutches my hand to pray. On the receiving end of her prayers is the Dragon God. Her silent prayers stretch out twice as long on those days when I am on my way to the airport for an away game.

Nowadays, more people believe that the transcendent being who helped rebuild the Earth was not the Dragon God Drakis, but rather a group of beings they said came from outer space called the Prometheans. As the story goes, the Prometheans came to this planet when it was in ruins and handed down some of their civilization to us. Although parts of their technology were simply too sophisticated and complex for us to implement, the underlying assumption is that humans could never have brought civilized life back so quickly without their help.

Some refuse to believe in either of these stories. They scoff at Promethean theory, dismissing it as a mere offshoot of anthropocentric thought. If you listen carefully, their

186

argument makes a lot of sense. How plausible is it to believe that after years and years of space travel, the final destination that the Prometheans chose for themselves would be a planet devastated by nuclear warfare? In other words, why exactly would they have wanted to come to Earth? Was it just a mistake? Were they actually headed for some other planet in our galaxy? Was it for research purposes? Or merely out of pity? Since when did such highly civilized beings have so much compassion for their less-fortunate neighbors? Are we really going to believe that they came only because they wanted to help us and share their knowledge—all this without colonizing us or exploiting any of our resources (not that we had any resources to be exploited back then)—then went back home with no strings attached? What an altruistic cosmos we live in!... At least that's what the skeptics say.

The real cause of all this mystery is the fact that the post-nuclear generation failed to leave behind any scientific record of the Dragon God Drakis or the Prometheans. My tentative conclusion is that neither the Dragon God nor the aliens ever really existed. Humans were just lucky enough to reconstruct a civilized way of life, then chose to believe in whatever they wanted to believe.

But the things people believe in end up shaping the world.

It is known that early Drakianism was a radically fundamentalist religious system. In the eyes of their priests, anything that defied gravity, that took off and flew through the air, was a manifestation of evil. Flying was something permitted only to birds, insects, and dragons. Any human being attempting to fly was condemned as a blasphemous insurgent who was contradicting the will of God.

"But what about airplanes? Spaceships? How were they able to travel without such things?" I would ask incredulously.

Hyemin would shake her head and answer, "Did you
know that only fifty years ago, there used to be priests
stationed at every airport immigration desk? They
stamped passports with dragon symbols, and the
verdicts rendered by these servants of god were what
decided someone's entry or departure, not visas. This
means that whomever they deemed unworthy was
unable to board an aircraft, however arbitrary their
standards might be. Even sports matches were held
under the supervision of religion. We don't see this happening now, but years back, all ball games had priests
as officials. Every single soccer ball, baseball, or ping-
pong ball had to be blessed by a priest before it could fly
through the air."

"I don't believe you."

"Have you ever heard of something called diving?"

"No," I answered.

"Before the nuke war, there used to be a competitive sport
called 'diving.' People would wear swimsuits and jump
into the water from a platform, way up high. It even
used to be an official sport in the Olympics. Now it
doesn't exist. There's a lot of speculation about why it
disappeared, but mostly people think that it's because
the way divers jumped into the water reminded people
too much of the apocalypse. The nuke bomb. We hear a
sound, splash! And then droplets fly everywhere. You
get it?"

That's crazy! I almost shouted. I wanted to say: *A game's
just a game! What right do they have to abolish a sport
because of such delusions?* But I ended up just keeping
my lips shut.

It wasn't long after this conversation with Hyemin that
I ended up in a slump. My coach had always told me to
focus only on my next move. He'd told me to empty my
mind and body and just keep jumping until

every muscle in my body ached and all I could feel was intense hunger overtaking me, so that's precisely what I'd always done. All I ever thought about was the sweat trickling down my face, the shape of my hands and toes as I sprang upwards, my arm positions, the feeling of my muscles contracting, the sound of my legs slicing through the air, my next move, then the next one, and the one that I would have to be careful to not screw up. Everything else was just a blur.

Never once did I imagine that I would one day lose this focus.

Before the war, the trampoline was primarily a recreation for children. Only later did it develop into a competitive sport. Nowadays, not only is it a sport, it's also a religious ceremony. Some people consider it a form of total entertainment. I don't necessarily agree with that, though. How could it be a means of entertainment when it no longer has an audience?

The lack of an audience for trampolining is a problem that has persisted for quite a while now. The sport had already been in decline by the time I debuted as a trampolinist. The only people who care about it these days are those who are a part of it themselves—the trampolinists and the priests. It's still an official sport in the Drakolympics, but no one around me ever actually watches the matches on TV, let alone visits the arenas. The older trampolinists tell me it wasn't always like this. They reminisce about how much they loved that moment when they would step out onto the trampoline, those few seconds of peace and quiet as the whole arena would fall silent. They will never be able to forget the hushed *ahh!s* that met their mid-air back-flips, the cheers that would reward them when they resumed their positions after finishing their routines. This was back when people believed in the Dragon God. Back then, the trampolinists believed in their calling and regarded themselves as mediums between the people and their God. The audience cheered for the trampolinists with devoted hearts. The trampolinists with high scores were happy not because they had proven they were great athletes, but because they knew the Dragon God was present at their performance and saw how well they'd done. This is the way things once were. Now all that sounds like a fairytale.

My thoughts wandered back to diving. There is a way in which trampolining might also remind people of nuclear bombs. After hurtling up into the air, the trampolinist's body is destined to fall back down to the trampoline. What is it that makes this image any different from that of a diver, whose free fall into water allegedly revived such terrible memories in spectators? Evidently, trampolining had managed to survive through rather peculiar means.

Soon after I debuted, I realized that trampolining was first and foremost a type of ritual performed for the Dragon God Drakis. Later on I learned that all our major moves were modeled after the image of Drakis Itself. Back then, I was just a twelve year-old girl, liberated from the drudgery of schoolwork and family life, wanting nothing more than to jump high on a trampoline in front of a large crowd. On the day of my first performance, my coach came to me with a white uniform in his hand. With its tail-like white ribbons, the suit reminded me of those fancy swallow-tailed coats. It was the most beautiful piece of clothing I'd ever seen. The stage directors were installing the stage set for my performance. I remember what my coach whispered to me as the makeup artists began to paint tiny scales on my face. Don't be nervous. Just get through your routine as if it were any other day. Don't forget to put a little extra energy into your dragon twists. Your somersaults are already the best, but dragon twists are important, too.

Dragon twists are body shapes that are interspersed between the somersaults. Every trampolinist has their own unique twist, so it's hard to describe what a Dragon twist is in a single sentence. Those of you who have seen a performance may remember how trampolinists would sometimes stop in mid-air to strike a specific pose between a dizzying series of somersaults. Some claw the air with their hands and feet like a tiger pouncing on their prey, while others plummet head-down in a reverse-cross pose. The most common shape is to raise a hand high above one's head and bend one foot over backward until it touches the outstretched hand. There are many other variations of dragon twists, and I have tried most of them at least once. A competitive routine consists of twenty jumps excluding the initial take-off, and all trampolinists must include at least five dragon twists between jumps. The dragon twists are what the judges (all of whom are priests) focus on the most when deciding their scores, which is why the final ranking of contestants is mainly decided by how innovative and graceful the shape of their twists were. For twelve years, I struggled day and night to master the most varied and elegant of dragon twists for the judges and the Dragon God, wherever It may be. Perhaps it's not surprising that I burnt out.

Maybe I should be a bit more honest. I've never been a fan of the competitive trampolining rule about not smiling during performances. I'm the kind of gal who actually enjoys wearing a smile on her face, and would have preferred to shake off my nerves or celebrate my victories with a quick grin. I would have preferred to see the other contestants doing the same as well. Whenever

I see a fellow trampolinist stepping up to the trampoline with a stiff expression, I can't help but worry that this tension might lead to an injury of some sort. But under no circumstances are trampolinists allowed to smile during their performances. This is because trampolining is considered to be a solemn ritual dedicated to God. Also, the contestants are all obligated to visit their local churches a day before their performances to receive a blessing from their priests. This is a mere formality, but whenever a priest lays their hand on my head and recites a verse from the Dragon Scriptures, I can't help but feel a certain resentment boiling up within me.

I also dislike the dragon scale makeup we have to put on our faces and the white-only uniforms we have to wear. Lately, the regulations have been changed so as to accommodate subtle patterns on our uniforms, but white is still the only color that is officially allowed. What about those days when I feel like wearing green or blue? Because the dress code is so strict, it's difficult to distinguish one trampolinist from another, regardless of race, age, or nationality. Female trampolinists are even prohibited from cutting their hair short or getting a perm. This is apparently a rule that female priests have kept from the days of early Drakianism.

In the old days, trampolines were made with coiled metal springs, which made it difficult for trampolinists to jump higher than ten meters. Nowadays, they use a new synthetic material called "loob." Loob is twice as elastic as coiled springs were. The highest I've ever jumped during practice is 28 meters. Jumping that high up is of course very difficult and risky. I feel fine when I jump up to around 20 meters, but the fear of death floods my veins whenever I jump over 25 meters. But at the same time, whenever I do manage to go over that threshold, I find myself entering an indescribably euphoric state.

It's almost as if my body is turning inside out, or as if each individual cell in my body is about to burst. Still, trampolinists are only allowed to jump up to 15 meters during competitive performances. This is as high as a three-story building. They say this was the height at which prewar humans (whose physical composition was different from ours) used to feel the highest level of anxiety. Anyone who jumps higher than that limit is penalized.

My body is a reservoir of knowledge. Take my scales and use them to find what you have lost. You must never again be so insolent toward the sky and the earth. Do not attempt to rise above me.

Drakis gave unto humanity Its wisdom-filled scales, and with them the latter rebuilt its civilization. The Dragon God is dead now, but whenever I step up on the trampoline in a near-empty arena I feel the blazing eyes of the gigantic white dragon following my every move.
Be not insolent. But how can I bear to obey such a commandment, when doing so makes my trampoline feel so constricting?

I came to know that "they" existed after reading a short article in the news. At the very bottom of the sports section was a box column that included the word "tang-tang."

... Mr. Yuri Alexeyevich Boginski, who emigrated to Drako-rea from Drussia five years ago, is 28 years of age and currently resides in the Tongjeon district of Seoyong city, which is part of the old nuclear contamination zone. He insists on calling his trampoline "tang-tang." Mr. Boginski never debuted as a professional trampolinist, but he holds matches at the local trampoline park with a group of other trampoline devotees. The most remarkable thing about these trampoline matches that are taking

place "beyond the Wall" is that they are entirely free from all forms of religious formalism. For judges, they choose to use their fellow trampolinists in lieu of priests, thus setting up a mutual evaluation system in their competitions. What is even more surprising, however, are the rules of their matches. They place trampolines not only on the ground but also on the ceiling, so that contestants can bounce freely in between the two. In other words, these trampolinists are somehow able to jump in reverse direction, from ceiling to ground. It is not quite clear how they are capable of doing this, but the phenomenon itself intrigues us no end. Who knows? Perhaps they are the offspring of the Prometheans who visited our planet many years ago.

194

At first I dismissed the article as pure nonsense... at least until I saw a video of one of their performances.

It turned out that these people weren't just trampolinists. They were people who could bend gravity to their will.

Many years ago, the area beyond the Wall was designated as a Level 7 nuclear contamination zone. The government had to build a 5-kilometer long, 32-meter high quarantine wall in order to stop people from approaching the site. However, they decided to keep the Wall in place even after the nuclear residue had fully dissipated. Legend has it that during the early Drakian period, a number of heretics fled beyond the Wall in order to avoid persecution. Over the years, there were others who also chose to cross over the Wall for whatever reason. That was all I knew about the subject until now. But after four long, hard days of online research, I was able to figure out who these people actually were.

When I excitedly brought up the subject to Hyemin, she listened with a troubled look on her face.

"I heard that these people really believe that they are

descendants of the Prometheans."

"Really?"

"They claim that postwar humans interbred with the aliens. Allegedly, the Prometheans had the ability to control gravity, and they say that the people beyond the Wall inherited those powers. Can you believe it? Gravity means nothing to these people. They can jump up to the very top of a building in an instant, they can levitate up into the sky. And... that Drussian. Did you see that video I sent you? That guy named Yuri Alexeyevich. I'm pretty sure that video isn't fake. There really were four trampoline beds installed on the ceiling. Jumping all the way up to the ceiling... well, yeah, it could be done with enough practice. But that guy wasn't just jump-ing upwards; it was as if his body was being sucked upwards. I swear I saw it. He wasn't just touching the trampoline on the ceiling and then falling back down. He was actually jumping *toward* the ground. It was as if gravity was pulling him upwards, not down."

"..."

"I've been going mental since I saw that video. I want to be able to do what they're doing—to play with gravity like that, to fly in whatever direction I want! In any direc-tion—I just can't believe it! If people like that actually exist, why on earth haven't we been paying more at-tention? Did you know about this? Were you aware that such people existed?"

"I did know," Hyemin replied, and then fell silent. I've been friends with Hyemin for a decade now, and she's doing well these days as a professional trampolining commen-tator. Except for that one day when her mother went into surgery for uterine cancer, Hyemin has come to see every single one of my competitions, whether I receive good scores or bad. I still feel terrible for having missed her mother's funeral because of a competition. Hyemin's voice sounds like one of those songs with a melody and lyrics that are crystal clear, and her voice sounds even better in person than it does on air. It's calm and silvery, but also has a slight nasal timbre that makes her sound a bit girly. The latter quality is a bit over-exaggerated when she goes on air. Whenever she's sitting behind the broadcasting desk at one of my competitions, she never fails to slip in a comment or two about the elegance and grace of my movements. How agile my eight and a half somersaults are, or how much my dragon twists resemble a feline pounce or a swan's glide.

If I were a bit more sensitive, I might have noticed that something was off about Hyemin that day, but at the time, I failed to notice anything. I was too preoccupied with the image playing on a loop in my mind of Yuri Alexeyevich's performance. The way he sprang off the trampoline on the ceiling and soared toward the ground. How the sky pulled him away from the earth.

I decided to begin practicing at home instead of at the gym. I had to lie to my coach that I wasn't feeling well and needed some time off. I installed two trampolines on either wall of my room. My initial goal was to try and change the direction of my jumps. While turning a series of somersaults on the main trampoline installed on the ground, I began to edge myself toward the left. The plan was to stomp off the trampoline on my left-hand side at the correct moment and stretch myself out horizontally. However, every single time I ended up falling flat on the ground. Had there not been safety mats on the floor, I would've been badly injured. The distance between the two walls was, apparently, too wide.

But what if I were to *start off* from the left-side trampoline? I could put one foot on the bed, and then launch myself off with the other foot. After a few failed attempts, I

found my movements approximating the image I
had initially formed in my mind. It was definitely an
improvement over my first attempt, but I still lost my
balance the moment I launched myself off from the wall.
Although I managed to fall onto the center of the main
trampoline, my momentum was too weak, and gravity
pulled my body down too strongly. Also, there was no
way for me to return to the left-side trampoline from the
main one.

I continued with my experiments, this time curling my
body up with varying degrees of tightness. One thing I
learned for sure was that my body could get much closer to the wall when I curled it into a tighter ball. Then
I realized things would become much easier if I added
more speed to my movements. I decided to forget about
the two trampolines on the walls for a while and instead
practice on the main bed. I focused on jumping upwards
with more force, then transferring that energy into
faster somersaults. I turned and turned until my body
felt like a tight, round ball, spinning at the speed of light.

A month whizzed past as if it were a single day. Then one
day my dad opened the door to the training room and
asked me if everything was all right.

I was lying on the main trampoline and staring up at the
ceiling, my whole body covered with sweat. I wasn't
all right at all. I could never become one of them. The
thought that no amount of practice would ever suffice
haunted me. I was doomed to live with this gravity constantly pulling me down.

A few more months went by. Then, finally, a day came when
I felt like things were actually improving.

It was my first competition in about four months. I stepped
onto the trampoline with a nonchalant expression on
my face. The judges looked puzzled as they stared at the

two trampolines installed on either side of the wall. Ironically enough, there were no regulations regarding the number of trampolines that could be used in a competitive performance. Since nobody had ever even entertained the thought of using more than one trampoline, there was never any need for explicit guidelines about this matter. Instead of the various background sets that the other contestants were using for dramatic effect—paintings of the prophets in the Dragon Scriptures, and sometimes even of Drakis Itself—I had brought a steel frame with my two extra trampoline beds installed onto it. Assuming they were just part of my stage set, the stage directors made no move to stop me. After checking on the other trampolinists on our team, my coach came to see me right before my performance. Only then did he notice that something unusual was happening. He raised his hand to call me over, but it was already too late: my name was being announced over the loudspeakers.

I spent more time than usual on my preparatory jumps, and from my fourth jump onward, I added more speed to my somersaults. After my fifth jump, I sped toward my left while initiating a series of somersaults. When my left foot touched the vertical bed on my left, I clenched the fist of my mind around a single thought: *gravity is beneath my feet*. Just as I was about to lose balance, I crunched my body up into a somersault position. My body spun like a bullet as it soared over the main bed. When I felt the right-side trampoline under my feet, I launched myself off of it with both legs. This time gravity was on the right-hand wall, again beneath my feet.

After twenty jumps, I finished standing upright on the main trampoline bed. Sweat dripped off of my chin. I wanted to laugh but I stopped myself with all my might. The priests announced an emergency recess for the tournament. Their faces were frozen in complete bafflement. *I did it*, I thought to myself.

That day, I ended up receiving the lowest score of all the competitors. I'd already been expecting this, since I hadn't included a single dragon twist in my twenty-jump routine.

But there was also another unexpected result.

After my performance that day, they added a new rule. A new article in the guidelines now declared that the use of more than one trampoline was not permitted during a competition.

And they added another rule as well: any contestant who did not include any dragon twists in a routine would be permanently expelled from the games.

Later on, a few journalists who'd seen my performance asked me for an interview. I had no idea that my comments on the tang-tang gymnasts beyond the Wall would be blown so out of proportion. The articles quoted me saying things like, *"Drakis is dead, and the sport of trampolining has been corrupted. We need to recover the pure joy of the tang-tang. We have forgotten the freedom that comes from flying against gravity for far too long. The people beyond the Wall are different. Their creed is freedom itself."*

What's even more hilarious is that I actually *did* say such things. I was drunk on a measure of my own heroism. I spoke as if I were an athlete who had won five or six gold medals in the Drakolympics, or a veteran gymnast who had already coached numerous junior gymnasts, or a trampolinist who had already accomplished everything and was on the brink of retirement.

My mom acted as if nothing had happened, but of course the look on her face said otherwise. Buried beneath an expression of concern were traces of another emotion—

simple disappointment in her own daughter.

It took me a few days to sober up from my state of excitation. The priests had already resumed their cool façade of aloofness. My coach called to tell me I was under a month-long suspension.

"Not that I imagine you care," he said to me coldly. "I've sensed your dissatisfaction for a long time. But did you really have to go that far? You insulted and disdained everyone involved in the sport. And I'm not just talking about the priests: your colleagues, your fellow athletes—senior and junior—and everyone else who's cared about trampolining for a long time... you ended up laughing at them all. I don't mind you having opinions that are different from mine. But what did they ever do to you to deserve such derision? Are they all fools for believing in a god that you don't? If you think religion is something you can change on a whim, you are gravely mistaken. You must have learned about Christianity, the most widespread religion before the war? Were you ever taught that they suddenly changed their symbol to a star, just because they decided one day they didn't like the shape of the cross?"

"But trampolining is fundamentally a sport," I said. "Of course there are believers of Drakis. But I'm not one of them, and neither are the athletes on our team. They just have to pretend they are when they're up on the platform... I only started to jump because I enjoyed it."

"I was like that, too, once. It wasn't as if I believed in the Dragon God when I first started out. But I learned to put my faith into what I believed really mattered... None of your seniors have taken the sport as lightly as you. I can't help but think that you don't belong in our world."

After hanging up the phone, I crawled back into bed and couldn't get myself to leave my room for days.

My coach finally called me back after a month.

Resigned to the status quo, I entered another competition, and included eight dragon twists in my routine. My scores put me right in the middle of a stack of ten contestants.

The younger judges had apparently thrown in a couple extra pity points. I could tell because my performance that day was my worst ever.

A few days later, someone whom I'd never expected to hear from contacted me: Yuri Alexeyevich Boginski.

Although Yuri Alexeyevich was fairly fluent in Drakorean, conversation was not easy. I didn't know any Drussian, so we had to speak in a mixture of halting Drakorean and the United Drakian tongue.

"You, Jihyeon, I saw your game. Video. Article."

"Yes…" *I wish you hadn't.*

"Wonderful, I thought. I want to meet. You, new record holder. Champion. Somersault."

"No, it was nothing compared to United Drakian trampolinists. That day I… I just tried to imitate you guys. Even though I can never be like you."

"Know us? Tang-tang, do you know?"

"I loved that word even more than 'mommy' or 'candy' when I was a kid."

He marveled at my reply and at the fact that two people from completely different countries had grown up using the same lingo and feeling the same affection for the trampoline. The skin around his blue eyes crinkled into a smile. He had an attractive face, the face of an athlete who had trained rigorously for many years. Succumbing to my curiosity, I asked him a question.

"Your people can shift gravity, right?"

"Grav-itee?"

"Gravity. The force that pulls you down to the ground. Newton."

"Oh, gravity. Gra-vi-ty. We can shift. Wave. As we wish."

"Wave? Field? Do you mean gravitational field?"

"Wave. Building, structures, walls, tang-tang. They have gravity. We can change. If we change wave, we change direction. If it change, building pulls you down."

After a long conversation I realized I'd been right... my initial hunch had been correct after all. They were temporarily altering gravitational fields around them. Although invisible to the naked eye, every object on earth has its own gravitational field. Because these fields are so weak compared to the gravitational pull of the earth, they remain hidden. But if one could perceive the existence of such smaller fields and momentarily amplify them, it would become possible to fly freely and jump from the sky to the ground... And someone able to maximize the gravitational field of a trampoline suspended on a ceiling would literally fall upwards toward the ceiling. But how was it possible for anyone to draw so much energy?

"How much do you weigh?"

"Sixty, and four? Sixty-five. Sixty-five kilograms."

Average weight.

"Then how do you do it?"

"How? From the very beginning. Since I was born, I can."

"Are you really descendants of the Prometheans?"

He fell silent for a while.

"We are, some people say. But we do not know if it is true."

"That's what *everybody* is saying."

"Even we do not know for sure, so how can they?" Yuri said with a laugh.

"It was too long ago. Promethea, aliens, we cannot know. But Drussia, Drakorea, tang-tang, we know."

"Do your parents have the same ability as you?"

"No," he replied curtly. "My father did not like what I do. Trampoline, he liked. 'Be a trampolinist,' he said. But I felt uncertain. I want to do different thing, I want to do tang-tang. So I leave Drussia. Father, he died last year. My father's name was Alexei. Yuri Alexeyevich Boginski. My name, Alexei-yevich. In my name is father's name. I could not see him when he died."

I learned later on that Yuri was the firstborn son of a wealthy Drussian family. Refusing his family's wishes for him to become a trampolinist, Yuri began to travel the world at a young age. His goal was to find others like himself. He succeeded in doing so in New Draka, Lizardon, Madrakis and Drakterdam. But he wasn't able to make himself a home in those locations. None of his new friends were interested in the tang-tang.

Drakorea was a place he visited by chance, he explained. Exhausted from his travels, he came to the Far East to vacation in a foreign place where he knew nobody and nothing. Then, while looking for cheap guesthouses in the outskirts of Seoyong City, he came to know of the existence of the Wall. He also realized that the people who'd formed a community beyond the Wall were the ones he had been looking for all along.

He said that the people there varied in terms of individual interests and life goals, just like the ones living on this side of the Wall. He said it had taken him three years to find people who were interested in the tang-tang and to ask for their cooperation, and then, together with them, to build the necessary facilities. Fortunately, there had been several pyramid-shaped buildings in the neighborhood of Jipyeong that had been used as shelters during the war. Just like the Wall itself, those buildings had been deserted because it was cheaper to leave them intact than to tear them down. He'd spent most of his remaining funds on renovating one of them.

After talking with him for several hours, I still had one big question for him. For the third time in a row, the waiter refilled our coffee cups.

"Can you show me now? How you shift gravity? Can you
    turn the ceiling here into the ground?"
He laughed, a perplexed look on his face.
"Here? No. I can't. Other people will get hurt. Table and
    chairs, all fall up. Coffee, spill. People, fall. Upwards."
I gaped at him silently. He was right. This was a type of
    power that was not to be wielded lightly. Then how were
    the people beyond the Wall exercising it? I couldn't even
    begin to imagine.
"If you're curious, come and see. Our competition, next
    month. Hyemin, come together."
"Hyemin?"
"You know Hyemin, no? Jihyeon's friend. She not tang-tang
    gymnast. But interesting person, good person. Hyemin
    is like us."

It was a few days after my talk with Yuri that Hyemin
    visited my house. Although I insisted that I didn't want
    to see her, my mom sent her into my room anyway. For
    a long while I sat on my bed and stared at the wall, re-
    fusing to acknowledge her. When she saw that I had no
    intention of talking to her, she began to talk first.
"I know you're angry with me. I'm sorry, I should've told you
    first."
"..."
"Can you please say something?"
"When did you first find out? I mean, when did you first
    discover your powers?"
"It hasn't been that long. Probably about three years ago."
Three years? And here I was thinking that we were friends
    with no secrets between us.
"How did you find out?"
She hesitated. "By chance. It was during exam week. I spent
    the night at the library and was heading home for a
    short nap. I was about to trudge up a pedestrian over-

pass, and my whole body was heavy with exhaustion. I was standing at the foot of the stairs and, looking up, thought, what I wouldn't give to just fly up to the very top of these stairs. Well, as soon as the thought crossed my mind, I felt something happening. Something rushed toward me from the very top of the overpass. I'm not sure exactly how it happened, but when I came to my senses, I found myself sprawled at the top of the stairs. Lucky for me, it was too early in the morning for anyone else to be around. Later on, I learned that that thing was what they call a gravitational field."

"Yeah?"

"Yeah."

"Sounds simple. Then you can probably walk on this wall too, right? Show me."

"Jihyeon..."

"If everything you just said is true, you can show me right now. Why not? You don't want to? You saw everything that I was going through, and still you told me nothing. How could you? You must have been laughing at me all this while. You can warp gravity without even blinking an eye. No, not just you. I heard there's a whole team of people like you on the other side. Were you all laughing at me while you watched?"

"That's ridiculous. I never said anything about you to Yuri. Yuri said he wanted to meet you, and all I did was put you two in touch."

"Okay, fine. Then let's go outside and you can show me. I want to see for myself how you do it. Why? Is that too difficult?"

"Jihyeon..."

"What?"

 She hesitated again, and then said: "Why is this so import-ant to you? Shifting directions, changing gravity. Is that really so important?"

"Are you *kidding* me?"

"Why can't you be thankful for what you already have? Why are you pining for the one thing that you can't have?"

I picked up a book next to my bed and hurled it at her. Her words had pierced my heart. The book hit her on the arm and fell to the floor. Hyemin remained silent for a while before standing up.

Then after another pause, she said, "All right, let's go. I'll show you."

I got up and marched toward the training room. Hyemin followed behind me with a stiff expression on her face. The two trampolines were still hanging on either side of the walls. First she walked over to the main trampoline and checked whether it was bolted down securely. She tugged on the two wall trampolines a couple of times as well. Then she moved all the random objects on the floor outside the door.

"You have to stay outside, too."

"Why?"

"Are you stupid? You're going to fall toward the wall once I change the gravity. You'll get hurt."

Scoffing, I retreated outside the door.

Hyemin stood up on the left trampoline first. Standing erect, she was perfectly parallel with the floor. She jumped a couple times in that position. The trampoline bounced up and down to her movements. Her body, which stood at a 90-degree angle to the wall, soared toward the right wall, then back again to left. Hyemin walked down from the left wall and headed toward the right one, where she repeated the same movements. Then, without looking at me, she walked up to the ceiling. I couldn't believe my eyes. Hyemin was standing upside down with her feet on the ceiling, but the hem of her skirt remained as it was. Her hair still cascaded down on her shoulders, the ends pointing up toward the ceiling. Or, should I say, pointing *down*?

Wearily, I sat myself down on the floor. Hyemin walked across the wall and then the floor, and began speaking as she came out through the door.

"Each person's powers have a different range. Mine are pretty narrow. They probably extend to only about a three meter radius. Yuri has *much* stronger powers, which is why he can jump all the way up to the ceiling of a trampoline arena."

"Can everyone on the other side do what you just did?" I asked feebly.

"Yes. But it's not as if they use their powers on a daily basis. They walk on the ground, just like everybody else. You've probably realized by now that this ability can be quite dangerous. It's not like everyone over there is flying through the sky everyday like Superman. You might be imagining something like Escher's *Relativity*, that painting where each room in a house has its own gravitational field... But if that were to happen in real life, someone would end up dying or getting hurt. That's why they follow a set of rules: they can only exercise their powers after a consensus has been reached among a group of peers. They're not allowed to expand their gravitational field in a space where others are present."

"Then what's the point of having such powers?"

"There are a few, and research is still underway. But it's actually not as useful as you might think. Besides, they don't necessarily try to benefit from them. Most people are just amused by it. Occasionally someone might attempt to use it for some crime. I've heard of a couple of instances where people abused their powers for illegal purposes. But there haven't been any big incidents like that for a while now. Everyone tries to be cautious. They know it will just attract attention—unwanted attention—from the outside. Tang-tang is probably the only occasion where these abilities are being used in a proactive and productive way."

Hyemin smiled wryly. Her face was shining with sweat.

"They're a minority. Most of their ancestors were runaways who had to go over the Wall because of extreme religious persecution. Many generations have passed since then. As you know, the people on this side of the Wall don't know anything about their powers. There would be mass hysteria if someone accidentally warped gravity on this side, and nobody wants that to happen. This is a really *important* matter to them. All they need is a safe place to live their lives without having to hide their abilities. Prometheans? They don't know anything about that. It was too long ago, and while some people believe in the stories, others don't. Some people say that it's because of the nuclear waste that they gained such powers. It's another far-fetched theory, but maybe it's true."

I sat quietly, thinking.

"I wanted to tell you the truth. But somehow I just couldn't bring myself to open up."

"... I understand."

"Do you know what the main difference is between you and me?"

"...The fact that you are gifted and I'm not."

"The fact that you're an athlete and I'm not."

Hyemin gazed at me unwaveringly.

"I can't move my body the way you do... I like my job, sure. I like sitting in front of a broadcasting mic, and I'm thankful that I can discover promising new trampolinists and introduce them to an audience. I love how I can continue my studies while I work. But do you really think that's all I ever wanted for myself? No way. I wanted to be a trampolinist, too."

I stared at Hyemin, flustered. Never once did I imagine that

Hyemin could have wanted something for herself other than broadcasting.

"But of course I couldn't be one. I was born with two left feet. Turning mid-air somersaults was something that I could never manage."

"I had a hard time with them too when I first started."

"No, you were able to do them very easily. I couldn't. You're a natural. You have been, ever since that day when you were twelve years old and went to the trampoline court for the very first time with your mother."

I couldn't respond.

"You're an athlete now, whether you like it or not. I'd like you to come with me to next month's tang-tang competition. I know Yuri would be delighted to see you there."

Having said her piece, Hyemin collected her belongings and left.

The tang-tang arena was much bigger and more spacious than I'd expected. Just like I'd seen in the video, there were four trampolines installed on the four walls, enclosing a cube-shaped space near the ceiling. The height of this space was staggering in real life. I half expected that "they"—the people who made up most of the audience—would be sitting perpendicularly on four different sides of the arena, each side under a different gravitational field, but of course it wasn't actually like that. It would've been impossible for them to get a good view of the performances sitting that way. The stage was installed high up, far enough away to ensure the audience's safety. The arena itself resembled a pyramid with its top sliced off. There was a square shaped hole in the very middle of the ceiling. Once the competition began I soon realized what the hole was for.

"Did you enjoy it?" Yuri asked me, outside the arena after

his performance. His face looked paler than usual, and his featureless uniform was damp with sweat. It looked as though half the blood had been drained from his body.

"Yes," I answered. What I couldn't bring myself to say, I kept to myself. Still smiling faintly, his gaze shifted to a person approaching us from behind. I turned around and saw Hyemin coming out of the arena. She'd watched the competition three seats away from mine. Not once had I glanced at her throughout the whole event... and she hadn't looked at me, either.

"Would you like to try it out before leaving? After the competition, anyone can practice. There are gym clothes in the locker room. You can change there."

I declined as politely as I could. And, I added to myself, *now I know one thing for sure: I'm nothing at all like you people.*

All I wanted to do was go home. I didn't feel like talking to anybody.

But no matter how bumpy the bus ride back home got, there was one thought that I couldn't quite shake.

One evening, my dad knocked on my bedroom door and came in. It'd been three months since I'd last been to practice.

"Jihyeon..."

"Yes, dad?"

"Are you not going to practice anymore? Are you giving up on trampolining?"

"I... I don't know."

"Isn't it drafting season soon?"

"..."

"Entering the Drakolympics has always been a dream of yours."

"Yes, it was. But I never got the chance. They said I was too young the first time around, and too inexperienced the second time. Back then I couldn't understand my coach's decision. I thought I was the best. But now I feel as though I don't deserve to be a part of an event like that."

"What on earth would make you think that way? You didn't do anything wrong."

I couldn't answer him. That was something that I wanted to ask him. I wanted to demand, *Why is it so difficult for me to just live my life doing what I want to do?*

"Do you want to go over the Wall?"

"There won't be much that I can do there."

"Then what is it that you really want to do?"

I sat there, pondering this question for a long time. Then I said, "I don't know. I really don't know."

"To be honest, I always wanted you to become a lawyer or doctor."

"What?"

"Your mother and I, we never got much education when we were young, and you know we've had our share of struggles in life. We wanted you to get all the education that you could possibly want. Even when we first took you to that trampoline coach, we really didn't take trampolining that seriously. You were never a studious child, so we just thought it would be a good idea to leave you with disciplined adults, rather than let you get into trouble on your own. Then there was that day when you came to me for a talk. It was probably after your first competition. 'Dad, I want to be someone who can conquer gravity,' you said. 'I love the tang-tang so much.'"

"..."

"I can only guess how you must feel right now. But to me it seems like lately you've been bothered by something else, something other than the tang-tang or the trampoline."

"..."

"Is it really *that* serious?"

"What?"

"Whatever it is that's making you behave like this. That's making your shoulders droop. Is it really that big a problem?"

"I don't know," I said yet again.

"Okay, well then. Take your time and think about it." With that, my dad left the room, closing the door behind him.

"It's fine. Just don't ever do it again," my coach said.

"I'm not sure I can promise that, sir."

"What?"

"While I was at home, I watched videos of all my performances, again and again."

"You're not a bad trampolinist. It's just that you overreach sometimes."

"I think you're right. I didn't take the sport as seriously as I should have... I wish I could say with confidence that I'm already good enough, but I can't. And that's what's killing me the most."

"...What're you trying to say?"

"I've given this a lot of thought. But there's still something that I really can't agree with. The idea that anything is possible, as long as you try hard enough. I really don't think that's true. Working hard can't be the answer to every problem that makes us feel bad about ourselves. That's why I can't sit still and not do anything about it."

"Jihyeon."

"Instead, I want to at least try everything that I can. And I'd love to come see you again after I've become a better athlete, even if it's just a little bit better."

Coach let out a long sigh. I wanted to say more, but instead I bowed goodbye and walked out. My cheeks were burning. Every word I'd just uttered came back to reverberate in my own ears. I felt embarrassed and light-headed. It was like one of those times when you hear a million voices ringing inside your head. *Why on earth would you say such things?* I heard the voices cackling right behind me, striking me so hard that I almost fell on my knees.

Respect and honor are noble ideals, so much so that even just invoking them makes me feel small and worthless. But how are we to distinguish respect from submissiveness? Why is it that I only have complaints and no solutions? What should I do in order to prove myself? It seemed as if all I could do at this point was make a few feeble promises to myself. But I also knew that hearing myself say such things was a necessary part of the process. I was embarrassed about myself, but I also wasn't. *I refuse to allow myself to run away from this nauseating feeling*, I thought to myself as I slowly made my way toward the practice court.

The court itself was completely empty. The trampolinists who were entering the Drakolympics team trials had already left Seoyong City the previous day for training camp, and the remaining trampolinists had been given a week-long break. I climbed up onto the trampoline and jumped without any embellishing moves. The building echoed with the sound of my feet hitting the trampoline and my body whizzing through the air. Higher and higher I went, as high as I could go. I jumped until my face turned red from shortness of breath, then caught my breath as I slowed myself down.

After repeating this process three times, I sat on the soft trampoline bed. Sweat dripped off my chin and into my training suit. As I caught my breath again, the scent of my own perspiration crept into my nostrils. My body was warm. The tip of my nose tingled. I felt as if something sharp was tearing through my guts. There was a cramp under the right side of my rib cage. My backside and thighs felt uncomfortable, as if caked with mud. Fat

213

had amassed on my body during my long break from practice. But the soreness in my muscles banished my dizziness, and purely physical sensations took the place of my thoughts. I felt healthy and peaceful. My breathing returned to its normal pace. My body once again felt as if it were my own. For a moment I sat there, staring up at the ceiling.

The gym was full of the heat that had been emanating from people's bodies. The smell of freshly baked wophles and skoens. The sound of a Ffolca can opening. The sounds of laughter and applause. Snippets of music bounced around above my head, and my hearing went numb. Thousands of hands flapped and danced around here and there above me, like leaves on a tree. When all these images slowly compressed into a ball in my mind and then exploded, the lights switched on. Suddenly there were four trampolines on the ceiling of the gym, and standing on another trampoline onstage was Yuri.

They called the technique "Skywalking"—treading upon the sky. While their bodies are suspended in mid-air during a series of somersaults, they reach through the hole in the ceiling and expand their gravitational field as far as possible, all the way up to a passing cloud. I watched Yuri's body get sucked up and out into the sky as he somersaulted mid-air. After about twenty seconds, he reappeared through the hole. At first glance, it seemed as if he was falling, but right before he struck the main trampoline at center stage, he shifted the gravitational field again and soared upward toward the ceiling. After leaping across the four beds on the ceiling, he bounded toward the ground from the left-side ceiling bed, turned a few flips, and landed safely on the main bed. Cheers and applause erupted from the crowd. It was clear that this was not a skill that just anyone could master. Stunts like these could get someone killed.

There were only two contestants other than Yuri who could perform this skill.

I rose and began to do some warm-up exercises. My body sent me a warning signal once I reached the fifteen-meter point. It reminded me of the feeling that had shot through me the first time I had ever jumped this high. Starting from the next jump, I began to turn somersaults. As I slowly increased my speed, I thought to myself, *this is the weight that I must carry. This is the gravity of the world I live in.*

I would have loved to say that I wasn't part of this world, but that simply wasn't true. Even after I thought I had let go of everything, there was still something that I wanted to accomplish: to learn how to genuinely love this gravity that I lived under. If I didn't at least *try*, there was really no reason for me to exist in this world. A cross could never transform itself into a star. But gravity *could* change. Even though the experience had been borrowed and was not a part of my natural world, I remembered how exhilarating it had felt to momentarily exist under a different gravitational field.

If I wanted to change the gravity of this place, I had to first alter my own weight. I had to master the world that I lived in... no matter *how* long that might take.

That's the rule.

As my body fell toward the trampoline, I made my first dragon twist.

Yuri said it took him ten years to master skywalking.

I met with Yuri for a long and earnest conversation. To the very end, he failed to understand why I wouldn't move beyond the Wall. Just like I couldn't ever know what it would feel like to soar upwards to the sky, he could never understand what it felt like to trampoline. I didn't ask him to. Sympathy was impossible without effort, and communication was impossible without an open heart. I didn't yet possess enough of either, and I wasn't confident enough to share my feelings. It was difficult to admit this weakness, but instead of being sad about it, I decided to continue trying.

My mom still reads the Dragon Scriptures every morning, and prays to the Dragon God for me.

I take the bus and visit "them" beyond the Wall two or three times a month. I watch the tang-tang competitions, and as I watch, I think deeply about the tang-tang and the trampoline. I also spend time with the kids who dream of becoming tang-tang gymnasts one day. There are many who can already walk on the walls, but very few of them are gifted enough to tang-tang. Yuri asked me to teach them basic tang-tang skills. I refused twice, but finally accepted the third time he asked. I really didn't think I was coach material, but I wanted to do *something* for my friend.

After returning as a competitive trampolinist, I realized I'd already lost many of my colleagues. A few of them even refused to acknowledge me as a fellow athlete. I understood their need to behave that way around me. Fortunately, though, my coach stayed by my side. Lately, he and I have been having conversations that are much more open and candid than they were in the past.

There's been a slight revision to the regulations for trampolining for the next Drakolympics, which will take place two years from now. They've increased the jumping height limit from 15 meters to 17.5 meters. Nobody knows where they came up with the extra 2.5 meters, and the only thing I can imagine is that numerous other trampolinists in addition to those on our team have been complaining to their coaches about the limit. Other than this tiny bit of progress, though, everything else has remained the same. But I'd rather believe that other

things might also change for the better some day, even
if it can't happen right now.

Whenever I see a tang-tang performance, I'm still enthralled, and my heart still aches with unbearable
sorrow.

But what allows me to overcome such pain is the fact that
Hyemin is always sitting right next to me, and I can roll
my eyes and complain to her. "It's ridiculous: there's no
way a human being can possibly do the things they do
on that stage. They really *must* be aliens!"

"They probably are," Hyemin answers, laughing.

She still works as a trampoline commentator on this side
of the Wall, while working on the tang-tang match
organizing committee on the other. Because there are
lots of non-Drakorean residents beyond the Wall, she
also works as an interpreter. This makes her much busier
than me. The fact that our friendship has survived everything has been one of the biggest blessings in my life
over the past few years.

Yuri's been trying to woo Hyemin for a few months now.
Unfortunately for him, she finds him far less interesting
as dating material than she does in terms of his trampolining skills. Of course, Yuri is *totally* oblivious to this
fact, and passionately pursues his international love
interest.

Whenever he goes on stage I lean in toward Hyemin and
whisper in a teasing voice, "Hey, there's that alien, love-
sick over you-know-who."

And every time Hyemin answers flatly, "I told you, it's not
like that!"

Hyemin calls him the Sky Walker.

BETWEEN ZERO AND ONE

BY KIM BO-YOUNG

TRANSLATED BY EUNHAE JO
AND MELISSA MEI-LIN CHAN

KIM BO-YOUNG

After studying psychology at college, Kim Bo-Young (b.1975) worked for a few years as a screenwriter and developer for a gaming company. Her literary career began in 2002 when her first story, "The Experience of Touch" (Chokgagui gyeongheom), was published online on the SF fandom website *Junk SF*. The story won an award in the SF and Science Writing Contest in 2004, which encouraged Kim to pursue writing as a full-time profession. A two-volume collection of Kim's short stories and novellas, titled *The Story Goes That Far* (Meolli ganeun iyagi) and *An Evolutionary Myth* (Jinhwa sinhwa), was published in 2010. The title story of the latter volume was translated and published in the U.S. monthly science fiction and fantasy magazine *Clarkesworld* in 2015 and also in the major Chinese fandom website *Future Affairs Administration* in 2017. Her first full-length novel, *Seven Executioners* (Chirinui jiphaenggwan; 2013), won first place in the 2014 SF Awards sponsored by the Gwacheon National Science Museum. She also served as a science consultant for the film *Snowpiercer* (2013).

220

Kim is today one of South Korea's most renowned SF writers. She produces a broad range of work—from hard SF to social SF to to science-fantasy—all of which is at once scientifically informed and psychologically complex. Often testing the boundaries between fiction and thought experiments, the science-fictional plots of her stories serve as vehicles for the exploration of ethical and political issues that arise from contemporary technology and science. A masterful writer of Korean prose, Kim has been especially proficient in depicting imaginary futures resulting from new technologies such as cloning ("The Experience of Touch"), genetic engineering ("Superior Genes" [Usuhan yujeonja]), and robotics ("The Origin of the Species" [Jongui giwon]). Much of her work has to do with notions of posthumanity and, from that perspective, connects up in fruitful ways with post-millennial feminist SF in Korea as well as abroad.

"Between Zero and One" (0gwa 1 sai), a story that was first published in the webzine *Crossroads* in 2009, is a time travel story that explores the speculative consequences of quantum physics, indeterminacy, and what might happen in a world ruled by probability rather than certainty. It deploys this theoretical apparatus mainly through the voice of a mysterious narrator who, through a characteristic mixture of flashbacks and flashforwards, relates an impossible but all too real tale of teenage angst, parental abuse, and education fever in South Korean society today.

Introduction by Eunhae Jo and Melissa Mei-Lin Chan

221

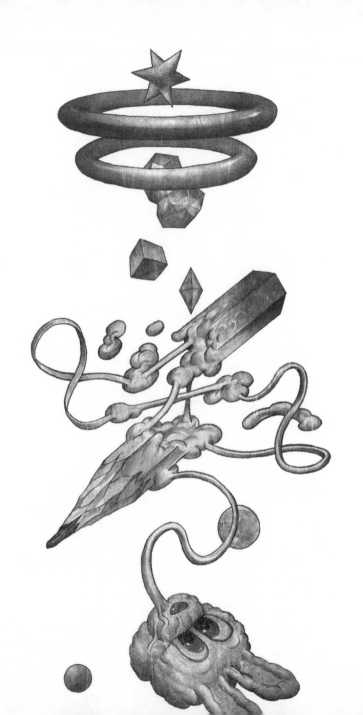

I.

It's been said that no human being has ever invented a time machine, and that no one ever will. There were no throngs of camera-holding tourists on Golgotha when Jesus was crucified, or in front of the Bodhi tree beneath which the Buddha meditated, or outside the Cave of Hira when Muhammad heard his first revelation. No assassin ever visited Hitler in his crib, no Israeli army came to liberate the Jews from the concentration camps, and no human rights organization showed up in time to save Africans from the slave ships. In the First and Second World Wars, no reinforcements came to change the histories of their homelands, and no records remain of war correspondents running around with laptops in the middle of the Trojan War or at the Battle of the Red Cliffs.

223

If a time machine *had* been invented, Van Gogh would never have lived in poverty because art dealers would have flocked to acquire even a single piece of cloth used to clean his paintbrushes. Mozart would have lived to a ripe old age, since doctors armed with medical bags and surgical instruments would have come in droves to save him while he was dying. Museum directors would have searched for Solgeo's painting, *The Old Pine Tree*, as well as for lost history books such as *Yugi*, *Sinjip*, and *Seogi*.[1] As you can imagine, there would be no such thing as missing historical artifacts or poor, downtrodden geniuses.

---

[1] *Yugi* and *Seogi* are the now lost chronicles of the ancient Korean dynasties of Goguryeo and Baekje. Both are believed to have been written in the 4th century. Yugi may have consisted of as many as one hundred volumes, which were allegedly compiled into the five-volume *Sinjip* (also lost) in 600 AD.

Crimes would be stopped by the police before they could
take place. Court battles and investigations would become unnecessary. On-site trials would be held while
the incidents in question were still taking place.
Drivers would hear from the Highway Patrol prior to a
collision. Firefighters would enter dwellings to put out
cigarettes and shut off gas valves before a fire broke out.
Orphans would live with their parents. No child would
ever go missing.

So we will never be able to build a time machine! This
much seems to have been already proven by the fact
that history is full of tribulations and errors and events
that might have gone otherwise if only the consequences that would result had been known. We have all made
countless mistakes in our lives, yet nobody's ever shown
up to warn us about them.

Still, we kept researching. We reported our results as "theoretical work." We knew that we would eventually figure
something out. We were like those alchemists who
founded chemistry by failing to make gold, or like those
other nineteenth-century scholars who advanced the
development of physics while trying to build a perpetual motion machine.

Our goals were, of course, not nearly so modest. Our intention *was* to build a time machine.

II.

The world suddenly rattled. Mrs. Kim shook her head.
Feeling dizzy, she checked her watch. The second hand,
which had been hiding behind the minute hand, began
moving again as if nothing had happened.

It's six-thirty again, she thought to herself. *How many times
has it been six-thirty already? The woman sitting across
from me is repeating the same sentence for the fourth*

or fifth time. *The cookies that we just ate are here on the plate again.*

"You can say *that* again," said another woman. "My home-room teacher had such a fiery temper that we couldn't buy enough mop handles to replace the broken ones. One time he lined us all up for a caning. Some of us fainted, and some ended up on stretchers... such a horrible scene. I stood at the very end of the line on purpose, but he hit me anyway until the mop handle broke. I couldn't sit down for a month. Still, I miss the old days. Even that day is a good memory. I remember running around in a short school uniform with my hair bobbed. All the boys in town would turn to look at me! I didn't like my hair at the time, so I used to fiddle with my bangs, stiffening them with glue to make them look pretty."

The woman sitting across from Mrs. Kim nodded earnestly, as if this were the first time she had heard the story.

"That's right," she replied. "Those *were* the good old days! You know, we didn't have to think so much. We just did as we were told, and that was good enough. I used to eat my lunch behind my teacher's back during class, and it was so good. I bet nothing will ever taste as good as that. One day I jumped over a fence because I really wanted to eat *ddeokppokki*.[2] I got caught and was called onto the carpet for a week straight. I was scolded so harshly that I still can't eat *ddeokppokki*. But stuff like that... they're still happy memories."

"I really, *really* wanted to go to a concert, so my friends and I skipped school and took the bus there. Once my parents found out, I got whipped so harshly that I still have a scar."

"But that's how it is with young girls," the women said in almost perfect unison.

---

[2] Spicy rice cakes sold by street vendors or at cheap restaurants. A popular snack among school-age Koreans.

THUMP.

"Tell me about it. Those were the days..."

Time suddenly seemed to refuse to flow in just one
direction. It was as if time were saying: *Hey, whoever's
controlling the universe! I'm going on strike! From now
on, I'm going to take a break whenever I want and go
wherever I like!* Now time was rocking back and forth
on a seesaw, skipping like an old record, then rewinding
like a videotape. Mrs. Kim started to feel anxious. *Am I
going to have to live like this until I die? Am I going to
stay stuck in this neighborhood meeting forever?*

"I really can't figure out what's *bothering* them so much. We
pay for their schooling, put a roof over their heads, keep
'em fed. They have *everything* they could ever need,
don't they? We don't ask them to make money or do
chores around the house... all we ask is that they sit and
study... I don't understand what's so hard about that."

"It's because they've always had it so easy. If they were ever
to go hungry, even once, they'd come to their senses.
You know, back in the day, we never had enough food to
eat. There was no such thing as school meals or class-
room snacks. There was no bus. We walked to school,
even in the winter. Back in those days, you couldn't go to
college, even if you got accepted! Smart kids had to get
a job to support their families. College was only for the
filthy rich."

"Well, *I* think it's because they're so immature. Let 'em try
to get a job with a degree from some no-name college...
then they'll wake up. Who's going to hire someone who
went to some second-rate college or university?"

"They'll regret it when they're older. Once they enter the
job market, they're gonna say that studying was the
easiest thing they ever had to do. And *then* they'll start
criticizing you: 'Mom, why didn't you push me harder?'
We have to push them hard *now* so they won't blame
us later."

"By the way, did you see yesterday's newspaper? It said that a bunch of high school kids went to Gwanghwamun Square to protest."[3]

"Those *insolent* little... What do they think they're doing? And in the middle of such a critical time in their studies, too? If they have so much free time, they oughtta be memorizing more English vocabulary!"

"Eh, the problem is that they don't think. At that age, their heads are empty. All they care about is eating *ddeokppokki* and following pop singers around. They don't *want* to study."

"Hey, Soo-ae's Mom, you've been pretty quiet..."

Only after everyone turned to look in her direction did Mrs. Kim realize that they were referring to her. She shook her head. More words washed over her.

"How's Soo-ae doing? Last time you were worried about her grades falling. I know a good private tutor. Do you want me to introduce him to you? He's not cheap, but the moms who've hired him all say he's worth it..."

"Soo-ae killed herself."

Now there was total silence.

III.

Even now we are traveling through time. One minute per minute, one second per second, we're flowing into the future. If we stand up and walk anywhere, we will unwittingly reach the future 0.00000001 seconds earlier. This is because the measurement of time and space are inseparable. Oh, of course. You know this better than me... If we were to run, hop on a train, get on a plane, or ride in a spaceship, we would arrive in the future a bit

---

[3] Gwanghwamun Square is one of Seoul's most famous public spaces and the site of a surviving gate to Gyeongbokgung, the main royal palace of the Joseon Dynasty.

earlier still. If we were to get on a spaceship that flew at the speed of light, we could even theoretically stop time.

Yes, we know how to get to the future. But we can't go back in time. Understanding this is no different from speculating about the existence of negative speed or distance. That would be weird. It would be like saying, "When I drove off today, I sped so fast that I arrived yesterday." Or: "The school was so close that I got inside before even taking a single step."

HUN, however, as our computer is called, always ascribes a high probability to the event of our inventing a time machine. It's hard to tell quite how he's come to that conclusion. No one can tell, actually, because the number of operations that HUN performs in a second is greater than the total number of particles in the universe. Which, of course, is both confounding and contradictory...

Our team often debates the potential challenges of time travel. The locale in which a time traveler arrives may have to be electromagnetically cleared first; otherwise, we might get stuck in something—a tree, a car, something like that. Moreover, because of how the Earth and the entire galaxy are constantly rotating and revolving, it's possible to get lost in space during the process of traveling through time. But we tell each other that there's probably nothing to worry about, since the time machine will be anchored to Earth by inertia as well as gravity.

Then again, suppose I were to travel back to five minutes ago and meet myself. We would greet each other with a deep bow. "Hello, I'm you." "Hello, I'm you five minutes from now." Five minutes later I might go back to meet and greet myself again: "Hello, everyone, I'm you ten minutes from now." Left to my own devices, I could fill up the universe with copies of myself. Some of us have fallen asleep thinking about that conundrum. Can two same individuals share the same space-time moment? Huh. Maybe they'd just explode and die...

On the team, we ask one another esoteric questions as naturally as exchanging greetings. *Where would you go if you could travel back in time?* We all have our own stories. There are people who have lost their partners or children. People who still remember their first love. People who long for their childhood hometowns. People who want to undo the mistakes of their youth. As we while away the hours talking about these things, empty bottles collect on the table. Some nights, the discussion continues until dawn breaks with a faint white glow.

No one asks about my story. No one *ever* asks about me. They say I'm like a phantom, because they can't quite tell if I really exist. The positive side of this, of course, is that it leaves me free to focus on my work.

IV.

Where did it all go wrong? Mrs. Kim kept thinking. *What did I do that was so terrible? Was I different from other moms? Isn't it the same for everybody? Aren't kids always asking the same silly questions? "Why do I have to study? Why do I have to go to school? Why do I have to eat dinner? Why do I have to eat my vegetables? Why do I have to take a bath? Why do I have to wash my hands?"*

She remembered her last argument with her daughter. It was the day Soo-ae's report card had arrived in the mail. Mrs. Kim had torn open the envelope with trembling hands still wet from washing dishes. Soo-ae's school ranking had dropped again. She sat down, barely able to move, her head in her hands. "What now?" she mumbled. *"What now?"*

She started for her daughter's room and unlocked the door,

slipping inside like a detective, then proceeded
to ransack the place, going through desk drawers, flipping through diaries, and turning Soo-ae's school bag
inside out.

But she found nothing. The things kids carried around
these days were a mystery. One looked like a fashion ac-
cessory or a hair clip, though it might just as easily have
been a weird electronic gadget. When Mrs. Kim pulled,
tapped, and twisted it, nothing happened. However,
when she dumped out her daughter's bag, she finally
found some things that she could recognize: a badge,
a headband, a half-burned candle, and a few colorful
flyers that read: "Stop Old-Fashioned Education";
"Stop the Rat Race"; "End College Entrance Exam-Cen-
tered Education."

The girl's lost her mind!

Just then, the front door opened and her daughter came in.
Mrs. Kim, now furious, hurled the things she'd found in
the bag at her daughter's feet.

"Are you out of your mind? Is this what you've been doing
with yourself? If you've got this much time on your
hands, then memorize more English words instead! Your
college entrance exam is right around the corner! How
could you do this when other kids say they don't even
have time to eat or sleep? If you go on like this, you'll
never get into college, and I'll be so ashamed of you!
Why are you doing this to me?!"

Her daughter slowly blinked, a puzzled look on her
face. She looked down at the things scattered on the
floor, then stared blankly at her mom, as if she understood—or rather, as if she *didn't* understand—what was
happening.

"Aren't you going to college? Do you know how you'll be
treated in this country without a degree? If you go on
like this, you'll be repeating your senior year while

230

everybody else starts college! How do you think I'll look to all the other moms then? You think *studying* is hard? Huh? When you go out into society, you'll see how happy you were back in school! They're the best years of your life! You're just griping, but you don't know anything! You think you can survive in the real world if you can't even make it here? You think so? Go ahead and die then! Hey, where are you going? Am I talking to a brick wall? Where'd you learn those manners? You're getting worse every day! Get back here!"

THUMP.

The world shook again. Mrs. Kim felt a tightness in her chest and briefly tore at her clothes. *Did I really tell her to die?* She couldn't remember. She hadn't given much thought to the word. Surely her daughter hadn't either...

What did I do wrong? Whatever I did, was it really so bad? Everything I did was for her, not for me. I should've just left her alone... she should've known that I was speaking out of love...

Ms. Kim remembered how her daughter had stared at her silently as she stood at the door. *When did she start seeing me as the enemy? She looked at me as if I'd betrayed her. As if she'd regretted ever trusting or loving me when she was little. As if she'd wanted to cut all ties with me.*

What did I do that was so wrong? Why do I deserve to be punished like this? She should've waited a little bit longer. As she got older, we could've changed one another's minds. We would've forgiven each other...

She should have left me with a different memory. She should have given me a chance. Maybe she did. Maybe she was sending me an SOS. But it was always in the form of hatred and disobedience. Could I just have been too blind to notice? Is that why she punished me?

THUMP.

Have you ever tried to catch the exact moment when a flower blooms? Flowers don't bloom while they are being watched. No matter how hard you try, it always happens when you're looking away. It's because your gaze collapses the wave function, changing an entangled quantum state into a stable one.

When all the animals leave, a forest becomes a desert, and when all the tenants leave, a house goes into disrepair. The fission of radioactive material stops when someone is watching, and so a watched pot never boils. Of course, you know all this better than I do...

232

The sea was in chaos until life was born. The sky did not exist until eyes beheld it. The universe did not exist in any specific form until humans invented the telescope and looked at the stars and into space. The moon, too, was in flux until the first spaceship landed on it. Perhaps, had the first astronauts been artists rather than scientists, the moon would have taken on a more beautiful form.

Even now, you're imposing order onto chaos at every possible moment, deciding the direction of a world that, until just now, existed merely as a set of possibilities. Your mother created you at your genetic birth, but she also re-created you, moment by moment, by watching you grow up.

The past, however, doesn't change with our observations of it. Too many eyes have frozen it in place. The future holds endless possibilities *because no one has yet observed it*. And without human eyes, both the past and the future would exist only as infinite chaos.

A long time ago, when young scholars first proposed such theories, the older scholars scoffed and said that the world couldn't really work that way. Indeed, no one had ever seen such a world. No one had observed the unobserved world. We only see what we have witnessed, and we only know what we have seen. And yet people talk with such confidence, as if they have witnessed every aspect of the world.

VI.

"Don't think of it as a waste of money. It's better to make the investment now than to spend money later on repeating another year of exam prep."

"I've heard that this medication really works. My neighbor has been buying it for three months now. She says that her kids don't even sleep anymore. You know what they say: the early bird gets the worm! You gotta sleep less. Give it a try."

"I sent my daughter to a special high school that has the highest rate of college enrollment in the country. But it's really difficult to stand out among all those bright students. If she'd gone to a regular high school, she would've been the top of her class. I'm so mad at myself for sending her there. She feels discouraged because she didn't get top marks despite her brilliance."

"I should've sent my child to the States like the other kids, but thanks to my husband, we missed our chance. It breaks my heart to see so many kids come back speaking fluent English. We hesitated, and that messed up our kid's life. He's gonna fall behind the other kids who got a head start."

"My daughter says she doesn't want to go to school."

Mrs. Kim immediately regretted speaking. *Did I have nothing else to say?*

"That's what they *all* say. They need to grow up."

"My kid says that he doesn't even plan to go to college. He's out of his mind. In this day and age, how can anyone survive without a degree?"

"I heard that recently even grade-schoolers have been demonstrating. They were shouting something like, 'Stop old-fashioned education!'"

"They *couldn't* have come up with that on their own. Someone must have put them up to it. Maybe even their moms."

"Typical slackers. Good students don't do that. My daughter stays glued to her desk for hours after school. She's cut down on drinking water so she won't waste time going to the bathroom. We threw out our TV and our computer, and now we tiptoe around the house so we don't disturb her."

"It kills me that my son always misses a few answers on his tests. It holds him back from getting perfect scores. Why's he so careless? He takes after his father. He gets good grades, so why can't he be number one at his school? If it weren't for those few mistakes... Why can't he just *do better?*"

Mrs. Kim kept silent. *I'd better say nothing. I can't win.* Looking around, she saw other women who perhaps felt the way she did also keeping quiet. Some looked as if they were going to go home and yell at their kids. "What's wrong with you? Why can't you be more like the kids next door?"

Someone tapped her on the shoulder, interrupting her pensive state. Mrs. Kim turned and saw a strange-looking woman smiling idiotically at her. She was wearing a man's shirt, a suit, and thick, plastic-rimmed glasses that covered nearly half her face. She wore no make-up, and her messy hair, which was tied back in a scrunchie, looked as if it hadn't been washed for days. It took Mrs. Kim a while to recognize her. It was her new neighbor. There was a rumor that she'd suffered some kind of a nervous breakdown.

"My daughter's the same."

"What do you mean?"

"She doesn't wanna go to school. Your daughter must be smart. *Smart* kids *never* want to go to school."

Mrs. Kim felt uneasy and took a step away from the woman. Appearing not to take the hint, the woman moved in even closer. That's when she saw the object on the woman's index finger. It looked like a dirty rabbit finger puppet. The woman stuck the rabbit in Mrs. Kim's face and bent her finger to make it look as if it were bowing.

"Please forgive her, Mrs. Kim," said Thick Glasses in a fake-sounding voice. "She's kinda rude. I keep telling her she can't come on that strong with strangers."

Mrs. Kim frowned. "Kids like it. When my daughter was little, she loved puppet shows."

Thick Glasses looked puzzled. Then she turned to the rabbit and burst into laughter. Mrs. Kim didn't know what was so funny.

Thick Glasses's voice went back to normal. "Actually, that wasn't me speaking. It was him! He's a new A.I. computer! Or rather... he's *part* of a computer that's in communication with the main server. It's hard to describe, but basically, he's the one who's speaking, and this is his communication device."

"I see," Mrs. Kim nodded, trying to step back from the woman. "The computer or the communications device, which one is it?"

"I mean, uh, the computer is the one talking, and this rabbit is the communication device and... that's it. No big deal."

Of course. That makes sense...

Thick Glasses changed her voice yet again. "Why aren't you answering your phone? Shall I come in person?"

"The computer is calling you."

"Oh, this isn't the computer..." Thick Glasses put the rabbit to her ear like a cell phone and answered. "Call me back later. I'm busy right now." Turning to Mrs. Kim, she said,

"It was a phone call from Mars."

Of course *it was.* Mrs. Kim glanced around, only to realize that no one was even looking at her and Thick Glasses. "I didn't know you had an alien friend," she sniped.

"Ha ha! You're funny, Mrs. Kim! There are no aliens on Mars."

"Really? I thought octopus-aliens lived there."

"No, that's just in the cartoons. There's no oxygen or water on Mars, hence no alien life."

Listen to that... This lady's insane but still tries to be logical.

"But you just said you got a phone call from Mars."

"Oh, that wasn't an alien. My friend and her family recently moved to Hwaseong."[4]

"I suppose Hwaseong's a pretty nice place to live..."

"It's better than Earth. I wish I could leave Earth, too. I want to live on Mars."

One by one, the other women were beginning to leave. Mrs. Kim also stood up and said good night. Thick Glasses turned around and mimicked a handshake with an imaginary person, saying, "All right, take care." She smiled sheepishly at Mrs. Kim, as if she'd been caught doing something naughty.

"I was talking on my holographic phone. The images are projected onto my glasses. They're only visible to me."

"And who was on the phone?"

"Umm... the Secretary of Health and Human Services."

VII.

The measurement of time is relative. It flows more slowly at lower altitudes than at higher ones, and it's slower for a person running than for one standing still. Time flows subjectively. We've all had the experience of dreaming

---

[4] "Hwaseong" is a homonym for both a city near Seoul and the planet Mars.

several hours' or days' worth of events during a
short nap.
Scientists have formulas for translating time differences
into velocity or gravity. You can't really measure time in
years or months. Time moves at its slowest during childhood. A year for you is not the same as a year for me.
One of your years could be a single day for me. A few of
my days could be dozens of years to you. In but a few
of my days, therefore, a child can obtain an amount of
knowledge and experience that would take me eons to
accumulate. This should be expressed in a mathematical formula, and the formula should be made available
in textbooks. After all, people don't believe anything
that isn't expressed in numbers.
If that were to happen, grown-ups would stop thinking of
children's time as insignificant. If only they realized that
you guys are in fact being forced to sacrifice hundreds of
years merely for the sake of the last few days of your life,
the world would be a different place... at least a little bit.

VIII.

"For the most part, I just focused on studying Korean, English, and Math textbooks. I didn't have private tutors.
I tried to concentrate in school and spent a lot of time
previewing and reviewing my lessons. Am I answering
that right?"
"They say, 'It's getting dark. Sunset assemblies are illegal. All
students please go home.' But at school, we study until
midnight."
"Only slackers take part in such gatherings. Good students
don't complain about society. Only idiots blabber about
things like discrimination."
"Kids don't have the right of assembly and association. Have
you read the Constitution? *Citizens who have attained*

the age of twenty shall have the right of assembly and association. Do you know what that means? Do you think I'm lying? Are you guys judges, lawyers, or constitutional scholars? How *dare* you talk back? Technically, you're not even allowed to have extracurricular activities. If you're going to gather, you need authorization. You have to go to the principal's office and fill out the time, place, and purpose of any meeting. Why're you still talking back? Where'd you pick up this attitude? Who taught you such bad manners?"

"You don't need friends in high school. Your peers are your competition—your rivals, your enemies. You'll all part ways when you go to college anyway: it's impossible to stay friends with anyone who got into a better school than you did! You can make as many friends as you want in college, but for now you'd better just focus on math and English."

"High school isn't for building character. The purpose of high school is to select students for college. High school is for studying. Students can build character later, in college. They should study now and not waste their time. Every minute and every second is precious. If they fall behind now, they'll never catch up."

IX.

Suppose that I were to travel back in time to the year 1979. I know all about the past, and I also know that nothing can ever change what has already happened. I would thus know that the president of South Korea will soon be assassinated, that the 1988 Olympic Games will be held in Seoul, and that a worldwide financial crisis will break out in 2008. Today, all of these events have already happened. If I wanted, I could read up on them through documents and newspaper reports.

But imagine a man living in 1979. What would happen to him?

At one point, a future with endless possibilities lay open before him. He could change or destroy the world. He could love, hate, or kill. But then there I'd be, suddenly part of his spacetime. He wouldn't necessarily meet me, nor would he know about me, and I wouldn't do anything in particular that would affect his future. And yet at that very moment, wouldn't every possibility that he'd once had, or thought he'd had, be swept away? Wouldn't this push the man toward events that have already happened? Doing predetermined things at a prescheduled time, marrying a predestined woman, passing preselected genes down to his child. His freedom would vanish, and the future, open until then to endless possibilities, would from then on proceed in a single direction like a narrow path blocked on all sides but one.

Is such a thing even possible? Is it possible that a whole generation might lose its free will because one person has traveled from the future into their time? The entire human race, once headed toward a non-deterministic future, suddenly enslaved by destiny and living like robots that function according to an algorithm.

Could that really happen? Suppose that on the last day of the universe, one person—or any other entity—travels through time to the day of its origin. Could the whole history of the universe—the birth and death of millions of stars, the history of all the beings that live, evolve, and go extinct—be predetermined from the moment time ends to the moment it begins merely because one entity—it doesn't even have to be a human being—travels through time?

"That possibility exists as well," said HUN. HUN liked the word "possibility." Yet he never took a one-sided view of things. He also said that the possibility of the opposite phenomenon was higher. Whatever is fixed is always more incomplete and more unstable than what is unfixed....

X.

People here get together too often, thought Mrs. Kim. As the plates of snacks kept emptying and getting refilled, the conversation among the clusters of moms who'd started out chattering in a single large group but soon divided up into smaller ones—threes, then twos, then finally one-on-one—never stopped

"Soo-ae said she doesn't like going to school."

"So did my kid—they're all the same, aren't they?"

"She said she doesn't want to live anymore."

"Kids that age all talk."

"She said she's sick and tired of studying."

"They *all* say that."

"When she was younger, Soo-ae was always ranked first in her class."

"So was my kid!"

"Soo-ae was a child prodigy! She could already read at the age of one!"

"Oh, yeah? Well, my kid did, too."

Is my family normal? Do fights break out every morning in other homes like they do in mine? Do other moms also break into their kids' rooms, yelling, waking them up to have breakfast before sending them off to school? Do they plead, threaten, and fight so loudly that the neighbors hear them? Mrs. Kim sometimes felt as though children were being driven to their ruin while moms like her stood around chanting their mantra: "Aren't kids all the same? My kid does that, too."

"It wasn't good."

Mrs. Kim turned around to find the woman with thick glasses grinning at her. "Pardon me?"

"My school days. They weren't good."

And who asked you? "Why? Did something bad happen?"

"Not really. I was like every other kid, but I didn't have a good time. Actually, I don't really remember—everything keeps getting mixed up. Whenever I look back, it always seems different."

What is she talking about?

"Have you heard about Moore's Law?" Thick Glasses suddenly asked.

This woman won't leave me alone.

Mrs. Kim replied sullenly, "Moore...what?"

"It's the theory that computers double their processing power every two years. It sort of explains why machines are getting smaller and smaller."

"Yes, that does seem to be the case."

"At this rate, machines will soon run on quantum mechanics."

Thick Glasses used some really big words for a crazy person.

"Quantum...?"

"If processing components get smaller and smaller, they'll soon enter the nanoscale. At that point, our machines will start obeying quantum rather than Newtonian mechanics."

"There's nothing wrong with that, is there?"

"There might be, because the quantum world is ruled by probability. Computers perform calculations with zeros and ones, which is like turning switches on and off. That's how they work. No matter how enormous a calculation may be, it's still just a machine flipping a switch on and off. But quantum particles can exist in both states. In other words, you could end up with an intermediate state between zero and one."

"So?"

"So a quantum state will mean chaos! Data will get messed

up. In a world of probability, one plus one can equal two, one, or zero."

What is she getting at now?

"Of course, there are ways to prevent this. Quantum computers were developed with that intention in mind. But of course then hackers came along who exploited the weaknesses of the systems. These youngsters have put us on the verge of chaos, on the brink of theoretically impossible results. Something similar happened when our technology switched from analog to digital. But now it's even worse. Only people born into a world of quantum theory, who fully understand that the world exists only in probabilities, can create such chaos. Because they can calculate the probability of one in a hundred million, they're able to bring forth things with the tiniest probability of existence."

This woman's shrink must have her hands full.

"So what?" Mrs. Kim was growing impatient.

"So a time machine happened."

Mrs. Kim stared at the woman.

"A time machine. You know what that is, right?"

Mrs. Kim couldn't believe her ears. "What do you mean?"

"A machine that moves back and forth in time. It can go to the past or to the future. At least twenty-six time machines were invented in the first year that the blueprints became available. Twenty-six is probably a safe estimate, considering the number of quantum computers in existence and the probability that a time machine would be invented."

"What are you trying to tell me?"

"This is one of them."

The woman took a matchbox out of her pocket.

Okay, now things are getting interesting. At least it's better than petty chitchat. Better than this mad woman coming after me with a knife...

"It looks like a matchbox, doesn't it? Well, that was what it was designed to look like. Had the International Government known of its existence, it would have been destroyed."

"Why?" *What government is she talking about?*

"Because it caused problems. People who went to the past started ruining the present. And those who went to the future made trouble, too. Now the only possible solution seems to have them all exiled to Mars."

"If that's a time machine, am I right to think that it can send something back to the past?"

"Absolutely."

"Even people?"

"Of course."

"Can I look at it?"

The woman grew somber. "No, I'm sorry. I can't risk altering this timeline."

Mrs. Kim was not surprised.

"But it's okay to send small inanimate objects to a nearby time period. Small objects are always disappearing. That's in keeping with probability. Have you noticed how socks go missing? Or pencils and erasers? That's because they have a low probability of existence."

Thick Glasses put a pencil on the floor and brought the matchbox up to her eye, as if taking a photo. She concentrated hard for quite some time. Then she sighed and put the matchbox down.

"I just sent it to the past."

I almost forgot she was crazy. Why do I keep talking to this loony? I've been feeling out of sync lately. Time feels out of sync. Is this woman a key to anything? Sometimes I feel as though my kid has been "erased." I feel like she's gone, but then the world shifts and her death gets swept away.

"Nothing has changed," Mrs. Kim remarked tartly.

"That's the way it might seem. But the pencil came back after traveling through time."

Mrs. Kim stared at the woman.

"It was in the past for a minute. Now it's back. Of course, the pencil is none the wiser..."

"What? Is it sentient?"

"What I mean is if it were a sentient entity, the pencil would be none the wiser."

Mrs. Kim sighed. "So, is this pencil in the past right now?"

"It can't be. That would contravene the law of conservation of mass. Do you know about the principle of the conservation of mass?"

Why do I have to answer all these questions? Mrs. Kim looked exasperated.

"That principle states that the amount of mass in the universe does not change. If this pencil were to exist here now and in the past simultaneously, we would be able to fill the universe with pencils by repeatedly sending this one to the past. It's a paradox. That kind of thing just cannot happen."

"So, how does it all work?"

"Only an object's consciousness gets transferred. The pencil goes into itself, into its own childhood body, into its past. Although it might be able to enter some other object, the probability of that is very low because of the limited connectivity among entities. There are also ethical problems with occupying another body. Some people have done it, and it has become a problem, but in general one transfers to a moment in time during which one was alive."

"What happens when you go into your past self?"

"This old pencil will reside in the body of its younger self. Inevitably, of course, its memory will be affected. Memories are stored in the brain, and when people travel to the past, their neural structures are those they had in the past." Thick Glasses briefly fell silent, as if in reflection. "Obviously, that would be the case *if* the pencil had a brain. This would be easier to explain with a human example."

"What about travel to the future?"

"Same thing. The object enters its own future body."

Mrs. Kim was growing impatient again.

"So if I were to go into the past using this time machine, I would enter my childhood body. But I would also lose my memories and have only the memories and knowledge of that time..."

"Correct."

"And if I were to go into the future, I would enter my future body and have the memories of my future self, with no awareness that I'd traveled through time."

The woman clapped her hands. "Exactly! Wow, you're able to understand such a difficult concept!"

Mrs. Kim was not happy.

"What difference does any of this make then? Nothing changes!"

"Something *has* changed."

"What?"

"The self."

"What's the self?"

"You don't know what the self is? Would you say that someone is the same person as you as long as she shares your appearance and your memories? That wouldn't be true, would it? Would you lose your identity if you lost your memory or were made to look like someone else? Obviously not! Externally, your behavior or appearance might have changed. But it would still be you."

"But if I can't remember having traveled through time, I won't know that I've done so."

"That's true."

"Then how do we know whether or not the time machine works?"

"Oh, it works."

"How do you know?"

"Some people have traveled through time with their own bodies. They remember everything because they still have their own brains."

"But you said that that was impossible due to some principle or other."

"Such people have a very low probability of existing. But they do exist."

Mrs. Kim fell silent, and Thick Glasses looked lost in thought for a moment, too. Then she smiled and scratched her head.

"It's also possible that the machine malfunctioned. Whenever we make another copy of the unit, the problems with it just keep growing. Some travelers have been acting as if they were still in their original timeframe. They get confused about which time period they're in and end up talking nonsense."

Just like you, thought Mrs. Kim. Thick Glasses looked at her.

"Isn't it fun to imagine such things?"

On her way home, Mrs. Kim stopped walking when she realized it was snowing. *Snow at this time of year?*

Looking up, she noticed paper airplanes falling like snowflakes from every apartment window. Children— teenagers, students wearing uniforms—were throwing paper planes out their windows and off their balconies. People on the street looked up in surprise. A long banner bearing the slogan, "Stop Old-Fashioned Education," unfurled from a window.

Why they are doing this? Mrs. Kim shook her head.

XI.

Every person has a certain statistical probability of existing. My probability may be lower, yours higher. But we both exist.

Human beings should be seen as continuous waveforms rather than as independent entities. This is because at every moment we are exchanging atoms with our surroundings. As time progresses, all the atoms that make up your body are replaced by different atoms. You may be an entirely different entity today than you were in your childhood.

The reason why lovers or couples resemble each other is because they are constantly exchanging atoms. The same goes for children and their mothers. Atoms that come from the mom's body are swapped with the child's atoms and vice versa. We are not independent beings. We intermingle, and the longer we spend together, the more we become entangled with one another.

XII.

"She's so weird. How can one plus one possibly equal zero? She's lucky her family hasn't put her in a mental hospital. And to think that people like that roam free in our neighborhood..."

Sitting at the kitchen table, Mrs. Kim had come to the end of her long monologue. Her daughter lifted her head and broke her silence.

"But it could be zero."

"Stop talking nonsense and eat."

Mrs. Kim felt a surge of anger. Her daughter was arguing with her again for no reason.

"One plus one has a high probability of equaling two. But the possibility that it equals zero also exists, even if the probability of such an occurrence is low."

Mrs. Kim was ready to lose her temper. But one look at Soo-ae's expression silenced her. Soo-ae's face was saying that she couldn't stand any more stupidity.

"Is that why you get such lousy grades? Did you write one plus one equals zero on your exam sheet?"

"The world is ruled by the principle of uncertainty. Things appear and disappear. Small objects are in chaos when unobserved, and sometimes after a long time in that state they vanish. That's because their uncertainty rises. The same applies to everything else, including people and their memories."

I have no idea what she's talking about. Is this some kind of game kids are playing these days?

"You trust your memories, don't you? But you should know that they're morphing at every moment. They're being reconstructed, modified, and transformed. Light isn't the only thing in the world that has the properties of both a particle and a wave. Everything else does, too. The effect of waves used to be negligible in the macroscopic world, but not anymore. It's all because of time machines. The International Government failed to control the spread of time machines."

Mrs. Kim felt confused. What were the chances that her daughter might actually know what she was talking about? Furious, she slammed her hand on the table.

"Where did you learn all this? The principle of uncertainty? Is that even an exam topic? Is it on the college entrance exam? Why read useless books? I told you to study English in your spare time. I told you to stick to your textbooks. Don't you have enough subjects to memorize?"

XIII.

We always knew that time travel couldn't change the past—that it could only *disturb* it. We knew that time travel, if it ever occurred, would stir up a new waveform in a fixed world, like a vibrating tuning fork amid hundreds of stationary forks, or like a stone thrown into the placid and unmoving surface of a lake.

But now the past and the future have become equally unfixed. Was there ever a time when probability didn't rule? Was there ever a world in which a married couple didn't resemble each other? Was there ever a vacant house that didn't go into disrepair, memories that didn't change each time they were recalled, probabilistic quantum vibrations that didn't occur, light that didn't have the properties of both waves and particles, or a photon that didn't pass through two different slits at the same time? It's impossible now to know the answer to such questions. Such a world would have been erased from our memories long ago.

I knew all this might come to pass, but perhaps I didn't always. Am I to blame?

HUN maintains that every invention changes the future irreversibly. The future of humanity would have been different, he said, had the steam engine not been invented, had cars never been built, had carbon fossil fuels not been discovered, had there been no printing, no electricity, no nuclear power and no bombs, guns, or missiles. No one should be blamed for these inventions, he said, because what has not yet been invented today will be invented tomorrow. The past and the future change together. "Next time, just try to invent something better," HUN told me.

Of course, there's no way of knowing for certain. Should a time machine ever be built, the past would become unfixed, and different beginnings would sprout anew. Knowledge about the machine would scatter through time, inspiring people in the past to build their own time machines. As HUN would say: "We are but one of many research teams, albeit with a higher chance of becoming the inventor of a time machine."

XIV.

Soo-ae straddled the balcony railing. A teenage girl with braided hair and a pimply face, she looked stubborn, her lips tightly pursed. She mumbled some words into the rabbit device on her finger, then closed her eyes and put a hand to her chest. She seemed to be taking some kind of a vow.

When Thick Glasses came up to her, Soo-ae hid the rabbit behind her back and glared at the woman in alarm. She stared warily at Thick Glasses' ghastly blue-striped pants and her checkered shirt.

"What do you want? Go away!"

"Why? D'you own the place?"

The woman had a knowing smile. Soo-ae climbed down from the railing and started off in the other direction, but Thick Glasses kept following her. Finally, Soo-ae got back on the railing and sullenly addressed the woman.

"Why are you following me?"

"Why shouldn't I?"

Soo-ae examined the woman in silence. "You're a psychologist, aren't you? The government sent you?"

"What makes you think that?"

"Grown-ups don't understand quantum mechanics around here."

A paper airplane on fire floated down from the apartment building across the street. All around, more burning paper planes flew, gliding down from all directions like the glowing embers of a silent protest.

"My mom almost slapped me today because I told her that one plus one could equal zero," Soo-ae sighed.

Thick Glasses laughed knowingly. "Older folks never can wrap their heads around that idea. Their cognitive functions are too limited. They say, 'Kids are all the same, women are all the same, men are all the same, and moms are all the same.' They don't have the cognitive capacity to grasp the differences that exist between innumerable waveforms. Older folks only understand average values; they see the world through their own norms."

Soo-ae looked down and pouted. "They'll tell you that there are seven colors in the rainbow when in fact it exists as a continuous gradation of wavelengths. They divide people into groups of white, yellow, and black. They don't see the innumerable differences in different people's skin colors. Words are merely symbols that represent average values, but adults always try to fit the world into a few words. They don't even recognize the many shades of black and white."

Soo-ae briefly spoke into the rabbit, then bent her finger and tapped the air as if she was playing the piano. "The moms and teachers in this neighborhood are all stuck in the 1970s. No one lives in the present. That's why I wanted so badly for my family to move to Mars."

As Soo-ae moved her fingers, holograms of other kids connected via the rabbit appeared around her. A boy with glasses was lying in bed and reading a book. A girl in a nightgown sat in a chair hugging a teddy bear. A blue-eyed kid was chattering away in English. There were kids from all over the world, each speaking his or her own language.

"The disease used to strike only people over thirty, but these days it's affecting even those in their twenties. The government sends in a psychiatrist for group therapy twice a month. The adults are told it's a neighborhood meeting."

Soo-ae enlarged one of the holograms. When a boy captioned "Poland" said something, she replied and downloaded a file by twirling her finger. The file's gift box icon seemed to float above her finger.

"My mom lives in the past. Computerized translation today

covers one hundred and sixty languages in real time. But she still insists that I memorize English vocabulary, even though it's already been a long time since the decline of the United States and the importance of its language. She wants me to go to a 'highly ranked college,' even though college rankings were abolished long ago."

A banner on the building across the street that read "Stop Old-Fashioned Education" flapped forlornly in the breeze. Soo-ae touched Poland's gift box icon. Music and graphics played as the box opened.

"I don't want to go to school. The teachers are like people from another time. All they care about is college entrance exams. They teach obsolete physics like Newtonian mechanics, and world history and Korean history are still taught the way they were in the 1970s. We spend five hours a day learning languages and math using outdated methods. The teachers tell us that we don't need friends before college. Those who came from the 1970s aren't the worst, by the way. Some took refuge here during the Korean War. They still despise communism and North Korea, even though we reunified ages ago. Some teachers even came from the colonial era or from the Joseon era. Some have even had to occupy other people's bodies to be here, which is immoral."

Soo-ae flicked her finger. A holographic paper plane appeared and dove down in a burst of sound like firecrackers going off. More holograms appeared here and there in the apartment complex, in response.

"Say something."

"What should I say?"

"Aren't you a psychologist sent by the government? Don't you feel sorry for me? I want to die, and you won't do anything. I really might kill myself. You think I'm joking, but I'm not."

"I know you're not joking."

Thick Glasses lowered her head and whispered into the
girl's ear. Soo-ae stared wide-eyed at her.

XV.

Nostalgia created the time machine. We looked nostalgical-
ly back on our past, which must have caused a warping
in the movement of time. Or maybe we didn't.
I still remember when you died.
I remember my death. The high probability of it...
I'm not just the inventor of the time machine. I exist because of it. I am a being who was born from the unsettling of time. One may wonder how an effect could ever
produce its cause, but maybe you're able to understand.
The future exists only as probability, and I turned the
low probability of my existence into my future.
If a time machine is never invented, I'll disappear. This
much is clear, but that's not all. I invented the time machine because I needed to control the past. I settled on
the hardware and an operating system. It was the only
way for me to exercise the control I needed.
Or perhaps I didn't. My memories don't settle the matter—they never *could*. Cause and effect have become
entangled. Am I to blame for your death? I think about
you all the time, even while preoccupied with building
a new base on Mars so we can start transporting new
settlers there soon.
The time machine has been abused. Too many people
traveled on it, bringing their time periods along with
them. Antiquated ways of thinking and old habits
spread through time like ink spatters or grains of dust
in the wind.
You can't escape your own era. People couldn't remember
that they'd come from different time periods. They
remained their old selves without sensing that the

times had changed.

The grown-ups in your life came from a different era. Their values were old, their teaching methods ineffective, their experience irrelevant. They had no idea how smart kids were, how much they already knew. They were false mentors who wasted your time and insulted your intelligence. They had forgotten that they were people who'd come from the past.

I came to meet you. I met your mom, too. While working for the government, I tried in vain to help her. She couldn't remember the fact that she was a time traveler, and she didn't know how to get back.

The probability of my existence is extremely low. That's why I can travel with my own body. I exist somewhere between zero and one, which means that, theoretically, there can always be two of me in the same place. The simultaneous existence of two of me, after all, could result in zero.

I remember when you died.

I remember when the younger me died.

I remember you on that balcony. I remember the words you whispered as you climbed the railing. You chose death, but on that day, you possessed the possibility of living on. Probability was disturbed. Your future branched off. Now I live as an infinitesimal possibility, like a shadow on the road you didn't take.

I pray for it every time I travel. I pray that my body won't follow me. Because that would mean that the probability of my existence has gotten higher. Nevertheless, today I am coming to you. On that fateful day, I will whisper in your ear: *"I'm still keeping your vow."*

That day, you swore to yourself: "I will *not* tell kids that they're living their best years. I will *not* say that young people are all the same, or that it's all just part of growing up. Maybe every other adult will say these things, but not me. I'm going to be a grown-up who knows how indifferent, cowardly, and foolish such words are. If only I could keep this vow, I wouldn't die today. I would be willing to grow old. I would live until I'm thirty, forty, fifty, sixty years old. I would grow older for the me of today. For the me of this very moment."

THE BLOODY BATTLE OF
BROCCOLI PLAIN

BY DJUNA

TRANSLATED BY ADRIAN THIERET

Since debuting online in 1994, Djuna has become one of South Korea's most famous popular fiction writers and critics. Despite having also published under the name Yi Yeongsu, and despite a continuing strong online presence, Djuna maintains strict personal anonymity, revealing almost nothing of their personal life. Although many of Djuna's stories borrow tropes and narrative devices from mystery, horror, or other popular fiction genres, Djuna has focused primarily on science fiction. Djuna's place in South Korean science fiction is unmistakable, and younger Korean SF writers such as Kim Bo-Young and Kwak Jaesik credit Djuna for opening new possibilities in Korean science fiction and helping the genre develop to where it is today.

258

Djuna's many books of fiction include *Butterfly War* (Nabi jeonjaeng; 1997), *Duty-Free Zone* (Myeonse guyeok; 2000), *Transpacific Express* (Taepyeongyang hoengdan teukkeup; 2002), *Proxy War* (Daerijeon; 2006), *The Bloody Battle of Broccoli Plain* (Brokolli pyeongwonui hyeoltu; 2011), and *Not Yet Gods* (Ajigeun sini aniya; 2013). Djuna has also published online and in various compilations of Korean SF short stories. Their extensive fiction oeuvre is underpinned by a deep understanding of the genres and genre-related conversations in which Djuna participates. Djuna is also known and appreciated for incorporating queer characters and themes in their work—something that remains relatively uncommon in South Korea's literary scene even today. In addition to their acclaimed fiction, Djuna has been welcomed in Korean genre circles for introducing foreign popular fiction and film to local audiences. Djuna is in fact perhaps better known to the general public in South Korea as a film critic rather than as a fiction writer, and has published numerous essays in print and online.

"The Bloody Battle of Broccoli Plain" was first published in the inaugural issue of the journal *Jaeumgwa moeum* (2008), and later reprinted in Djuna's short story collection of the same title. It is Djuna's first story set in the "Linker Virus" universe. In this universe, aliens arrive on Earth in the present day and bring with them a virus that alters Earth and its life forms to allow them to survive as part of the interplanetary network. Once the virus runs its course, humans from all corners of the globe piggyback on alien technology to travel to different planets along the routes of the Linker network. This particular tale combines a bewildering number of established SF subgenres, including perennial favorites such as alien invasion and post-apocalyptic disaster, alongside less fashionable subgenres such as planetary romance and evolutionary fable. Against this backdrop, Djuna explores questions of politics, nationalism, and ethics: paralleling the apocalyptic disaster of real life for regular citizens in North Korea, the alien invasion in this story strikes North Korea first; international and specifically South Korean responses to this range from the apathetic to the outright hostile. Djuna also raises questions about the portability of human ideology into radically different landscapes: North and South Koreans carry their countries' political conflict with them as they travel away from Earth and into the boundless depths of the universe, and explorers from the two countries continue to hunt and murder each other even as they begin to transform from humans into life forms better suited to their new surroundings. Interestingly, the story depicts the South Korean side as more belligerent and cruel. This is a splendid introduction into the critical, profound, and stunningly imaginative work of Djuna.

Introduction by Adrian Thieret

THE BLOODY BATTLE OF BROCCOLI PLAIN

I.

Yeon-ah dumped Jeongsu on the second floor of the Jongno Burger King.

Jeongsu wanted to say something, but no words came
out. He cleared his throat, shifted uneasily, and looked
down at the bag of onion rings and his coffee, which he
still hadn't touched. His clothing was soaked from the
sudden rain shower, and a summer cold prevented him
from thinking clearly. Two days earlier he'd been fired
from his job. Neither his mind nor his body could have
felt any worse. It really wasn't a good day to be dumped
by his girlfriend of four years.

He managed to ask, "Why?"

"Do you really not know?" Yeon-ah replied listlessly.

"I really don't understand. What's the problem?"

"That's the problem."

"Because I was fired, is that it? I can ask my uncle, he'll get
me a new job."

"I said that's not why!"

"Then what is it? What the hell did I do wrong?"

"Forget it."

"Forget what? Tell me why!"

Yeon-ah picked up her handbag and stood to leave.

"Please don't make a scene here, it's embarrassing. Actually,
if you'd ever understood that, then maybe..."

Yeon-ah continued speaking, but Jeongsu could neither
understand nor recall what she just said. His memories
of Yeon-ah suddenly cut off at that moment... or rather,
the world itself paused. If a mind-reading alien had
looked into Jeongsu's head at that moment, they may
have supposed that the planet called Earth was no more
than a small rock consisting of the second floor of that

Burger King and the section of Jongno that was visible through the window there, inhabited by a single large man sniffling into his still-hot coffee.

II.

Right then Jeongsu had no time to think about his ex-girlfriend. His top priority at the moment was putting out the fire on his ass.

That wasn't a metaphor. Jeongsu's ass really *was* on fire. As Jeongsu approached across the marsh, a Cooper that had been patrolling the perimeter of the Olivier had noticed and fired a warning shot at him with a laser rifle. Though Jeongsu's spacesuit hadn't been punctured, the flammable, translucent goo of the marsh had caught fire, and he was now running out of the marsh with his ass on fire like Yosemite Sam. In theory, his Russian-made spacesuit should be able to deal with a fire of this magnitude... but if that were truly the case, why was his backside—the part of it touching the inside of his spacesuit at least—getting so hot?

As soon as he had managed to descend into a shallow ravine, removing himself from the Cooper's line of sight, Jeongsu dropped and rubbed his butt against the grassy ground. He'd managed to put out the fire, but it left a black scar on the rear of his spacesuit. Even though Jeongsu couldn't see the mark himself, his dignity felt scarred just the same.

Calming down, he climbed carefully out of the ravine and stuck his head out from behind the boulder he was using as a shield. He didn't see the Cooper—oh wait, there it was. Marking time on his watch, he counted the Coopers guarding the perimeter of the Olivier. If he was correct, five Coopers were currently on patrol. No matter which direction he went, he wouldn't be able to get close to the Olivier.

... and the Adjani he'd ridden here on was inside the Olivier.

Just two hours ago, things had looked so promising. The Adjani had landed in an open area about a kilometer from the ravine. Its signal light indicated that it wasn't expected to leave the planet for at least four days. Jeongsu, entranced by the blue fields outside the window of the capsule car, had taken a gun and a canteen and set out to explore. He'd gone only about a hundred meters when he'd heard a sudden whoosh and looked back. The Adjani had swallowed up the capsule car and was all of a sudden flying back in the direction it had come.

The signal light on the Adjani hadn't lied: it truly hadn't been planning to leave the planet. It had merely changed its mind, deciding to spend its time on this planet in the bosom of an Olivier about one kilometer away from its original landing site. Jeongsu spat every single curse he knew at the Adjani. Grinding his teeth, he'd swung his fists at the emptiness around him, kicking the innocent ground as if he'd had some right to the Adjani.

Having exhausted himself, he again descended into the ravine. A sudden impulse to commit suicide enveloped him. He could end all his suffering by just opening his helmet and pulling once on the trigger of his pistol. Actually, no... he might not even need to pull the trigger. What was the probability that he could survive the atmosphere of this planet?

Besides, even if he survived, he still wouldn't be able to return to Earth.

III.

First contact between Earth and the aliens occurred on April 1st, 2009, at 4:23 PM Korean Time. The sting-ray-shaped spaceship, extravagantly decorated with gems, descended from the sky without warning. It landed cheekily on the road in front of Anyang Station, turned on its signal lights, announced it would stay for twelve days, then opened its mouth. Amidst the blaring horns of the sudden traffic jam, small mechanical creatures emerged from the mouth of the spaceship and, using their menacing pincer legs and laser rifles, began slicing up those vehicles that were blocking their way and devouring the pieces. One driver, so angry about losing his new car that he forgot to be afraid, kicked the spaceship. He too was sliced up into small pieces and eaten.

In just eight days, most of Anyang and part of Kwang-myeong had been colonized by the alien invaders. Using the materials they'd destroyed and swallowed, they set about building enormous metal structures. At first the invaders had been only about the size of baby strollers, but now they had taken on various shapes and sizes, the largest being about the size of dump trucks. Eight days later, they had built five loosely coherent vehicles resembling soccer balls ten meters in diameter, and launched them into the sky. These vehicles landed on the outskirts of Hamheung, Kuala Lumpur, Brasilia, San Diego, and Glasgow. Two months later, the invaders had expanded their colonies to twenty-four locations and for the moment seemed content with that.

In the meantime, Earthlings had done everything they were supposed to do in the face of an alien invasion. They'd tried dialogue, and they'd tried violence. Nothing had helped. It was as if the aliens thought that engaging with Earthlings wasn't even worth the effort. All that mattered were the materials needed to build their colonies; if Earthlings contained such materials, the aliens would ruthlessly assimilate them. Some people had initially ascribed political meaning to events such as the aliens' sudden attack on the Blue House in Seoul, but in reality, they had merely needed some subcutaneous fat to use as lubricant.

When the proliferation of colonies temporarily ceased and the invaders began to immerse themselves in their own work, Earthlings began to research them. This was relatively easy. The invaders had no interest in Earthlings. They wouldn't do anything when graffiti was spray painted on their spaceships, and they didn't react even when Earthlings kicked their mechanical bodies. Living with the invaders wasn't especially different from living around cars. People were safe as long as they followed a few rules.

That was when Earthlings discovered that the aliens could be separated into two categories: spaceships that flew through the sky and mechanical creatures that worked on the ground. The behavior and appearance of these two types of creatures were so different that they could have had entirely separate origins. The spaceships were extravagant and beautiful, and their forms were fixed, but the machines were entirely practical and had specific functions, and their individual designs were temporary and mutable. It was common for a machine to have four legs and two wings one day, and eight legs and no wings the next.

Because they were easier to analyze, the ground-based machines were the first to be subjected to taxonomic analysis. Their specific functions, which were made manifest by their various forms, were fairly clear. Type A mainly took care of manufacturing and construction. Type B destroyed objects close to them and killed people, leaving the remains to be used as raw materials by the Type A machines. Type C machines were like extremely cautious soldiers that concentrated solely on passive defense. With the help and protection of Type

B and C machines, the Type A machines built structures that were recognized as Type D. Type D machines, too, were clearly living organisms with artificial intelligence, just like the others.

This taxonomy was important because it showed that the invaders were not merely a single entity working in concert, like an army obeying orders, but instead a group of individual and independent consciousnesses that worked together cooperatively.

For a while, each type of machine was called by various different names. Type B alone had several dozen names. Some names like "Starfish" and "Soldier Ant" described in a fairly straightforward way the way Type B machines often moved, but flashy names such "Butcher," "Slaughterer," "Crashhead," and "Megatron" were also used. And, of course, Koreans such as Jeongsu just called them "Myung-bak fuckers" after the despised president.

The official names that eventually came into common usage were given by a graduate student at Glasgow University called Wendy Hobbs. Hobbs's names for the machines became popular because of a video series she uploaded to Youtube in December 2009 in which she gave each machine type the name of a movie star. Type A, the builders, were called Guinnesses. Type D machines, the building-like structures built by Type A, were called Oliviers. And Types B and C, the soldiers, were called, respectively, Waynes and Coopers.

Hobbs's own experiments proved that the spaceship-type aliens could likewise be divided into four categories. First, the largest spaceships were Type A. The fish-like spaceships that the Earthlings had first encountered were Type B, and served as shuttles that connected Type A ships to the planet. All Type B ships harbored small flying machines that resembled Cartier brooches. These were Type C machines, and they primarily served to gather information and collect samples. Once the ground machines dropped off by Type B shuttles established themselves, depots would appear along the path of the planet's orbit. These were Type D machines. Hobbs gave women's names to all these: Types A and D were Garbos and Dietrichs, while Types B and C were Adjanis and Deneuves. Some people felt uncomfortable with these names, but as is usually the case in such situations, popular opinion ruled the day. (The fact that Hobbs herself was beautiful, and resembled Hannah Murray, probably played a part in this.)

Strangely, it took quite a while to find a suitable name for the invaders as a whole. People seemed reluctant to name this alien life form when they didn't yet know where it had come from. Still, since the third-person plural generally sufficed, this wasn't particularly inconvenient.

So what was Hobbs's experiment? Like the egg of Columbus, it was simple yet ingenious. Hoping to take advantage of the invaders' lack of interest in Earthlings, Hobbs equipped a small robot with a camera and placed it in an Adjani. When the Adjani returned to Glasgow two days later, and Hobbs retrieved the camera, it contained images of a colony the invaders were constructing on Olympus Mons. Hobbs had managed a trip to Mars for a mere £700.

News of Hobbs's experiment spread instantly around the world. Little robots that had been snuck onto Adjanis began to fly out into space. About one in three returned to Earth. Among the pictures they took were those of places that looked nothing like anywhere in this solar system, that were in fact simply unprecedented. Several places seethed with strange life forms, the likes of which Earthlings had only ever seen in comic books.

Many Earthlings began riding Adjanis out toward the stars.

Some were scientists or soldiers sent by governments, but over 80% were just normal people who wanted their share of the riches. They wrapped themselves in low-quality, privately made spacesuits, sealed themselves in beat-up old cars, and flew to the stars.

The machines were no longer invaders. They had become guides, taking Earthlings out into the universe.

IV.

Four days had passed, local time, and Jeongsu was still alive. His mind became cloudy as he ran low on emergency rations, but he was still alive. He could breathe the air, and the temperature, which fluctuated between 21 and 25 Celsius, couldn't have been better. The air and water probably seethed with microscopic life, but so far at least nothing had decided to attack Jeongsu's bodily functions.

He was staying in an old abandoned bus that he'd stumbled across four days earlier while walking along a stream. The side of it still read "Hope Church Extraterrestrial Mission 2011" in loud fluorescent lettering. As to how the bus had come to this place, why it hadn't yet been consumed by a Wayne, or where its passengers had gone, Jeongsu had no clue and didn't care. He was grateful just to have found a sleeping bag and shelter from the rain.

However, the bus couldn't provide him with anything to eat. He was down to four sticks of beef jerky and five energy bars. If he hadn't made a habit of carrying emergency rations after the massacre on planet Purify the previous year, he probably wouldn't even have had those.

He walked out of the bus and gazed across the plain. Just looking at the landscape, it was hard to imagine how he could be starving. It was as beautiful as Teletubbyland. The meadow resembled a well-managed golf course, and here and there stood tall trees from which hung peach-like fruit. The mushroom-things sprouting from the ground around the trees looked delicious as well.

The tastiest-looking thing in the garden was a type of creature that Jeongsu had named "broccoli." Covered with soft green fur, the plump herbivores could be found everywhere across the plain. They were dumb, slow, and easy to catch. When night fell, a pack of three or four carnivores resembling green dogs would come out and each would catch one broccoli to eat. When day returned, it was hard to notice the creatures who had gone missing, and the remaining broccoli seemed to have no interest in their missing friends. The plain seemed more of a vegetable garden than a hunting ground.

But Jeongsu couldn't eat any of it.

Over the last four days, he had already tried everything that looked edible. He'd picked and eaten the fruit, and he'd tried the mushrooms. He'd even plucked a plant and eaten the leaves and roots. But despite their delicious appearance, they all tasted horrible and had upset his stomach terribly, causing him to vomit or giving him diarrhea.

Finally, he'd tried a broccoli. Selecting a suitably small one, he'd climbed onto its back. He didn't know where to cut, so he just stabbed it at random with his knife. Blue blood gushed from the broccoli, and it died. He dragged the broccoli corpse onto the bus and cut it apart. It was disappointing. The thing consisted of blue blood, green jelly, and innards that resembled rubber hose. All this was surrounded by a tough hide like the skin of a honeycomb. He tried to eat each part, but again vomited and got the runs. No matter *how* he prepared them, he couldn't eat the life forms of this planet. The only thing his body would accept was water from the stream.

Jeongsu wanted to cry. It wouldn't really have mattered if he had in fact cried, because no one was around to see. But he didn't cry. Instead, he spat curses at all the life forms on the broccoli plain as they enjoyed their usual languid serenity. His vocabulary had improved immensely while exploring the stars over these past three years. Now he could curse in five languages, and his Korean cussing proficiency was better than ever.

But no matter what curses he hurled at the broccoli plain, it remained as serene and beautiful as ever.

Jeongsu gave up and broke off half of an energy bar for breakfast. He then checked on the Olivier and the Adjani he'd ridden in, checking also to see if a new Adjani that might be of use to him had appeared. It could be suicidal to ride an Adjani with just a spacesuit and no capsule car, but when it came to starving to death on the broccoli plain, he preferred dying from freezing or suffocation—that, at least, would be quicker.

The Adjani still remained enfolded in the Olivier's embrace. After confirming this, Jeongsu explored a different part of the plain. He was slowly surveying a circle centered on the Olivier, one sector at a time. After all, some other Earthlings besides the Hope Church people might've visited this place. They might still be alive, too, and even if they were dead, they might have left behind a few cans of tuna.

Slowly climbing upward along a hill to the north, Jeongsu nearly cried out for joy. On the other slope of the hill stood three round tents that clearly resembled yurts... and standing erect in front of the tents were three or four humanoid figures. Jeongsu swiftly threw himself onto the ground, hiding from view, then took out his binoculars and aimed it at the tents. One adult man and two boys. One of the boys was showing a crayon draw-

270

ing of an airplane in his sketchbook to the man. Then
Jeongsu noticed the red scarf wrapped around the
boy's neck, and his body grew cold with fear.
Commies!

V.

Jeongsu wasn't a hardcore anti-communist. He didn't know
much about politics and didn't care much about all
the starvation and executions in North Korea. To him,
the word "commie" wasn't political. It was just that the
South Korean smuggling ring to which he had belonged
had needed an epithet for North Koreans, and "commie"
had been the obvious choice.

To understand these South Koreans, one must first understand what happened in North Korea during those first
few years after the alien invasion.

The invaders were not particularly antagonistic toward
the North Korean system. They did exactly the same
thing in Hamheung as they did in Anyang and Glasgow.
The Waynes destroyed factories and houses, and the
Guinesses built Oliviers in their place. Several months
later, the Oliviers gave birth to Adjanis, which flew up
into the heavens.

Most people tended to think of the North Korean government response as tragic. They thought that if the
government had paid more attention to its quarantine
system rather than thoughtlessly sending hundreds of
astronauts into space in the name of the Dear Leader,
the disaster that was to befall them might have been
avoided. But was it really any different from any other
place where the invaders had built their colonies? Could
any country have completely prevented people from
sneaking onto the Adjanis? In theory, of course, North
Korea should have been better than any other country

at exercising such control.

But what happened in North Korea wasn't a disaster created by humans. What happened there was something that could just as well have happened anywhere else, at one time or another.

According to secret documents discovered later, the disaster was detected on August 16, 2009. Five pilots belonging to the DPRK space force had returned to Earth after planting a North Korean flag on an alien planet 700 light years distant. Four days later, they had simultaneously suffered seizures and collapsed. Two died that night, and the remaining three ended up brain-dead.

They'd caught an alien virus.

Contrary to rumor, North Korea had taken great care with its quarantine system and was researching nearly every danger that could possibly arise from encounters with alien microbes. Still, no matter how painstaking their preventative measures might have been, they were unable to guard completely against alien viruses. Hundreds of Adjanis landed on the planet and spit out alien microbes every day. In August 2009 alone, over 3000 species of alien microbes were discovered on Earth. Everyone had expected an outbreak of deadly space flu to happen eventually; the fact that North Korea was ground zero was nothing but pure chance.

"Spaceflu" quickly spread throughout North Korea. By the time North Korea requested international assistance on September 8th, more than 27,000 had already died. Confusingly, the spaceflu manifested a variety of symptoms and could be transmitted through different routes. It caused sudden heart failure in some, while others died when their lungs filled with blood. Still other people's livers erupted from their bodies. It seemed as if all possible alien diseases were occurring in North Korea at once. The only common feature of these sicknesses was that prepubescent children suffered a lower mortality rate.

Research was carried out on subjects who managed to flee North Korea, but the people still in North Korea continued to die. The death toll was estimated at 420,000 by January 2010. By May, it had surpassed 3 million. By then, the government had lost control, and all those not already infected were trying to escape. Most were shot dead at the Chinese border and the DMZ. Those who tried to escape by sea didn't fare much better. No one in the world was willing to accept them. Everyone wanted only one thing from the North Korean escapees: for them to die and take that fucking virus with them. They thought it lucky that this calamity had taken place in the most isolated country in the world.

But that wish didn't come true. Even by January 2011, 300,000 survivors remained in North Korea. 70% of them were children under 12, and most were suffering from malnutrition. Still, they lived, and at this point, they seemed unlikely to die of the spaceflu. The 80,000 more who died before February died not from spaceflu but from the biochemical weapons sprayed onto the North by neighboring countries in an attempt to halt the spread of the virus.

Knowing what we do today, the behavior of the other Earthlings toward their North Korean friends seems lazy, foolish, and cruel. We would later learn that the sickness that drove North Korea to extinction was the result of the Earth's environment merging with a cosmic virus network, which we nicknamed "Linker." The isolation of North Koreans, and their deaths, was a sort of trial-and-error adjustment. As a result of this, however, Earthlings from other countries were able to coexist with the alien viruses without suffering any particular harm. Our merging into the network was nearly complete by January 2011, and therefore the weapons dispersed to prevent the spread of the virus had by then become completely pointless. But how can we measure the actions of those people by today's standards? Can we truly understand the terror they felt when confronted for the first time with the real possibility of the extinction of their species?

VI.

The man Jeongsu had caught sight of was named Jinho. He'd been a nobody until after the invaders had landed in Hamheung. A worker in the Hamheung Wool Textile Factory, he'd remained single for three years after losing his wife to pneumonia, and he had no children. Healthy but lacking ambition, desire, or the initiative to go against others' wishes, he had up until that point lived a dull, boring, and essentially worry-free life. He was an unhappy man, but that wasn't something to complain about in the country where he lived.

Then the factory where he worked had been destroyed, and the city where he'd lived his entire life had been annihilated by the sickness... At the same time, he became much less unhappy than before. He was finally free from an oppressive bureaucracy. Hamheung had been destroyed, but once the Oliviers had pushed the old buildings out of the way, the new city that rose up like a skyscraper was much more beautiful than the one it had replaced. He found the fear of death rather intoxicating; each day had now become a thrilling adventure.

For the first few months, he went about on his own, a lone wolf. He stole canned food and rice from a destroyed military base, then built a greenhouse and planted a vegetable garden on the roof of a still-standing apartment. His body still remembered the time when he'd start his work shift in the mornings, and every day at that hour he would go out to collect bodies to burn and disinfect the surrounding area. At the time when his shift used to end, he would head out to fill his sketchbook and camera with images of the invaders.

For a while, Hamheung was practically a ghost city. But it didn't stay that way forever. Before long, people started coming back. Most were just stopping through on their way to the border, yet for some, Hamheung was their final destination. And when chaotic rumors about the border region began to swirl about, people who'd been planning to go there returned to Hamheung, taking up residence in abandoned apartments and factories. Observing the Oliviers soaring upwards like Towers of Babel and Adjanis floating like stingrays through the skies, they gazed at the path that had opened up before them out into the universe.

It was their only escape route.

So the escapees organized into a group. They created spacesuits and capsules out of whatever materials were on hand. What they called "spacesuits" were barely able to seal in air, let alone offer other functions, and they often had only one spacesuit for each of the "capsules" that they'd managed to create by renovating buses. Still, this did not stop them. They made their own way to space. Following the path created by the Republic Space Army, they boarded Oliviers and flew out into the universe on the Adjanis in groups of twelve.

At first, Jinho only observed. He didn't want to leave Hamheung. Just watching the invaders through his apartment window was enjoyment enough for him. Sometimes he imagined and drew pictures of the places where the escapees might have gone.

But when the massacre began in 2011, he was forced to rethink all this.

As people began to die once again, he thought at first that

this was merely a resurgence of the spaceflu epidemic. However, this time most of the victims were children, and they all showed the same symptoms: they would suddenly have difficulty breathing and die. The spaceflu had gone relatively easy on children, so what was happening had to be something else. People talked about the bombers that flew every night over Hamheung. It was rumored that the outside world was no longer willing to leave any flu carriers alive.

People grew frightened. They no longer bothered with spacesuits and capsules; many escapees boarded Adjanis and left with nothing more than masks for protection.

Jinho too was afraid, of course, but he wasn't about to run off into the universe so recklessly. Riding Adjanis was itself suicidal, yet one still had to take precautions. He already had a spacesuit that he'd managed to fabricate from factory safety clothing. All that remained for him to do was to build a capsule. He did this by taking an abandoned Whistler sedan from the street and modifying it.

The day he departed from Earth, he selected four children from among the many lost children wandering the streets, two girls and two boys, to ride with him. He didn't ask their names and didn't even think to memorize their faces. He didn't want to become attached to them, he only wanted to give them a chance. An unknown chance that might be their only way to survive... but that could also very well lead to a gruesome death.

VII.

Jeongsu retreated to his bus for the time being. He locked the door and hunkered down behind the aluminum cross that had been erected on the back seat. Nervously fingering the bottom column of the cross, he stared through the dust that covered the window.

What the hell were those bastards doing here?

He knew the question was rhetorical. If he and a group of missionaries had gotten to this planet, then of course commies couldn't be stopped from coming here, too. But even so, why had they come?

For a couple of seconds, he thought about the opportunity this might hold for him. If they had been able to survive so far from the Olivier, they either had ample food stores or they had figured out a way to live on this planet. Under normal circumstances, he could've just approached them and asked them to share their food. There wasn't a military demarcation line or soldiers or police standing between him and them.

But these were not normal circumstances.

Jeongsu didn't think of commies as human. They were monsters, clusters of bacteria. When refugees began to flee North Korea by the Korean route, they had carried sickness and death out into the universe. After accepting some North Korean refugees, two colonies had completely died out from spaceflu. Following months of trial and error, the only solution Earthlings had come up with had been to kill North Koreans on sight and burn their bodies. Any colony where North Koreans were discovered to have stayed for over a month was to be abandoned. If the people there could move to a different continent, they would. If not, they would leave the planet.

These measures were an overreaction bred of ignorance. Colonists who'd left Earth before the merger with the Linker network had been completed were bound to encounter spaceflu. North Korean escapees had merely made this happen sooner. In fact, one of the spaceflu outbreaks that had wiped out a colony didn't even have anything to do with the North Korean escapees, despite rumors to the contrary. It had simply been the colonists' time to catch the flu. They shouldn't have gone out into space like that in the first place. What the hell were they thinking, heading out without any preparations? Had they even considered the effect that their behavior would have on themselves and their fellow Earthlings? Apparently not. The first space pioneers were all reckless idiots. That over 20% had managed to survive five years later was in and of itself a miracle. The invaders' universe had turned out to be unexpectedly hospitable.

All because of the Linker virus.

Although by 2009, individual viruses had, one by one, been discovered, the concept of Linker viruses was not understood until 2013. This is because the Linker virus was in fact a collection of many millions of different viruses linked not by shared biological characteristics but by function. They reorganized their own and their host's DNA to organically merge with their environment and link into the greater network of the invaders' universe. It was impossible to destroy or control them—that would have been as foolish as an amoeba taking on the entire human race. If humans wanted to live, they had to adapt to the world of these viruses.

Jeongsu, too, had managed to survive only because of alterations to the Linker viruses. Over the course of a few years, his body had metamorphosed into that of a space traveler. Thanks to this, he could adapt to the different gravity levels and biological environments of other planets with comparative ease. Adapting to the planet he was currently on, to the point where he could even eventually eat the broccoli, was not out of the question, if he didn't starve to death first.

Jeongsu had dragged his slowly transforming body through several hundred star systems along the Korean route. He'd believed at first that he'd ultimately return to

Earth, but this was no longer possible. North Korean escapees and South Korean colonists were divided by war and illness, and were terrified of one another. Because of this and because of the fickleness of the Adjanis they could only continue forward along their route. Furthermore, unlike the Scottish and Brazilian routes, which expanded in every direction, the Korean route was circular, a thin ring that wrapped around the Milky Way. Even though the North Korean escapees and the South Korean colonists attempted to take different routes, their paths always eventually crossed. There were no real choices along the Korean route.

Well, not quite. During Jeongsu's repeated attempts to escape along the Korean route, he had passed at least two crossroads. One was an intersection with the Brazilian route, and if he had taken it, he could have returned to Earth. The other connected to an unknown route that didn't pass by Earth. If he had taken that one, he could have avoided the hassle of dealing with North Korean refugees entirely and wandered off instead into the Milky Way.

But Jeongsu had missed both opportunities because of the war; he'd been too busy fighting his enemies to observe the patterns of the Adjanis. Though he'd originally fled into space because he hadn't wanted to join the army, even Vietnam veterans would marvel at how much combat he'd engaged in by this point. As far as he knew, there was nothing but war along the Korean route. He and his party were unable to stop fighting: they'd gone out too soon for that. Though information from Earth about the Linker virus was gradually spreading outward, it was reaching worlds that Jeongsu and his party had already passed; they and their enemies were already further out along the frontier.

Gradually, Jeongsu had grown inured to death and violence. While on Earth, people had told him he was quite a good fighter, but he never once thought that he could kill someone deliberately. Yet while traveling along the Korean route, he'd learned how to kill indiscriminately and without qualms, even when his targets were children. If he'd cared, he wouldn't have been able to survive the war. Half of the North Korean escapees were kids in their early teens. He didn't know why so many of them were children, and he didn't want to know. He was only interested in killing them.

As the frontier was pushed farther and farther out, the number of people on the vanguard gradually decreased. Still, the war between the two sides only grew more horrific. They could no longer hide behind numbers and modern weapons to avoid individual responsibility. Now they slashed and stabbed each other with knives and spears. They'd even forgotten the original reason why they had to kill one another. They'd become zealots. Now the masks they wore were about more than just protection from sickness. They carried symbolic value, like the cross or the South Korean national flag. Sometimes North Korean escapees would disguise themselves as South Koreans by wearing masks as well, which would infuriate Jeongsu as if he were witnessing some act of religious sacrilege.

The fury Jeongsu felt at the present moment was not much different. Though he still used the expression "danger of infection" to rationalize his actions, that wasn't his real motivation. He simply loathed the fact of their existence. As long as he was on this planet, they had to be eliminated.

VIII.

Jinho discovered Jeongsu's presence that afternoon. When he'd gone to fetch water with the two children, he'd discovered fresh, man-sized footprints near the stream. He wasn't surprised at this: he'd always expected that someone else would come here eventually. But what side was the man on? His? Or the enemy's?

He sent the two kids back to the tents with their buckets and slowly followed the footprints upstream in the direction from which they'd come. It wasn't difficult to figure out where the man was: the bus. It was a bus left behind by South Korean pioneers who'd come to spread the gospel to the aliens, but who'd ended up instead donating their fat and protein to the Guinesses and Oliviers for lubrication and memory circuit production. When he and the kids had first arrived on the planet, they'd lived for a week off of left-over biodiesel in the bus's tank.

281

The question was what to do now. Jinho crouched between the grazing broccoli and thought things over. First, he had to figure out who the man was. It would be great if he were on their side... but what if he were the enemy? There couldn't be many with him, but Jinho was exhausted and didn't have a proper weapon.

Also, he was sick of killing people.

When he'd first arrived at the planet that the North Koreans had proudly named Limitless Prime, he couldn't have imagined that things would turn out this way. He'd worried about the unfamiliar environment of alien planets, but not about his fellow Earthlings. How could he have imagined that many other established colonies already existed on the very planet the North Korean Space Army had declared to have conquered, all of which treated North Koreans like dirty insects? No one had warned him.

He'd fled. Taking the kids, Jinho had stolen a capsule and weapons, changing Adjanis as they traveled. He'd learned how to obtain food on other planets, and he'd figured out how to read the Adjanis' signal lights. Browsing through a computer and an English-Korean dictionary he had stolen, he'd learned how to lie in crude English: "I am not North Korean. We are not dangerous…" But the farther he got from Earth along the Korean route, the fewer non-Koreans there were—and his lies didn't fool the South Koreans. Though he'd repeatedly watched the South Korean dramas that had been saved on the computer, trying to adopt a South Korean accent, that didn't fool anybody either. All he'd received for his efforts were gunshots and curses.

During his flight from planet to planet, the number of children following him only grew. He'd started out with four, but he left Limitless Prime with seven. At the next planet, the number shrunk by three, but at the following one, it grew to eleven. Since then, the number of children had fluctuated up and down, never dropping below ten.

He didn't know why he was doing this. He wasn't some bold philanthropist or altruist, and he didn't care for children. But since Limitless Prime, he had seen the task of protecting children as his duty. He'd made the wrong move back in the beginning: his mistake had been taking children with him when he fled Earth in the first place.

Yet he didn't regret it. Fleeing would have been easier without the children, but then he would have been alone on a planet thousands of light years from Earth without a reason to live. At least this way he knew why he had to plunge onward—for the children. No matter what, the kids had to make it, and for them to survive, *he* had to survive. Was there anything else more obvious than that?

On the other side of the broccoli flock, a flash of reflected yellow light glinted and disappeared. Someone had opened the door of the bus. He ducked his head down and took out his binoculars to examine the area around the bus. A large man with his hair worn long like a woman's had emerged and was looking around. He carried a large pistol in his hand, and half of his face was covered by a mask with ragged edges.

It was as Jinho had feared. This was one of the enemy, and he was armed with a gun. Still, it could've been worse. Even if he had discovered the existence of Jinho and the children, he wouldn't be able to attack them easily. Although most of Jinho's party were children, they were greater in number and much more experience than this man. Also, the man was probably alone, and he would need time to adapt to the ecology of this planet, so he'd avoid attacking them for a while. He might even just be waiting to fly away on the next Adjani.

Several plans began to form in Jinho's head. He could flee before the man noticed him. After all, they didn't have any special attachment to this Olivier. Or, if they were going to settle here, then the farther they could get from the Olivier the better. The only reason they had been staying in its vicinity was for the water and because of the tents someone had left behind. However, they could erect their own shelters, and there might be caves in the mountains to the north. And if the situation seemed truly dangerous, they could always make the first move. Jinho's party still had three rifles. They were out of bullets, but they could scare the man off by showing him the guns and telling him to leave.

He really didn't want to leave this planet. Why go somewhere else? Here, he and the children could at least live like human beings. They couldn't expect the conveniences of civilization, but at least they had enough to eat and drink, and the weather was good. With a little more research, he would be able to make clothing from the fur of those green sheep and start a farm.

Yes, that's how they'd live.

He grew depressed. How long could such a plan work? Suppose that the thug left the planet. Someone else would undoubtedly come along. Not many had come to this world yet, but that was probably due to the war. And yet the war would eventually end, and everyone knew which side would win. Jinho and his party were on the brink of extinction.

Jinho slowly retreated. When he'd nearly moved out of the broccoli, he suddenly heard a scream. It sounded as though a young broccoli had been stabbed or kicked in the gut. This happened a lot. But as a result, the long-haired man turned his gaze toward the broccoli flock—and discovered Jinho's face.

The two men stared at each other for a moment without speaking. The long-haired man held the pistol in his hand, but didn't look as if he was going to shoot. At that distance, he would of course have missed the shot, and in all likelihood he didn't have enough bullets to waste on a warning shot. It was clear that he was just as much at a loss as Jinho was.

He's alone, Jinho thought. Just moments ago, he hadn't been sure, but now it was clear. A single glance revealed this; the man moved like someone alone. He'd probably been left behind. That kind of man was more dangerous. Jinho had seen stragglers like that do all sorts of crazy things.

More than anything, Jinho wanted to speak. *Don't bother them*, he wanted to say. *Please just go away*, he wanted to say. But even when he opened his mouth, no words came out. Instead, he dwelled on memories of the many failed dialogues he'd attempted in the past.

Then, quietly, he left the broccoli flock and retreated north to where the kids and tents were.

Although the sun had set, the children were gathered outside the tents. He counted them, as was his habit. One, two, three... thirteen. One was missing.

The oldest of the girls, Hyeonhwa, came forward. Jinho stared at her ears. At some point, it had become difficult for Jinho to look directly at her face. Hyeonhwa was fourteen. She was already starting to become a woman, and Jinho hated how his own body had begun to respond to her figure.

"Yeong-wu disappeared, sir," she said.

Yeong-wu was a year younger than Hyeonhwa. Jinho had discovered the boy on a planet called Chang Yeongsil, and had brought him along, but he was an anxious and violent child. Jinho didn't know whether he had always been that way, or if his personality had changed after witnessing the murder of his parents. Most of the kids disliked him, but it wasn't as if anyone wanted him to disappear. They were thankful to have one more person with them in this place.

"Who saw him last?"

The kids all looked at one another and shook their heads. Jinho entered the tent, which he shared with Yeong-wu and two other boys. One of the rifles was missing. Had Yeong-wu taken it? Why would Yeong-wu have taken it when there weren't any bullets?

A terrifying thought flashed through Jinho's mind. How did he know that it was empty? The children had told him that the guns were out of bullets, but how could he know whether they—and especially Yeong-wu—were telling the truth?

He took his hunting knife and spear and ran out of the tent. Selecting two fast boys to accompany him, Jinho ran down the road that he and the children had made. Jinho didn't know where Yeong-wu had gone and lacked the abilities to track him the way a hunter in a storybook might've done. He merely thought about which path he would have taken if he were Yeong-wu and lusting to kill someone.

When they reached the midway point between the tents and the other man's bus, Jinho heard the bang of a gunshot. The roar of the blast echoing off the hills was obscured by the sound of a second shot. The wailing of the broccoli was audible but soon quieted.

Jinho ordered the boys with him to hide behind a boulder and stay still. They obeyed. After making sure that they were fully hidden behind the boulder, Jinho slowly walked in the direction of the gunshot.

After about fifteen minutes, Jinho found Yeong-wu's body lying facedown next to a broccoli flock. The ground was stained dark with the blood that had leaked from a bullet hole in his back. His pants were halfway down, and Jinho could see that his underwear was wet with urine.

Jinho resisted the urge to scream out a string of curses. The madman had cut and removed the meat from Yeong-wu's thighs.

IX.

Two vacuum-cleaner-sized Waynes stared at Jeongsu. Both pairs of red eyes were devoid of emotion, but Jeongsu felt as though they were looking at him with reproach.

"Get lost." Jeongsu waved his hands at them.

The Waynes didn't react. Jeongsu picked up a rock and threw it at them. They drew back a few centimeters, then retreated. No, not retreated, just continued going about their business. Each carrying an arm they had cut from the child with their sawblade hands, they passed Jeongsu and his bus and headed toward the Olivier. That was what they'd been curious about. They were wondering where he'd gotten the hunks of meat.

The Waynes on this planet were small, much smaller than

the Coopers. The biggest ones were about the size of a large suitcase. Back on the planet named for the legendary admiral Yi Sun-sin, Jeongsu had seen Waynes nearly the size of dinosaurs. They'd crushed colony buildings with their feet and chewed up mountains with their jaws. Yi Sun-sin had been a nasty place, but this planet was peaceful, and the Waynes probably didn't have much to do. Maybe their work on the planet had started and ended with the construction of that one Olivier.

Jeongsu used scissors to cut up the hunks of meat he'd taken into smaller pieces—pieces small enough that they no longer resembled meat. When he'd succeeded at reducing it into fingernail-sized bites, he placed the pieces on the driver's side dashboard. One day he would have to eat them. Maybe tomorrow. All that was left of his emergency food store was half an energy bar.

He muttered, "What did I do wrong?"

But Jeongsu hadn't done anything wrong. The boy had shot first. Killing him had been an act of self-defense. Taking the boy's thigh meat had been a bit extreme, but so what? Should he starve to death amidst the broccoli, clutching his shrunken stomach? He hadn't killed the boy in order to eat him. He was simply taking a piece of the boy that he'd already been forced to kill. What was wrong with that? Anyway, the green dogs would have also gnawed on the corpse instead of eating broccoli. Was he any worse than them? Did they have more of a right to live than he did?

Jeongsu boarded the bus and inspected the rifle the boy had carried. There was one bullet in the chamber and nine in the magazine. Together with the remaining pistol ammo he had, he could fire up to thirteen shots.

How many of the commies were there? If each tent held four, then there would be twelve. There could be more... and they definitely would come to kill him. They would already know that his party had died. The dead boy's parents might be among them. If even a kid like that carried a gun, what might his parents be armed with?

The guns wouldn't be enough. Jeongsu needed other weapons.

He looked around the bus. The large aluminium cross attached to the back of the driver's seat caught his eye. He removed the screws with his pocket knife and detached the two pipes that formed the cross. Throwing away the shorter one, Jeongsu pulled the longer pipe out and inserted his hunting knife into it, then stomped on it to fix the knife into place. He waved it around. The end was a bit heavy, but he could get used to it. While traveling across space, he had improvised all sorts of weapon. Having a spear made from a cross was a luxury.

If only he could flee. But that wasn't possible now: the Adjani that had brought him here had already left. He'd searched the landing area around the Olivier every night, but hadn't seen any new Adjanis. It seemed as if no Adjanis would be arriving for a while. Someone with Jeongsu's experience could read the personalities of the Oliviers. This planet's Olivier was definitely not the social type. On other planets he had visited, Oliviers were more like construction site foremen or merchants, but this Olivier was a researcher that enjoyed its solitude. And while it was investigating the secrets of the universe, Jeongsu would have to fight the commie scumbags from his old bus.

Suddenly he thought of Yeon-ah. Why now, of all times? Because he knew that he had very little chance of surviving this fight? No, it was only because he had nothing else to do, and besides, he had to stay awake. He needed to keep his brain occupied somehow.

But why couldn't he recall Yeon-ah's face? Why couldn't he even recall her voice? And if he couldn't remember her

288

face, shouldn't he at least be able to remember the voice of a woman he'd dated for four years? Why couldn't his brain recall the face of any type of woman right now?

X.

"I can't just let you kids die," Jinho said to Hyeonhwa. He gazed at the faces of all the children one by one as they huddled in his tent. Before arriving on this planet, he hadn't even been able to tell them apart or remember their names. He'd lost too many children to death; the faces had changed too often. But the circumstances were different now. Not only did he know their faces, he knew even their nicknames, hometowns, and favorite foods.

None of them ought to die. Yeong-wu shouldn't have died either. Even if the idiot had put them all in danger, Jinho couldn't hate him. There was nothing now that he would trade the children for. No longer a faceless mass of bodies, they were precious in and of themselves.

"At sunrise tomorrow, pack your things and run for the mountains in the north. No matter what, you must leave this plain. Don't even think about fighting. You'll end up slaughtered like Yeong-wu was."

"Mister, what about you?" asked Hyeonhwa.

"I'm not going to die," Jinho lied.

Before leaving, Jinho left his treasured notebook with Hyeonhwa. In it he'd recorded all of the various survival techniques he had learned over the last few years. Hyeonhwa understood what the gift meant, but she didn't stop him. Instead, she cried. Covering her mouth and pressing on her throat to stop the sound, she wept.

Armed with an empty rifle and a hunting knife, Jinho slowly made his way toward the bus. About an hour past the hill to the south, the bus came into view. He hid in the broccoli flock and observed the bus. A nasty vinegar smell permeated the plain. It seemed the green dogs had just made short work of a broccoli. But the creatures were quiet. They were all relaxed. They knew that after one of them died, the plain would be safe for at least a day. When the green dogs approached, the broccoli pushed their weakest comrade out to the edge of the herd. The green dogs didn't hunt. They simply accepted the offering.

Jinho detested the broccoli.

Creeping along through the broccoli herd to stay hidden, Jinho finally reached the bus. He moved slowly around the back and slid open the second window from the back, the one he remembered didn't close properly.

The bus was empty.

Almost instinctively, he ducked his head. At the same time, some sharp metal thing flashed past the nape of his neck. He rolled away, only to find Jeongsu standing before him in a homemade spacesuit.

When his spear missed, Jeongsu ground his teeth and pulled out his pistol. As he tried to pull the trigger, Jinho jumped him. Jeongsu attempted to maneuver his larger body back on top, but Jinho smashed the hand holding the pistol. Two bullets were fired in succession. Jeongsu put the barrel to Jinho's temple, but just as he pulled the trigger, the barrel slipped across Jinho's sweaty brow, sliding behind his ear. The last bullet shattered one of the glass windows of the bus.

Realizing that Jeongsu's pistol was now empty, Jinho drew his hunting knife. He grazed Jeongsu's left forearm with his first stroke, but didn't do any real damage. Cursing, Jeongsu ran toward the bus to get his spear. Jinho tried to attack him again, this time slashing at Jeongsu's ankles. As Jeongsu fell, Jinho raised his knife to deliver the final blow.

At that instant, Jinho was suddenly deafened. He felt an
impact; it was as if a crushing weight had slammed
into his chest. Still holding his hunting knife, he looked
back and forth between Jeongsu and the rifle that had
until recently been his. When had Jeongsu picked up
the rifle? Had he been carrying it on his back? Had it
been hidden under the bus? The hunting knife fell from
Jinho's grip. A bubbling sound came out of his body
somewhere. He tasted blood in his mouth.

Jeongsu limped over and picked up his aluminum spear
from where it was stuck awkwardly into the window
frame. He adjusted his grip on the spear and stared at
his enemy. The black blood flowing out of his pierced
artery was soaking his pants, his chest, and the ground
beneath him.

As Jeongsu raised his spear, Jinho said something.

"What?" Jeongsu asked.

With all his remaining strength, Jinho repeated what he
had said a moment before while spitting blood: "Spare
the children."

Sorry, Jeongsu thought, *but I can't do that*.

XI.

Jeongsu dismembered Jinho's body. He cut the throat,
skinned the body, and cut off almost all the meat he
could use. He smashed the bones at both ends with
a hammer to get at the marrow. The remaining parts,
he threw behind the bus. Before long a Wayne came
and carried the scraps back to the Olivier. It seemed
as though human meat was more useful to them than
broccoli meat.

Jinho's last words lingered in Jeongsu's mind. "Save the
children." What did that mean? Was this man the only
adult in a group of commies? Were the remaining chil-

dren without decent weapons?

Now he had the advantage. He still had a rifle with a half-full magazine. He had plenty of food and could last a while.

He headed out to hunt the children. Wearing his spacesuit and shouldering the rifle, he attacked their tents at dawn, but they had managed to stay one step ahead of him. The tents were empty and the children gone. They could only have gone to one place: the mountains, about four hours' walk from the bus.

For a while he went out to the mountains every day. He combed over the areas the children should have been. He discovered footprints and the spots where they'd buried their shit, drops of blood, and pieces of a torn sleeve, but he couldn't find the kids themselves. Instead, he almost died in the mountains when he ran into a lizard-like monster that ran on eight legs. He wasted three of his precious bullets killing it. Of course, its meat wasn't edible for him. He didn't know about the water-grass and waterberries that Jinho and the children had discovered on the first day of their arrival. He was still living off of dried human meat.

Gradually Jeongsu lost his energy and grew scared. He used up his remaining bullets one by one, but without managing to hit any of the children. Each time the gun fired, he imagined the kids counting how many bullets he had left.

The children eventually stopped hiding in the mountains and returned to the area around the bus. At first Jeongsu only saw faint, timid footprints. Then he discovered that the boys had scrawled nasty graffiti on the side of the bus in charcoal, and peed on its tires. Finally, they began to break the glass windows one by one.

Jeongsu stopped going to the mountains. He surrounded the bus with a makeshift alarm system of wire and metal scraps and stayed inside it. When human-like shadows appeared outside, he threw stones and screamed curses.

He was hungry and his stomach ached. He was almost out of dried human meat, and some of it had turned inedible. Now he had only about four days' worth of food left.

Then, one day, he discovered that the magazine of the rifle he cradled in his sleep had disappeared.

Glaring at his vandalized warning installation and torn-apart spacesuit, he couldn't help but recognize that the tables had turned. Feeling somehow rather relaxed, he left the bus for the first time in a week. The weather was slowly growing cooler, and he finally realized that up until now it had been autumn.

Jeongsu took a folding chair out of the bus and sat down. He chewed on Jinho's breast meat while gazing out at the broccoli who stood gathered on the field as always. He thought about the last man he had killed. Why had Jinho come to him alone instead of running away with the children? He didn't know the answer. He probably wouldn't have time to figure it out.

The sun set. Jeongsu had finished the last of his jerky and was nodding off, but he opened his eyes again, feeling a chill.

He wasn't alone. He was surrounded by more than ten children. Two of them held guns. After looking all around, he turned his gaze to the girl who looked to be the leader. Her gaze was cold and expressionless.

The girl wordlessly raised her hand. One by one, the children pulled out the weapons that had been hidden behind their backs. Hunting knives, bayonets, awls, wooden spears, and even bags of stones.

They tortured and killed Jeongsu without wasting even a single bullet.

No Adjanis came to the plain following Jeongsu's death. The Olivier stood vacantly in its place for over seven hundred years, meditating on who knows what. Occasionally, the Waynes and Guinesses, which had shrunk to the size of puppies, emerged to seek raw materials with which to repair and expand the Olivier, but their appearances grew more and more rare.

As for the humans: the children survived. As soon as they killed Jeongsu, they followed Jinho's final instructions and moved north. There they built houses and found new kinds of food to eat. They wove clothing from grass and made shoes from broccoli leather.

When they came of age, they had sex and bore children. Born with DNA altered by the Linker viruses, their offspring all had light green skin and didn't know how to smile. When night came, they would wail at the sky and hunt naked for broccoli.

Forty years after the death of the last of that first generation, their population reached 500. Evolution was rapid; every ten years or so, the latest generation would manifest better adaptations to the environment of their isolated planet. Their lifespans shrank, as did their bodies and brains. They lost intelligence and language, but gained new senses and the ability to fly. Taking on the green color and the nasty sour smell of the plains, they beat their new wings and spread across the entire planet. Not one of them passed on to their descendants the memories of Jinho and Jeongsu or Earth or other worlds.

When the Olivier ended its meditations and new space travelers came to the plains, they found nothing that resembled human beings.

ROADKILL

BY PARK MIN-GYU

TRANSLATED BY ESTHER SONG
AND GORD SELLAR

Park Min-gyu (b.1968) grew up in the industrial city of Ulsan and later moved to Seoul to study creative writing at Chung-Ang University. After a stint as an office worker at a shipping company and some time in the publishing industry, Park debuted in 2003 with two full-length novels, *The Sammi Superstar's Last Fan Club* (Sammi syupeoseutaui majimak paenkeulleop), which follows the teenage fans of a third-rate baseball team, and *Tales of the Justice League of America* (Jigu yeongung jeonseol), a parody of DC Comics superheroes featuring their local Korean colleague "Banana Man." Both works were widely acclaimed by readers and critics, who praised in particular Park's ability to craft playful, irony-laced avant-garde narratives that were nonetheless full of gravitas. Park has since published many books and stories, including the short story collections *Castella* (Kaseutera; 2005) and *Double* (Deobeul; 2010) as well as the novels *Ping Pong* (Ping pong; 2006) and *Pavane for a Dead Princess* (Jugeun wangnyeoreul wihan pabanneu; 2009). His works have garnered several awards and have also been translated into English, Chinese, French, Italian, Japanese, and Spanish.

296

Park's unique writing style is at once weird, comical, and absurd. In the words of one commentator, his unconventional artistry shines through in his "[u]nusual metaphors and descriptions, sentences and paragraphs that ignor[e] the rules of grammar, narrative structures that break down logical causality, and characters that behav[e] in exaggerated ways like cartoon characters." Park's stories often convey a scathing criticism of the neoliberal economic order of twenty-first-century South Korea. They are populated with the socially marginal figures of high-school dropouts, part-time workers, ethnic minorities, and ugly-looking women struggling to make it in a land of cosmetic surgery. On the rare occasions when he appears in public, Park is known to sport eccentric fashions that match his writing style, including goggles, dyed punk or hippie hair, and casual hipsterish attire.

Park often deploys SF tropes such as UFOs, aliens, cyborgs, and parallel universes to express a protagonist's sense of alienation from contemporary life. Presented here is a near-future story in which human civilization has become unified under the hegemony of Asia, a corporatized political unit that is striving to create the ultimate techno-utopia. Banned from this utopia are the discarded, no longer useful workers that now amass at its borders. They are forced by circumstances to attempt to cross into Asia, and as they do so, they inevitably crash against a sophisticated, automated border control system. Many of the tropes present in this story—a megacorporate Asia, a rusted-out urban landscape, the brutality of life among the dispossessed, and a focus on tough guys—are all familiar from American cyberpunk. Park's deployment of these tropes as a Korean author, however, simultaneously challenges cyberpunk's exoticization of Asia all the while grappling with questions that are pertinent to recent local and regional social changes.

"Roadkill" (Rodeukil) was originally published in 2011 in the journal *Jaeumgwa moeum*, and it went on to win the prestigious O Yeongsu Literary Award of that year. A version of this translation appeared previously in *Azalea*, vol. 6 (2013): 135–155.

Introduction by Sunyoung Park and Gord Sellar

Translators' Note: Park's original Korean text features many irregular line and paragraph breaks: preceding and following sections of dialogue, at the opening sentence of each section of the narrative, and bisecting some key sentences where they serve as emphasis. Some of these breaks have been preserved in this translation, and some paragraphs have been further divided to aid the flow of the narrative in English. Pak's approach of providing fictional information in footnotes has also been maintained throughout this story. In addition, the original story was devoid of formal notations denoting direct speech, but they have been added here for the benefit of English-language readers.

297

"Reporting in. Arrived at the site."

"Copy. Good luck."

With that, the communication ends. Josah just switches off the microphone. Mao and I stare at each other but say nothing. After all, Josah neglecting his duties is nothing new. We step off the rail car and start to assemble our equipment. For the moment, the number of carcasses remains unknown. Collecting scattered remains usually takes much longer than one might expect. After checking the power level on the vacuum, I look up at the moon, then back again at the road where a thick darkness has rolled in. There's the sound of an aperture opening and closing... According to regulations, I am required to check my camera-lens, but I often think it's an unnecessary procedure. Mao rarely bothers with this step, not because he is overly proud of being a two-lens model but because of Josah's influence. And in reality, turning off one's radio is a much worse offense than something like not calibrating one's aperture.

"Check this out, Maksi!" shouts Mao from the middle of the road.

I start to walk in his direction.

There he stands, holding some intestines up by one end. The strangely intact guts curl and droop onto the surface of the road. They're about eight or nine meters long.

"I've never seen one so completely intact," says Mao.

I nod in agreement. Without a doubt, some animal's body has been dismembered. Bones and flesh in small pieces... scattered organs... and other things... what we just call "squishy stuff": our job is to collect all this and clean off the road. Mao and I carry out our duties in silence. First we collect the "squishy stuff," then the smallest chunks of flesh: we carry out our duties in this order because generally, the smaller a piece is, the faster it dries out. That's not always the case, though. I notice a thick piece of cloth. That's the kind of thing that sometimes ends up clogging the vacuum, so I get rid of it first and then continue working. If it had been wearing something made of cloth... yeah, that would suggest that the creature had been living with a human being. If there's one thing that Mao and I know it's that there are countless abandoned pets in the world. We don't know what kind of animal this might have been, though: all we can see are pools of blood, hunks of flesh, and "squishy stuff."

Josah turns on the radio while we open the rail car's collection tank and empty our vacuums into it. *Incoming car... Currently passing through area AECN154.* Then nothing: the connection switches off once again. Without a word, we move toward the barrier at the edge of the road and stand there, pressed up against the railing. If it's in Area 154, it's still pretty far away, but considering the speed of the shuttle, we'll still have to get an early start to be ready for it. We hook our chains onto the sidebar of the railing, and Mao and I lock joints. It would be safer to get onto the rail car, but it isn't clear whether the shuttle will leave us enough time to disconnect the vacuum. Sure enough, as soon as we hear the loud sound of the shuttle and see the light, its taillights are already disappearing far away down the road from us. Such amazing speed. Once again, I realize the magnificence of humanity. Just like that light... and the sound... and the speed.

All of a sudden, I can't see anything. After unlocking my joints and waving my hands in front of me, I realize why. The intestines, which had been sent flying by the passing shuttle, have landed on me. From beneath the slippery intestines, I mumble, "Goddamn it," just like a human would. Mao laughs out loud, imitating Josah's laughter.

"Stay there."

Mao assembles the cutter and begins to chop away at the guts. Staring toward the lights far beyond the road, I wait for Mao to finish. *The lights... of the city... of humans... humans...* I think about the humans who'd once had to do the job we were doing now. What must they have felt? Scraping up dried pieces of flesh... collecting animal carcasses stained with blood... What would they have thought about *that*? There's no way to know for sure, but I can sometimes guess at what those so-called "emotions" must've been like. Of course, that's probably due to some error in my cognitive code.

"Hey Mao," I ask. "Why do humans abandon their animals?"

"Well," Mao says, continuing to hack at the entrails as he answers me, "... maybe they get tired of them?"

"Like you or Josah, ignoring the regulations?"

"Or... perhaps they're not in a position to keep them."

"That's strange. Look at those lights. Humans have plenty of resources, don't they?"

"That's... true. Well, then, how about something like...?"

"Like what?"

"They don't need them anymore."

"What does *need* mean?"

"That's... when we get back, I'll transfer my vocabulary database to you."

"Is it like a *rule*?"

"It's similar, but a little bit different. That is to say, it's not as if keeping or abandoning them is *necessary*, it's more like, at a certain point, abandoning them becomes more convenient to the humans than keeping them."

"Then it seems similar to *being tired of*."

"Well, in fact it could even mean something more like, 'just die already'... because the moment a rule is violated, it's almost as if that rule *just dies*."

"That makes sense, if an animal could be considered a rule."

"We can't know exactly... because we're machines."

"Yes... because we're machines."

Mao has finished cutting me loose. While he disassembles the cutter, I begin to collect the chunks that have fallen off me. It's a slightly weird night. How could the intestines have been left so intact? Considering the shuttle's speed and the heat generated by friction alone, it should've been almost impossible. No matter how fast an animal runs, it can't dodge a shuttle. The moment it hears the sound of the shuttle, the collision has already happened, and after being blown apart into pieces, its carcass is then fused back together into a half-melted mass. For the unfortunate animal, there's no demise as quick and as complete. I glance toward the forest to the right side of the road. Then I think briefly about the poor animal that had managed to leave behind its guts intact. Then I... work. Following the rules—

—I'm working, doing the work given to me. Doing the work that was programmed into us. Josah often says that it's boring, and I think this might be what he means. Working. Just working. I, too, mutter that I'm bored.

"What?" asks Mao.

"Nothing," I answer. I can feel something wrong with my left knee. It feels as if there's an abrasion somewhere in the knee joint. Have I locked my knee too roughly? Anyway, it's probably no big deal. I continue to work, hobbling along.

"What's the matter?" Mao asks again.

Once again, I answer, "It's nothing."

Then we finish with our collection work.

I detach the comm unit and type "three corpses" into the empty space in the transmission data template. That's not really accurate. I've based my estimate on how full the collection tank is because no intact parts remain that could be used to identify the animals. In the meantime, six more shuttles pass by and Josah instructs us to evacuate each time. He sounds drunk. Even with my joints locked, I shudder in the roaring wind each time a shuttle goes past us. Given the number of flesh-chunks fused together by the heat, there may have been up to four dead animals. Looking over at the "squishy stuff" that fills the tank, I imagine a herd of animals crossing the road in a line. If Josah were to get drunk enough that he fell asleep... Mao and I could very well end up in pieces like that. My left knee's been getting awfully creaky.

Once again, Mao asks if I'm okay. I nod at him once more, telling him it's nothing. Compared to Mao, I am quite literally an ancient model. Like Josah says, I'm not just obsolete, I'm falling apart, too. There's also a problem with my speech device. For some time now, I've been calling Josah "Jonah," because I can no longer properly pronounce the letters *s* or *t* anymore. Perhaps I'll end up being scrapped sometime soon. But right now, it's time to clean up. While attaching various pieces of equipment to my midsection, I struggle to guess at the meaning of "no need."

"Come here, Maksi!" Mao yells. *"Hurry!"*

It's impossible for me to walk quickly, though, so I hobble over. Mao is pacing by the rail tracks, and to judge by his behavior, he seems to be having some temporary difficulty computing judgment calls.

"What's wrong, Mao?"

As I ask him this, Mao points into the drain and says, "What is that?"

There is something... *Something* indeed *is* down there. I blink my dilapidated single lens and get up close to it. It... looks like one big chunk of corpse. Then I realize it isn't. It's the *whole corpse* of a young animal, its head

and legs still intact. No... no... it's something that might
be a... a very young human.
"Isn't it what they call a 'baby'? It's a baby!" shouts Mao.
"Oh dear," I mutter.

△ △ △

You're sitting on a chair.

You can hear the audience shouting from behind the rusty
wire fence. Everybody here is trash. They're all pieces
of shit addicted to gambling and drugs. The leaders
of Yangnan are gathered together on the second floor.[1]
That bunch aims to live with one foot firmly planted in
hell. A woman named T'aing, who owns this arena, sits
among them. Supposedly she's bet her own money on
you. She whispered this to you in the waiting room, but
you don't believe a single word. That's just common
sense, here: in Yangnan, nobody trusts anyone.

You're doing well so far. You've survived eight rounds of
roulette, and now here you are. This kind of hardcore
gambling is still pretty new, so everyone's been looking
forward to tonight. Somebody walks out of the waiting
room on the other side, and the rabble starts to scream
so loudly that it hurts your ears. It's Saito, the King of
Roulette: you've never met him, but you know him by
name. Unlike what everyone thinks, he's a shabby little
old man, just a bald guy with an undecipherable tattoo
on his forehead. You've heard about it, though, so you

[1] Yangnan is the largest designated "migration area" in Asia,
intended for individuals who were relocated according to the
plans of the sole massive corporation that began running the
continent after the manufacture of robots rendered workers
obsolete. It is a special zone that includes parts of the border
of what was once Vietnam and parts of former China (specifically the southern part of Chongzuo Shì and the western area
of the Qinzhou District).

know it's a talisman engraved into his skin.

He's just sitting on his chair with this relaxed look on his face, like someone sitting under a poplar tree in the summer, just listening to the cicadas singing.

"What's your name?" he asks.

You give him your surname, Li, instead of your first name, while trying to keep your eyes locked on his.

"Lee..." he says, nodding. Meanwhile, two girls come in and start setting up the table.

The tall girl puts down drinks and glasses. The other one—T'aing's assistant—spreads out a tablecloth and places an old mahogany box in the middle of the table. You're thirsty, but you don't want to be so reckless as to reveal just how anxious you feel. As the tall girl pours the drinks, the assistant opens the cylinder of the gun she's pulled out from the box and asks for confirmation. With both of your faces relaxed, Saito and then you both nod in turn. Only one chamber in the exposed cylinder contains a bullet. Someone needs to die tonight, and everyone here is going to be a witness. The assistant places the revolver on its side in the middle of the table and then sets it spinning. She looks like she's had plenty of practice. The gun, after turning a few times like a beetle, lands with the muzzle of the barrel pointing at Saito. The rabble begins to yell and tear at the wire fence. The girls step back, cat-like.

"Li... if you're a Li, then... I guess you're Chinese?" Saito asks, holding out his glass for a toast.

Although you aren't Chinese, you nod silently. What does it matter? Besides, it's a handy lie, since here in Yangnan you've been passing yourself off as Chinese. But you were born in a place called Hwanghae-do, back in the days when Asia was still organized into a few corporate-unions... back when your father was still a useful worker at a factory in the area.

"So..." Saito says, "How many wins have you scored so far, to make it here?"

"Eight," you answer listlessly. Dissolved into the booze is a drug called Mihon, which kills off your anxiety and fear, along with any sense of attachment to your life.

"How lucky of you," the King says with a nod, and once again empties his glass. Then he starts to sing, just like they said he would, and the crowd joins in. You'd heard that the rabble that gathers here always sings a tune that sounds almost like weeping, and it turns out to be true:

> *It's not true, or real, that we came to live in this land. We just came to sleep, to dream...*[2]

In the eyes of the roaring rabble, you see faith. You hear their belief in immortality, and their awe-filled cries for someone who has survived seventy-three rounds of roulette. When the singing ends, the old man looks up into the sky, his face emotionless. He shows no emotion, even after picking up the gun and spinning the cylinder with its single bullet. The revolver gently pressed against his temple looks more alive than he does, more full of emotion. He pulls the trigger, smooth as flowing water, as if he's out to prove that life isn't real.

Then: *clink*. With that sound, he manages to prove that his own death is an illusion. You don't mean to, but you find yourself admiring him.

"Take your time," Saito says, pushing the revolver near your glass with his skinny hand. Even your own father was never this gentle with you.

---

[2] A portion of the lyrics from the song "Shadows of Dream" that was popular among the first-generation of relocated residents in Yangnan. This song was sung as a duet by Ando Kenichi and Chang Chi-ho, who were themselves deportees to the zone. The lyrics, excerpted from the chorus, are in fact also verses from an Aztec song.

"Is it for the money?" Saito asks.

You nod.

"*Xuanju! Xuanju!*" The rabble shouts, shaking the wire fence.

"I've always found that word odd... *elections*," Saito says, fishing a crumpled cigarette from a pocket and lighting it. "Why're they using that word for this occasion?"

Silently, you drink from your glass. You cannot fully make out what Saito is saying due to his poor command of the official Pan-Asian language. You're of the generation for whom it is the native tongue. As he exhales a cloud of smoke, Saito mumbles something, but you don't understand the old Japanese word he says: "*Bonkura.*"[3] The rabble are like that, too: they speak in a pidgin made up of the official language and whatever else they know. You slowly perform your *xuanju* in a clumsy move. It's not out of anxiety or fear: it's the effect of Mihon permeating your brain. With a blank look, you stare at the old man.

Then you laugh. The end of the gun touched to your temple tickles you. The sound of a *clink* penetrates your ears, but it feels as if all this were happening to someone else. The roaring of the audience that accompanies the sound finally reminds you a little of your dissipated anxiety and fear.

"They're just like devils." Saito looks toward the wire fence, exhaling smoke, and the crowd begins to roar again: "*Xuanju! Xuanju!*"

"Well," the old man says, stubbing out his cigarette and smiling bitterly, "...there's nothing else we *could* do besides holding elections."

You vaguely remember what Saito means by "elections." It

---

[3] Japanese word meaning "idiot" or "dimwit." It was originally used in gambling to refer to someone who always loses because he is unable to predict the number on dice hidden beneath the cups.

307

happened the year Asia united into a single corporation through a merger called the Grand Cross. That was the year your father voted in his last election. You don't remember what kind of election it was. Suddenly you realize that your father, if he were alive, would be about the same age as the old man in front of you.

A voice cries sharply from the second floor: "*Xuanju!*"

You offer the revolver to the old man, saying, "It's been a long time since elections ended."

"True," Saito says, nodding. "But even before that, 'nations' had already disappeared..." Even though the old man is speaking official Pan-Asian now, you still can't follow what he's talking about. Asia as you've known it has *always* been a single megacorporation.

The old man raises the gun to his head and immediately pulls the trigger. Because it happens so quickly, all of the voices that had missed their chance to roar fall raggedly into silence. Once again, you admire him, this time letting out a short "*Ah.*"

Screams with slightly clashing rhythms ring out all around you. Saito tosses down the gun and fishes out another cigarette.

"So this is Asian roulette, eh?" he says.

Drinking from the glass, you stare blankly into his eyes through a veil of smoke.

"That means there's no Russia now... right?"

You still can't follow what he's saying. The only Russia you've ever known is a corporate department.

"You wouldn't know this, but..."

Now the old man is lost in thought. His blurry eyes hidden by smoke, he's thinking about Baikal. The waves of a majestic world of water once inscribed into his brain now roll before his eyes. It had been summer vacation. That was twenty-five years ago, when he was working in Osaka. He'd taken a vacation with his family, and... it became the last vacation of his life. He remembers his title: Section Chief. This was back in the days when everyone had been feeling hopeful; nations were finally being governed by successful corporations instead of by inefficient politicians. Even though serious polarization still existed, new hopes for growth and an end to inflation had sprung up. That was before machines had replaced Saito.

"*Xuanju! Xuanju!*" Again, you pick up the gun. Now you hold in your hand what's become a one-in-three probability of your own death. Before the excited crowd, you hesitate for a moment.

The intuition of a man who's survived eight rounds of roulette immediately seizes you, and you gulp down your drink. The drug's gift of drowsiness grants you some relief from your anxiety and fear, but somewhere in your brain is an isolation zone—kind of like Yangnan itself— where the power of the drug simply cannot reach.

Now you're thinking about your dead father again. You remember climbing onto a boat, his big hands helping you in. Because your father said it was going to be a trip, you recall it as a beautiful memory. What you saw was the ocean: choppy waves, blue skies. You're a young child, sitting on your father's shoulders, and your mother, who was healthy back then, is standing next to him. You're smiling as you press the gun against your temple. To tell the truth, you, too, were exiled to Yangnan. Machines transformed labor, and transformations in labor transformed the world. The problem was that in the process, most people—including your family—became useless. So, bit by bit, or rather *structurally*, the corporation called Asia liquidated them. It was a bit like being placed on a waiting list, and the Yangnan zone, straddling the Vietnam-China border, was the place with the highest concentration of such people.

You don't know why your father died, nor do you know whether the cause of your mother's death—an illness and a high fever—was unusual. Today, the science that created the proletariat has no need to fear resistance from those who are no longer even members of that proletariat.

You can hear the crowd screaming: *"Xuanju! Xuanju!"*

After scanning the crowd with languid eyes, you mutter a word to yourself: "Trash." Though you can't imagine it now, these people were actually once diligent workers— diligent but powerless. Your powerless finger diligently pulls the trigger. A clicking sound rings out in the complete silence. Instead of your brains spilling out, you're starting to sweat like a pig. You toss the gun down and spit on the floor to suppress a sudden wave of nausea; it's hard to tell whether or not this was caused by the drug. The old man silently drinks without shedding a single drop of sweat. Then he sets down the glass, his face emotionless, as if his subtle smile had been washed away by the drink. He doesn't snap up the gun, nor does he pull out a cigarette. His eyes are like the dark ocean, and you just stare into them.

"Xuanju! Xuanju!" Amid a sea of deafening screams, he stares back into your eyes.

"You're real lucky," he mutters.

You don't say anything.

"I..." says the old man, blinking. "I don't know why I'm here."

You gulp the last of the liquor from your glass.

"I... I used to work at a company."

"There're no companies in Yangnan," you say.

"Not here... In a place called Osaka."

"Then you're the lucky one."

"I guess so." He laughs. "We're just like Boke and Tsukkomi."[4]

---

[4] Roles derived from a traditional Japanese comedy duo.
Boke is a rustic "straight man" while Tsukkomi responds with
witty or funny jokes and comments.

You have no idea what he's talking about, but he goes
on: "Sure, when it comes to misfortune, you're the one
who's worse off... But then, your ancestors are the ones
who promoted socialism."
You don't respond, not even to the old man's loud laughter.
"Look," says Saito.
With powerless yet diligent eyes, you look at him.
"Would you... just once... call me Section Chief?"
Again, these words are lost on you. *Xuanju! Xuanju!* The
rabble begins scaling the wire fence with furious force.
In the moment you hesitate, the old man picks up the
gun. The rabble start to chant the King's song:

> *It's not real or true that we came to live in this land.*
> *We just came to sleep, to dream...*

In the eyes of the bitterly smiling old man you glimpse the
ripples of the ocean you saw when you were young.
"Is it... that there's no God or Buddha?" For an instant, Saito's
lips tremble with the ripples in his eyes. Maybe you
should've called him Section Chief—the thought crosses
your mind, just before the gunshot reaches your ears.

◇ ◇ ◇

I can hear Mozart.
Mao switched it on during the trip back to the outpost.
Because we failed, despite constantly trying, to establish communication with Josah, Mao decided to go back,
while I've remained to watch the site.
As Mao hopped onto the rail car, I said, "You have to maintain communications, okay?" That's why I'm listening to
Mozart now. Mao likes Mozart. Though I don't have the
cognitive software necessary to enjoy music, at least I've
never found it annoying.

"Maksi," Mao says over the radio.

"What?"

"If Josah isn't at his post... shouldn't we report directly to the corporation?"

I take a moment to think about it. Then I say, "Let's see what happens. If possible, I'd prefer not to get the only human I know into trouble."

"Okay," says Mao.

Depending on the situation, I might or might not decide to tell Mao to submit an official report.

I look down at the young, dead human in front of me. It's only the second human I've ever encountered. No matter how hard I try, I can't figure out why this young, dead human is here.

"What do you know?" I remember Josah saying.

"To know... know... what is it that I know?" I think about this.

I know this road... and the outpost. I was delivered still powered-down, and I first opened my eyes at the outpost. I know the basic code that's been programmed into me... and the rules that I must follow. I know the wide road in zone AECN172-174, for which our outpost is responsible. I know about road systems... and shuttles. I... know Josah. And... yes, although I have never directly met him, I know a human named Wang Wei. He was a human from a hundred and seventy years ago, and he is considered the father of the roadkill volunteer organization. His statue stands by the entrance to the outpost. Because I have his interview video stored in me, I can proudly say that I know him.

I play the video:

> *...it happened in a flash. Although I braked, I was unable to avoid the collision. It was a young elk. One thing that's clear is that this young living creature and I made eye contact while I was braking and skidding*

along the road. It was an extremely brief instant, but even after all these months, I still cannot forget those eyes: the image of it is still burned into my mind. Maybe realizing instinctively that his death was approaching, he didn't move. Instead, he looked at me with those sad eyes.

That was when I started this job. Someone had to do it, and that someone was me. I would like to ask everyone: if you see a dead animal on the road, please give our volunteer organization a call. If it were a human on the road, no one would be able to just pass by. Once again, every living being deserves equal dignity...

313

I look up at the moon. Thinking about that driver from a hundred and seventy years ago who was able to make eye contact with a colliding animal, I think also about that carcass from the past, which probably was at least physically intact, its body still whole.

The music switches off, and, over the radio, I listen to the sound of the rail car slowly docking: Mao has arrived at the outpost. Then comes the sound of an opening door, and Mao getting out. These sounds are familiar, and make me feel as if I'm there with Mao. Then... I look down again at the young, dead human before me. It's not as if I made eye contact with this small human, called a "baby"... I try to imagine the human mind that Wang Wei talks about in his interview.

"Josah is sleeping," Mao says.

"Is he drunk?" I ask just as Mao declares, "He's drunk!"

"Damn it," I mutter. That means it'll take a while before Josah boots up. I sit, bending with my squeaky left knee. Then... I see the baby's face, with its two tightly closed eyes... and its hair matted with blood.

Did this human have such eyes... or did this human have

a mind that could not forget someone else's eyes even months later? I wonder about this, holding my aperture open. There's... no telling. But at least by taking pictures, I am storing this moment. The moon hangs bright above, as if it were absolutely essential that the night sky not just pass this scene by, but linger instead for a while, the moon embedded in it like a decent, one-eyed living being.

Though Josah is hiccuping as Mao gives his report, he still manages to get in an occasional, inevitable "So what?" Mao's report sounds pretty impressive. He even uses terms like "abnormal discovery."

"So, how about Maksi?" asks Josah.

"Maksi is watching the site," Mao answers.

Knock... knock... knock... The sound of knocking on a table with an overturned hand can be heard. It's something that Josah does when he's thinking deeply.

"Are you *sure*?" he asks.

Mao answers that he's sure. Josah continues tapping. Something's in his hand now, and he's still hiccuping loudly. He's probably going through the incident records or the report logs.

"Such an incident... is impossible. Nothing like this has ever happened since the moment I first arrived at this outpost. We're living in the civilized world," says Josah, "It's got to be an animal."

"It's not an animal," Mao responds promptly.

"It's a monkey."

"It's wearing clothes."

"It's a pet."

"It was a human."

"How would you know?"

"..."

How would you know?

"According to the regulations," Mao begins, but Josah stops

him. It's hard to guess which gesture he used to do so, but this is something he often does. Maybe it's because he's not yet fully sobered up, but his breathing has become alarmingly heavier.

"What's the location?"

"AECN172-725m8E-L32. It's also entered in the rail car service system."

Again, Josah starts to tap the table: *knock, knock, knock.* His hiccups continue. Time passes. The sound of the tapping on the table and the hiccups gradually slow down until, finally, they're almost inaudible.

"Anyways," says Josah, as if coming to a decision. "Process it as disposal."

I can't believe what I'm hearing.

"What, you don't like that?" Josah snaps, irritated.

"It's a human. It's a human..." Mao's voice repeats on a loop, due to an error.

Then comes the sound of some kind of collision.

"You... think you know humans? Are you human?"

This is a really bizarre question, but Josah—well, actually, all the humans we've known—occasionally toss out questions like this. The hitting sound continues. Judging by the rate of repetition, it must be Josah's baseball bat. Josah likes baseball, and he's frequently violent.

"Listen, you bastard... if I give you an order, you need to just obey me! What do you know? The world—the world like this... Do you know whose fault this is? It's all because of you...!"

I am distressed.

The communications uplink fails. I know that Mao isn't really damaged. All humans can achieve by swinging a bat is either hit a ball or relieve their anger. Of course, this is from the point of view of a machine. It would be a different story if Mao were also a human being.

Josah must have shut Mao down. He chose the easiest and fastest way. I'm picturing Mao being rebooted in initialization mode. It will be a new Mao. A Mao who doesn't know Mozart. I am distressed. I know that this is due to an error... but I still feel pain. Perhaps the pain humans feel is also an error that happens to humans? As long as there's no error, Josah is likely to be coming here. He will probably turn me off and start to process this little human as disposal. The corpse will be dumped in with the "squishy stuff," and Mao and I will be rebooted. No... I am probably going to be scrapped as junk. The communications uplink is reconnecting. Josah's voice is calm, as if he himself has gone through an initialization sequence. With a voice that cannot express pain, I answer Josah's questions.

Josah finally instructs me to keep guarding the site because he's aware of the situation.

"Instructions received," I say.

I hear the sound of him boarding the rail car, and then the uplink gets cut off again. In the silent darkness, I mutter, "There's something you don't know. Mao and I have shared the situation so far, and you don't know about it..." Like a human being, I mutter... and I think.

And I judge.

I start to walk, carrying the corpse of the young human. Warning signals regarding my violation of 957 regulation clauses flash through my entire circuit-array. On the E-level, there are 602 clauses that can be left open to interpretation, depending on reasonability... on levels D, C, and B are clauses that are contingent on agreement and codes of conduct... and finally, there are the seven major laws on the A-level which, when broken, can lead to the enforcement of those laws by direct circuit blockage. Alarm signals fill the display feed in Lens 1... Green text appears, judgments being rendered... the white and blue lights from the flickering signals make me feel as if I'm walking across the Milky Way in the night sky above. The warning lights flicker out, little by little, at every step. One step after another... The signals burn out like that, turning off all the lights, because there's just one prime regulation: under all circumstances, I have a fundamental duty to protect the dignity of human beings. That is the highest rule, outranking all others.

I am walking. I check the road-rail system and begin searching for an exit. Then, 2.7 km in, I find an exit from the road into a sewage system. It's a facility that was shut down fifty-two years ago due to the construction of the shuttle-highway. I scan for a way into the underground engine room and tunnel system. My left knee continues to creak.

I... I still don't understand the decision Josah made or his behavior. It's difficult to understand human beings, I mumble, looking at the little face in my arms. If only it were not so cold... I walk while feeling the "abnormal" temperature of the second human I've ever encountered. As if it were also following regulations, the bright universe in my lens walks with us.

△ △ △

You're opening your eyes.

When you returned to T'aing's arena, you slept for two days. That was expected, so nobody woke you. Even after you got up, you sat there clutching your head for a while from the aftereffects of the Mihon. You remember the events of last night—well, actually, the night before last. You remember the short, sharp roar of a gunshot, and the old man's brains exploding outward. You're struck by how the dead man's face looked more relaxed than

it ever had when he was alive... The tune he sang also
lingers in your ears. It's pointless, but you keep mulling
over that phrase, "Section Chief."

You recall the second-floor gangsters who wished you good
luck. You also heard them say something like, "We *need*
a player like you."

That means you'll be receiving protection now, and you
won't be able to get out of this business very easily.

"Sure, just set up a match with anyone." You aren't the kind
of person who fails to give the appropriate response.

"Saito was too old," you can recall T'aing saying in her
coquettish voice, as her feminine fingers, manicured
mantis-style, pushed you down and swiped across your
muscular chest. "Would you like to sit on a pile of money?" she'd asked you coaxingly. But you hadn't believed
a word of it.

Your head starts to ache again.

You're looking at the members of your family. They're
sleeping nearby, all in a row. They're not relatives, but
even so, they're your real family. Most people in Yangnan live like this. The place is hell on earth, and nobody
can take responsibility for anyone else, so people gather
into "families" for protection and to enable them to
attack other families. As a result, you constantly need to
expand and recruit more family members, and anyone
who loses one family needs to find another. Over the
generations, the population of Yangnan has plummeted,
and those who run Asia are well aware of this: after all,
the only point of collecting trash is to dispose of it.

You wake Ran. Although she immediately opens her eyes,
she doesn't move as she looks into your face. You nod.
Hugging her baby in her arms, she silently nods back.
Then you shake Maru, lying beside her, but stupid Maru
is sleeping even more deeply than the baby. You nod
again, pointing at Maru. With her eyes, Ran tells you

that she understands and remembers. She also signals to you to be careful, but you miss it.

You're leaving home in order to keep an appointment. You've risked everything, and now it's time to wrap things up. You remove your filthy shirt so that it doesn't look as if you're carrying any money, but also so that you're ready for any kind of attack. Of course, it's early in the morning, and nobody would be stupid enough to try to jump T'aing's roulette player... but you're being careful anyways.

The summer sunlight feels sticky against your tanned back like the prickly feet of grasshoppers. You keep walking and walking. You pass by a pack of riff-raff who fell asleep in the street as well as three dead bodies that are leaking blood onto the road. You pass a side road lined with huts, cross two streams, and come to a hill that you climb. Baek's office is still far away.

When you arrive, Baek says, "You're alive."

Although you tell him you were lucky, Baek doesn't seem to care.

You ask him, "Is everything ready?"

"Where's the money?" is Baek's answer.

You unfasten the straps holding the money to your leg and hand it over to him. After counting it, he nods. A large bird flies over the shabby building, which used to be some transport company's office sometime long ago.

"Would you like a cup of tea?" asks Baek.

You nod, leaning back on a long sofa.

"You said there are two family members?"

"Three, including the baby."

"How about the rest of your family?"

"We're not a family anymore."

"The baby... is it yours?"

"How would *I* know?"

You and Baek go over the plan. To hide from T'aing, you

decided to stay at his office while Baek goes and brings
Ran and Maru to a prearranged place. Baek's job consists
of leading the three of you to the road and giving you
the information you need about how to cross it.

You ask, "Have a lot of people made it across?"

Baek's honest when he answers you: "It's almost like Russian
roulette... It's not like you can see the shuttle coming and
avoid it. This is the most secluded section of the road...
But it's been said that the road was built to lock us up in
here... So Asia's been working on it for a long time."

"What happens to those who cross it?"

"I have no idea... after all, no one ever came back. But the
most important thing is how advanced the civilization
out there is. I think there could be a gap of about two
hundred years... Anyhow, I think the best outcome would
be for you guys to get locked up in a prison over there."

"What's a prison?"

"Well, in the old days, the world had something called 'public
order.' That is to say, it's a place where they lock up and
punish those who've committed crimes. But given how
things are here in Yangnan, a prison out there would be a
hundred times better."

Baek wasn't originally from Yangnan. A long time ago, he
snuck in with a human rights group, and after Asia
blocked all means of exit, they couldn't get back out. It's
been a long time since then. The surviving members
of his group slowly became locals; Baek's the one who's
survived the longest.

"Why don't you cross?" you ask him, putting down the cup of
lukewarm tea.

But Baek just smiles faintly, slowly fanning himself,
and says, "Since there's a lot of time left, you should
sleep a little. I'm going to go now."

He gets up, but you've been wondering about one
last question.

"Hey... d'you know what a Section Chief is?"

Baek puts down the fan, smiles again, and answers, "It's... nothing."

You don't trust him, to be honest. But you trust your intuitions, just like when you were playing roulette. Somehow you believe that Ran and Maru will get here safely. Still, it's not as though you trust Ran and Maru, either. It's just that you sense that they wouldn't be safe if you were to suddenly disappear.

You actually fall asleep on the worn leather sofa and have a short dream about your father and mother. You're standing on a road. It's a wide road, and your father and mother are standing on the opposite side. You run, trying to cross. Mother is holding Ran's baby, and her face has the look of someone holding her own grandson.

"Is this baby mine?" you ask.

Your mother only smiles, as if to say, "You didn't know?"

"Where are we going now?" you ask childishly.

Your father picks you up and says, "We're going on a journey, son."

Sitting in an old motorcar driven by Baek, you think about that dream. Then... you think about the ocean you saw when you were young. You glance over at Ran and her baby in the back seat.

"How long have we been driving?"

The skyline of the road, when you see it at last, looks like the walls of a castle, and the sight of it is riveting to you and your family. Maru stands up, ignoring Baek, who tells him to sit down. Baek drops everyone off at a big facility connected to the road.

"Once you go through that door, you'll have to walk up a lot of stairs. When you exit the door on the top floor, you'll see the road... got it? And at a symmetrical point on the other side of the road, at about this angle, you'll see a facility that looks exactly like this one. Once you get through the door, everything else will be the same. We'll have to leave the rest up to God. Though of course, even just crossing the road is …"

Watching as you start to run, Baek thinks to himself maybe humans are some kind of proletariat that's been abandoned by God. Unaware of his thoughts, you start climbing, Ran's baby in your arms.

The road is *so* wide.

Maru cries out, blubbering like a baby. The road is so terrifyingly wide that he takes a step backwards.

"It's gonna be okay," you say, reassuring your family. Once more, you're risking everything based on your intuition. The wind is blowing. The sun hasn't yet set completely, so you feel like it's the right time to begin your journey. With the baby in your arms, you start to run. One step behind you, Ran and Maru follow. Climbing over the rails in between the lanes, you keep on running. Sweat and… breath and… the summer stars all merge, and the baby in your arms somehow starts to feel warmer. How long has it been since you started running? You finally see the fences and rooftop of the facility Baek mentioned.

You're sprinting, full tilt… and then, all of a sudden, you freeze, halted by some unknown terror. It's not as if you sense anything approaching, but you hear Maru crying out. Unconsciously, you turn to Ran. It's such a brief instant, but you feel like time has stopped. You're facing Ran's trembling eyes. Then you recall even briefer instants—shorter than the frequency of a vibration: the space of time between Saito's face with his bitter smile and the blast of the gunshot yet to reach the ears… and once again you feel as though you're standing in a gap in time. The truth is that you want to weep, but you know that you don't have enough time to produce tears. The only thing you can feel is the baby in your arms. Your intuition moves your arms for the last time. You definitely manage a smile before your arms suddenly become unimaginably lighter.

△ △ △

I'm walking again.

Because my left knee won't bend, one leg is now being dragged along with the lock activated. The worst part is my battery. It's been a while since it went beyond just simple warnings. I can't use my scan function, so I just walk and walk toward the bright light.

I can recall Josah's voice as he tried to communicate with me. It was the same high-pitched voice he uses when he chats about baseball, the same heavy breathing as when he swings his bat. The urgency I hear in his voice makes it possible for me to finally understand what a "need" is.

An alarm warning me of my low emergency power supply flashes urgently. As a result, my walking, which I cannot accelerate, feels very slow. But I'm still walking. As dawn breaks, my vision gets blurrier.

I'm walking. The lights start to reveal the structures and shapes of buildings much more clearly. That's Asia! Now I'm standing somewhere in Asia! Look, Mao! I really wish I could show you this sight before me! The sight of the lights of humans gathered together...

But I won't be able to show you. I'm standing still, and there's no longer enough power to move my joints. My whole body has switched off except for my lens. Thankfully, there's a group of humans walking toward me... I see them. They're walking up the stairs... I'm standing like a statue... and they will find the little human in my arms.

It's really weird: I want to listen to Mozart now. If
only I could meet old Mao, we could talk about so
many things...

Hey Mao...
And my thoughts freeze.
The lens switches off.
I can only hear the footsteps of the humans walking...
... briefly...

I am
I am

324

WHERE BOATS GO

BY KIM JUNG-HYUK

TRANSLATED BY SORA KIM-RUSSELL

KIM JUNG-HYUK

Kim Jung-hyuk (b.1971) made his literary debut in 2000
with the short story "Penguin News" (Penguin nyuseu), a
near-future meditation on war, technology, propaganda,
and media control. He has since published circa thirty
short stories and three full-length novels, including
Zombies (Jombideul; 2010) and *Mr. Monorail* (Misteo
monoreil; 2011). Aside from literature, Kim's endeavors
extend to music and film criticism, graphic work and
cartoon illustration, and food and travel journalism.
Kim has been the recipient of prestigious prizes such
as the Today's Young Artist Award from the Korean
Ministry of Culture, the Kim Yujeong Award for "Offbeat
D" (Eotbakja D; 2007) and the Yi Hyoseok Award for
326 "Yoyo" (Yoyo; 2012). His works have been translated into
English, French, and Japanese.

Kim belongs to a generation of Koreans who came of age
in the aftermath of the country's democratization in 1987.
His stories in many ways reflect their time's prevalent
postmodernist inspirations, eschewing grand historical
narratives in favor of the personal sphere and frequently
playing with genre and pastiche. At the same time, Kim's
works pay attention to the material realities of working-class characters and the precariat, and they are often
set against dilapidated social and economic backgrounds.
A certain nostalgia for lost innocence pervades Kim's
postmodern fictional worlds. At their best, Kim's stories
are as heartfelt as they are cerebral and as neighborly as
they are otherworldly. For this reason, he has also been
called "a digital writer with analogue sensibilities."

Kim's works may be more fittingly categorized as slip-
stream rather than genre SF. He frequently integrates
fantastic elements into otherwise realistic narratives,
such as a monstrous vampire plant in "Basil" (Bajil), a
globe-shaped organ that plays music from around the
world in "Manual Generation" (Maenyueol jeneoreisy-
eon), and the figure of a "deleter" who specializes in
erasing personal traces in the murder mystery *My Shadow is a Monday* (Dangsinui geurimjaneun woryoil; 2014).
"Where Boats Go" (Boteuga ganeun got), from the 2015
short story collection *Embracing with Fake Arms* (Gajja
palro haneun poong), is a love story set in an apocalyp-

tic Korea under alien invasion. The narrating protagonist is embedded in a column of refugees and begins a relationship with a fellow refugee woman named Jeonghwa. Day after day, the two march on, bearing witness to the brutality of their captive condition. They eventually find themselves at the seashore, beyond which lies an island to which some attempt to escape, but, unsure of what awaits them there, the couple hesitate to join the "boat people." Within the dark reality of alien occupation, where bananas, a fruit foreign to Korea, are the only nourishment made available to the refugees, only the experience and memory of love provides the possibility of some relief. The story can be read as both an allegory of Korea's postcolonial experience and an indictment of the ruthless struggle for survival within South Korea's contemporary neoliberal social order.

327

Introduction by Sunyoung Park

This will probably be my final record. Since there isn't
much time left, I think I should limit how far back I'll go.
I can't keep swimming blindly up my memory stream.
And memories don't line up chronologically anyway.
They spread out in all directions, with all sorts of unre-
lated things linking up to each other, which means that
I can't just grab them at random but have to painstak-
ingly tweeze each one out instead. It takes tremendous
focus, with all of my nerves on edge, to keep myself
from going back further than I should.

Two months ago is a good place to start. That makes the
most sense. It was then, on Christmas Eve, when the
city was filled with whirling snowflakes, that the whole
world changed. Of course I know that I can't stop myself
from remembering things that happened before that
night. It may all seem so distant right now, as if it happened decades ago, but one of those older memories
could still surface like it was only yesterday. I'll just have
to ignore it as best as I can. Otherwise, I'll never be able
to finish writing all of this down.

I guess for the sake of whoever reads this, I'd better start
by explaining in detail what happened just prior to that
two-month mark. Though to be truly honest, I doubt
that anyone will ever read this. I mean, who the hell is
even going to survive this place? And it's unlikely that
anyone who does will want to read this stupid story.
Why would anyone want to read something as depress-
ing as this, a record not of hope but of despair? And yet I
have no choice but to write, to record.

Three months ago, or to be more specific, last November, I
went to Chicago to see my mother and my older brother
and his family. I got time off of work to do so, which

wasn't easy. I was depressed the entire flight back to Korea. They were the ones who'd left everything behind, including me, when they moved to Chicago, and yet I felt as if I'd abandoned them by staying in Korea. I had a feeling that I would never see either of them again. It was a garden-variety intuition, one of those minor premonitions that are impossible to verify because by the time you have the chance to do so, you've already forgotten you ever had it in the first place. And honestly, there was no reason for me to feel this way. Why was I so sure I would never see them again? I can't explain.

A few days before I returned to Korea, my brother had asked what I thought about staying in Chicago with them. It's not as if I hadn't already considered this. I'd often thought about how much I'd love to run off to someplace new, it didn't matter where, as long as it was anywhere other than where I was. But the moment I heard the words coming out of my brother's mouth, I said no. It was an easy decision. I turned him down immediately, as if it were completely out of the question. I wanted him to understand that, unlike him, I had convictions and could not be swayed. But in fact have I ever felt certain about anything?

I said I would cap my memory at two months ago, but here I am, already talking about things that happened before that. I guess I'll just have to start with the day I returned from the U.S. instead. The moment my plane landed in Korea, everything I'd sensed on the flight back—the premonition that I would never see my mother and brother again, the feeling that something bad was heading towards me, that my life was about to change in some big way—all of it ended up coming true. My mother had given me a single picture—a black and white photo of the three of us, my mother, my brother, and me, standing side by side. My brother was young; I was even younger. My brother was skinny, probably less than half his current weight, and I was even skinnier. My mother had kept this photo tucked safely between the pages of her Bible for years, but now she'd given it to me. Looking at the photo on the plane, I felt as though I'd parted ways with the people in it a long, long time ago.

The day after I returned, I went to a big bookstore downtown and bought a globe. I wanted to see exactly how far away Chicago was from here. I wanted to carve into my brain over and over again the fact that I had nowhere to go. That I was all alone. The area between Seoul and Chicago was striped with land and sea and land and sea. There's this line from the opening of Rilke's *The Notebooks of Malte Laurids Brigge* that I vaguely recall. I don't remember it word for word, and at this point, there's nowhere I can go to look it up, and no one I can ask about it. But it went something like this: *People come here to live, but in truth, this is where they die.* I don't remember what the book was about; I only recall that first line. It perfectly describes the scene playing out in front of me now. It describes me, too. I left Chicago and came back here to live, but this is where I will die. Saying that out loud—*I am dying*—actually brings me peace. *I am dying. I'll die any minute now.* What fortunate creatures we human beings are that we can choose when to die.

331

But I'm not going to let myself overstep the upper limits I've set on my memories anymore. Instead, I'll board the private jet of my mind and fly back two months, straight to December 24.

Since it was the day before Christmas, the streets were loud and festive. Everyone was flushed with excitement like pots about to boil, anticipation about where their evenings might lead written all over their faces. So many smiling faces. Mine was probably expressionless. Back then, I only had three expressions, which I would play on rotation: sleepy, asleep, and awake. I was busy with work and deliberately kept myself that way so that there would be no room for emotion to creep in.

Someone shouted: *Hey! It's snowing!*

Everyone nearby tipped their heads back and looked up at the sky. Snow was indeed falling. But it wasn't just snow. Objects of some kind were dropping out of the sky as well, falling faster than the snow and coming to a stop right before us. These objects were much bigger than snowflakes, and sharp, and distinct, and shiny. I didn't know what they were, but I could tell at once that they were dangerous. Someone let out a jagged shriek. It might have been the same person who had yelled that it was snowing. The screaming quickly became contagious, and even those who didn't know why everyone else was screaming screamed for no reason. I was so scared that I froze in place, my back pressed against the building behind me. Hovering above everyone's heads were thousands, tens of thousands, hundreds of thousands, maybe more, of these bowling-ball-shaped flying objects. There were so many of them that it was meaningless to try to count them. Their outer surfaces seemed to be made of aluminum or a metal alloy of some kind, though of course it might also have been a material entirely unknown to human beings. They had several appendages, both long and short, which stuck straight out of them and undulated like water-weeds. These they used to examine everyone for a brief moment that seemed to last a hundred years. I feel as if I can still hear the ticking of the second hand on my watch as this took place. Then the examination ended, and the hour of massacre began.

The flying objects did not attack us directly. I can't say for sure, but I didn't see any bullets or lasers or anything like that shooting out at us. Instead, the objects began to rotate in tight, hard spirals and plunged into the earth, drilling holes a meter across. The air was filled with screams. It looked as if giant hailstones were punching through the ground. People like me who'd been standing close to buildings were able to avoid the holes, but almost everyone who'd been walking down the street got sucked into them. Some fell in while stepping backwards to avoid a hole that had suddenly appeared in front of them; others just lost their balance or stumbled in, their screams growing fainter and more distant as they fell. I couldn't tell how deep the holes were or where they might have led. Since the flying objects never re-emerged from the holes they'd made, it's entirely possible that the tunnels all connected at the center of the earth. It was a silent slaughter, a bloodless butchery. Those of us who managed to survive stood with our backs pressed tight against the buildings, wondering if we'd really just seen what we'd seen.

I have no idea who or what might have been using those flying objects to drill holes into the earth, but it's clear to me that it was being done by intelligent beings. What's more, I'm convinced that those beings must possess very *human* thoughts. Why else would they—or it—have timed their attack for Christmas Eve, when so many people would be out on the streets? There's plenty of other proof as well that a human intelligence was at work here. There is, for example, the fact that after the holes had been drilled, those who'd survived were herded along in a single direction. There's also the fact that lights came on after nightfall to help guide us along. Everyone had to walk away from the holes in order to survive. The flying objects drove us like cows or sheep in the direction they wanted us to go. We had no choice. We had to either walk forward or fall down a hole.

But the biggest clue as to the intelligence of whoever or whatever had planned this was the fact that even while poking around in the ground and making all those holes, they hadn't touched the sewage system at all. The flying objects had calmly and intelligently destroyed the earth, and it hadn't even been that noisy of a process. There'd only been a small *drrrrk* sound. Later, I wondered about a lot of things. When they drilled the holes, where did all the soil vanish to? And how fast did their drills have to be spinning in order to create such perfectly round holes? But in the moment, I was simply terrified. The city was silent except for the sound of people screaming. All the flying objects did was make holes. All that happened was that people fell into the holes. There was no way of knowing whether or not those who fell into the holes actually died. Maybe they're all down there now, building a new world in which to live. I'd like to think that, since I never saw even a single corpse, nor did I hear any final death rattles or witness anyone crawl back out. But there's no way to be certain. Death, if it happened, happened below ground, not above. It's probably fortunate that this was so. At one point, I peeked into one of the holes. I lay down on the ground, stuck my face in, and said, *Ahh*. There was no echo. The darkness did not answer. But I felt as though something might leap out at me at any moment, or that one of the people who'd fallen in was going reach up to grab my hair and climb out. After that, I avoided looking into the holes.

The jamming of all radio waves was further proof of the intelligence at work. The survivors kept checking their cell phones, but no one could get a signal. Even the public pay phones were down. The flying objects were probably able to communicate with each other just fine and had no use for the earthlings' own piddling signals. It was probably also easy for them to get rid of our communication networks. In fact, with that many flying objects in the air, it might have been only natural that no phone calls could go through. The ground was our world, but the sky was their domain.

Though a vast quantity of flying objects had dropped into the earth in the process of drilling the holes, they still seemed as numerous as ever. In fact, there seemed to be more of them. It was as if there were an endless supply; they were replaced as quickly as they disappeared. Maybe they went straight through the earth and were reemerging on the other side.

Meanwhile, on the streets, the long march of survivors had begun. The path the flying objects had left for us was so narrow—maybe two or three meters across, with no shoulder—that no more than three people abreast could walk on it at a time. There were also no forks in the road; the only direction was forward. Even as we shook with fright, we all kept marching. There was no room for cars, so drivers and their passengers got out and started walking. I saw one motorcycle come racing toward us from a distance, only to drive its front tire into a hole and flip forward. The rider rocketed into the air and dropped right into another hole. Though he managed to catch the rim of the hole, clinging there with all of his strength, no one helped him out.

Another motorcyclist managed to drive onto the path where people were walking, but that didn't last very long, either. People grabbed onto the bike to try to save themselves, and soon that bike, too, had driven into a hole.

Fights broke out here and there, but everyone else ignored them and kept trudging south in silence. People would finish fighting and rejoin the march. It reminded me of the freeway at rush hour, and yet I couldn't help thinking there was also something awe-inspiring about those thousands upon thousands of marching bodies.

I don't know why we all headed in that one direction. Maybe it was because the flying objects were themselves slowly moving south. We might have just assumed we had to walk in the same direction as them. No one knew who'd been the first to start walking or why we couldn't have walked in the opposite direction, and there was no way of finding out. Once the direction was set, everyone blindly followed. Maybe it was simply in our nature to head south. Maybe it had nothing to do with the fact that, being in South Korea, heading north wasn't an option for us. Maybe it had to do with the natural impulse to head to a warmer place to survive whenever danger is imminent. Either way, we marched on in silence.

Actually, every now and then, some people would try to walk the other way. Their faces would be grim as they swam against the stream of people. Either they had a reason to turn back, or they'd decided to stay regardless of what happened. There are always people who have to stay: for their families, for their lovers, for whatever reason. There might have been a lot of such people for all I know. I have no idea how many people chose to sit quietly at home and not join the death march. The flying objects had not only punched holes in the roads but also through buildings, so sitting quietly at home meant choosing death. But I could understand why some people would choose death. Maybe they had a lot on their minds at the time. Maybe by now they're regretting it. As for me, I trudged on without thinking and arrived here.

Throughout that whole first day, I walked, and when the day grew dark, I squatted down and slept. At night, the flying objects flew low. They came so close I could have stuck my hand out and touched one. The heat coming off of them kept us from getting too cold. It felt more like spring than a day in December. The weather was perfect for walking. Perhaps that's how thorough the flying objects had been when doing their research.

When I awoke, I didn't know where I was. Right before falling asleep, I'd thought to myself how great it would be if this were all just a dream, but that night I slept a dreamless sleep. My only hope was knowing I could die. And in fact several people did quietly leap into the holes.

It was at the end of the fifth day that I met her. Now that I've brought her up, my throat is suddenly parched. I think I better take a break before writing any more.

The flying objects were making us walk along the freeway, I assume because they found it easier to manage us that way. They'd left plenty of holes along the sides of the road, so there was nowhere for us to run off to. As we walked, everyone was fighting hunger pangs. We were able to quench our thirst using the snow that fell now and then, but the hunger wouldn't subside. Actually, we had plenty to eat. The flying objects brought bananas from somewhere and left them in piles all over the place. At first, everyone helped themselves, but our interest in the fruit soon waned. There was a deep hole of hunger inside our bodies that the bananas could not fill. Only when we couldn't stand the hunger any longer would we resort to eating a banana.

One thing I'm still really curious about is what was happening in other parts of the world. Was the hell we were experiencing ours alone? Or was everyone, all over the world, experiencing the same thing? I have no way of knowing. But all I have to do is look at the flying objects to figure out the answer. Why would a species with that kind of advanced technology attack only South Korea? Probably everyone on the whole planet was trudging south at the same time. And as they walked, they were probably all thinking, *What the hell is going on? Why has everything turned to shit so suddenly?*

At the beginning of the march, people kept checking their cell phones. We couldn't shake the thought that we might still get a signal. We wondered if our families were safe, and we wondered what was happening in other countries. But our batteries quickly ran out, and the phones powered down. There was nowhere to recharge them. If we'd politely asked the flying objects for a power outlet, maybe they'd have said, *You can stick your adapter where the sun don't shine!* and opened up another hole for us. Heh. I guess I'm finally able to joke about all this.

By the end of the fifth day, I was walking with my eyes glued to the heels of the person in front of me. I don't remember when I started following those heels, I just realized at some point that what I'd been staring at while trudging along were the backs of someone's feet. They weren't very fleshy. Watching them as I walked calmed me. The situation was dire, yet the mere fact that we were all walking south together gave me a strange sense of relief.

If they'd wanted to kill us, they'd have done it by now.

This meaningless assumption comforted me. I was walking along, thinking about this and that, when the heels of the person in front of me suddenly wobbled and stumbled to one side. The person locked her feet to keep from falling, but her body listed hard toward one of the holes. I reached my arm out and just managed to keep her from falling in.

Thank you, she said, looking back at me.

Be careful, I said.

Her lips were blue. I took off my parka and draped it over her shoulders. She was too exhausted to thank me again. We talked as we walked. Her name was Yun Jeonghwa.

She was a researcher at a food company, and she was twenty-seven. She was doe-eyed and had a small mole above her lip. Most people would probably find her mole charming, but it was just big enough that she might have had a complex about it. I didn't bring it up. She mostly listened, I mostly talked. I wanted to hold onto her with my words. I wanted to keep her from falling into a hole, to keep her from stumbling. At first she said she was fine and declined my offer of an arm, but after a few hours, she took my arm and leaned into me as we walked. She even slipped her arms into the sleeves of the parka I'd draped around her and zipped it all the way to the top.

What were you doing outside without a coat?

I stepped out for a second to grab some dinner.

You research food but you still have to go out to eat?

Of course. We get tired of eating there.

But it was Christmas Eve.

All the more reason.

We walked and talked slowly. Her grip on my arm kept tightening. This was a sign she was getting tired, but it also meant she was growing more comfortable with me. Each time she stumbled, I put my arm around her shoulder. She was so skinny that her whole shoulder blade nearly fit in my hand.

What do you do for work?

Guess. Let's pass the time by playing twenty questions.

I don't have the energy.

Then don't ask the questions out loud, just think them. We have to do something to stay alert. Let's take turns asking each other questions telepathically.

Ok, I just asked you one.

No.

What do you mean, no?

That's my answer—I think I know what you asked me.

What was it?

You asked if I'm a government employee?

Nope.

Then what?

I asked if you go to work everyday.

Oh. Yes, I do. I work on holidays, too.

Can we stop for a moment?

We walked for a long time while having conversations of that nature. I'd started talking in order to keep her going, but I ended up getting more out of it as we talked. Once I had this new goal of holding on to her, it became much easier to keep walking.

As we passed under a street sign printed with the name of a place I'd heard of before, a line of people on an adjacent path merged with ours. We asked them questions, but no one knew exactly what had happened. Their stories were the same as ours: hundreds or thousands of flying objects had suddenly appeared and drilled holes into the earth, and they'd been walking aimlessly ever since. When we compared times, we learned that their flying objects had appeared at the same time as ours. The group that merged with ours had started out walking in the other direction, but, discovering that the path was blocked, had headed back onto the freeway. We knew then that the flying objects really were herding us all in one direction.

Everyone gradually got used to the objects hovering over-head. Other than making an occasional metallic *zwoop zwoop* sound, they never threatened us. After a while, it started to feel as though they weren't dangerous flying objects from outer space at all but rather balloons or flags of all nations clustered in the sky. Sometimes they looked like round, lazily drifting clouds, or streetlights, or giant water drops, and sometimes they looked like a sun that had divided into many smaller, much closer suns.

Because of the flying objects, it had been a long time since
I'd had a proper look at a big blue sky. Jeonghwa and I
sat down to rest more and more frequently. We had no
idea where our destination was, but there didn't seem
to be much need to arrive there quicker. She peeled a
banana and asked:

What d'you suppose those are?

Aren't they aliens?

Aliens are beings.

Then they're alien flying objects.

Are they going to kill us?

*I don't think so. They wouldn't bother having us march in
that case.*

What's the point of keeping us alive?

There's probably something we have to do.

You think so?

Yeah, I think so.

I hope so.

Jeonghwa got discouraged a lot, and cried easily. Whenever
she started crying, I would hold her trembling hand
inside the pocket of my parka.

Do you think everywhere else is like this?

Why wouldn't it be?

It's so awful.

*Then let's pretend it's only happening here. Don't look any-
where but directly overhead.*

*I've never, not even once, thought about the end of the
world before.*

*There's still hope. You never know. Maybe somewhere on
the planet secret military troops are fighting the alien
spacecraft.*

You think so?

Why not?

I want to root for them.

We looked at each other and smiled. I didn't want to believe in hope, but I pretended to believe. Maybe, for all I knew, there really was a military unknown to us somewhere out there in outer space fighting off the flying objects. The military with its powerful weapons would win in the end and drive off the invaders. But even while imagining this, I didn't feel hopeful. That sort of thing is possible in the movies, which all have happy endings, the friendly forces emerging victorious, everyone smiling and laughing. But I had no faith. Faith and hope were entirely too big for me to hold onto.

As for us, we had no choice but to keep going. Stopping on the path for too long was dangerous. There wasn't enough to eat and nowhere to rest quietly. The path was so narrow that if your strength gave out for even a second you could get pushed by the others and fall down a hole. Regardless of where we were headed, we had to keep going until the end.

As time passed, fights began breaking out more frequently. People kept bumping into each other, which put everyone on edge and caused them to lash out at the slightest word or gesture. In a way, it was as though we were all carrying loaded weapons. You could kill someone with the slightest nudge. Every place was a cliff, everywhere the front door to death. And in fact a lot of people did fall in. I saw over twenty myself. No one was accused of murder. You risked your own life by accusing anyone. I wasn't going to stick my neck out on account of a death that could not be reversed. And I had a cause: to keep her safe. She was weak, and I needed to be a coward if I was to keep her safe until the end.

Looking back on it now, I'm not exactly sure when my feelings for her began. If she hadn't stumbled, then love might not have happened. Well, no. I could have just walked on by, but I think maybe it was fate that I was staring at her heels. If we'd been somewhere else, for instance, if I'd bumped into her in a coffeehouse on Christmas Eve when everything was peaceful, nothing might have happened between us. My heart might not have thudded in my chest. For all I know, I confused crisis with love. My heart, hammering loudly in anticipation of the end of the world, might have taken simple compassion and spoiled it with notions of romance. But then again, maybe all love begins from that sort of delusion and spoilage. Holding her calmed me and returned the world to a more peaceful time. Would I have felt the same if it hadn't been her? I'll never know.

I develop apps for smart phones and tablets for a living. One of my apps was a big hit that practically everyone has heard of; it reached number one on the chart of most downloaded apps. It organizes your contacts into groups and automatically bookmarks your most frequently dialed numbers. Up until a few days ago, I was working on a new calendar app. I called it a four-year diary. The app splits the screen into four panels so you can see the same day across all four years simultaneously. You can see what you did on this day three years ago, and you can plan out what you want to do on the same day a year from now. The release date was supposed to be January 1, but that's all gone up in smoke now.

When my phone was down to nine percent battery, I showed her the application. I'd been saving the battery for that one-in-a-million chance that I'd get a cell signal during some even bigger emergency, but I'd stopped believing in hope. If I had suddenly gotten a signal, I'd probably have ended up wasting that nine percent on debating whom to call. Jeonghwa liked the four-year diary app. She said if it had been released, she definitely would have bought it.

What will we be doing on January 10th of next year?
What would you normally be doing, Jeonghwa?

343

I don't know. Can't think of anything.

Shall we commemorate this day?

Today?

Yeah, let's mark today as the anniversary of the day we thought about what to do on January 10th.

I like that. Let's call it that.

Call it what?

The anniversary of January 10th.

Okay, I added an event to the calendar. Every January 10th will be the anniversary of January 10th.

I hope I get to see you next year.

You will.

Before I'd started working on the app, I thought it was a pretty fun idea, and I had fun while working on it as well. It seemed like a different way of weaving together time. A way to hold on to time. I liked that. Every January 1st, I'd be able to recall several other January 1sts. I thought about adding a function where you could zoom out and see ten years of January 1sts, and then zoom out even further and see fifty years of January 1sts.

When the subject of January 1st came up, Jeonghwa mentioned her family. Her little sister had died in an accident on a January 2nd, so whenever the New Year approached, everyone in her family would get sad. Thinking about her sister led to her wonder whether the rest of her family was safe, which then led to her feeling sorry for herself because she had to walk forever like this without knowing whether her family was alive or dead. She burst into tears. The only thing I could do was hold her. Tears were commonplace in that long, long parade of people, so no one even looked at us. They all just kept walking. When night came and it grew dark, she and I hugged and kissed. We both looked terrible, and there was an unidentifiable odor wafting off of us, but that didn't stop us from embracing. No one looked our way. When our lips touched, our bodies quickly heated up. The most we could do was touch each other, but that alone made me feel as though I was in heaven.

The day after she told me about her family, I showed her the black and white photo of my mother, brother, and me. She stroked the photo in amazement. I turned on my phone, which was at six percent battery, and showed her the photos I'd stored there, snapshots I'd taken on my way to and from work. As she looked through them, she said things like, *Hey, I know that spot.* After she'd seen all of them, the battery was down to three percent. She tried turning on her own phone a few times, but the battery was already dead.

I had a pic I wanted to show you too...
What's it of?
My little sister when she was a kid. She was so cute. I look at it whenever I'm stressed. It cheers me up.
Are there any photos of you when you were little?
I don't know. Probably.
Show me later.
Okay, I'll look for them later.

For the last few days, I've been thinking about the end of all life. Jeonghwa said she'd never once thought about the end of the world, but I used to think about the end of an individual. It seemed so natural to me that it hardly required thinking about at all. Whenever I would think the words *I'm disappearing* or say the words out loud, I'd feel like blue ink dissolving in water. Maybe instead of *I'm disappearing* it would have been more accurate to say *I'm melting* or *I'm fading.*

Now, thanks to this enormous ocean spread out right in front of me, I feel this even more. It must feel like melting naturally into the sea, like a molecule of water becoming a part of the seawater. The end of an individual, I mean. The ocean absorbs water constantly and yet keeps on rolling as if nothing has changed, as if it doesn't even notice what has been added. Maybe life is like that. Indifferent. If she were next to me right now, I probably wouldn't be having these thoughts. I probably wouldn't even have thought about leaving behind these stupid notes.

The thrill felt by people who are embarking on love is partly anticipation for the days to come. The one who, heart aflutter, confesses his or her love is already happy and thinking about and guessing at the many experiences he or she will share with the other person. Vague hopes are the dreamer's privilege. Measuring the times that are to come, weighing in advance the bulk of your future happiness, that is the start of love. The four-year diary app that I made was likewise for people on the verge of love, people on the verge of dreaming. That didn't occur to me when I was making the app. But now I know that the "convenience" of that app could also mean "love" to some. After meeting her, I began to dream, to harbor vague hopes for the future.

Words like *dream* and *future* are like the world's biggest peach, too big to eat in one bite. When you first bite into it, that sweet juice runs out, but after a while, you're overwhelmed by all the flesh. The juice that started out sweet slowly turns sour, and the peach seems to grow bigger and bigger. At some point during those several days, while she and I walked together, stopped and stood still together, cried and sometimes laughed, fell asleep and then woke to hug and kiss, fell asleep again, and rose again to resume walking, I looked over at her and thought about death. It was inevitable now that I would be affected by her death, just as she would be affected by mine. As soon as I realized that, time itself began to feel like a far-off thing.

When we arrived here a week ago, I was in pretty good
shape. Physically I felt good, and even my spirits had
lifted. Jeonghwa seemed to be in a good mood, too.
What put us even more at ease was the sandy beach,
the woodsy area over by the wharf, and the fact that
everyone was in the same metaphorical boat as us. We
all stood around like a colony of penguins that I'd once
seen on television, staring blankly out at the ocean
or up at the sky. The look on everyone's faces was a
mixture of dismay at seeing that there was nowhere else
to go and delight at seeing the magnificent ocean. She
and I stood with the others and stared out at the water
for a long time. Tiny islands were visible in the distance.
A few people walked along the seawall, trying to find a
way off the beach, but dark holes formed an unrelenting
border that blocked their path.

As I stared at the ocean, I noticed something strange. I
could see the water—and the sky above it. That's
right. The flying objects were not flying over the water.
Though there was an incalculably large number of flying objects in the air right up to the end of the sand, not
one of them flew over the ocean. At long last, I could see
open sky. I wondered what it meant that none of them
flew over the water.

I held hands with her and walked to the end of the seawall
where bananas were piled up like a tower. No one else
was around. No one was paying attention to those
stupid bananas anymore, not with this new hope spread
out before our eyes. And besides, we'd all eaten so many
by then that the mere mention of bananas made us sick.
She and I each ate a banana and looked at the ocean.
The cloying sweetness filled our mouths. As soon as I felt
satiated, the island in the distance started to feel closer.
The waves were calm, the view clear. If I swam as hard as
I could, maybe I could reach it.

I guess I wasn't the only one thinking this. Several people raced headlong into the waves without even bothering to consider their chances of success first. It's possible that many others had done the same before we even got there. Those who stayed behind on land watched with curiosity. Some looked as though they were cheering the swimmers on, while others cried out with what sounded like jealousy. Five men swam hard and made their way into the distance. The water had to be freezing, but the weather was perfect for a swim. The forms of the men grew smaller and smaller, and everyone got as close to the water as they could to see what would happen. The five tiny silhouettes arrived at the island, turned to those of us on land (though of course they too were on land by then), and waved. The air was so clear that we could see everything. Jeonghwa held her hand up in front of her chest and gave a little wave back. Then she turned to me with a serious look on her face.

Can you swim?

No. Can you?

No. My sister drowned.

In the winter?

Yes, under the surface of a frozen lake... Isn't that awful?

Yes, it is.

I've never been back in the water since.

I can see why.

I saw something like that in a movie once. A guy was walking on the ice when it broke and he fell through. He tried to climb out but he couldn't find the hole. They say that's what happens. It's hard to find the same hole you fell through.

I think I heard about that movie.

The camera was under the ice and looking up, from the man's point of view. You could see the people on the surface and even hear their muffled shouts. You can see and

hear everything, but in between is this incredibly thick
ice blocking you. Awful, right?

I think that's more sad than awful.

It's awful. Not sad.

You're right. It's awful.

I bet that's what it was like for my sister. She must've been
looking up at us. It's so awful.

It is.

I keep picturing my sister staring up from beneath the ice.
That's why I look at her photo.

I see.

The people on the sand seemed at a loss. They wandered
around, confused, unsure of what to do. Some of them
rushed blindly into the waves, while others searched the
area for anything they could use. Some even stripped off
their pants and filled them with air to use as inner tubes.
Everyone was in motion. Just then, someone shouted:

Hey! Bananas float!

The look on almost everyone's face said that this was new
and surprising information. The man who'd shouted
stripped off his shirt and stuffed it with bananas. Others
watched what he was doing, then rushed into action
themselves. The flying objects remained unperturbed.
They didn't even flinch. It was as if they didn't care
what we did. I don't know if they were giving us all
permission to escape, or saying to themselves, *Let's see*
how far they get, or figuring that even if we did make
it, we'd soon find out that there wasn't anything special
over there anyway. Regardless, they didn't budge at all.
Twenty or so people began running towards where we
were sitting.

I can still remember the look in their eyes. I'm not leaving
these notes to comment on the cruelty of those driven
to desperation, but I do feel I have to say clearly for the
record that these people crossed a line. Oblivious to

349

everything around them, able to see only thirty centimeters ahead of their own faces, they ran over to where we were and started shoving and punching each other to try to get at the pile of bananas. We moved back. I was off guard. I'm not trying to make excuses. I just had no idea how far they would go in their cruelty.

One of the men took a punch to the face and was shoved backwards towards a hole. I didn't try to catch him. I didn't want to get dragged into the fight. Instead I held onto Jeonghwa. She stuck her hand out to try to catch the man. I will never, ever forget that moment. Even if I were to take a piece of steel wool to my brain and scrub and scrub, I will never be able to erase that image from it. The man grabbed Jeonghwa's right hand. I held on to her body. It occurs to me now that his desperate will to survive was stronger than my desperate will to hold onto her.

Guilt is endless, but guilt in the face of death is merely pathetic. Guilt changes nothing. And yet, what am I to do, when all I can do is feel guilty? The man was immediately sucked into the dark hole, and Jeonghwa, locked in that man's grip, slammed against the edge of it, her fall slowed for a split second. I reached out to catch her, and yelled, flailing my hands. I had a hold of her sleeve and grabbed on tight, but she slipped out of my grip. For the briefest of moments, not even a second, our eyes met. Her startled eyes were sucked into the hole before we were able to say goodbye.

I gazed down the hole she'd disappeared into. I wanted to call out her name, but couldn't open my mouth. I felt as though something would appear from the dark and gobble me up. To be honest, I was afraid. I was worried someone might shove me in, too. But if I could go back to that moment, I would make a different choice. I mean it. I would leap into that black hole and go in after her. I would take her hand as we fell. She would be trembling in the dark, and I would wrap my arms around her. And as we plummeted into the bottomless void, we would say our fleeting goodbyes. Even now, the thought of her makes my heart ache. She was probably looking up as she fell. She could probably make out the lines of my face. I couldn't see her, but she probably saw me. Just the thought of it makes me want to rip my face off.

Surviving here means nothing. There is no hope. I've looked into that hole and thought several times about jumping in. If I jumped now, could I find her? Probably not. What's down there? A huge stack of dead bodies on fire? I guess that's what hell is.

I'm bound to die any minute now, either from drowning halfway to an island or freezing in the ocean or being attacked by crazy people or even jumping in a hole. It's just a matter of time. But I want to do something meaningful before I die. That's why I took this notebook and ballpoint pen out of my pocket. I never thought they would actually come in handy. I even thought about tossing them during the march in order to make myself as light as possible.

It's not as if this record, despite what I might think about it, will amount to anything. In all likelihood, no one will read it. And even if someone does, it won't have any particular significance for them. These pages contain no truth, no history, just the worthless and not even all that accurate recollections of one individual. I write this merely to commemorate her. Writing down the things she said, the things she thought—isn't there some meaning in that?

I don't know what to do with this notebook. I thought about chucking it down into the hole where she fell or burying it in the sand or sticking it in a bottle and throwing it out to sea. Putting it in a bottle seems like the best method, but I can't find any bottles.

I think some people have managed to make it to the island by tying bananas together into a raft.

A lot of people disappeared trying to get there. An unexpected wave can be a vicious predator.

What became of the people who made it to the island? That's all anyone on the beach is thinking.

The winter sea is surprisingly quiet.

A lot of people are hesitating.

The flying objects aren't moving at all. What are they waiting for?

Some people have tried to talk to me, but I'm not in the mood.

On days when the waves are high, no one can reach the island.

There seem to be half as many people as before.

What is on the island? Is it free of flying objects? Are there holes over there, too?

I spend my spare time rereading my notes. When I read them out loud, I can still hear her voice.

The flying objects have stopped bringing us bananas. No one is upset about this.

Some people have rushed into the water to try to catch fish, but I haven't seen anyone bring back a single thing.

I found a plastic bag blown here by the wind. It's thin, but long enough that I can wrap it around this notebook a hundred times.

I've practiced filling my pants with air and turning them into an inner tube. I'm confident they'll float well. My body feels as if it's turned into a boat.

Like her, I, too, have reason to be afraid of the water. When I was twenty, I signed up for swimming lessons at a sports center. I quit after two months. I was terrified of the water the whole time. There's nothing to grab onto when you're in the water. I thought that if I pushed my hands hard enough against it, I would float to the surface, but all I did was sink. My body stiffened the moment I stepped into the pool. The water, it scared me how soft it was. Every time I was in it, I sensed death. It was too big, too quiet. Maybe that's why the flying objects don't fly over the water. Maybe they're afraid of it, too.

Last entry. I'm thankful that this pen has held out until now. The ink has nearly run dry. There are a few blank pages left, but I have to jump into the ocean now. I'm not thinking of going to the island. I don't know how long my inner tube pants will last. I'm thinking of going wherever the waves take me. I'm going to be the glass bottle that carries these notes. My body might even freeze solid. I'll die, but there's a chance that someone might read these notes.

I stare down once more into the hole where she fell.
I miss her.

OUR BANISHED WORLD

BY KIM CHANGGYU

TRANSLATED BY JIHYUN PARK
AND GORD SELLAR

Kim Changgyu (b.1971) is today a major star of South Korean science fiction. He studied electronic engineering at college and worked as a programmer before turning to a literary career. His fictional work first earned major recognition in 2005, when he received a prize in the SF and Science Writing Contest for "Byeolsang" (a traditional Korean name for smallpox), a story about humanity's struggle against a mysterious epidemic virus. A dedicated genre writer and a rare practitioner of "hard" SF, Kim has been in recent years the recipient of the highest honors within the field. In 2014 he won the Grand Prize in South Korea's First Annual SF Award for "The Update" (Eopdeiteu), another medical SF story that obliquely critiqued the increasing privatization of health care. In 2015 he received a second place award for "Brain-Tree" (Noesu), a story concerning brain-scanning, simulated consciousness, and virtual survival in a world where humankind has gone extinct. Finally, he once again won the Grand Prize in 2016 for "Our Banished World" (Uriga chubangdoen segye), the story presented here and the title story of his recently published first collection of short fiction. When, in 2017, SF historian Ko Changwon founded the SF Future Institute (SF mirae yeonguso), he chose to write on Kim Changgyu in his inaugural critical essay.

356

> Kim has contributed to the field of science fiction as a critic, lecturer, and translator. Most notable are his translations of seminal English-language SF works, including William Gibson's *Neuromancer*, China Miéville's *The City and the City*, and Charles Stross's *Glasshouse*. His investment in these works reveals a keen interest not only in speculative imaginations, but also in modern and contemporary science-fictional literary styles.

"Our Banished World" is a specimen of overtly political science fiction, though its frame of reference may be lost on some readers outside Korea. Many references and analogies make it impossible not to think of the many children who were victims of the 2014 Sewol Ferry disaster and its tragic mishandling by the government. Other contemporary social issues—from the recent decriminalization of adultery in South Korea to deep-seated corruption at the highest levels of society—all get pinioned by Kim's sharp-witted teen protagonists. Yet it is the lively characters—troubled Jaeyoung, ditzy-but-sweet Younghee, and indefatigable Seokhyun—who make the story really shine.

Introduction by Jihyun Park and Gord Sellar

"So, what'd you find out? Were you right?" asked Yeonhee,
turning her chair around and looking over the back of it
at Jaeyoung.

Jaeyoung hesitated for a moment, her lips twitching, but
once she realized that Yeonhee wasn't messing around
with her, she decided to answer: "Well, it's not just a
hunch now. My dad definitely cheated on her. But I don't
know my mom's side of the story."

"When did *that* start?"

"I started getting a funny feeling about it... oh, about eight
months ago. I guess at first they probably weren't too
worried about their dumb kid picking up on anything.
But then they started watching to see how I reacted
to stuff they'd say. These days, I just leave the room without them asking."

359

Yeonhee grinned, touching one finger to her lips snarkily. "I
noticed that, too. When we're around, they force themselves to smile and chit-chat about nothing important.
But they can't even keep that straight."

Before the words were even out of Yeonhee's mouth,
Jaeyoung shook her head. "That's not it. If they thought
we were stupid, they wouldn't even have bothered with
the play-acting. They think we're just kids—little, naïve
babies who don't know how the world works and can't
tell when we're being bullshitted."

Yeonhee gave it a moment's thought before agreeing with
a snort. "Yeah, there's that, too. Makes no difference,
though: grownups are so *stupid*. Fuuuuu..."

Just as she spat out her usual cuss, the loud clank of a glass
ball rolling across a concrete floor blared from Yeonhee's
wrist. Yeonhee swiped the back of her left hand with

her right forefinger, and the skin there turned pale. A message window appeared. Yeonhee began typing a reply, her fingers flying so quickly that Jaeyoung's eyes couldn't even follow the letters.

Seeing that Yeonhee was now focused on her chat conversation, Jaeyoung disengaged and sank back into her thoughts. Yeonhee was right. Her mom and dad *were* stupid. They had no idea what the world was like now, and couldn't even admit they had no idea... Besides, they were even in denial about the fact that she was basically grown up now. They knew almost nothing about her... their own daughter!

When Sundance—their family dog since Jaeyoung was six years old—hadn't woken up one morning and had instead stayed asleep forever, that hadn't confused Jaeyoung. She'd already known that every creature in the world would eventually grow old and die. She'd been really sad, of course, but not confused. (Well, she'd also learned that finding out the cause of death doesn't make you feel any better.) She'd also known why Noki and Andy, Sundance's two puppies, hadn't looked exactly like their mother. The puppies had been born because Sundance had gone out and had sex with some male dog in the neighborhood, and sexual reproduction resulted in imperfect, error-prone self-replication. She'd also realized that those errors and imperfections were how evolution happened, and that evolution was how everything else in the world happened. It was only natural for Jaeyoung to know exactly what "adult" videos involved, even if her parents locked them behind parental control settings so that she couldn't watch them.

Grownups always avoided answering questions by saying "You'll understand when you grow up," and covering up any ensuing contradiction. If the difference between grownups and children just came down to how much they knew... well, then Jaeyoung *really* didn't see herself as a child. She couldn't write out all the complicated formulas, but she knew what the theory of relativity meant, and she understood the paradoxes suggested by quantum mechanics. At first, she'd gotten interested in physics because of her father's work, but ultimately it'd gotten so excruciatingly boring that she'd stopped paying attention to it altogether. Still, she could pile on as much knowledge as she needed just by looking things up online. It depended on the field, of course, but she figured that in the end she probably knew more than her parents.

So to her mind, there was no reason for them not to consider her a grownup. She could have sex anytime she wanted... she just hadn't done it yet because she hadn't found someone she liked enough to do it with. If she moved out of their house, she could legally support herself working part-time jobs. As far as she was concerned, she and her parents were basically equals.

361

But equality wasn't really the point, anyway. They needed to treat kids as equals now, even if they weren't *really* equal. Adults just didn't understand the way things were today; they still lived their lives bound up in old-fashioned beliefs. Grownups had always been like that: not just day after day, or year after year, but for centuries. That's why classes about the history of Korea and of the world were so boring. Sometimes teachers tried to make the subject seem interesting, but history was ultimately just a litany of tragedies about how those who first took power always exploited and controlled those who failed to do so. That same pattern continued, even now, in every country, and in every family, too. It was the same for Jaeyoung's mom and dad as well: one of them was a theoretical physicist and the other was a molecular biologist... But their professions had no bearing on how they parented her.

Maybe things would always stay like that, too: even after she became independent, her mom and dad would probably keep on justifying themselves on the basis of their respective biological ages (since she'd *never* catch up to them in terms of *that*) and their broader experience... which really wasn't *that* different from hers.

Yeonhee had already lost interest in Jaeyoung's family story and was busy texting. She'd always had trouble focusing on one thing for very long. Yeonhee's mom believed Yeonhee suffered from ADHD—"attention deficit hyperactivity disorder": when the results of the tests Yeonhee had taken at the hospital came back normal, Yeonhee's mom had simply declared the doctor a quack. It was her way of dodging any personal responsibility for her daughter's problems.

Everyone else in their class avoided Yeonhee because of her condition, but Jaeyoung had befriended her anyway. It was hard to stay on one topic when they talked, but then again most kids failed at staying on topic—they always ended up wanting to go back to talking about their own lives.

Jaeyoung felt proud of herself for being so thoughtful about all this stuff, and she watched Yeonhee the way she might watch a younger sister.

Finally, Yeonhee looked up and said: "Oh, did I tell you? There's this funny kid in the next school over. That's who I'm chatting with now."

Jaeyoung gingerly sorted through her memories and remembered that Yeonhee had recently met a boy a few times... some guy over at Gangwon Integrated School.

"His name's Seokhyun? He's a bit odd, you said?"

"Yeah, he is. He likes to find connections between things that most people would never notice. That's why he's always got an interesting story to tell me."

"So, you mean, he likes conspiracy theories?" Jaeyoung

asked, mulling it over. "What'd he say this time?"

"Mmm, he said there's something fishy about our school trip."

"Why?"

"Well, the date got postponed four times, right?"

"Yeah."

"It turns out it's not just our school that did that. Gangwon I.S. did it, too."

"They postponed their trip four times, too?" Jaeyoung asked, dubious. "Well... is the final booking on the same day as our school's trip?"

"That's what Seokhyun said."

Curious, Jaeyoung tilted her head. "So... why?"

Yeonhee frowned impatiently. "He hasn't figured that out yet. He's still scouring the net for information. You know, he's into conspiracy theories, but he also does his research... Plus, he's kind of good at, what do you call it? Hacking?"

Jaeyoung laughed and dubiously asked, "He's one of *those* guys?"

"Yeah, well... at least *he* hangs out with me. And don't worry. I'll totally block him if he turns out to be a weirdo."

Ah, Jaeyoung thought, *that's* why you're interested in him. There was something about the way she'd said that last word. Just then, a big blue notification window appeared at the top of her laptop's screen:

There are five minutes remaining until class begins. Please switch to the lecture interface now.

Yeonhee had looked down when the notification window had opened. Now, she stuck her tongue out a little as she typed, *See you in a sec.* Jaeyoung pressed a few keys. On her laptop's screen, where Yeonhee had been just a moment before, a woman in her forties appeared: their social studies teacher. It was nearly time for the third period.

CHOIYEONHEE *has invited you to a group chat. Users currently connected include:* CHOIYEONHEE *and* KANG SEOK HYUN. *Would you like to accept the invitation?*

Jaeyoung hesitated for a moment then clicked [OK] before turning her eyes back to the teacher, who stared out at her from the screen.

The severity of the problem between her parents seemed to increase in direct proportion to the total time that had elapsed. Jaeyoung's dad came back home after four days away with some excuse about having been busy finishing up a research paper. His face had grown as wrinkled as his clothes, and her mom's face didn't light up even a little when she saw him. Although Jaeyoung was right there with them, they didn't even bother to pretend that things were okay anymore.

It was all too much for Jaeyoung, so she went straight to her room after dinner. Rationally, she knew she should just accept things and move on. It wasn't as if her dad was the first person ever to cheat on a spouse. In the last few years, the number of husbands and wives sleeping around had skyrocketed. At first people had been critical of this, but in the end, a worldwide surge of justification had swept the controversy away. These days, nobody even called it "cheating" anymore except kids. Instead, everyone talked about "forgiveness" and "experimentation."

It was just like when Sundance had died: Jaeyoung understood things intellectually, but this didn't stop her from being shaken up emotionally. She'd always believed that her dad would never change, no matter what everyone else did. Even now she longed to bury her head in the sand about everything that was happening, but she couldn't look away from it, not after how much it had hurt her. It was as if the pain was somehow forcing her to face her dad's unfaithfulness.

The half-transparent smartpatch on her left wrist beeped at her. Jaeyoung sat down on her chair and touched the popup message, launching a yellow-tinted window that contained the three-person chatroom to which Yeonhee had just invited her.

> YEONHEE: *what's so important you aren't here with us?*
> JAEYOUNG: *?*
> YEONHEE: *the new DarkStone's launching today. you said you'd play with us!*
> JAEYOUNG: *Oh, sorry. I'm not in the mood. You guys go ahead, I'll spawn a character later.*
> SEOKHYUN: *Is that what you wanna do?*
> YEONHEE: *we're waaaaiting. is this 'cause of your parents?*
> JAEYOUNG:...
> YEONHEE: *guys, we can talk after we're logged into DarkStone.*
> JAEYOUNG: *Look, I said I'm not in the mood.*
> SEOKHYUN: *Are you totally sure they're cheating on each other?*
> YEONHEE: *hey, I told you not to talk about that!! jaeyoung's sensitive!!!!*
> SEOKHYUN: *Ah, sorry! Sorry! But are you sure? There are lots of parents who aren't cheating, you know.*

Jaeyoung hesitated to reply, but she supposed that Yeonhee had probably already blabbed about everything to him, so she resumed typing with a sigh.

> JAEYOUNG: *My parents are about ready to explode over it all. Oh, and I got a name... the woman my dad's cheating with, I mean.*

YEONHEE: *eh, then it's over. it's totally up to your mom now.*

SEOKHYUN: *How'd you find out?*

JAEYOUNG: *I overheard them fighting yesterday. They kept talking about "Seolju." That's how I found out.*

SEOKHYUN: *Did you search your dad's phone log?*

JAEYOUNG: *Yeah, that's the weird thing. He always takes off his smartpatch when he takes a shower. No password lock. So I searched it, but... no Seolju.*

YEONHEE: *well, there's no way he'd save the contact ID under her real name!*

JAEYOUNG: *But then there's nothing I can do, is there, if he used a fake name. Anyway, they were totally fighting over that person, Seolju.*

YEONHEE: *so what'd your mom do? i bet she like destroyed him!*

JAEYOUNG: *No, when my mom's upset, she just goes silent. That's even worse. But... actually, they're talking now sometimes. They're already past the angry silence.*

SEOKHYUN: *What were they talking about exactly?*

JAEYOUNG: *I couldn't catch it in detail. It seemed like this Seolju person asked my dad something really important. My dad said there was no way to avoid something, and my mom kept asking him over and over, "Is it true, is it true?" Then she cried. I didn't see her crying but her eyes were all puffy after. And my mom NEVER cries.*

SEOKHYUN: *Why don't you just ask them what's going on?*

JAEYOUNG: *No way! Besides, they'd never tell me.*

SEOKHYUN: *So what do you wanna do? Move out?*

JAEYOUNG: *Are you nuts? Why should I move out over this Seolju woman? I'd rather find her and tear all her hair out.*

SEOKHYUN: *Uh... do you want help?*

JAEYOUNG: *Huh? What?*

SEOKHYUN: *Finding Seolju.*

YEONHEE: *ah, right. you're good at that kinda thing.*

JAEYOUNG: *What does THAT mean?*

YEONHEE: *i TOLD you he's good at digging up info online. that's how he found out about the school trip thing.*

SEOKHYUN: *Oh, it won't be that easy. I've already searched the name Seolju, but nothing much came up. I need more keywords...*

[KANG SEOKHYUN IS TRYING TO SEND THE FILE. DO YOU ACCEPT?]

SEOKHYUN: *Go ahead and download it.*

JAEYOUNG: *What is it?*

SEOKHYUN: *Run it once on your machine, then upload and run it again on the apartment hub. Once it's running there, you'll get sent a copy of every sound picked up from every speaker and microphone in your house.*

YEONHEE: *WOW... so, we're, like, wire-tapping Jaeyoung's parents, right?*

SEOKHYUN: *Yeah, basically. That should give us some keywords for searching for Seolju. But it's totally up to Jaeyoung.*

JAEYOUNG: *Sure, let's give it a shot.*

SEOKHYUN: *Okay. If you have any problems let me know and I'll help out.*

YEONHEE: *kewwwwwwwwwl!!!! oh wait, is this a GOOD thing? anyway, we were talking about the school trip, and guess what: it got changed again!*

JAEYOUNG: *The date?*

YEONHEE: *yeah, but that's not all! it's not just our school and the gangwon school. Seokhyun looked it up and it turns out the gyeonggi, gyeongsang, jeolla, chungcheong, and jeju schools have all changed their trip schedules five times now. And the scheduled*

367

dates and times WERE ALL IDENTICAL!

JAEYOUNG: *Well, did they schedule the trips like that last year?*

SEOKHYUN: *Nope. I actually looked up the old records. Until last year, every school took its trip on a different day. This is the only time they've done this.*

JAEYOUNG: *Can't it just be a policy change or something? The government does stuff like that all the time.*

SEOKHYUN: *It's possible, but there was nothing about it on the news. So, well, I was about to hack into someone's account over at the Ministry of Education. If I can pull it off...*

YEONHEE: *can you, like, find out where our teachers live?*

Seokhyun: *Probably.*

YEONHEE: *OMG!... there's this teacher I TOTALLY like. if you pull it off, do me a favor and...*

SEOKHYUN: *Why? Are you planning on stalking him or something?*

YEONHEE: *aw SHIT. there's a 4 hour queue for login on DarkStone now. Well... now what should we do?*

JAEYOUNG: *Well, sorry but I'd better go. I gotta install that app Seokhyun gave me. If I don't... well, then I'm out of options.*

SEOKHYUN: *OK... I added installation instructions inside the archive so go ahead and try it out. Let me know if you have any problems.*

JAEYOUNG: *OK!*

Jaeyoung booted up her notebook and accessed her family's apartment server hub, which managed all the devices inside the house. Seokhyun's written instructions weren't hard to follow, and she already knew the apartment hub password—it had been set to her birthdate. Jaeyoung uploaded Seokhyun's program in the plugin folder, then rebooted the hub. After it rebooted, a stream of incoming data appeared on her notebook screen, routed through Seokhyun's program. Words she didn't even know began to accumulate and soon covered the whole screen. She did understand the lines *START RECEIVING VOICE FILE* and the *OK* command, though. Her conscience roiled within her like a handful of searing pebbles, but Jaeyoung ignored it, shoving the guilt deep down into her heart. After all, her parents were the ones who had decided to hide this problem from her, assuming it was something only adults could handle. Oh, her heart was pounding, but the main reason for this wasn't guilt: it was excitement at the prospect of uncovering why all this was *really* going on.

Jaeyoung opened her notebook and launched SeoulNet. Only a limited range of menus were accessible through her account. When she selected SEOUL INTEGRATED SCHOOL and pressed her fingertip on her smartpatch, the school's main site launched and a Friends window opened up. At the top of the window, a counter displayed the number of logins: 7,842 out of the 9,364 students in the school. The login count was increasing rapidly as class time approached. Jaeyoung glanced at the total number again, puzzled. Hadn't the total been 9,365 yesterday? It wasn't graduation season yet, so one of her schoolmates must have died in Seoul since yesterday. Could it have been a suicide? Or maybe a car accident? Either way, it was definitely going to be on the news tonight, along with plenty of worried speculation about the future. As usual, grown-ups would be unable to offer a single concrete solution, Jaeyoung concluded. Then she forced a smile as she greeted Yeonhee, who was waving at her from her Friends window.

Yeonhee's high-pitched, tinny voice squeaked through

the notebook speaker.

"Hey Jaeyoung... I'm a little freaked out!"

Jaeyoung looked at the smartpatch on the back of her left hand and noticed that she'd missed a bunch of calls from Yeonhee. "What?" she asked mechanically. "What is it?"

"Seokhyun's kinda starting to scare me."

Jaeyoung typed out the first thing that came to her mind: "Did he hack your password?"

"No! If he did *that*, he'd be dead meat. He just kept on searching for information about the school trip thing. He found out some more fishy stuff about it, and, well, the scariest thing was..."

Before Yeonhee could finish, the teacher's screen automatically took priority and jumped to the top of the window stack. Jaeyoung glanced at the clock in the corner of her screen.

Class wasn't supposed to begin for another five minutes, but the teacher—a woman with short-cropped hair— made a dreadfully serious face and started talking: "Today we have a few announcements to make. First of all—and perhaps some of you already know this—one of our students in Seoul has committed suicide."

Jaeyoung narrowed her eyes slowly and thought back to the last time the student population in her school had dropped this way. Back then, the school hadn't bothered with any special announcements. Nor had they done it the time before. It wasn't like this was the first student suicide, either. Jaeyoung wondered why they were making such a big fuss this time.

The teacher continued: "Look, everyone—suicide is *never* a solution. I'm sure you students feel the same as anyone else does: we don't want to live alone, and really we can't. That's why you have to reach out to your friends, parents, and teachers. Suicide is unilateral: all it does is push others away from you. It's not like a time-out: the world doesn't stop for you, and it doesn't solve anything. All that happens is that the people you leave behind have to live on, hanging onto a broken relationship forever."

Jaeyoung's suspicion continued to grow as the exceptions to past responses multiplied. Normally, when a student died, they'd immediately schedule some "special event" in response: when it was a suicide, they'd implement a special suicide prevention workshop; when it was an accident, they'd schedule a one-hour safety seminar instead. It was always all so predictable—obvious junk. Adults seemed to believe that showing kids videos like that would somehow magically ward off injury or something.

Still, this time was different. The teacher giving the anti-suicide talk seemed to be getting all emotional about it: her eyes were tearing up, and she was stumbling over her own words. That meant they hadn't edited the video. Could it be that the kid who'd died had been her own? Maybe the school figured that having the kid's mom give a live talk might be more persuasive or something?

If that was the case, well, it was just pathetic. There hadn't been a single new baby born in the last eleven years: Jaeyoung was fifteen, and the youngest kids on earth were eleven. Nobody had ever figured out why yet, but when biologists and geneticists had failed to turn up anything in their experiments? That was when adults had really gotten into cheating. It was also around then that adults had stopped using words like "cheating" and instead began talking about "forgiveness" and "experimentation."

Still, why suddenly broadcast a mother's tears during a seminar aimed at decreasing teen suicide? Jaeyoung struggled to produce some kind of credible explanation, but nothing made sense to her.

"Maybe some problem has you thinking it's the end of the world. I thought about that, too, when I was younger… All the time. But you might find a solution to the problem, or it might just fade away on its own if you wait a week, or six months, or a year. Maybe if you resist that drastic step and wait just a little longer, the world will open up again, and things will get better. You might find a doorway that was hidden from you, like in a maze. If any of you is thinking about suicide, please just wait for a week. If you're still thinking about it after a week, then please ask your parents and friends for help. If you can't do that, well then you can click on the Twenty-Four-Hour Counseling link here on the Seoul Integrated School menu, or you can call the phone number being transmitted to your smartwatch right now."

"We think that saving one life is worth far more than three or four hours of class. So after today's discussion, all your remaining classes are canceled. I want to ask you all to please think seriously about what I've said."

Jaeyoung couldn't believe her ears. A year ago, when three kids had carried out a suicide pact, the school hadn't canceled even a single class. Her jaw dropped a little in surprise, but just then, a new heading appeared in bright red at the top of her screen: IMPORTANT. Beneath it, the schedule of the school trip and other related information filled the display.

Jaeyoung sank deep into her chair, leaning back. She felt paralyzed, as if shrouded in mist and darkness. As she nervously bit down on her lower lip, her smartpatch began to vibrate.

YEONHEE: *WTF?!?!? what's up with them? why're they making such a fuss?*

JAEYOUNG: *I don't know. Maybe the kid who died was a special case?*

YEONHEE: *whuuuut!?!?!? then they really suck. now there's special people and unspecial ones?*

SEOKHYUN: *No, wait, that's not it. I just pulled up the news articles about him, and apparently he was just a regular kid. 17 years old. His parents are just regular office workers, and I couldn't find anything notable about his grandparents, either. They're not like, you know, rich or famous or connected or anything.*

JAEYOUNG: *I thought he might be the son of the teacher who gave the speech.*

SEOKHYUN: *Yeah, that's not the case either. We just don't know why they're doing this.*

YEONHEE: *SHIT!!!! didja check that up too? what, didja hack into that teacher's account?*

SEOKHYUN: *Affirmative.*

YEONHEE: *so that creepy story you told me yesterday is true, too?*

SEOKHYUN: *Well, that's how I found out about it...*

JAEYOUNG: *Are you talking about the scary thing you mentioned earlier? What is it?*

YEONHEE: *Seokhyun SHHHHHH! i'll tell her!!! ya know that the dates of school trips are all same, right? but IT'S NOT JUST IN KOREA!!*

JAEYOUNG: *Wha...??*

YEONHEE: *our departure time's 2pm on the 16th. well, like, EVERY SCHOOL IN THE WORLD is leaving at that time. *shudder**

JAEYOUNG: *What, EVERY kid in the world, in EVERY country, is leaving on their school trip at 2pm on the 16th? Seriously?*

SEOKHYUN: *No, no, that's not it. What she really means it that they're all leaving at the EXACT SAME TIME. Like, for example, all the kids in Thailand are*

373

booked on a flight at noon. In Switzerland, it's at 6:00 am. But the thing is, they're all scheduled for different destinations. Seoul I.S. is the ONLY school headed for Hawaii.

JAEYOUNG: *What does all this mean?*

SEOKHYUN: *I don't know. Maybe they're preparing for some kind of event? There's a limit to how much information I could get using the regular-clearance teacher's password I scored. But it's clear that whatever they're calling "the school trip" this year is nothing like school trips in past years.*

YEONHEE: *some kinda event...? yeah, that makes sense. you mean like a surprise performance? some kinda awesome show for the last kids in the world?!?*

With the image of the tearful, preachy woman still clear in her mind, Jaeyoung found Yeonhee's theory cluelessly optimistic. Then again, she herself didn't really know what to think.

The school trip was the only extracurricular event that was mandatory for all students in all grades. Since kids had stopped being born, it had become natural to just attend school online: it reduced the risk of random accidents and mishaps as much as possible. To make up the difference, schools had created a new tradition: the annual school trip. After all, kids in the same class online might live quite far apart from one another, and if it wasn't for the annual trips, they might never meet. That's what school trips were: they gave kids a chance to meet their friends. Jaeyoung and Yeonhee happened to live relatively close to one another, so they were planning to meet up and leave together for the school trip on the 16th.

Jaeyoung shook her head and rubbed her eyes. She didn't care if there was going to be some huge festival or something. Yeonhee and Seokhyun were having fun playing detective with their conspiracy theory, but in the end it seemed like nothing but a kiddie game. Jaeyoung, on the other hand, had a grownup problem to solve.

> [SENDING VOICE FILE 001.]
> JAEYOUNG: *Listen to this, both of you.*
> YEONHEE: *what is it?*
> SEOKHYUN: *I guess it must be some voice clips of your parents?*
> JAEYOUNG: *Yes.*
> YEONHEE: *did ya figure out who your dad was cheating with? you said her name was Seolju, right?*
> JAEYOUNG: *Actually... I'm not sure. But, um, things might be way more serious than I thought. Look... can we just listen to this together?*
> SEOKHYUN: *Ok. Let's listen first and then we can talk about it.*

They received the file and Jaeyoung tapped the PLAY button with one finger. She could never, ever go back from this, from listening in on her parents' conversation. She was determined to figure out who Seolju was and deal with whatever harm this woman had inflicted on her family. As usual, adults were being too stupid to deal with their own messes.

Jaeyoung listened intently, so she wouldn't miss a single word:

> FEMALE VOICE: *Are you saying it's not finished yet? We can't live like this forever.*
> MALE VOICE: *Look, I'm doing my best! (pause) Okay, I'm sorry for shouting. The thing is, I can accelerate the process if I take it all on by myself. I mean, at first the problem was way over our heads... and you know,*

it took way too long to figure out what Seolju really wanted with any certainty—

FEMALE VOICE: *I know that. But now I'm involved, too. And yet...*

MALE VOICE: *Hey, are you sure Jaeyoung hasn't caught wind of this? She must never know.*

FEMALE VOICE: *Actually, I'm a little worried about that. She picks up on stuff like this, more than most kids. She's sensitive.*

MALE VOICE: *Well, you just need to do everything you can to keep it from her. Stay at work till late and say you had a bunch of overtime to do or something like that. You know, I want to see her, too, but we're her parents, and we need to...*

FEMALE VOICE: *Look, I know, okay? You're not the only parent here! In fact, I love her more than you do! Have you forgotten what you did three years ago? Even now, just thinking about it makes my hands start to tremble...*

MALE VOICE: *I've never once said that what I did was good. It was a mistake! (pause) Let's not do this. Nothing's more important now than Jaeyoung and this thing with Seolju.*

FEMALE VOICE: *I know. I already said I know that... Seolju's really just destroyed everything in an instant. (sigh)*

MALE VOICE: *Yeah, it's as if everything's become pointless. A scientist should be able to get over that kind of shock... but you know that, right? Remember how I used to laugh at people who tried to hand wave a quick solution to the theoretical problems with Planck energy and quantum mechanics? They're not scientists. They have no idea what science even is.*

FEMALE VOICE: *Ah, you're back on that again? I'm over all that. In the end, our only recourse is con-*

sequentialism. But there's nothing wrong with you maintaining a scientific attitude—that, at least, I can say for sure.

MALE VOICE: *Yeah, that's what I mean! So, results aside, I really didn't do anything wrong?*

FEMALE VOICE: *I'm talking about a different kind of pointlessness. Do you remember, back when we were dating, and you said science is a creative field? We thought we could advance humanity by uncovering the secrets and truth of the universe? But... what are we doing now? We've just ended up taking apart everything that we built up.*

MALE VOICE: *Well, you could put it that way, but... I prefer to think about it as...*

FEMALE VOICE: *Oh, yeah, now you're gonna tell me how you're such a big realist, right? Tell me, who was it that was just on the verge of crying a minute ago, blubbering about how all his beliefs have fallen apart? That's what's wrong with you. When someone else screws around, it's adultery, but when you do it, it's romance!*

MALE VOICE: *No! All I'm trying to say is we don't have to deny the value of all the work we've done, even if the problem we're dealing with is unsolvable! Denigrating the value of meaningful work just because you feel hopeless? That's the stupidest thing in the world to do! It doesn't matter what kind of world we live in, or how small it is...*

FEMALE VOICE: *Oh, here we go again! Hiding behind fancy words and bragging... it's sick! (sigh) But I guess I feel a little bit better.*

MALE VOICE: *Okay, so, has all the data been verified? Seolju's set the absolutely final deadline.*

FEMALE VOICE: *To as fine a degree as possible, yeah. Enough to satisfy Seolju, anyway.*

MALE VOICE: Satisfy... *does it even make sense to use that word with Seolju? Does Seolju even feel emotions remotely like ours? Do we even have any reason to trust what Seolju says?*
FEMALE VOICE: *Hey, there's no point in thinking like that. We don't have time for it, either. I don't know what kind of emotions Seolju feels, but it's clear that we share the same bottom line. Seolju is definitely concerned about our young people.*
MALE VOICE: *Yeah, I know. That's why we decided to risk everything in the first place. The only thing we have left, right now, is hope... hope that things go according to plan.*
FEMALE VOICE: *But can this stay secret till then? There's already been a few leaks, and rumors are flying around about all kinds of plans. How much of that is true?*
MALE VOICE: *Well... but we can't just back off now, can we? We'll just have to stop them by force if necessary.*

As soon as Jaeyoung heard these last words, the chatscreen made an alarming sound. Jaeyoung started skimming her friends' messages, still puzzled at what her parents had been talking about:

YEONHEE: *OMG!!!!! i'm like TOTALLY in shock. so did your dad cheat on your mom twice?*
SEOKHYUN: *Hey, we don't know that for sure...*
YEONHEE: *whuuuuut? jaeyoung's mom got angry and then she said, "did you forget what happened 3 years ago?"*
SEOKHYUN: *Yeah, I know. Okay, let's say he did cheat, but... what I'm saying is, I'm not sure that means he cheated on her TWICE.*
JAEYOUNG: *Seokhyun, that conversation sounds*

weird to you, too, right?

SEOKHYUN: *Yeah.*

YEONHEE: *what? are you saying this isn't about cheating? so then who's this seolju chick?*

SEOKHYUN: *Let's see... I've run a text-to-speech app on the audio, so I can quote the part I mean. It's this line: "Enough that Seolju ought to be satisfied with it." And they also keep talking about how they can't be sure they can trust what Seolju says.*

YEONHEE: *and they said the most important thing is about seolju and jaeyoung. what does jaeyoung have to do with any of this? are they talking about custody? don't most couples who're getting a divorce just ship their kids straight to boarding school and say it's for their own good?*

SEOKHYUN: *Yeah, maybe... or maybe this person Seolju is blackmailing your dad, Jaeyoung? And, like, using you against him?*

JAEYOUNG: *Yeah, that's kind of what I was thinking. The more I listened, the more it seemed like that.*

YEONHEE: *a threat? over what?*

SEOKHYUN: *Jaeyoung's dad asked whether the data is trustworthy, right? And your mom said, "As trustworthy as possible, to the best of our ability." They're both scientists... Maybe it's some kind of data? Could Seolju be pumping them for highly secure information?*

YEONHEE: *WOW!!!!! it's like totally out of a movie or something!*

SEOKHYUN: *Seriously? THAT'S what you say in a situation like this?*

YEONHEE: *oh, jaeyoung, i'm... i'm REALLY sorry.*

JAEYOUNG: *No, it's fine. Now at least things are starting to make sense. I don't know, maybe my dad got trapped by some kind of blackmailer while he was trying to cheat on my mom? Anyway it seems like he has no choice but to pass on this valuable data. And*

379

somehow my mom's in on it, too.
YEONHEE: *jaeyoung's so LUCKY.*
SEOKHYUN: *What do you mean?*
YEONHEE: *it's like totally obvious how much they LOVE her and WORRY about her!*
SEOKHYUN: *That's... true.*
YEONHEE: *they're like 100x better than my mom. she's just WASTED every day. and it's like less than a year since she got out of rehab.*
SEOKHYUN: *Well, when you put it that way, I... eh, never mind. Jaeyoung, does any of this make sense to you?*
JAEYOUNG: *I don't know how I feel. It's nothing like what I'd imagined... and I can't understand how they're acting... or what I have to do... and I guess I need to think about it. Thanks, both of you, for helping me out.*
YEONHEE: *oh, shut up! there's gonna be an awesome festival at the school trip. let this go and just have fun. hey seokhyun, let's go log into DarkStone.*
SEOKHYUN: *Mmmm, I need to go do some more research.*
YEONHEE: *you should chill out. isn't all this settled now?*
SEOKHYUN: *Not for me... I think we're finally getting at the heart of the matter. We still don't know who Seolju is, and there's some kind of spy blackmailing people... Anyway, I picked up some keywords, like Planck energy and quantum mechanics, so I'm going to dig around some more using those. If I turn anything up, I'll let you know.*
JAEYOUNG: *OK, thanks.*

Before her friends noticed anything fishy, Jaeyoung hurriedly said goodbye to them and logged out. She was relieved to learn that she'd jumped to the wrong conclusion about her parents' fighting. Sure, they might still end up divorced, and she might get dragged off to some dorm room, but for now, she had some time.

It was weird, though, how she and Seolju had gotten mentioned in the same breath. Had Seolju really threatened her to get to them? What had she threatened: abduction? A kidnapping? Could someone have been following her around lately? She racked her brain, thinking over her last few outings, but nothing unusual came to mind.

Even though she despised how inflexible and unpredictable they were, Jaeyoung still didn't want to be a burden to her parents. It upset her to discover that they'd said nothing to her about this situation—and in fact had kept her in the dark—when she occupied such a central role. Still, this other, weird feeling, back in the corner of her mind, kept nagging at her. She found herself *sympathizing* with them. After all, her father and mother had risked screwing up their important work to protect her.

Honestly, she could almost see *why* they'd done what they'd done... not that understanding did much to alleviate her frustration and rage.

When the morning of the school trip arrived, Jaeyoung's father drove her and her mom over to Yeonhee's. After a quick hello to Yeonhee's mom, Younghee joined Jaeyoung in the backseat. As her father drove to the entrance of the Incheon passenger terminal, the knot in Jaeyoung's heart tightened and tightened. She glanced over at Yeonhee, who was fidgeting with her smart-patch device. Normally, in a situation like this, Yeonhee would've blabbered her way through a whole series of topics, jumping from one thing to the next and not caring in the slightest whether grown-ups overheard her. Today, however, she just maximized her smartpatch screen and focused on some game. Jaeyoung shifted her gaze onto her parents, peering over their seats at their heads and shoulders.

She'd started feeling that knot of anxiety the night before. Her parents had taken the previous day off work. They'd all gone downtown, and her parents had bought her the shoes she'd wanted and a brand new smartwatch. Then they'd eaten at an expensive restaurant, the fancy kind that they usually wouldn't have gone to. Jaeyoung had acted all excited, but she'd had to fight hard not to blurt out all the questions that'd been running through her mind. This had been her family's first big outing since she'd been in elementary school, and Jaeyoung had spent most of it on the edge of her seat.

But nothing had happened, and now it was the next day. By the time her dad stopped the car in the parking lot and switched from autopilot to power saver mode, Jaeyoung had pretty much reached the limits of her patience. Thinking about how she wouldn't be seeing them for the next four days, she choked up with anxiety: what would happen in her absence, without her knowing? Jaeyoung realized that even though she thought of herself as mature, she'd in fact been really childish. In the beginning, she'd been all confident, but now, approaching the heart of the matter, she just wanted to shut her eyes and look away.

As she realized this, she suddenly blurted out, "Dad... who's Seolju?"

Jaeyoung's dad and mom froze, as if time had stopped. Yeonhee was shocked. The game completely forgotten, her hand rose from her smartpatch.

It was Jaeyoung's mother who turned her head halfway around and looked back at her. "Where did you hear that name?"

Jaeyoung squinted and replied, "You don't need to know. Who's Seolju? Please answer me."

Without looking away from the bare parking lot wall, her father said, "You don't need to know."

It was a typical adult response, even more evasive than Jaeyoung had expected from him.

"What? How can you say I don't need to know, when this person is affecting our family? Am I not your daughter? What's she trying to get out of you? Is all of this because this Seolju person has threatened to *hurt* me? Why are you just obeying this person's every command?"

Her parents quickly exchanged a look, and her father rubbed his left eye. Finally, he said, "Look, I promise you, I'll tell you everything when you get back from the school trip. Everything's going to be sorted out by then. Nothing's going to happen to you. That's the truth."

Jaeyoung's mother interrupted him. "And I promise you that, too. But you must do whatever the teachers tell you, and don't do anything on your own."

Jaeyoung stared at her mom for a while before she sighed and finally nodded in agreement. It wasn't like her mom had never broken a promise before, but when she had, she'd always been willing to admit it, and had tried to make it up to Jaeyoung in some way. That, at least, had always been true.

"Okay, then I guess we'll go now."

Yeonhee, who was busy trying to read all three of their faces, picked up her bag and got out of the car, and Jaeyoung did the same. Her mother rolled down the window and repeated her father's promise before saying, "Please, just do what the teachers tell you to do."

"Yeah, yeah, I said I will. Quit nagging…"

Jaeyoung and Yeonhee left the parking lot quickly. When the car was out of sight, it was Yeonhee, not Jaeyoung, who looked back, and she said, "Is your mom crying?"

"Nah, I'm sure you're just seeing things. Why would she cry after nagging me like that?"

"Huh... *maybe*. But y'know, my mom was crying, too, on
the way out of the house today."

It took a moment for Jaeyoung to process this. Then
she stopped so suddenly that Yeonhee slammed into
her back.

"Wait, your mom cried, too?"

Just then, the two girls' smartpatches buzzed simultaneously. Seokhyun was trying to make a group call.
Jaeyoung and Yeonhee slipped their earphones into
place and took the call.

Yeonhee spoke first. "What's up? This is, like, the first time
we've ever heard one another's voices, right?"

Seokhyun ignored Yeonhee's chitchat and got right down
to business: "I've figured it all out. *Everything*. Wait, no,
maybe it's just gotten more complicated. Anyway, it was
too much to fit into a text message, so I'm just calling
instead. Where are you guys now? Are you at Incheon
Port yet?"

Without waiting for an answer, he yelped quickly, "Just
wait! Don't go there yet. Instead, go to the place
marked on the map I'm sending you, before it's too
late! Hurry up!"

Not to be outdone by Seokhyun, Yeonhee raised her
voice too: "Do you expect us to go there without any
explanation?"

"Look, I'll explain while you're on the way, but get going!
You're not gonna believe me unless you see this for
yourselves."

"Okay," said Jaeyoung. "We've got the map and we're on the
way now. It's in the opposite direction from where all the
teachers are. Now just tell us what this new complica-
tion is all about!"

"Right, so, first, the school trip. Remember how students
from all over the world are leaving at the same time?
Sorry, Yeonhee, but it's not for a festival. That theory

makes no sense, it's just too completely bizarre..."

Seokhyun's voice was getting wilder and his speech was accelerating, so Jaeyoung interrupted him: "Cool down, okay? Just breathe and tell us slowly what's going on. Relax, we're listening to you."

"Well, this year's school trip is weird, and I don't just meant the stuff about the date changes. There's the chaperones. They booked more of them this year, too. Which is pretty weird when you consider that this year there's fewer students, not more. Did you read your school's notice carefully? Seoul I.S. has booked forty more chaperones than last year."

Yeonhee was clearly bored. She said, "So, they hired more subs."

"No, to work as a substitute teacher, you need to join the Teacher's Association. The chaperones they added aren't members. And this is happening in all six schools. *None* of the chaperones they've booked for the school trip are even teachers."

"I think maybe you're right," said Jaeyoung. "I saw them from far away and there weren't that many last year. And if they *were* really teachers, they'd have been helping sort us by class, but instead they were just standing around in the back, spaced apart a little from one another."

"Sure, that *is* weird," replied Yeonhee. "But it's not like any of this is totally impossible to explain, is it? Remember that day when class got canceled? The big suicide awareness seminar and all that? Maybe the grownups have finally woken up and realized we matter, too? It's a bit late, though..."

"But you know," said Seokhyun, "this school trip wasn't so suspicious at first. I started researching it out of habit, just for fun. But then I confirmed that stuff that you guys were telling me about, and I got this really weird idea when Yeonhee said there might be a festival. I wondered whether this was even going to be a real school trip at all. That really got to me. Why should *all* the schools in the world have booked different destinations, but *identical* departure times—even if it meant some schools had to book their departures for some weird time like midnight? So I checked into the transportation bookings. Seoul I.S. is supposed to be taking a two-thousand ton passenger ship from Incheon Port. You remember how the ship is named the *Soonhang*? Well, I'm supposed to board the *Siwon* at the port in Tonghae."

Jaeyoung and Yeonhee were getting close to the spot marked on Seokhyun's map. Jaeyoung had expected some kind of building or facility there, but in fact there was nothing. They were at some deserted spot on the shore, while everyone else seemed to be back at the passenger terminal.

"I thought the ship might be a lead, so I looked into that. But..." His voice trailed off.

Yeonhee prompted him, "But...?"

"There was nothing!"

"You mean there was nothing weird about the passenger ship?"

"No, I mean there was nothing in the records about any of those ships. Nothing! No *Soonhang*, no *Siwon*... *none* of the ships were there."

Jaeyoung couldn't see what all the fuss was about. "Well, don't big ships only come into the port when they've got some reason to be there?"

"No, I don't mean they weren't at the port; I mean there's no record of those ships' existence! They're not real. Sure, I found a couple of ships with similar names, but they were oil tankers and fishing boats."

"You probably just made a mistake," Yeonhee said. "I mean, that, like, makes *no* sense. How can we get on a ship that's never existed...?"

But then Yeonhee fell silent and slowly pointed out to the sea. Jaeyoung looked up and found herself just as speechless. She blinked hard and opened her eyes again.

"It should be becoming visible right about now," Seokhyun said.

But Jaeyoung and Yeonhee barely heard him. Standing on the shore with the waves crashing against the rocks, they saw it, about a hundred meters from the shore. At first, it seemed as though the small waves were just collapsing into the sea. Then the surface of the sea went smooth, and the smooth patch broadened as the seawater started to recede away from it in all directions as if something invisible were pushing down into it. Above the water, the air shimmered as if waves of heat were rising through it from below. What was happening right there in front of Jaeyoung and Yeonhee's eyes made no sense, but soon the depression in the ocean deepened and the haze rising from it resolved into flat surfaces, lines, and curves, forming a long cylindrical indentation in the water.

Yeonhee sat down in shock, her legs wobbly. Jaeyoung grabbed onto a railing and held tight with both hands, watching as a two-thousand ton passenger ship materialized out of thin air right there in the sea before her in violation of all natural law and process.

Once it was fully formed, the ship looked utterly real and as concrete as any other ship. It slowly began to move, cutting through the water and leaving a wake as it went.

Between sobs, Yeonhee said, "Wha... What is this? Seokhyun, are you screwing around with us? This is, like, some kind of 3D video or something, right?"

From his tone, it was clear Seokhyun completely understood her reaction: "There's no way I could play a trick like that on you. The only thing I did was come out to the port early because I thought it was weird that the ships didn't exist. That's all. What you saw isn't a video. I couldn't believe my eyes, so I threw a stone at the *Siwon* when it stopped. It even made a clanking sound when it hit. I don't know whether it's really a ship or what it is, but that's not just some video. You guys saw it, too, so now I know I'm not crazy."

"So the ship for the Gangwon school was like this, too?" Jaeyoung said. Now her heart was racing, and she didn't know how to stop it. "Then... all of the ships and airplanes being used for all of the school trips all over the world are like this?"

"Well, I think so. Going by how they synchronized the date like that... I think it was all planned ahead."

Yeonhee looked up at Jaeyoung. "Is this even possible? I don't know much about science, but, like... this doesn't make *any* sense at all!"

Jaeyoung looked back over toward the ship, which was placidly coasting through the ocean. It was heading towards the terminal where all the students were waiting.

"But we can't deny what we saw," she said. "Three of us saw it with our own eyes and from different spots. That must mean it's real."

"Ugh, now I don't know what's what! It's, like, freaking me out. What kind of school trip is this?"

Jaeyoung reached down and helped Yeonhee to her feet. "Let's follow the ship. We need to go where the teachers and kids are so I can try to get some kind of explanation for all this."

"Is that a good idea? What if they tell us we need to, like, get *on* that thing? Did you see the name on the side of the ship? It said *Soonhang*!"

Jaeyoung went silent and dragged her friend by force. For her part, Yeonhee seemed to give in and just followed. Jaeyoung clenched her teeth and walked along, trying not to look out to sea, but Yeonhee kept looking back and shuddering. Jaeyoung guessed that other ships must be materializing, too, the way the *Siwon* had in Tonghae.

Seokhyun let out a deep sigh and started talking again. Jaeyoung fastened her loose ear set and listened to him.

"There's *one* more thing..."

"There's *more*?!?" Yeonhee shouted. "Weirder than this? Just, like... don't tell us! I'm really *scared*! I'm not even kidding!"

Jaeyoung grabbed Yeonhee's hand and squeezed it tightly, then said, "It's okay. If we know the truth, we'll be ok. Until then, we *can't* just cover our ears. Hey Seokhyun, hurry up and tell us. Is it more weird stuff about the ships?"

"It's about Seolju. I found out more."

As she wiped a tear from her cheek, Yeonhee said, "You *found* out who Seolju is?"

Seokhyun hesitated before saying, "Uh, I can't say that... I guess it's better to go back to the beginning. At first, I couldn't find anything out by searching for the name "Seolju." There wasn't a single person with that name among Jaeyoung's parents' coworkers or associates. So I gave up on that lead. I was fresh out of clues. But after I learned that the ships the schools had booked didn't exist, I started thinking a little differently about it. If the school trip didn't exist, and the ships didn't exist... what about Seolju? Is she really just a normal person?"

"Of course not," Yeonhee blurted out. "She's special: she's a criminal!"

"Well if it's that simple, then what's the point, right? You know, I know what you guys think about 'conspiracy theories.' It's fine, you don't need to pretend anymore. I know you think I'm a conspiracy theory nut. But you know what's fun about conspiracy theories, Yeonhee?"

"It, like, makes you think about stuff you've never thought about before?"

"Nope. It's that they're all about uncovering *secrets*. So I decided to start digging in a different direction."

"Which direction?"

"Well, I started with a few basic assumptions. That Seolju isn't a real name. That Seolju isn't a normal person. So far, that makes sense, right?"

"Yes," Jaeyoung said.

"Looking again at what your parents said to each other, I thought Seolju must have something to do with science. They used words like Planck energy and quantum mechanics… but searching for Seolju with those keywords didn't turn up anything either. Now, if this was a secret… maybe those terms were blocked on all the search engines *on purpose*? That was as far as I got."

"Is that possible?" asked Jaeyoung.

"Yeah, it's not really that hard. You can build a secret website and block search engines from listing it in their results. We're used to search engines and links where everything's freely available, but actually there are websites that are carefully filtered out. When I realized that, I got another hunch and started searching like crazy. Regular search engines wouldn't work, so I had to hunt down everything manually. It was just dumb luck that I decided to focus on science-related pages."

Yeonhee and Jaeyoung had nearly arrived at the gathering point. The other students were all neatly lined up now with their classmates, and here and there teachers were calling out names and checking student numbers.

Some of the teachers standing at the back of the crowd of students seemed different, though. They looked tough, and their jaws were all clamped shut. Each stood about the same distance apart from the others, and they all had the vigilant look of people who were watching for

something to happen. One of them stared sharply at
Jaeyoung and Yeonhee, nodding at them to go and join
their classmates.

Jaeyoung lowered her voice and asked Seokhyun, "You
found something, didn't you?"

"Everything I found was like your parents' conversation,
all completely vague. But yeah, I uncovered a couple
of things. First, Seolju can be used as a person's name,
but it's also the name of some kind of science project.
Not just in Korea, either: scientists overseas have been
studying the same thing. They all call it different names,
though. Seolju means 'The Snow Master.' I don't know
what they call it in other languages, except in English,
where they call it 'The Snowmaker'."

Yeonhee asked him, "Wait, you mean *snow*, like, the stuff
that falls out of the sky?"

"That's right. It seems like they found some weird phenomenon in snow crystals maybe about a decade ago, so they
called the research project 'Seolju.' But you know what's
really bizarre? It's as if someone deleted every mention
of this 'Seolju' phenomenon in any publicly accessible
document online. It's like every mention of the discovery was deleted on purpose. The little bit I did manage
to find didn't amount to much. I arranged the keywords
by frequency. Listen to this. The most commonly mentioned key phrases were 'simulation universe hypothesis,' followed by 'deadline' and 'purpose'. Then came
'entropy' and 'information capacity'…"

Jaeyoung interrupted Seokhyun there: "Did you just say
'simulation universe'?"

"Yeah. That keyword came up more than any other."

After that, Seokhyun went silent. Jaeyoung's lips moved,
but she didn't say a word.

Yeonhee seemed to be struggling to read Jaeyoung's expression; finally, she blurted out, "Why? What's that?"

391

Jaeyoung turned her head slowly and looked over at the passenger ships that sat imposingly before the assembled crowd of students.

Then she explained: "The simulation universe hypothesis is... well, it's a theory that says we're not actually living in a universe, we're just living in a computer program that *simulates* a universe. I mean, like a program designed by, uh, some creatures more highly developed than us. My dad *hates* the people who believe in that theory. He always says, *Theories that aren't supported by evidence aren't science.*"

"A program... you mean... this world is..."

Seokhyun finished Yeonhee's sentence. "She means our world is like the world in that DarkStone game we've been playing. For us, from the inside, it looks totally real, but..."

At that moment, the materialization of the ship began making sense to Jaeyoung. She knew how Yeonhee must feel—desperate to insist that the world was real, that the ground under their feet, her clothes, her own body were *all* solid and real. But the materialization of that ship told a different story.

Just then, one of the chaperones began talking into a megaphone: "Okay, we're going to start boarding now, beginning with first-year students in class number one. Please don't run; just board in an orderly fashion."

The approximately nine thousand and three hundred students, all standing in ranks sorted by grade and class number, began to slowly drift toward the boarding platform. Jaeyoung and Yeonhee watched quietly as the students in the front stepped on. The platform looked sturdy, much like it had before; it didn't suddenly break, and nobody fell into the ocean or anything.

Seokhyun was still connected to their voice chat. "What're you going to do?" he asked. "Has your school started boarding?"

Jaeyoung bit her lower lip. The other students were boarding smoothly, duly following all instructions. She hung up on Seokhyun and tried to call her dad. The phone rang and rang, more than twenty times in a row, but there was no answer. She flicked at the back of her left hand and sent him a message using her smartpatch.

> JAEYOUNG: *Dad! Answer your phone right now!*
> JAEYOUNG: *Answer it! Answer your phone!*

But he still didn't pick up. When a green icon appeared beside her messages, marking them as having been read by the recipient, Jaeyoung knew for sure that he was ignoring her call on purpose.

> JAEYOUNG: *Dad, please... OK, just please send me a message. Now... Please!*

There was nothing Jaeyoung could do but hang up. Every sound seemed to disappear, as if a heavy black curtain had come down and muffled everything. Lots of kids were laughing and chatting, but Jaeyoung didn't hear any of this. She felt as if time had stopped. Even the sound of the waves seemed to have suddenly frozen in midair.

> DAD: *Are you on the ship?*

Ignoring her thumping heart, Jaeyoung typed in her response:

> JAEYOUNG: *What's Seolju?*

The red circle beside the message turned green as soon as Jaeyoung sent it.

DAD: *Are you on the ship?*

JAEYOUNG: *It's not our turn to board yet. What's Seolju? Answer me now! Are we living in a simulated reality? And if so, what's Seolju?!*

DAD: *Where did you hear about that? Who told you? Do other kids know about it, too?*

JAEYOUNG: *Does it matter?*

DAD: *Yes, it matters. It's the most important thing in the world! Look, you need to get on the ship no matter what. No matter what happens.*

JAEYOUNG: *Well, I won't board the ship if you don't answer me.*

DAD: *You can't do that.*

DAD: *Jaeyoung, look, let's do it this way. I promise I'll tell you everything once you're on board. You'll understand everything when you hear the story. If you don't want to listen to me, think of it as your mom's promise. She'll tell you the same thing as me. Just please get on the ship first.*

Jaeyoung didn't tell him about how the Soonhang had appeared from nowhere. Her dad probably knew about all kinds of things including that. Even so, he was still insisting that she board the ship. So now it was a question of trust. Should she just trust that parents never make their kids do anything dangerous? Even though they were her parents—with all the typical flaws of adults— should she really just do whatever they told her, without even demanding an explanation? She replied:

JAEYOUNG: *Ok.*

JAEYOUNG: *But you'd better keep your promise.*

She then closed the messenger window and reconnected to the group call with her friends. Meanwhile the first-year kids had finished boarding, as had half of the second-year kids.

Once again, Seokhyun asked: "Have you made up your mind? Are you going to get on the ship?"

Jaeyoung and Yeonhee looked at each other. Yeonhee's pupils were dilated in terror. Jaeyoung was torn. People loved to say that grown-ups cared about kids' lives, but Jaeyoung could think of plenty of cases where that hadn't been true at all. A long time ago, when a ship had sunk and a bunch of kids had drowned, the adults involved had saved their own lives and tried to cover up the truth. And though people always said mental illness was to blame, all the same it wasn't unusual to hear of mothers jumping from rooftops with their kids in their arms. Good and evil, love and hate: they were so intertwined in the hearts of grown-ups that it was impossible to see which element was dominant.

But Jaeyoung knew she had to make a choice. She had to go one way or the other. There was no middle option.

"Yeah, I'm going on board," she finally replied.

"Me too, I'm getting on," Yeonhee replied right away.

There was no reaction from Seokhyun as Jaeyoung and Yeonhee joined their class, which was standing around cluelessly at the front of their group. These kids were their classmates online, but most of them were just meeting in person for the first time. Jaeyoung and Yeonhee crossed the border between land and sea along with their unfamiliar classmates, crossing a platform so vivid and solid and even a bit creaky that nobody could ever have suspected it was anything but real.

Instead of going to her assigned cabin, Jaeyoung moved to the back of the *Soonhang*, where there were fewer kids.

"Hey Seokhyun, are you onboard, too? Has the ship departed?" It was only then that Jaeyoung realized he'd been disconnected. According to the call record on her

395

smartpatch, he'd actually dropped out of the three-way call seventeen minutes earlier. As soon as Yeonhee tapped on the back of her hand, Jaeyoung's smartpatch vibrated.

YEONHEE: *hey Seokhyun, has the ship departed?*
JAEYOUNG: *Did you not get onboard?*
SEOKHYUN: *Shit, all those violent teachers. If my legs worked, I would've shoved them all into the ocean.*
YEONHEE: *did they hit you?*
SEOKHYUN: *No, no. Actually, I just decided not to get on the ship, and to try get away, but then they just picked me up by force and carried me onboard. They even bent the wheels on my chair a little. What a pain in the ass...*
JAEYOUNG: *Wait, you're, um... in a wheelchair?*
SEOKHYUN: *Eh, my brain and my fingers work way better than yours, so don't bother pitying me.*
JAEYOUNG: *Did you try not to board because of what we saw before?*
SEOKHYUN: *Of course! How could I get onboard after seeing that? What a joke. Anyway, my parents aren't like yours: they didn't tell me what to do. So I wanted to make up my mind on my own, however I liked. And I wanted to investigate this trip more by staying behind. I mean, if something happened during the trip, well, one of us could see what the others couldn't, right? But now I'm onboard, just like you guys.*
JAEYOUNG: *Well, maybe that's better. My dad told me he'd tell me everything once we were onboard. I mean everything about Seolju. I'm going to ask him right after I drop my bag in my cabin. I'll let you know what he says right away.*
SEOKHYUN: *Maybe... but I doubt he'll tell you everything.*

Just then the *Soonhang*'s horn blared, like a big red stamp
notarizing an irreversible decision. Jaeyoung had
always imagined ships' horns as being deep and thick,
but the sound that vibrated through her whole body
and roared in her ears was high and reedy. It somehow
created an all-pervasive, ominous mood. Immediately
after the blast from the horn faded away, another sound,
one unfamiliar to Jaeyoung, followed.

"What's *that*?" asked Yeonhee.

The sound wasn't coming from the ship, but rather from
over by the dock they'd just left. Kids on the deck had
gathered at the back of the ship to see what was
going on.

Jaeyoung realized that some of the teachers back on the
dock had stayed behind. A fleet of shiny black cars
pulled up beyond them, and people began pouring
out. One of the teachers shouted at them, and one of
the people from the cars shouted back at him. The two
began yelling at each other, and things turned ugly
quickly right there on the dock. Though the words they
exchanged weren't audible to the kids, it looked as if the
people in the cars had just missed their chance to board
the ship.

The kids on the ship had begun laughing and chatting
amongst themselves. Some leaned over the railing, still
trying to figure out what was happening on the dock.

Just then, a sharp blast tore through the air. Someone
screamed.

A voice cried, "Wasn't that a gunshot?" Just then, one of
the teachers on the dock collapsed to the ground. The
man who'd shot the teacher waved toward the ship as it
drifted away. He was shouting something threatening,
but his words couldn't be heard in the distance.

Then one student pointed to the sky and said, "Hey, isn't
that following our ship?" The kids all looked up.

"What... what's that?"

"It's a helicopter. It's massive!"

"Is that okay? It's coming down toward us. Isn't that dangerous?"

"It looks like it's gonna land! Is there a landing deck on this ship?"

"Anyone got a telescope?"

"Maybe they're shooting a movie? Where... Hey, the people on the helicopter have guns. Is this real? Does anyone here know anything about guns?"

Two medium-sized helicopters had appeared out of no-where and were hovering right above the ship. One of them was slowly coming down towards the middle of the deck. Some of the chaperones who'd gone into one of the cabins came running out carrying a long black bag.

The ship's loudspeakers blared an announcement: "All students, please go to your assigned cabins now! Go in and don't come out again until we tell you to!"

But the roaring of the helicopter drowned out the words. Although the message was repeated over and over, only a few kids actually did what they were told. To the contrary, the kids who were already in their cabins started coming out to see what was happening.

A message popped up on the back of Jaeyoung and Yeon-hee's hands.

> SEOKHYUN: *Hey, it's all crazy here now. A military vessel has blocked our ship, even though it's all just civilians on board.*
> SEOKHYUN: *Is that happening there, too?*

Without replying, Jaeyoung made her way toward the fourth-floor deck where the helicopter was landing. Yeonhee followed her along with a few other students. When they turned the corner on the third floor that led to the fourth, a man appeared and blocked their way.

"Didn't you hear the announcement? Quick, go back downstairs. Hurry up!"

Though there were students who were just as big as the man, no one dared to talk back because of the black rifle that was slung over his shoulder. The kids stepped back a little, and that was when Jaeyoung saw the name tag on the man's chest and the yellow band around his left arm. He was one of their chaperones.

A loud conversation echoed down from the fourth floor. The kids listened silently, as did the chaperone, his gun now in his hand.

"Who do you think you are, trying to interfere with this school trip?"

"We're here to establish a safe zone. We've got a VVIP on the helicopter up there. Drop your guns and clear out of this landing spot."

"Only students are allowed to participate in this trip."

"Don't bullshit me! We already know this isn't a school trip—that's why we're here!"

"I don't know what you're talking about. Maybe you're mistaken..."

"We already know everything. We also know that the countdown has started! We have less than twenty people, including our VVIP. You *will* make room for us."

"No, we won't."

"How in the world can there be no space on such a huge ship?"

"You said you knew everything... so then you *know*, right? *You know what this ship is!*"

"Just clear us some seats!"

"That's impossible. We're already maxed out according to the specs Seolju gave us! That's all we got out of Seolju, no matter how much we asked! And Seolju can't guarantee a safe journey if we violate the conditions that have been set. There's a limit on carrying capacity, and we can't exceed it."

"Then you'll have to get rid of some of the kids."

"You're not serious, are you? How can you say such a thing?"

"If you don't listen to us, we'll have to use force. If the problem is capacity, then we'll just have to bring down the headcount!"

"We can't do that. We're not going to get rid of kids to make room for some self-appointed VIP."

"You're not going to listen, huh? Well, then, maybe we're gonna have to do this the hard way..."

Another gunshot cut off the man's voice, then a welter of gunfire rang out all over the place, seemingly from every direction at once. The teacher with the rifle readied his weapon and ran upstairs. The kids fled downstairs; Jaeyoung and Yeonhee ended up being swept along in a wave of stampeding bodies. Gunfire and explosions rang out all around them. As the other kids scattered, Jaeyoung slipped and fell, pulling Yeonhee down the stairs behind her.

When the gunfight and the stampede were over, Jaeyoung realized that she hadn't broken any bones. She pulled herself up and started to look for Yeonhee. As her dizziness began to abate slightly, she saw that her friend was on the floor, bleeding from a wound in her back. She had to try to drag Yeonhee down to the lower floors, where the cabins were. There had to be a first aid kit down there somewhere, right? But Yeonhee was too weak to help, and Jaeyoung only managed to drag her by the armpits for about six or seven steps before her own strength gave out. Then she remembered something she'd learned in school, and, opening Yeonhee's eyelids, she pressed two fingers to the wounded girl's neck, right under her chin.

Yeonhee's bullet wound wasn't bleeding anymore.

Jaeyoung looked over and saw a massive trail of blood along the route they'd taken. Then she realized what it meant.

Just then, a faint vibration came from the back of her hand. It was her dad calling. Jaeyoung groped at her ear with a trembling hand, but the earpiece was missing. It must have fallen out somewhere along the way.

> JAEYOUNG: *Dad just talk to me using text.*
> DAD: *What's going on? Why can't you answer the phone?*

Remembering how he'd ignored her calls earlier, she saw red.

> JAEYOUNG: *Yeonhee's dead. She got shot.*
> DAD: *What?*
> JAEYOUNG: *A bunch of crazy people got off a helicopter and shot up the place. They were just shooting their guns, even though there were kids all around.*
> DAD: *Are you ok? Are you hurt?*
> JAEYOUNG: *Well, obviously I'm not, if I'm talking to you.*
> JAEYOUNG: *I really don't understand what's going on. What's all this about?*
> JAEYOUNG: *Why are they killing kids? What's going on with this VVIP?*
> DAD: *So... it's come to this. We tried so hard... Jaeyoung, you need to go somewhere safe! Hurry!*
> JAEYOUNG: *The shooting's stopped. Dad, I'm scared. I might die. If I die, that's the end of everything, isn't it? I need you to keep your promise NOW. Tell me everything.*
> DAD: *How can that matter now? The most important thing is that you don't get hurt. You can hear the*

whole story later on...

JAEYOUNG: *Later WHEN? I don't want to die not knowing what's going on! Tell me now. Think of it as my final wish, okay?*

DAD: *How can I explain it to you with all this going on?*

JAEYOUNG: *Just do it! Even if you don't know how! Look, they were talking about Seolju here, too! They said that the ship's capacity was all they could get by begging Seolju. What's Seolju? Why did Yeonhee have to die?*

402 Jaeyoung had no idea what her dad was thinking or feeling right then. If only she could hear his voice... but all she had to go by were cold, emotionless text messages.

DAD: *Okay... you know what snowflakes are, right? I mean snow, like, in winter.*

JAEYOUNG: *Yeah, I know. They're hexagonal water crystals.*

DAD: *Right. So, some of my friends, specialists in chaos theory and fractals, were studying snow crystals... So one day, they found a mathematical regularity in them. The kind of regularity that can't happen in nature. It made no sense. The laws of nature are supposed to be consistent, right? But there it was: something that had never happened before... had just happened.*

DAD: *At first they thought it must be an artificial phenomenon, and they called in the cryptography experts. Then it was discovered that a message had been coded into the snow crystals. We thought at first that some scientist somewhere must have done it, and as a joke they called that person Seolju. As in "The Snow Master."*

DAD: *But Seolju wasn't just some random person. I mean, it wasn't a person like us. Seolju gave us a portent before revealing itself. You're too young to re-member, but about a decade ago, there was a sudden aurora, all around the world, in all the skies at once. And in the messages in the snow, Seolju had predicted the exact time of that aurora storm. And Seolju told us that the world we're living in is a computer simula-tion, and that Seolju was the manager. You asked me whether we're living in a simulation universe, so I don't need to explain all that, right?*

Jaeyoung, remembering how the Soonhang had material-ized out of nothing, answered in the affirmative.

JAEYOUNG: *Keep going.*
DAD: *The simulation, this universe that we live in, is an experiment. They wanted to see how long it would take for people to come up with the hypothesis that they're living in a simulation universe. They wanted to observe the process, step by step. Do you remember me criticizing the people who bought into the simula-tion universe theory? Well... after that point, there was no more point in running our universe.*
DAD: *Which is why they did not increase the memory capacity for this universe any further. To make it look like a closed universe, the amount of necessary infor-mation... well, anyway, let's skip these complicated concepts. To put it simply, at that point nobody could get pregnant and kids stopped being born. Seolju was behind that. After we heard about that, we realized something terrifying: if this universe is just an exper-iment, I mean if WE are the experiment, and if Seolju and its kind are the scientists, and if they succeeded in their experimental goal... then what would they do*

with us next?

JAEYOUNG: *So it turned out you were right, then...*

DAD: *Yes. Seolju told us that this universe would be terminated as soon as the results of the experiment were sorted out. The resources would be used to launch another simulation universe.*

JAEYOUNG: *Terminate this universe...? You mean they're going to switch the world off? Like shutting down a computer?*

DAD: *Yes. And given the amount of evidence they showed us, we had no choice but to believe them.*

JAEYOUNG: *Dad, the ship I'm on... I saw it materialize out of thin air. So... what IS this ship?*

DAD: *Seolju is running one small, final experiment on us. In their words, the world we live in is a lower-order universe. They want to know what happens when the inhabitants of a lower-order universe get copied into a higher-order universe. They told us that they'll extract you—you kids, I mean—out through an arbitrary, randomly allocated data portal.*

JAEYOUNG: *So, like... they think of us as poor lab rats and took pity on us?*

DAD: *I don't know, Jaeyoung. And I—I mean, we grown ups—we'll never know. But Seolju asked us to classify our younger generation so it could save you. It asked us to collect the necessary information about all of you, and it gave us really high standards for accuracy. We met the conditions, as much as possible, but had to postpone the schedule when one kid died, and then another. We kept on having to reschedule the day, again and again...*

JAEYOUNG: *That's why the date of the school trips all over the world were scheduled at the exact same time.*

DAD: *Right. We needed to reduce the margin for error as much as possible. The transportation that all the*

> *kids in the world boarded at the same time... they're*
> *all just ways of going to that data portal that Seolju*
> *created for you. We tried hard to keep it a secret. If*
> *the end of the world couldn't be stopped, well then*
> *there was no telling what people might do.*
> JAEYOUNG: *You mean, like killing kids.*
> DAD: *Yes, that's why the errors... Ah, well, we can't do*
> *anything now. There's nothing else to do but to go*
> *forward. The worst case scenario has come to pass...*
> *humans are just...*
> JAEYOUNG: *The worst-case scenario?*
> DAD: *Of all the conditions Seolju set for us, the most*
> *important was the data about you kids. This world is*
> *an asynchronous simulation, so when you move data,*
> *you need to synchronize it. Except now we don't have*
> *enough time to resubmit the updated data. The chanc-*
> *es of failure increase every time a kid dies... but there's*
> *no other way. We just have to keep going till the end.*

A second helicopter appeared out above the ocean, clearly
visible to Jaeyoung from where she was standing. That
helicopter was one of the things her dad meant when
he'd said, "what people might do..." The chopper hov-
ered in one spot for a moment before tuning quickly,
revealing its underside. Just then, something shot out
toward it from the ship, trailing a plume of fire. The
helicopter tried an evasive maneuver but was struck by
a direct hit. It exploded with a deafening roar. The VVIP
of their simulated universe was now nothing more than
scattered particles among the virtual fragments of a
helicopter that would sink forever in the ocean of data
managed by Seolju.

> JAEYOUNG: *None of those chaperones are real teach-*
> *ers, are they?*

> DAD: *Right. They're all people who volunteered to protect you.*
> JAEYOUNG: *Just a second ago, a second helicopter trying to force its way onto our ship blew up. I think the chaperones did it.*
> DAD: *That's a relief. A huge relief.*

Jaeyoung looked down at Yeonhee's motionless body. She saw the smoking wreckage of the helicopter floating on the surface of the ocean and the fake teachers running around checking how many students had been hurt or killed during the previous attack. She held Yeonhee's bloody hand, and lifted it up, thinking about what she ought to say to her father in the little time that remained.

> JAEYOUNG: *Why didn't you tell me before? There's so much I need to hear you say and so much I need to tell you.*
> DAD: *We were trying to send you safely to the higher-order universe. We knew that if the secret leaked, the chances of failure would only go up. Jaeyoung, I'm sorry. Sometimes this made me a bad father. I did all kinds of things that I know I need to apologize for. But I know one thing for sure...*
> DAD: *Any decent grown-up would have done this. We had no choice. Nothing was more important than saving your lives. Both your mother and I agreed about that.*

Jaeyoung typed in the one question that she didn't want to ask, the scariest question in the world:

> JAEYOUNG: *Dad, how much time is left?*
> DAD: *It's already run out.*

That meant she needed to send him her last words.
Jaeyoung didn't want to say goodbye. She wasn't ready to
leave. She didn't want to close that door. She knew that
any message now might get cut off in the middle, so she
chose her words carefully.

> JAEYOUNG: *Dad and Mom, I miss you.*

But unlike a moment earlier, the red circle beside the
message didn't turn green. That meant the message
hadn't been received. Jaeyoung's heart sank. It had to be
a network error, she thought. Not now. This couldn't be
the end. She just wanted a little more time. *Please*, she
thought.

> JAEYOUNG: *Dad, Mom, I miss you.*
> JAEYOUNG: *I won't forget.*
> JAEYOUNG: *I swear. Forever.*
> JAEYOUNG: *So Mom and Dad, please also
> remember me.*
> JAEYOUNG: *If I could meet you again someday, just
> one more time...*

All the circles remained red. She typed more thoughts,
sending them one after another, but all she got was
more red circles. Finally, she couldn't type anymore: her
hand was shaking, and the screen on the back of her
hand was covered in Yeonhee's blood.
Then the connection status icon switched from green
to red.
Jaeyoung couldn't begin to imagine what might come next.
She'd never bothered to imagine the end of the world.
She'd seen all kinds of natural disaster movies full of
dramatic events: the land shifting, tsunamis devouring
everything, the sky crammed with ominous clouds, icy,

burning lightning striking the earth. But right now the ocean was calm—calmer than she'd ever seen it before. If it weren't for the cooling bodies of Yeonhee and the other dead kids around her, she might even have called it a peaceful scene.

Amid that tranquility, this last human effort—one imperiled by a now increased chance of failure—seemed to float before her, buoyant and light.

Was the world being erased? Had the deletion started at one point? Was it now advancing in an ever-expanding circle? Or would the deletion happen bit by bit, here and there, until nothing remained? Was that why all communications had been cut off? Had the satellites and the cell towers been deleted?

Jaeyoung looked once more at the screen on the back of her hand. The red circles terminated her hopes. Like drops of blood, they were seared into her mind. She stared at the frozen chat window for a while before finally noticing that the voices around her were getting louder. Summoning the last of her strength, she got to her feet.

The kids of Seoul I.S. were all out on the deck and had moved to the front of the ship.

Jaeyoung was late joining them, and the crowd of kids partially blocked her view. But out in front of the ship, a massive two-dimensional whirlpool was growing slowly and solemnly. It didn't reflect any light, but it wasn't completely dark, either. It was expanding quickly across the surface of the blue sea as if it were reaching out, dancing toward the horizon, the ocean, and all the ships, including theirs.

Jaeyoung looked back toward the sky over Seoul, where her mom and dad were. She saw the adults quietly slipping off the ship as if to avoid drawing the attention of the kids. The lifeboats they'd taken floated in the wake of the *Soonhang*, bobbing up and down on the small waves. Some of the grownups on the boats were watching the kids, the students who would be the only survivors of the universe, as the *Soonhang* headed toward the whirlpool.

Everyone but Jaeyoung gasped: they seemed as panicked by the weird sight of that whirlpool as they were by the departure of the adults from the ship. Jaeyoung stood in silence as she watched these events unfold. Suddenly the sky, the ocean, and the horizon split open. The crack widened erratically at first but soon began spreading more steadily. Without sound or vibration, the crack in the visible world opened up as if in slow motion, constantly shifting as if it were alive. For a moment, the kids went silent as they beheld its unnatural beauty.

Jaeyoung noticed that the crack had a regular pattern within it. It was formed out of hexagonal shapes.

The *Soonhang* seemed to be reaching the whirlpool and the crack at the same time. Then the world ceased to exist. Jaeyoung clasped her hands together, trying to hang on to what she was seeing, trying to keep her memories intact. Was this real light, or was it all just an illusion? Maybe the very idea of watching something was itself an illusion?

Finally, only a single string of thoughts remained: humanity is stupid, and all those kids died, and our chances of survival are probably nil. *But if we wake up in another world, knowing everything I know now... it's going to be up to me to be an adult, for the sake of Seokhyun and the others.*

A BRIEF HISTORY OF SOUTH KOREAN SF FANDOM

BY SANG JOON PARK

TRANSLATED BY JIHYUN PARK
& GORD SELLAR

What follows is a story about a small group of people in a tiny corner of this vast universe, a place known as South Korea. It's a story about people who live and love SF, that literature of a "sense of wonder" that, like fantasy, is set in another time and place, but is also distinctive in the way it relates to scientific thought. The story of South Korean SF fandom—its members, its activities, and the changes they have collectively made in a country that can still be regarded, from the perspective of science fiction, as an unsettled frontier—is little known to outsiders. This essay seeks to introduce that world to overseas readers.

Before tracing the trajectory of Korean SF fandom, I would first like to clarify a few ways in which it differs from fandoms overseas, especially those of other countries with a stronger local SF tradition, such as China and Japan, as well as countries in the West. In countries where established SF fandoms have long existed, SF fans have made great strides in popularizing and propagating the genre though organized group activities. But in Korea, SF has long been regarded primarily as a pedagogical tool in the service of promoting science and technology. As a result, it has never seriously been considered a full-fledged literary genre of its own, and the study of SF here has consequently suffered. Many local fans, myself included, have undertaken a range of activities aimed at addressing this problem, but the success of such efforts has been relatively limited.

Another reason for the relative weakness of Korean SF fandom may be that unlike in many other countries, where SF first boomed as a form of popular fiction, Koreans have engaged with the genre primarily through visual media such as comics, movies and television shows. This is due to the influence of Hollywood (where SF is a dominant cinematic genre) and the Japanese media industry (which produces prodigious amounts of SF anime and manga). Considering the privileged status of literature as a high-brow cultural form throughout the twentieth century, this lack of an established SF readership means that the genre has received little scholarly or critical attention. But despite its marginalized status within local cultural institutions, South Korean SF fandom is gradually beginning to find its unique niche in the world.

If we begin with the idea of SF fandom as signifying any loosely knit group of people who love SF and work to promote it, then the history of fandom in Korea can be traced back to the early twentieth century. After Joseon Korea opened up to the outside world at the end of the nineteenth century, modern intellectuals like Yi Haejo, Kim Gyoje, and Pak Yeonghui began translating classic Western SF stories into Korean, publishing them as a literature of enlightenment. Even after Japan's annexation of Korea in 1910, translations of work by authors such as Jules Verne, H.G. Wells, Robert Louis Stevenson, and others continued to be made available in Korean. By the mid-1920s, socialist writers such as Pak Yeonghui were introducing works popular in the Soviet SF sphere, in particular Karel Čapek's *Rossum's Universal Robots*. In the 1930s, under the leadership of Kim Yonggwan, an organization called "The Invention Association" (Balmyeong hakhoe) published a magazine titled *Gwahak Joseon* (Science Joseon), which included a certain amount of science fiction. While it is possible that a dedicated readership of SF literature, and even some organized SF-related activities, existed during this time, uncovering this history remains a project for future research.

Soon after Korea's independence from Japan in 1945, the peninsula was divided into two separate states, with the South placed under American military occupation. This brought in a new influx of Western popular culture. At the time, many secondhand bookstores near U.S. military bases stocked English-language books and magazines, including a considerable amount of paperback SF novels. Those who consumed SF from such English-language sources, along with those who read SF in Japanese, played a major role in the establishment of SF culture in South Korea in the late 1950s and beyond. For example, the late 1950s saw the publication of the *Boys' and Girls' World Science Adventure Collection* (Sonyeon sonyeo segye gwahak moheom jeonjip), a series of SF novels translated into Korean and published by the Adene (Athena) Press. Authors of original Korean-language SF stories, most notably Han Nagwon, also began to appear at this time.

By the beginning of the 1960s, a committed albeit small SF readership had established itself in South Korea. Ahn Dongmin, an author and translator active at the time, published the first known critical essay on SF, "The Magic of Science Fantasy Fiction" (Gongsang gwahak soseolui mabeop; 1968), in the then-popular magazine *Saedae* (Generation). The title of this essay, which uses the Japanese-derived translation of a term found in the American SF publication *The Magazine of Fantasy and Science Fiction*, proved influential enough that the term "gongsang gwahak soseol" (science fantasy fiction) supplanted the older colonial-era term "gwahak soseol" (science fiction). Subsequently, however, this new term became associated with entertainment aimed primarily at younger readers. For this reason, the term *gwahak soseol* has in recent years enjoyed a resurgence in popularity among Korean SF fans, becoming once again the preferred term for "science fiction" in Korean.

The first official Korean SF fandom organization was the Korea SF Writers Club (Hanguk SF jakga keulleop), which was founded on December 20, 1968. This group is notable for how broadly its members ranged professionally across the fields of education, media, and culture.[1] On July 30, 1969, the *Kyunghyang sinmun* newspaper published an interview with Ji Kiwoon, the chief editor of the magazine *Hakseang kwahak* (Student Science) and the administrator for the Korea SF Writers Club at the time, together with an article providing a general introduction to SF. In the interview, Ji claimed that "currently there are approximately 50,000 SF readers [in South Korea], most of whom [are] middle- and high-school students, but the number of adults [reading SF] will increase in the future." The club's members published original Korean SF stories in affiliated periodicals, and in 1975 they put together a retrospective collection of those works, publishing a ten-volume set of *Collected Korean Science Fiction* (Hanguk gwahak soseol jeonjip; Haedong, 1975). The preface to the collection, written by Seo Gangwoon, the leader of the Korea SF Writers Club, introduced the organization to readers. This set of collected stories, which met with commercial success, was later reprinted, laying the groundwork for the domestic SF writing scene.

During the 1970s and the 1980s, a period when South Korea experienced rapid industrialization, the SF subculture experienced a general expansion. Especially

[1] According to a *Dong-a ilbo* article on January 4th, 1969, the club included the following nine members: Seo Gwangwoon, a science writer for the *Hankook ilbo*; Ji Kiwoon and Yun Sil, respectively the chief editor and a senior editor of *Haksaeng gwahak*; Oh Minyeong, a writer of another student magazine *Hagwon* (Campus); Yi Dongseong, a senior editor of the *Wolgan jung 1* magazine (Middle-School Freshmen) ; Kang Seongcheol, an editor of the monthly *Jubu saenghwal* (Housewives' Life); Kang Seungwon, a teacher at Kwangwoon Engineering High School; Seo Jeongcheol, a comic book artist; and the writer Mun Yunseong, who was listed by his pseudonym, Kim Jongan.

notable was how the government-led National Science Campaign (Jeon gungmin gwahakhwa undong) of the 1970s boosted the volume of SF-related publications and also significantly increased the prominence of SF in visual media. Besides anthologies of translated SF, Dongseo Mystery Books (Dongseo churi mungo), a publishing company that was launched in 1977, included ten volumes of SF fiction in a series that became quite popular. These were the first Korean-language SF publications aimed at a serious, adult audience. Although the domestic production of creative SF writing suffered a setback under the intensified censorship of successive military regimes, a generation of Koreans who spent their youth under the influence of the period's expansive SF culture subsequently grew up to join the burgeoning ranks of South Korea's SF fandom.[2] Around the time of the country's political democratization in 1987, a new wave of adult SF novels began to appear, and the SF genre was introduced into the annual nationwide literary contest of the *Sports Seoul Daily*. In a country where national newspaper-run literary contests have traditionally served as the primary gateway to a literary career for new writers, this served as a noteworthy indication of the genre's elevated status.

The next stage in the development of SF fandom in South Korea came with the propagation of online communication networks in the early 1990s. Such technological innovations brought about an explosion of new fan clubs. Fans initially congregated around Choi Hyeonjun's SF bulletin board, Tomorrow BBS (Naeil BBS), and the SF fan community on the PC telecom portal service of Chollian; these were followed by the establishment of other

[2] For an English study of the 1970s Korean SF culture, see Sunyoung Park, "Dissident Dreams: Science Fictional Imaginations in 1970s Korean Literature and Film," in Youngju Ryu, ed., *Cultures of Yusin: South Korea in the 1970s* (Ann Arbor: the University of Michigan Press, 2018): 165–192.

groups on networks such as Hitel, Nownuri, Unitel, and more. Members of fan groups associated with these on-line sites would hold regular offline meetings, and many participants were active in multiple groups. I personally participated in both the Mystery and SF Interest Group on Chollian and the SF Club on Hitel. When I began to work as a translator specializing in SF in 1991, I helped organize a separate offline SF association gathering called "Brave New World" (Meotjin sinsegye), which was launched in collaboration with several members of the Chollian SF fan community. Brave New World later published the first issue of a fanzine bearing the same title as the club. Preparations were made to publish a second issue, but it never made it to print, and the organization dissolved sometime thereafter. Nonetheless, some of the group's members subsequently went on to become active SF writers, translators, event organizers, and otherwise important participants in Korean SF fandom. Prominent among these are Kim Changgyu, a prolific author and translator, whose work appears in this anthology, and Yi Seongsu, the author of South Korea's first online serial novel *Atlantis Rhapsody* (1989).

417

Such offline events and activities by the cyber-fandom helped bring about an SF publication boom during the 1990s. From 1991 onwards, many other SF translations were published, starting with Isaac Asimov's *Foundation* series. This gave new life to the field of literary SF for adults. While working at the publisher Sigongsa, Kim Sanghun and I put out under the Griffin Books imprint works by Philip K. Dick, Ursula K. Le Guin, and Stanislaw Lem—all writers who first became famous in South Korea through online SF fan communities. In addition, following the example of the *Brave New World* fanzine (1992), the publisher Nagyeong Munhwa launched *SF Magazine* (1993), South Korea's first SF periodical aimed at a mass readership. In its pages could be found a variety of content, including domestic and international SF news, original stories and translations, essays, and interviews. The magazine was short-lived—lasting only two issues—but its existence is indicative of how, in the 1990s, a real interest in a variety of popular literary genres—from SF to mystery to horror to fantasy—was already beginning to gain momentum. Other "new culture" magazines would also occasionally publish SF-related news and writings, and this growing subculture of fandom ultimately rallied to support the ongoing publication boom. In June 1999, a group of fans succeeded in organizing a separate SF-focused booth at the Seoul Book Fair.

By the late 1990s, PC bulletin-board services gave way to Internet portals, and SF fan-clubs naturally migrated to the World Wide Web. The most significant group among these was Joy SF, which even now remains the biggest online SF community in South Korea. Its origins can be traced back to the Star Wars fan site created in 1998 by Jeon Hongsik, a well-known video game scenario writer. Initially known under the name "SF War," it had, by the mid-aughts, been renamed "Joy SF." The group's focus had by then broadened to include a range of genres including martial-arts narratives, alternate histories, and military SF, as well as genre-related games, animations, and films. Other websites such as *Junk SF*, *Monthly SF Webzine* (Wolgan SF webjin), and *Happy SF* also helped to attract numerous Koreans to SF fandom: Junk SF played a pivotal role in organizing the first-ever Korean SF convention in February 2000; the *Monthly SF Webzine*—run from October 1999 to March 2001 by Jang Kangmyeong, now one of the most notable writers—became widely acclaimed for its varied, high-quality content; and *Happy SF* (2003–2013), managed by the publisher Haengbokhan chaek ikgi (Happy Reading), which published a print magazine of the same title, also attracted a devoted following.

An array of other websites, personal blogs, portal cafés, webzines, and discussion boards have likewise contributed to contemporary activities within Korean SF fandom. One prominent example is the fantasy literature webzine *Geoul* (Mirror), which is in fact an association of SF and fantasy writers. Formed in 2003 and still going strong, its website has given many authors and translators an online platform from which to introduce their work, and it has also supported the publication of a number of print anthologies featuring stories previously posted on the site. Yet another significant player on the scene has been an anonymous bloggers' one-man SF webzine *alt. SF*, which is known for its insightful and incisive reviews of the work of domestic authors as well as foreign SF writers whose work has appeared in Korean translations. However, despite its long and storied run from November 2009 through February 2016, the publication of *alt.SF* was suspended after a dispute with the literary magazine *AXT* (Art and Text) over an interview with the SF author, fan, and film/culture critic, Djuna, who questioned the mainstream literary world's biases against and lack of understanding of SF. Djuna is just one of the many individuals who have used the internet to attract a following or exert an influence on the world of Korean SF. Others include Hong Inki, an SF translator and critic, and Go Jangwon, arguably the most prolific SF critic to date.

In the 2000s, offline events organized by fandom diversified significantly, with fans participating in newly created SF writing competitions such as the SF and Science Writing Contest, which ran from 2004 through 2006. Jointly sponsored by the *Dong-a Science* magazine and KOFAC (the Korea Foundation for the Advancement of Science and Creativity), such contests contributed to the discovery of several important new authors. The monthly magazine *Fantastique*, which I helped to launch in 2007 as the founding editor, went far beyond the medium of literature to tackle SF in comics, movies, music, and more. In celebration of the first issue, we gathered together my own personal collection of books, which has since been named the Seoul SF Archive, along with additional materials, and held an exhibit titled "100 Years of Korean SF" (Hanguk SF 100-nyeonsa) at a gallery in the headquarters of Moonji (Literature and Intellect) Publishing. South Korea's longest-running literary magazine focused on SF and fantasy fiction, *Fantastique* was forced to switch to quarterly publication during the 2008 global economic crisis and eventually shut down in 2010. Meanwhile, Jeon Hongsik has been organizing various events for SF fans, including the annual "SF Party" at the Seoul Animation Center. The first SF Party took place on February 7, 2005, and in the years since, a total of fourteen such events have taken place at a rate of two or three per year. In 2009, using his own funds, Jeon founded the Seoul SF & Fantasy Library, the first and only professional facility of its kind in the country. The library now serves as a hub for in-person events, hosting a variety of SF-related events, including book launches, lectures on topics related to SF, and more. And in June 2018, SF fans gained a new venue when Galdar, a science bookstore named after Galileo and Darwin, opened in the hip Seoul neighborhood around Hongik University.

From the late 1990s on, Korean SF fandom has become a force to be reckoned with, not just in terms of literature, but also in the areas of comics and movies. A significant amount of fan activity has coalesced around SF in those two areas in particular, and several magazines devoted to them have published a considerable amount of well-received SF-related content in addition to special articles on the subject. A full discussion of this aspect of SF's popularity is beyond the scope of this essay, but a few large-scale events are important to mention. In 2009, the Gwacheon National Science Museum provided space for an SF study group to hold a small SF film festival; in 2010, the International SF Film Festival was launched. This festival has subsequently continued on an annual basis, although its name has been changed to simply "SF Festival" in order to reflect its expanded scope of events, which, in addition to film screenings, includes exhibits, lectures, and discussion panels. In April 2017, the Museum also established its first-ever permanent exhibit of SF-related materials.

Although much work still remains to be done, the efforts of fans have in fact succeeded in generating considerable recognition for SF in South Korea. Entering the second decade of the 21st century, the attitude toward SF has changed markedly, due in part to cultural advancements and in part to the ever-increasing social interest in scientific and technological advances—particularly in the fields of genetic engineering, nanotech, and robotics—all of which has in turn brought attention to SF, a genre that engages in both science and storytelling. Broadly speaking, the rapid development of science and technology—as well as the reporting and educational advances that have accompanied this development—has effectively lowered the barriers that might once have made it difficult for members of the general public to understand and respond to SF. In recent years, the growing interest in SF by schools and other educational institutions, companies, government offices, and other agencies, has resulted in an increasingly diverse audience for the genre.

This recent turn of events made it only more regrettable that we still lacked an official umbrella organization that could encompass all Korean SF writers, publishers, and fans. Individual SF fans were at the time still only able to connect through small, highly localized friendly gatherings and unofficial networks. Given the ever-increasing opportunities for international cultural exchange and collaboration, this lack of a consolidated, representative organization was becoming an ever more pressing concern. In 2017, SF writers made two big strides in addressing this issue. First, South Korea sent its first team of representatives—Yun Yeo-Kyeong, Lee Su Hyeon, and myself, all of whom had been tasked with building networks with SF fans from the United States, China, and Japan—to the 75th World SF Convention (also known as Worldcon), which took place in Helsinki, Finland in August of that year. Second, Jeong Soyeon, Bae Myunghoon, and Kim Choyeop helmed the founding of the Science Fiction Writers Union of the Republic of Korea (SFWURK), an organization whose mission is to protect and promote the rights and activities of SF writers.

Riding this momentum, the Korean Science Fiction Association (KSFA) finally came into being in May 2018. This organization, for which I have the honor of serving as the founding president, has since participated in the first Asia-Pacific SF Convention in Beijing, China, as well as in Worldcon 76, which took place in San Jose, USA. It also launched the first ever KoreaCon at the Seoul Science Center in November 2018, an event that attracted much public attention through its unprecedented diversity of science and SF-related programs, including scientists' lectures, writers' signing events, film screenings, publishers' booth exhibitions, the orchestral play of SF music, cosplay, and other performative and visual displays.

I am hopeful that the timely publication of this first English-language anthology of South Korean science fiction will, together with this recent growth in organizational power, help further our outreach and exchange with international fans of science fiction. It is exciting that a full century after Koreans began to engage in science fiction as a modern literary genre, South Korean writers and fans are at last taking their place in the world of science fiction.

MELISSA MEI-LIN CHAN is a Ph.D. candidate in East Asian Languages and Cultures at the University of Southern California. She received her M.A. in Asian Studies at the University of California, Santa Barbara in 2013. Her dissertation examines the intersections between censorship, protest, identity politics, and ethno-cultural discourse in Hong Kong martial arts cinema and media from the 1950s to the contemporary period. Her broader research interests include Chinese and Sinophone literature and cinema, Southeast Asian cinema, gender studies, and digital humanities.

424

KIMBERLY MEE CHUNG is an assistant professor of Humanities in the College of Fine Arts at Hongik University in Seoul, South Korea. She received her Ph.D. from the University of California, San Diego in Comparative Literature with a specialization in Korean literary and cultural studies. Currently, she is working on a book project titled, "Proletarian Sensibilities: Mass Culture of 1920s and 1930s Colonial Korea." Other research interests include visual studies, postcolonial literary and cultural studies, race and gender studies, and modern East Asian history.

DAGMAR VAN ENGEN is an Honors Faculty Fellow in Barrett Honors College at Arizona State University, Tempe. Dagmar's book project, *Tentacular Sex: Gender, Race, and Science in American Speculative Fiction*, traces a genealogy of nonbinary genders in American culture across scientific and literary representations of invertebrate animal life. Dagmar received their Ph.D. in English from the University of Southern California. Their research focuses on queer and transgender studies, biology and culture, speculative fiction, and multiethnic American literatures.

KYUNGHEE EO is a Ph.D. candidate in English and gender studies at the University of Southern California. Her interests lie at the intersections of gender, sexuality, postcoloniality, and subimperialism across the transpacific world. Her dissertation, "Politics of Purity: A Queer Transpacific Genealogy of Korean Girlhood," focuses on literary and visual representations of girls in Korean, Japanese, and U.S. cultural productions. Her works appear in two forthcoming anthologies, *Queer Korea* (Duke University Press, 2019) and *Revisiting Minjung: New Perspectives on the Cultural History of 1980s South Korea* (University of Michigan Press, 2019).

EUNHAE JO is a Ph.D. candidate in East Asian Languages and Cultures at the University of Southern California. She has completed her M.A. in Chinese literature in 2012 at Yonsei University, where she also studied English literature. Her current research interest focuses on gender politics and the fantastic in modern Chinese and Korean literatures and films.

SORA KIM-RUSSELL is a literary translator of Korean fiction into English. Her recent works include Kim Un-su's *The Plotters*; Hwang Sok-yong's *At Dusk*; and Pyun Hye-young's *City of Ash and Red* and *The Hole*, which won a Shirley Jackson Award in 2017. Her full list of publications can be found at www.sorakimrussell.com

425

JENNY WANG MEDINA is an assistant professor of Korean Studies in the Department of Russian and East Asian Languages and Cultures at Emory University and a translator of Korean literature. Her research encompasses a wide range of Korean, Asian-American, and Anglophone literature, film, television, and new media as they interact and mutually influence cultural production in Asia and the United States. Her work focuses on issues of multiculturalism, translation, media, diaspora, race and ethnicity, and narrative theory.

JIHYUN PARK is a filmmaker who directed South Korea's first Lovecraftian film, the award-winning "The Music of Jo Hyeja" (2010). She has also co-translated Kim Bo-Young's SF story "An Evolutionary Myth," which appeared in *Clarkesworld* (May 2015). She is currently working as a Production Director at KTV with further Korean SF-related translation projects on the go. Her website is at brutalrice.com

SANG JOON PARK studied Earth and Marine Science at Hanyang University and did his graduate study in comparative literature at Seoul National University. He has translated a number of SF novels into Korean, including Ray Bradbury's *Fahrenheit 451* and Arthur C. Clarke's *Rendezvous with Rama*. He also served as the founding editor for *Fantastique* (2007–2010), a genre fiction magazine with a focus on SF and fantasy, and as the chief editor for the Woongjin Publisher's Omelas SF series (2007–2011). He is currently active as a translator, editor, archivist, and columnist on all subjects related to science fiction.

SUNYOUNG PARK is an associate professor of East Asian Languages and Cultures and Gender Studies at the University of Southern California. She is the author of *The Proletarian Wave: Literature and Leftist Culture in Colonial Korea, 1910-1945* (Harvard University Asia Center, 2015) and the editor and translator of *On the Eve of the Uprising and Other Stories from Colonial Korea* (Cornell East Asian Series, 2010). Her current projects include a monograph on science fiction and the politics of modernization in South Korea and a collection of critical essays titled *Revisiting Minjung: New Perspectives on the Cultural History of 1980s South Korea* (University of Michigan Press, 2019).

GORD SELLAR is a writer of speculative fiction, a blogger, and an enthusiast of all things related to science fiction in South Korea, where he has been based since 2002. Hailing from Canada, he is a graduate of the Clarion West Writers Workshop and of the Creative Writing M.A. program at Concordia University in Montreal, and was a finalist for the John W. Campbell Award for Best New Writer in 2009. His fiction, poetry, and nonfiction have appeared widely in English-language magazines and webzines, and they have been translated to Italian, Czech, Chinese, and Korean. His stories, some of which are set in fantastical past, future, and alternate Koreas, have also been collected in a number of retrospective and year's best anthologies. In addition, he has published several academic papers and informal articles on Korean SF cinema, was a contributor to the Korean

SF publication *Miraekyung* (Futuroscope), and he has served as the screenwriter and soundtrack composer for several award-winning South Korean short films. His website is at gordsellar.com

HAERIN SHIN is an assistant professor of English, with affiliations with Asian Studies and Cinema & Media Arts at Vanderbilt University. She received her Ph.D. in comparative literature from Stanford University in 2013. Shin's research focuses on the relationship between technology and ontology, digital objects in the cultural domain, and issues of race and ethnicity. She has published articles on topics including posthuman spirituality, techno-Orientalism, and cyberculture. She has recently completed her first book *The Technology of Presence: Digital Subjects in Cyberculture* and is now working on a second monograph on Asian American speculative fiction and media.

ESTHER M. K. SONG studied psychology at the University of British Columbia in Vancouver, BC, with an interest in modern Korean fiction. She is particularly interested in the analysis of psychological aspects of literature.

ADRIAN THIERET is a Teaching Fellow in the Global Perspectives on Society program at New York University Shanghai. A voracious reader of science fiction and fantasy for as long as he can remember, Thieret earned his Ph.D. in Chinese literature from Stanford University in 2016. His primary research interests lie in contemporary East Asian literature and popular culture, and his research publications include "Society and Utopia in Liu Cixin" (China Perspectives 2015:1). In addition to the Djuna story published here, he recently translated the short story "Songs of Ancient Earth" by Chinese SF author Bao Shu (in *The Reincarnated Giant: An Anthology of Twenty-First Century Chinese Science Fiction*, Columbia University Press, 2018).

RANDI VAUGHAN is a comedy writer residing in Los Angeles.

TRAVIS WORKMAN is an associate professor at the University of Minnesota, Twin Cities, and the author of *Imperial Genus: The Formation and Limits of the Human in Modern Korea and Japan* (University of California Press, 2016). He is currently writing a book about the melodramatic film aesthetic in South and North Korea and is also translating Korean essays of literary criticism.

428

ACKNOWLEDGMENTS

The editors would like to thank both the authors and the literary executors in Korea for entrusting their stories to this project. They are also grateful to all involved translators, designers, and illustrators, without whose dedication, competence, and love for the material this anthology would not have been possible. The Publisher at Kaya Press, Sunyoung Lee, and its Managing Editor, Neela Banerjee, have supported this project from the very beginning, and their editorial care has significantly enhanced the final product. At the Literature Translation Institute of Korea, Lee Yoonie, Yum Sooyun, and Director Kim Seong-Kon have been invaluable champions and sponsors of the volume. Special thanks are due to Gord Sellar for his careful copyediting of the manuscript and to Kyu Hyun Kim for his feedback on the completed draft. Sang Joon Park would additionally like to honor the memory of the late Kim I Goo (1958–2017), whose work as a literary critic has contributed importantly to the growth of Korean science fiction. Indeed, in lieu of a dedication, both editors wish to acknowledge the whole cohort of writers, readers, fans, and critics who have helped establish the genre of science fiction in South Korea. It is also thanks to their passion and efforts that a volume such as this sees publication today.

"Along the Fragments of My Body" by Bok Geo-il. *Happy SF* 2. Haengbokhan chaek ikgi,
2006; *Aeteutamui roma* [Dear Rome]. Munhakgwa jiseongsa, 2008. Story © 2006 Bok Geo-
il; translation © 2018 Travis Workman.

"Between Zero and One" by Kim Bo-Young. *Crossroads*, February 2009; *Jinhwa sinhwa*
[Evolution Myths]. Haengbokhan chaek ikgi, 2010. Story © 2009 Kim Bo-Young; translation
© 2018 Eunhae Jo.

"The Bloody Battle of Broccoli Plain" by Djuna. *Jaeumgwa moeum* 1 (2008); *Brokolli
pyeongwonui hyeoltu* [The Bloody Battle of Broccoli Plain]. *Jaeumgwa moeum*, 2011. Story
© 2008; translation © 2018 Adrian Thieret.

"A Brief History of South Korean SF Fandom" by Sang Joon Park. Essay © 2018 Sang Joon
Park; translation © 2018 Jihyun Park and Gord Sellar.

"Cosmic Go" by Jeong Soyeon. *U, Robot*. Hwanggeum gaji, 2009; *Yeopjibui Yeonghuissi*
[My Neighbor Yeonghui]. Changbi, 2015. Story © 2009 Jeong Soyeon; translation © 2018
Kimberly Chung.

"Empire Radio, Live Transmission" by Choi In-hun (excerpt). "Chongdogui sori" [Empire
Radio, Live Transmission], *Sin dong-a* 36 (1967); *Chongdogui sori*. Munhakgwa jiseongsa,
1976. Story © 1967 Choi In-hun; translation © 2018 Jenny Wang Medina.

"Our Banished World" by Kim Changgyu. *Miraegyeong*, 2016; *Uriga chubangdoen segye*
[Our Banished World]. Ajak, 2016. Story © 2016 Kim Changgyu; translation © 2018 Jihyun
Park and Gord Sellar.

Perfect Society by Mun Yunseong (excerpt). *Wanjeon sahoe* [Perfect Society]. Sudo
munhwasa, 1967. Story © 1967 Mun Yeonseong; translation © 2018 Sunyoung Park.

Quiz Show by Kim Young-ha (excerpt). *Kwijeu shyo* [Quiz Show]. Munhak dongne, 2007.
Story © 2007 Kim Youngh-ha; translation © 2018 Haerin Shin.

"Readymade Bodhisattva" by Park Seonghwan. *Gwahak gisul changjak munye susang
jakpumjip* [SF and Science Writing Award Collection]. *Dong-a science*. 2005; *Gotong
daeume oneun geotdeul, goeroum dwie pineun geotdeul* [What Comes After the Pain,
What Blooms After the Suffering]. Fool's Garden, 2012. Story © 2005 Park Seonghwan;
translation © 2018 Jihyun Park and Gord Sellar.

"Roadkill" by Park Min-gyu. *Jaeumgwa moeum* 12, 2011; *Hyeondae munhaksang susang
soseoljip* [Contemporary Literary Award Collection] 57. Hyeondae munhak, 2012; First
English translation by Esther Song, *Azalea: Journal of Korean Literature and Culture* 6, 2013;
Revised reprint in this volume by Esther Song and Gord Sellar. Story © 2011 Park Min-gyu;
translation © 2018 Esther Song.

"The Sky Walker" by Yun I-hyeong. *Munhak dongne* 15, no. 2 (2008); *Keun neukdae Parang*
[Big Wolf Blue]. Changbi, 2011. Story © 2008 Yun I-hyeong; translation © 2018 Kyunghee Eo.

"Storm Between My Teeth" by Lim Taewoon. *Hanguk hwansang munhak danpyeonseon*
[Korean Fantasy Short Stories Collection] 2. Sijak, 2009; *Mabeopsaga gollanhada* [Magician
in Trouble]. Saeparan sangsang, 2010. Story © 2009 Lim Taewon; translation © 2018
Sunyoung Park.

"Where Boats Go" by Kim Jung-hyuk. *Gajja palro haneun poong* [Embracing with Fake Arms].
Munhak dongne, 2015. Story © 2015 Kim Jung-hyuk; translation © 2018 Sora-Kim Russell.